DNAlien III

By
JIM WEST

Other Books by Jim West

DNAlien

DNAlien II

Page Left Blank intentionally

PROLOGUE

Deep beneath the Naval Air Station/Joint Reserve Base (NAS/JRB), Fort Worth, Texas, formerly known as Carswell AFB, there exists a facility dedicated to a single purpose: the creation of a new life form that combines the DNA of captured aliens with human embryos. That well-kept secret became at risk when Vicki Grubbs, one of the primary caretakers of the Genetic Embryonic Nucleus Enhancement (GENE) program, found her time left on earth dramatically shortened and her love of the product more important than her own well-being.

After conspiring with a sympathetic friend, she clandestinely removed the young man from what she determined was his ultimate future, his demise. Gene, as he was known to those close to the project, was slipped from within the facility the night before the cowardly attacks on the World Trade Center on September 11, 2001.

After making his way from the northern edge of Ft Worth, Gene is taken into the small rural areas of Texas by different individuals who think him to be one of the numerous illegal Hispanic workers who roam the countryside in search of labor.

Butch North found Gene walking north of Azle on FM 730, heading toward Boyd, Texas. He picked him up and hired him to work temporarily in his stables while his hired hand took a few days' vacation. After taking Gene around the country with him and his daughters, Mischelle and Jeannie, they meet two young ladies at a local cantina. That night, Gene becomes involved with one of them, resulting in the inevitable consequence.

Meanwhile, the government is urgently trying to locate their 'product' without letting the public know what they are so desperate to recover. They discover that Gene has been seen and quickly begin to monitor Butch North's movements through every method at their disposal. Unfortunately, they are always just one step behind as Butch and his friends keep Gene out of sight.

Once the involvement of Leslie Barber, the lady Gene became involved with, becomes known, Butch sends an old military acquaintance to get her and then ensures that Gene and the young lady are hidden from the enclosing snare the government is attempting to spring. As Gene and Leslie begin living together, they become a unique family, especially with 'Uncle Kevin' taking care of them and their soon-to-be-born child.

As the net tightens, plans that were begun months ago during Butch's trip to Del Rio must suddenly be enacted. Discovery of Gene, Leslie, the newborn, and Kevin is passed to the facility beneath the NAS/JRB, and dramatic measures are soon to be taken to regain Gene and the rest of those having knowledge of him. Kevin must get the family quickly and unobserved to the safety of Butch's friend in Del Rio, Texas.

CHARACTERS

Military

1. General Mike Nelson—Project Revive commander and facility commander.
2. General Gary Brown—NAS/JRB commander.
3. General Paul Modelle—White House/Presidential staff advisor and a senior member of Majestic Twelve (MJ 12).
4. Colonel Rick Erickson—Facility deputy commander and operations officer for Project Revive.
5. Colonel Karyn Lynch—Communications officer for Project Revive and the facility.
6. Colonel Amy Moore—Facility laboratory commander.
7. Major Jerry Fleenor—White House liaison.

Civilian

1. Butch North—Owner of the Equestrian Center of Aurora Vista.
2. Kevin Knox—Friend of Butch from Vashti, Texas, and former marine.
3. Tammy Terbush—Romantically linked with Butch.
4. Leslie Barber—Carrying Gene's child.
5. Mel Bailey-- Friend from Butch's assignment at Laughlin AFB, in Del Rio, TX. Known as El Sancudo, or 'The Mosquito'.

CHAPTER 1

Butch North needed to think quickly. The noose was quickly tightening around him and his friends. The phone call he had received from Major Jerry Fleenor told him that unless prompt action was taken, all would be lost. Kevin Knox had just taken Gene, Leslie, and the newborn from a small clinic outside of Ringgold just before the Texas highway patrolman found the flyer he had been searching for that described Leslie.

Butch made a quick call to Mel Bailey or 'Sancudo' to those that knew him well. Sancudo and his family, going back to his grandfather, were old-time residents of the Del Rio, Texas, area. Sancudo, meaning mosquito, was a minor villain who had operated between Mexico and the US for numerous years, as had his family before him. Just about any low-level criminal activity, which included 'coyote work' of bringing illegals across the border, was acceptable activity. He had never been involved in anything that would result in violence or drugs. There, he drew the line and knew that to cross it meant a lot of trouble for both his companions and the law on either side of the border.

He had met Butch during one of several trips across the border during Butch's assignment at Laughlin AFB and had helped him during one minor infraction of the 'laws' of Cuidad Acuna when the local police had tried to extract a bribe. Sancudo was just enough of a pest to the US Border Patrol that he had learned how to cross either way over the Rio Grande as necessary without their knowledge unless it was to his benefit to make them aware of his activities.

Now, Butch needed to get Kevin and Sancudo together as quickly as possible somewhere between Ft Worth and Del Rio. He knew Kevin would take the quickest route that avoided the major roads. Just how much of the network of County, Farm to Market, and State roads he might remember was questionable. He had to find someplace that would accommodate the rendezvous and give the least chance of detection.

Not to mention, he had to disappear long enough to enact the plan before his unavoidable capture by those year-long adversaries from the Naval Air Station/Joint Reserve Base (NAS/JRB), Ft Worth, Texas. Standing there in the main barn at the stables, he knew time was very, very short, and once captured, he couldn't help either Kevin or Sancudo protect Gene and his family.

The first thing he had to do was gain some precious time by getting away from the stables without being seen. That wasn't going to happen using either his truck or his easily recognizable 1962 Corvette. The government had been following those vehicles since their knowledge of Gene's time at the stables and the discovery of Butch's suspected involvement in thwarting their attempts to regain control of the situation.

Butch ran down the aisle shouting for Steve, his stable hand, to get to the office. As he opened the door and stepped inside, he turned on the small television that sat atop the refrigerator. The set only picked up local stations and was normally used to record either the foaling process or one of the security cameras located throughout the stable area. But, it would provide some noise in case there were any unwanted listening devices.

The minute Steve entered the office, Butch told him that he was leaving for a couple of days and provided him with a list of people and their numbers in case he needed any assistance.

"Where are you going?" Steve asked as he took the list and quickly scanned it.

"An old friend is in trouble," Butch acknowledged as he scribbled a few more notes on the tablet resting on the desk. "Here are a few reminders and who you need to contact if you have any questions about anything. I'll try to contact you as soon as I can, but I don't think you'll be able to call me. At least not for a few days."

"Anything I can do to help?" Steve questioned as he looked at the newest notes and directions.

"I wish there was," Butch answered as he wrote another quick note that he placed in his pocket. "But, if you'll keep this place running safely until I get back and check on my horses at the house, that's about all you can do for now. Any questions?"

"Lots," Steve replied. "But I guess you don't have time to answer all of them, and I don't even know all of them to ask."

"One more thing," Butch told him as he turned for the door. "I need you to put on my hat and drive my truck to Boyd. Don't ask why, but do expect to be stopped before you get there. Other than that, you know nothing about where I've gone or what I'm doing."

Steve frowned as he debated the request but could only shake his head and take the offered hat. "This has to do with that fellow you hired last year while I was on vacation, doesn't it?"

"I can't say, and you don't want to know anymore other than I asked you to take my truck into Boyd," Butch acknowledged. "Please take it out to Dan's Auto Shop; it needs an oil change. That's all you know if you get stopped. If you don't get stopped, wait for Dan to finish and bring it back here and leave my hat in the office."

"Am I going to get into any trouble for this?" Steve wanted to know.

"Nope, but they'll spend some time questioning you," Butch replied. "But they'll do that regardless of where they find you. Now, I've got to get going. You'll hear from me as soon as possible."

Sticking his right hand out, Butch somberly told him, "Thanks, Steve."

Firmly shaking the offered hand, Steve just nodded and answered, "Not a problem, Butch. You've been as fair and honest a man to work for or with that I've ever known. I know you'll take care of me and whoever else you're involved with."

As Steve headed down the aisle, Butch turned in the opposite direction and climbed over the fence that separated him and his neighbor. He knew that the white van parked in the driveway always had the keys in the ignition and that the note he stuck in the screen door would keep the owner from thinking it had been stolen.

Once he had the van started, he quickly pulled out and headed north on Old Base Road. Making the right turn on Highway 114, Butch pushed the van as hard as he thought reasonable toward Rhome. He certainly didn't want to be stopped for speeding right now, especially in someone else's van.

Once he had used the access road to cross Highway 287, he drove straight to the Woodhaven Bank, where he knew he could withdraw some much-needed cash. As soon as he entered, he took a withdrawal slip from the desk and stepped up to the teller's window.

"How much cash can I withdraw right now?" he asked.

"Give me a second," the teller replied as she punched Butch's account information into her computer. "How much do you think you need?"

"As much as possible from all of my accounts," Butch told her. "I need to use your phone while you figure out how much of my money you'll let me have if you don't mind."

Butch picked up the receiver from the lobby phone and dialed Tammy Terbush's cell phone number. As soon as it was answered, he told her, "Hey, I may not make it this evening. Something has come up that I really need to take care of."

Knowing that Tammy would understand that he wouldn't break any date without a good reason, he continued, "I'll get in touch with you as soon as I can, but it may be a few days. Other than that, I can't say more and need to get going as fast as I can. I sure do miss you, though."

Listening to her necessary protest about not getting to see him, he smiled and finally told her, "I'll call when I can, promise. Please don't try to call me until I finish what I've got to do. Promise me, okay?"

Hearing her promise, he hung up the phone and walked back to where the teller was printing a list of all the accounts Butch had with the bank. "Do you want it all?" she asked. "There's about $25,000 available right now."

"Yep," Butch said. "Let me have about $24,000 in hundreds and the rest in twenties, please."

"I'll have to get the manager to approve this amount," she reminded him as she made a call on the intercom.

"I know," Butch acknowledged. "And I bet you have some special form for any withdrawal of over $10,000, don't you?"

Renee, the branch manager, was stepping from her office before the teller had the chance to answer. "We'll see, Butch," she told him. "Do we need to discuss this in my office?"

"Might help," he answered. "Can you have the money gathered up while we talk? I don't have much time."

"Start getting it together," Renee told the teller. "I'll sign the necessary forms back in my office."

After a quick walk down the hall, Renee motioned for Butch to take a chair across from her desk. As she sat, she made a few quick strokes on her computer keyboard and asked, "Do I need to know what this is for?"

"No, ma'am," Butch said. "I'm not sure exactly what I'll do with it anyway. Maybe head to Florida and hang out with hookers until it's all gone."

"Sure," Renee answered, smiling as she finished looking at the data on her computer screen and making a couple of additional entries. "If there's one thing I know about you, it's that there's a certain lady I've seen you with that would have your 'nads if you even thought about that. And I don't mean it would be either of those two daughters of yours. Although they might do it also if you screw up this relationship the way you tend to do."

Butch smiled and replied, "Oh, she'd have more than just the 'nads; she'd take anything remotely connected to that particular area. I just don't understand women sometimes, you know?"

As they were talking, the teller appeared at the closed door and knocked. As she entered, holding a bulging bank bag, Renee held out her hand and accepted the money. "Thanks," she told her. "I'll take care of everything else. Please close the door when you leave."

The door closed softly, and Renee handed the bag to Butch. "Want to count it?"

"Nope," he answered, "I trust you."

Renee sat quietly, watching as Butch unsnapped two snaps on the front of his Wrangler shirt and stuck the bag inside. "Now," he told her, "I need you to trust me on something."

"Just what is that?" she questioned.

"I need to borrow your car."

"Let me see," Renee replied as she rolled her eyes. "I'm supposed to hand you $25,000, ask no questions, not provide notice of that large cash withdrawal, and loan you my car. Do I have that right?"

"Yep," smiled Butch.

"And, I guess you can't tell me why on anything," she questioned as she shook her head in disbelief.

"Only that I need a couple of days with no one knowing where I am or what I'm doing," Butch answered. "I'll even swap you a fine white van to use until I get your car back to you. How good of a deal is that?"

"Wonderful," Renee said as she dug into her purse, searching for the keys to her 'almost' new car that she was so proud of.

"Will you at least wash it before you bring it back?" she queried as she reluctantly handed him the keys.

"And waxed, if not now, later for sure," Butch said as he stood. "Thanks, Renee. You've been a great friend, and I'll explain everything when I can. I truly do appreciate what you've done."

He turned from her desk and reached for the doorknob, pausing for a second. Turning his head remarking, "By the way, the keys are in the van parked out front. If possible, could you take it back to the owner when you leave this evening? He lives just south of the stables, and his address is on the insurance papers on the visor. I'm sure he would appreciate having it back today."

Butch hurried out of the bank and crossed the parking lot to where the employees' cars were parked. Renee's semi-new red Mustang convertible was easily recognizable and was certainly well cared for. After unlocking the door and sliding across the leather seats, Butch started the engine and thought about what he needed to do next. After only a couple of seconds, he determined that right now would be the last chance to get back to his house and retrieve a few items. Even now, it may be too late, but he needed to give it a try.

As he pulled out onto the access road, he saw three black Suburbans speeding north on 287. Paralleling them as he approached 114, he was glad to see they continued toward Decatur and didn't exit to head toward his house. Pausing only slightly at the stop sign, Butch pushed the speed limit back toward Old Base Road. A short distance down that road, he entered the Aurora Vista development and took the shortest route through the homes until he came to Orion Court, the cul-de-sac that ended just south of his fence.

Parking the car, Butch jogged past the house that sat across the fence from his barn and quickly climbed over onto his own property. After a quick look in the barn, he verified that there were no unwanted vehicles either along FM 718 or parked at his house. Dashing to the house, he entered through the screened-in porch at the back and hurried to his bedroom. Once there, he grabbed his old suitcase and began throwing in socks, underwear, a couple of short-sleeved knit shirts, starched jeans and shirts, the money he had gotten from the bank, and his always-packed shaving kit.

Next, he took his 'going out' black hat from the hat rack he had made from horseshoes and headed into the kitchen. There, he retrieved the last of the money he had kept in case Kevin needed quick cash and found one of the last prepaid cell phones they had been using for communications over the last year. After stuffing everything into the suitcase, he opened the cabinet doors that enclosed the microwave. Taped beneath the bottom was the result of the DNA sample he had received from the Lewisville office. Sliding the envelope that contained the crucial information regarding Gene's abnormal genetic makeup inside his shirt, Butch retraced his steps until he was back to the barn. Then he climbed over the fence and carried his clothes and other items to Renee's Mustang.

Turning right out of the cul-de-sac onto West Aurora Vista Drive, he slowed slightly at FM 718 before heading south toward Newark. Still having seen no unwanted vehicles around his house, he sped away, knowing it was only a matter of time before the stables, his house, Tammy's house, and Kevin's place up in Vashti would be surrounded and searched. His only chance was to get as far away as possible and try to find a way to coordinate the rendezvous.

CHAPTER 2

Major Jerry Fleenor had just hung up his clandestine cell phone after notifying Butch of the need to disappear. After sliding it back beneath the front seat of his car, he hurried back toward the facility entrance. The phone call he had received from the Federal Bureau of Investigation (FBI) switchboard told him that a Texas Highway Patrol trooper had just minutes ago spotted what was considered to be one of their wanted fugitives. If correct, it provided the first positive information regarding Gene's or Leslie's location in several months, and the manhunt was about to renew with a vengeance.

His initial calls to Colonel Ericson and General Nelson would be the beginning of what he knew would be the final chapter in the nine-month search. Although he strongly disagreed with some of the methods that had been employed, especially what he considered unlawful actions against Butch North, his girlfriend Tammy, and other private citizens; he was still a military officer. Regardless of his personal feelings, he would continue to do his duty. Maybe he could even help moderate the repercussions of Butch's capture.

Hurrying back to the still functional command center that had been established during the initial phases of the hunt for Gene, Jerry plotted the location of where the trooper had seen Leslie and called the switchboard that had received the trooper's call. As soon as the operator answered, he directed her to call the number that had called in the information.

As he was waiting, Colonel Rick Erickson rushed into the room and asked, "Do we have a positive location?"

Jerry stood with the phone held to his ear and held one finger aloft as he asked, "Are you the person that reported the sighting of the fugitive from the Department of Defense (DOD) bulletin?"

After hearing that he had the correct individual, he said, "Please hold for a minute."

Jerry then turned to Rick and reported, "I believe so, sir. I called you and General Nelson as soon as I got the initial call and then called the switchboard to locate the caller. I am talking to him right now, and I'll know more in a minute or so."

Rick nodded and pointed to the map of northern Texas where Jerry had stuck a red pin, asking, "This where we think she is?"

"Yes, sir," Jerry acknowledged.

As Rick walked closer to the map, Jerry asked into the phone, "What other information do you have other than you believe you sighted our person?"

Listening to the trooper's detailed account of what had transpired with Leslie, Jerry's face turned white, and he asked, "What was that? Could you please repeat what you just said?"

As the trooper began again, he interrupted and said, "Please hold on for just a second. I'm putting you on the speaker."

"Colonel, you've got to hear this," Jerry told him as he transferred the call to the amplified speakers.

As soon as he heard the click and hum of the wall-mounted speakers, he said, "All right, please go ahead. Colonel Rick Erickson will be on the line also and be advised that we are recording this conversation."

The trooper's voice became distinctly official as he began reporting that he had stopped a speeding car just south of the Red River, and the young lady driving was panicking, and she believed that she was about to deliver a baby. Seeing her condition, both mentally and physically, he elected to drive her to the clinic where his own daughter had been born. Having called the doctor on his way there, he had been met by the nurse, and they had helped the lady into the examination room. Upon the doctor's arrival, he had left and started to return to the location of the lady's car.

He had thought that he recognized her face, and after searching through the numerous wanted posters in his folder, he became positive and called immediately. The FBI operator had directed him to return to the clinic to observe the individual and maintain contact but not apprehend her. Upon his return to the clinic, she had already gone. After questioning the doctor, he determined that she had delivered a baby boy and was immediately taken away by a man that the doctor recognized but couldn't identify. He further stated that the doctor had watched them leave in a truck, although he had protested their leaving without further medical examination. The doctor stated that he had given specific advice to remain and that he believed that the baby had some abnormalities that he couldn't explain, especially given the rapid departure of the patients.

"What is your exact location now, trooper?" Rick demanded.

"I'm still in Ringgold, which is just south of the Red River off of Highway 81," came the response. "Do you want me to remain here?"

"That's affirmative, son," Colonel Erickson replied. "I'm sending some people your way, and they'll need you to retell your story and give them any assistance they request. Do I need to contact your supervisor to clear any of this?"

"No, sir," came the reply from the speakers. "I can call in and explain. They will probably send a couple of more units to assist me if they think they need it."

"That won't be necessary," Rick told him. "If you need to clear your schedule and have a replacement take your patrol, that's perfectly fine. But I want you to remain available, and no additional forces will be necessary at this point. I will request any needed support from Austin myself."

"Yes, sir," came the reply.

"And," Rick added, "Please keep this line open in case we need to call you."

"That's not a problem. Will there be anything else?"

"Not yet, son, you've done a great job. Just stand by for further instructions, and thanks," Rick told him as he motioned for Jerry to disconnect the call.

"Do you want me to recall the team?" Jerry asked as soon as the speakers went quiet.

"Definitely," Rick answered as he studied the map denoting the small town of Ringgold. "When do you expect General Nelson?"

"Any minute now," Jerry responded. "With your permission, I'll call the General's secretary as well. Ms. Blevins can help locate all the personnel if I have any difficulty in finding them immediately."

"Certainly," the Colonel told him as he did a quick calculation of the distance from the NAS/JRB to the small country town. "I'll call the Base Commander and request any aerial photos or aviation maps of this area. We need to determine where we can sit our choppers down."

Jerry sat at the desk and pulled the recall roster from its file. The major players of the initial search were still assigned to the facility, and he knew that each individual would rapidly execute their portion of the recall pyramid. After notifying the top two names, he called Kathy, General Nelson's secretary, to gain access to any information she maintained in her office.

With that done, Jerry wondered for the millionth time if he had done the right thing in warning Butch North. And for the millionth time, he wondered what would happen to him if they ever found out.

CHAPTER 3

Kevin Knox and Gene had rushed from their home just north of Ringgold the second they had gotten back from fishing up on the Red River. Noticing the car missing caused initial concern, and once inside the house, it was confirmed by the note Leslie had left telling them she had headed for the doctor. Wasting no time, they ran back to Kevin's old pickup and slung gravel as they accelerated down the driveway.

"Crap," Kevin exclaimed as they turned south on County Road 2332. "I hope she's all right and not some premature problem with the baby."

Gene clutched the armrest and braced his feet against the floor as they bounced along the road. "Do you think she's okay?" he asked as he watched the trees along the road go flashing past. He didn't think he had ever been going this fast in a car during his entire life.

"Oh, I'm sure she is," Kevin answered, trying not to alarm him. "My ex-wife had several false starts. I remember rushing her to the hospital two or three times before she finally had our daughter."

"Is that normal?" Gene queried since he had never been around pregnant women or knew anyone who had discussed all the issues of going into labor.

"More or less," Kevin acknowledged as he tried to keep the ancient old truck from wandering too far from the center of the narrow road. "Especially with the first one, you've got to remember that this is Leslie's first time also. She probably just felt some pain and decided that it was time. I just wish we had been home to help her before she rushed off."

"It's my fault, isn't it?" Gene asked, looking forlorn and helpless. "If I hadn't wanted to go fishing, we would have been there with her."

"It's no one's fault," Kevin told him. "We all knew that the due date was coming, but that was just the doctor's guess. Mother Nature gets to make the decision as to the kid's actual birthday."

Just a couple of miles north of Ringgold Kevin spotted his car sitting beside the road and slid to a stop behind it. Both men jumped from the truck and ran to look inside. Seeing nobody in the car and no evidence of injury, Kevin frowned and looked off into the distance, saying, "What the hell is going on? Where is Leslie?"

Gene was looking practically scared to death as he stared helplessly into the vacant car. "Oh God, oh God, oh God," he kept saying, "What's happened?"

Kevin finally grabbed him by the arm and pulled him back to the truck, telling him, "She probably got a ride on into town with someone. We'll head for the clinic, and I'm sure she's there waiting for us. Probably embarrassed that she panicked, you'll see. It'll be all right."

Jumping into the truck, they sped on into Ringgold and came sliding to a stop just outside the clinic. Telling Gene to wait in the truck, Kevin ran into the small building that was the closest thing to a hospital in that particular part of the country. After he crossed the waiting room, he went to the examination room where he had brought Leslie for all of her checkups since determining she was pregnant.

The minute he entered the room, he saw the doctor holding the newborn and the nurse standing completely still with her hands on her face. A glance at Leslie's face told him that she was at least all right for now, but he had to get her and the baby out of there.

"Doctor, are they both all right?" he asked, looking at the baby and Leslie.

The doctor looked up from the baby and answered, "I don't know, I think so, but I've never seen anything like this."

Telling the doctor to hurry and get them ready to travel, Kevin rushed back out to the truck and told Gene that he believed Leslie and the baby were all right. As he was reassuring Gene, he pulled a cell phone from beneath the seat and called Butch.

After explaining the situation and discussing their decisions, Kevin ran back into the clinic just in time to see the doctor wrapping the child in a soft white blanket. "Can they travel?" he asked as the nurse handed Leslie her child.

"I assume so," the doctor replied. "But I strongly advise against it. She needs rest, and we need to see if there are any complications. And I'm not sure what problems this child may have, but I need to watch it."

Telling the doctor that it was impossible for them to remain there any longer, he asked Leslie if she could get up and stated that they needed to get to a specialist.

As he rushed Leslie and the child out of the room, the doctor asked where they were going and what was wrong with the baby. Kevin just replied that there was nothing wrong with this baby, and they didn't need to know where they were going. With that, he hurried them out to the pickup, where Gene was almost frantic with worry.

As they sped away from the clinic, his phone rang, and Kevin answered, knowing it was Butch. He wanted to tell him how everything had gone, but before he could begin, Butch told him to forget going home. Now, they were to start heading toward Abilene as he learned that they had been discovered.

Kevin reversed the truck and headed south on Highway 81 toward Bowie. The game had changed dramatically now. His plan to keep Gene, Leslie, and their child safely hidden in the dense woods just south of the Red River was over. He knew Butch was quickly working on some escape plan for them, and he could only wait to get the details.

Kevin slammed his hand against the steering wheel and exclaimed, "Shit, they'll find the car and trace it to me."

Leslie looked up from her baby and told him, "I had to leave it parked there; the highway patrolman that stopped me made me go with him to the doctor."

"What?" exclaimed Kevin, "You were taken to the clinic by the cops?"

"Yes," she answered, "After he pulled me over, I didn't have any choice! And I was scared that I was going to have the baby right there in the car. I didn't have a choice!"

"I know, I know," Kevin said, trying to reduce the level of panic and hysteria within the truck. "I just realized that we have even less time than I thought."

"What do you mean?" Gene asked as he stared in amazement at his newborn son. He desperately wanted to touch him or hold him, but at the moment, things were happening so very fast, and it was all too confusing.

"They already have our pictures," he explained. "I'm sure that's what Butch meant. Someone recognized you, and that must have been the Trooper. Now, he certainly knows about the car you were driving, and it won't take long for them to trace that to me. Do you understand why knowing the State Trooper found you means so much?"

"I see what you're saying," Gene acknowledged, still watching the baby's eyes staring back at him.

"Well," Kevin told them, slowing slightly as they passed Stoneburg, "I've got to get rid of this truck. Once they have my identification, they'll know every vehicle I own and will be looking for each of them."

"They've already found the car," he continued as he accelerated passing the small town. "Next, they'll find the truck I left in the garage at my place. That'll sure set them off. They've been looking for that truck ever since we started trying to hide you guys. If there's anything that will tie me to you and Butch, it's that truck."

Watching closely for any sign of police or unusual vehicles, Kevin then explained, "Once they tie me to the truck and car, they'll find out about the place where you've been living. There's enough stuff there to prove without any doubt who we are. Next, they'll run checks and find out about this old heap of junk."

Leslie finally took her eyes off her baby and noticed that Gene hadn't moved a muscle since they had left the clinic. Smiling at him, watching their child, she finally asked, "Do you want to hold our son?"

"I'm not sure," he answered. "I've never seen such a tiny person."

"That's all right," she told him. "Pretty soon, he'll be growing just as big as you. Hold him; he needs to meet his daddy."

Gene reluctantly took the baby in his arms and marveled at the tiny fingers and features. "He seems so helpless. I don't know anything about what to do; I've never seen a real baby before."

"Don't worry," Leslie soothed him as she put her hand on his arm. "I've had a little experience with some of my family's and friends' kids. I think I can figure it out."

"Aren't you guys forgetting somebody?" Kevin asked as he prepared to turn south on Texas State Road 59. "I'm pretty sure I know somebody in this truck that has raised children, well maybe not children, but at least a child. Are you two going to forget about me?"

"Certainly not," Leslie told him. "You've been like family to us since you first started hiding us. You can be his grandfather or great uncle, or whatever you want. We wouldn't dream of being without you around to help us raise him."

"Well, if I don't get rid of this truck soon, I don't think we'll have to worry much about being taken care of or who will raise that child," he told them as he started looking for county road 2127 that led to Post Oak.

"You guys remember that little trailer where I first brought you two together after I '*kidnapped*' Leslie?" he asked.

Not waiting for an answer, he continued, "Well, ol' Mikey Carmichael owned that land, and I happen to know that he kept an old 4-door Ford sedan up by his house. I'm going to make him trade this old truck for that piece of junk that's just been sitting there for the last year or so. I just hope it starts and the tires aren't flat."

Making the right turn onto 2127 and finding the gravel road that led to the KC Ranch that Mikey owned, Kevin heard the phone ring again. As he answered it, he saw the cattle guard that separated the road to the ranch house from the public road. Bouncing across the cattle guard made from 3-inch pipes onto the rutted gravel drive, he listened to Butch give him the next set of instructions.

"I'll be there," he said, hanging up the phone. "Well kids, slight change of plan. As soon as we can swap vehicles, we're heading for Stephenville. We'll stop for some supplies when we hit Jacksboro. You guys figure out what we'll need, like diapers and things, while I leave a note for Mikey. Can't let him think someone stole his car, and I've got to tell him to hide this old truck, or he'll be in almost as much trouble as we are."

They continued on along the rough road, bouncing back and forth as they crossed dry washes, and mesquite branches brushed the sides of the truck. Gene still hadn't taken their eyes off the baby, and it appeared to be just as interested in him. Leslie sat smiling as she watched the people she cared for most in the world try to get away so they could live like normal families. She missed her mother and wished she could share this joy with her, but she also knew how much trouble both Butch and Kevin had gone to trying to protect her and Gene.

Maybe someday they can be a real family again, with all her friends and the people she had known for many years. She surely hoped so, but for now, she was satisfied to be with her baby, its father, and the man who had spent the last nine months taking care of them. If she had to live the rest of her life with just these people, she would be happy. Yes, she would be very happy indeed.

CHAPTER 4

Butch sped south on FM 718, slowing as necessary for the single stop light in Newark, until he joined Business 287 leading into Saginaw. Joining the 820 loop around Ft Worth to the west, he finally decided on what he considered to be the best option, and it was fairly direct, reasonably equal distance for all concerned, and provided a relatively secure meeting point.

As he continued around the loop, he realized that he would be passing within a couple of miles of the NAS/JRB where this saga had begun for Gene and, ultimately, many others, either directly or indirectly. *"They'll probably never look for me to be driving right by their front door,"* he thought as he passed White Settlement Road that led toward the main gate for the base.

Upon reaching US 377, he exited the loop and headed toward Benbrook. Once within that suburb just southwest of Ft Worth, he pulled into the first large grocery store he came to. As he parked and walked toward the entrance, he saw several helicopters leaving in formation from the direction of the base heading north.

Once inside the store, he grabbed a basket and went to where the pharmaceutical items were on display. Quickly, he selected a box of Q-tips, a bottle of alcohol, a pair of nail clippers, small scissors, and a box of latex gloves. The next stop was to acquire a box of quart-size zip lock freezer bags, a box of gallon size, and a couple of permanent markers to write on the bags. The photo shop provided the digital camera, a 128 MB disk that had the required capacity for the pictures he needed, and 20 padded envelopes to hold copies of everything he would hopefully accumulate. Finally, he took a legal-sized yellow pad from the office supply area.

Placing ten prepaid cell phones in his basket, Butch stepped to the counter and waited for the sales clerk to total all the items he had acquired. Taking five $100 bills and several $20 bills from his pocket, he paid the clerk and carried his sack back to his car. Sitting in the parking lot, he dialed the Sancudo's number and spoke quickly as it was answered.

"How's your trip north going?" he asked.

"I need for you to stay on that road until you reach US 87 toward Brady," Butch told him when he learned that his friend was much further north than he had predicted. "Get back on 377 there and keep going north until you hit 281, then head south. About a mile or so south of where you turn, you'll see what you will recognize as two 4's on the crap table. Understand?"

Realizing that Sancudo knew very well that two 4's were known as a 'Hard Eight', he finished by saying, "Look on your right as you go a mile or so, and I'll be waiting there, probably inside. Any questions?"

Hearing that his instructions were going to be followed, he replied, "Great, I'll see you in about 2 hours or so. Be ready to take a package to your amigos on the other side of the river. Thanks, my friend. It's been a long time, but I do appreciate your assistance. 'Til I see you there, drive with caution."

Butch then dialed Kevin's phone and waited for it to be answered. Upon hearing Gene's voice on the phone, he immediately exclaimed, "Congratulations, little fellow, I hear you're a proud papa of a bouncing baby boy!"

He listened while Gene tried to explain how beautiful the baby was, how beautiful Leslie was, and how proud he was. Not wanting to dispel his exuberance, he waited a little longer than he wanted but finally told him to put Kevin on the phone.

Kevin spoke one word as he took the phone, "Asshole!"

Laughing, Butch responded, "So much love, so much love! Ready for some directions?"

"Okay, here's the plan," Butch started. "Do you remember the Bar-B-Q that our little friend Bandy loved when he was bull riding in college?"

Both men knew Mike Bandy and that he had gone to Tarleton State University in Stephenville. Kevin also knew of the Hard Eight Bar-B-Q restaurant located just across the street from the local airfield. They had flown down from Hick's Field with a friend of Butch's that just wanted to fly his much beloved Beechcraft Bonanza one sunny afternoon several years ago.

"Of course," Kevin answered. "Best eating for miles around. Are you planning on taking us out to dinner?"

"Depends," Butch said, "Have you passed Jacksboro, or are you still wandering around the scenic hills north of there?"

"Had to do a little auto adjustment," Kevin told him. "We're just about to hit the town. Navigation suggestions would be appreciated."

"Great," Butch smiled, "281 and an hour and a half will put you just about where you need to be. Think you'll recognize the place?"

"Not a problem," Kevin said. "By the way, everyone's so happy they're making me nauseous. Can I go home now?"

"Bull shit," Butch laughed, "You'd stick with your 'kids' through 100 miles of muddy road if you had to, and you know it. Take care, my friend, and I'll chew a rib with you later."

After hearing Kevin's final smart retort, Butch smiled and started the car. He knew that he could be parked at the Hard Eight in a little over an hour and would have plenty of time to get his packages ready for their arrival. He needed to make a few copies of the genetic results before he got to Stephenville, and seeing an office supply store just down the street, he knew they would have copying services.

The short drive south on 281 took only seconds, and after parking, he took the envelope from his suitcase sitting on the passenger seat beside him. He was hoping that since all the activity the people at the NAS/JRB had known about was north of Ft Worth, they would concentrate their efforts in that direction. This was especially true since Leslie had been spotted so far north, at least to his way of thinking. Maybe, just maybe, they would think they had tried to run across the Red River to that bastion of evil known as Oklahoma. Of course, if they really knew him, they would have known that was a most unlikely course of action.

The office supply store gladly accommodated his request, and Butch made 20 copies of each page of the report that he hoped would give him a little leverage against his adversaries when he was brought before them. If he could just manage enough time to compile all the things he thought would provide any strength in bargaining with those folks. A mighty big if at this point, but each precious minute they continued their southern unobserved movement gave him increased confidence.

Butch drove to the first gas station on the right-hand side of the road and filled Renee's car with fuel, checked the oil, and water level, and gave the tires a kick to do a quick cowboy pressure check. He remembered from his Air Force days the old adage of 'Kick the tires and light the fires,' meaning to do an abbreviated preflight of the aircraft and get the afterburners cooking for take-off as soon as possible. With the complexity of the later fighters, that was hardly enough to ensure you would make it out to the runway. He still marveled at the capabilities of today's modern jets and even more at the abilities of the young pilots taking them into battle.

As soon as he finished with the car, he walked into the combination gas station, convenience store, remote banking facility, auto parts store, and rest area. Paying with one of the $100 bills, he asked for a couple of dollars in change to use the phone. Accepting his receipt, he went to the rear of the store, where the restrooms and pay phone were located. *"This is almost a miracle," he thought, "Not many pay phones left with the accessibility of cell phones."*

After taking his personal phone from its tooled holder on his right side, he scrolled through the directory until he found the number for the Woodhaven National Bank in Rhome. After it was answered, he asked for the branch manager and waited for Renee to pick up the line.

Hearing her 'official' voice, he said, "No need to be so formal with me, Renee. I just wanted to tell you that it may be a couple of more days until I can return your beautiful little Mustang. If you would please be so kind, I want you to rent a car to use until I get yours back. I will pay for any expenses and will also pay $100 a day for the use of yours."

He listened to Renee tell him that she already had a car, one her husband had bought for their daughter, but it wasn't going to be used for at least a week. It seems the light of their eyes had committed some gross violation of proper etiquette and would be spending the next few days contemplating her transgressions.

Butch began to laugh as he listened to her eloquent description of the situation and told her, "Hey, I'm just a dumb-assed country boy. If your words exceed four letters, I've got to find a translator. But I do understand that the little sweetie stayed out a wee bit too long and will remain home until she can properly tell time, even if the clock has hands."

Again, Renee ensured him that there was no need for rentals, but Butch ended the conversation with, "Have it your way; I appreciate it. But I will pay fair rental rates for your car and I insist on taking you and the rest of your loved ones to a fine steak dinner up at Cow Camp Steak House when I return. End of negotiations, you are hereby dismissed. Oh yes, thank you. You've been a great friend."

Butch replaced the phone and entered the men's room to take care of one more urgent issue. Moments later, he emerged and headed for the doors. Spying the cold Dr. Peppers resting in the glassed-in cooler, he yielded to temptation and purchased a bottle for the hour-long drive down to Stephenville.

CHAPTER 5

Major Jerry Fleenor was still on the phone when General Mike Nelson entered the operations center. Quickly straightening his posture, he nodded in acknowledgment of his arrival and terminated the conversation as rapidly as possible.

Mike walked to the map where Rick was intently studying the area where Leslie was supposedly recognized. As he approached, Rick stood at attention and said, "Good morning, General."

"I hope you're right about that, Rick. Do we have a positive sighting of Ms. Barber?" he replied. "If so, that will be the first good news in over eight months."

"The report came from a Texas Highway Patrol Trooper up north of Bowie," Rick answered as he relaxed slightly. "He is certain that the lady he drove to a small clinic in that area is Leslie Barber. I'm working on getting a team up there as soon as I can to verify his sighting."

"What was the reason for him taking her to the clinic?" Mike queried. "I'm sure the state of Texas doesn't normally make ambulance runs, even in the remote areas."

"I don't have all the information, but it appears that she was speeding toward the small town of Ringgold when he pulled her over. At that point, she told him that she was about to go into labor and needed to get to the clinic that must be the only medical facility in that area."

Astonished at that, Mike asked, "Did you just tell me that she was having a child?"

"Yes, sir," Rick responded. "And if it is her, and if she has been with Gene this entire time, then there is only one conclusion to be drawn."

Shaking his head, Mike told him, "If true, our problems may have gotten worse. Have you located the doctor or whoever saw this lady? Are we even sure she did deliver a child?"

Shaking his head, Rick answered, "Not yet, sir. As I said, we've just begun getting a team to the area. As of right now, it's all speculation. But we will have proof of all of that as soon as we get people to the area. Unless you have any specific directives, I'm working with the Base Commander, General Gary Brown, to get a couple of helicopters to take some of our team to the location."

"No, that's exactly what we need to do," Mike agreed. "Do you need me to talk to General Brown?"

"No sir," Rick said. "I can take care of that, and as soon as Jerry gets all of your people here, we can decide who goes to take control of the situation up there."

"Is there any clue as to where our mysterious Mr. Won Dum Phuc is at this time? Or if Gene, Mr. Phuc, or even Butch North is still involved with Leslie?" Mike asked.

"Nothing positive on any of those people," Rick said. "But, as before, I still believe they are all tied together. There were just too many coincidences for them not to be jointly involved, regardless of the lack of concrete evidence."

"I agree with you," General Nelson told him as he turned from the map and faced Major Fleenor. "Jerry, where do we stand on the recall?"

"Sir," Jerry said, standing at attention, "The first tier was finished less than a minute ago, and they should have completed their contacts by now. I estimate that we will have everyone here within the hour, possibly sooner if they aren't too far from the base."

"Fine, have you called my secretary?" Mike asked.

"Yes, sir," Jerry replied. "I notified Kathy that she should come in as soon as she could and that we would probably need to get access to any of the files she stored from our initial searches. She told me she would be here in about 30 minutes or so."

"Excellent," Mike told him. "I'll get her to work as soon as she arrives. Has anyone set up the conference room?"

"Not yet, sir," Rick replied. "As soon as I finish coordinating the helicopters and make sure we have a safe landing area that can readily access the clinic, I will help Jerry get everything ready in there."

"All right," Mike said as he turned to leave the room. "I'll be in my office and meet Kathy. For now, let's concentrate on finding anyone up there who had any contact with Leslie. Make sure we can get that State Trooper's cooperation and, if necessary, contact their headquarters to ensure his availability."

Rick and Jerry returned to attention as Mike left the room. Once he was clear, Rick asked Jerry, "Is there anything else you can think of to help provide any more information before the meeting?"

"I do think I need to see if I can get any more information from the Trooper who saw her," Jerry answered.

"I will also see if I can get that doctor on the line and try to find out exactly what he saw and encourage him to remain there until we arrive."

"Make sure he secures everything available concerning the delivery of that baby," Rick directed. "If that child is our Leslie's, and if it is the result of a union with Gene, I want every molecule confiscated. And that includes sheets, instruments, towels, their clothing, I mean sterilize that area. We can take no chances of future evidence of a strange DNA becoming known to the public. That would be just about as dangerous as having Gene on Fox News."

"I understand, sir," Jerry said. "When we select our team to go, I think we need Colonel Amy Moore to command the team. At this point, it's more of a medical issue than an apprehension situation."

"That's probably the best thing to do," Rick acknowledged. "But that will ultimately be General Nelson's decision. However, I will support your recommendation."

Jerry paused a moment and then asked, "Do you think we need to bring that Trooper down, as well as those who were immediately involved with the delivery of the baby?"

"Possibly," Rick said. "But I think we need to verify the identity of this Leslie. Until we do that, we're just guessing. And I don't want premature celebration or conjecture until we absolutely confirm her identity. If the child is indeed the result of Gene's and Leslie's union, we'll know as soon as Amy gets some tissue to test."

"I've done about all I can except try to get the doctor's phone number," Jerry told him. "Do you want me to start building briefing folders for the conference as soon as I have their information?"

Colonel Erickson stood deep in thought as he contemplated the implications of a child with a genetic makeup involving their project. What was the result, and if recovered, where would this lead the program?

"All right," he finally said. "Try to get that Trooper on the line and expand our knowledge of the events and tell him to be prepared to come back with the team if General Nelson believes it to be necessary. Also, get that doctor on the line and try to find out what he knows. Advise him that he may need to come here also."

"I'll get that taken care of right now," Jerry said as he returned to his desk.

"Don't forget to determine if there are any other people involved up there," Rick ordered. "I think we need to have all personnel removed from that clinic and use the Trooper to accomplish it. Then direct him to make damn sure nobody, and I mean absolutely nobody, reenters that building."

Jerry picked the phone up and started dialing the number that the Trooper had given him.

"If that man has any reservations about doing what you ask, let me know," Rick told him. "Be sure he's aware that we can guarantee the state's full cooperation, and any reluctance on his part will not go well with future career opportunities."

"I'll be as direct as possible," Jerry replied. "I'm sure he will be fully cooperative, and we'll have no problems there. The doctor may be a little less inclined to abandon his facility or to provide any information. Doctors seem to have an issue with doctor/patient privilege things.

"I know," Rick retorted. "But, I think we can invoke national security to get around any ridiculous privilege issues. If he wants to play that card, I'll bet on my hand in this game. Furthermore, I don't care if he tries to use that leftist batch of ACLU idiots, either. In this game, we make the rules."

"Yes, sir," Jerry answered, waiting for the call to the trooper to be answered.

As Rick left the room to begin preparing the conference room for the upcoming meeting, Jerry shook his head and worried even more about the legality of the continued intrusion into these people's personal rights.

This talk of even more intrusion into people's lives further validated the concerns he had when he first decided to contact Butch North. Just how far this organization was willing to go to protect its program weighed heavily on his mind. Someone needed to step back and see if what they were doing was worth all the violations they seemed to be willing to take.

"Trooper," Jerry said as the phone was answered. "First off, what is your name? We neglected to ask you when we were talking, and I prefer to work on more of a personal basis."

Upon learning his name, Jerry told him, "Thomas, well, it's good to know you, sir. We really appreciate what you've done. It's good to know our law enforcement officers are doing such a commendable job."

Pausing while the complementary bone was being gnawed by the trooper, Jerry finally continued, "I need a couple of things from you at this point and hope you'll help us with them. Again, if you need us to contact your headquarters to assist you, we can."

Waiting for the response from the thinly veiled threat, Jerry continued, "I would like to talk to the doctor and anyone else there during the delivery. Exactly who was involved that you know of?"

As Thomas began telling him the names, Jerry scribbled the names of the nurse, Amber, and the doctor,

Adams. Then Jerry prepared to ask him to do what he personally hated to ask.

"Thanks, Thomas," Jerry told him. "Now, do you think you could persuade Doctor Adams and Amber to leave the clinic and lock the doors? Additionally, if there are any other people in there, they need to be asked to leave."

Waiting for the response, Jerry continued, "Once that's accomplished, we need you to make sure nobody reenters the facility and the contents remain undisturbed until we arrive."

Hearing that Thomas was planning on cooperating as best he could, Jerry asked, "Could you please ask Doctor Adams and Amber to talk to me? I'll be glad to call them if you can get me the number. Oh yes, when you get the people out of the clinic, I need you to remain there to guard the property. We'll probably be treating this as you would any crime scene, and your actions will certainly help secure the integrity of the investigation."

Thomas told him he would ask the doctor and nurse to talk to him, but he needed to hang up his phone while he went into the clinic. Jerry acknowledged, saying, "Call back when you get them available to talk or with their phone number. I'll be waiting, and thanks again, Thomas."

CHAPTER 6

Kevin had the sedan running as fast as he thought he could go on the rocky and rutted road leading out of Mikey Carmichael's ranch. It was a little smoother to ride in than the old truck he had left behind. The note explaining that he had taken the car and directions to hide the truck in the barn wouldn't be too much of a surprise for Mikey. He probably didn't know any of the details of what he and Butch had been doing, but he would do as he was asked and remain silent. Out here, a man didn't pry into another's business unless there was very good reason.

Not only was the ride smoother, but the extra room provided a lot more comfort for Leslie and the baby with them in the rear seat. Kevin was anxious to get into Jacksboro and get some supplies. All the things they had bought and kept at the place north of Ringgold would soon be evidence against them. But, more importantly, they ran a risk every time they entered a public store. He didn't believe they could get pictures or information on them out so soon, but he didn't want to take any chances.

Kevin pulled into the gas/convenience store and told Gene and Leslie to remain in the car while he filled it with gas and found as many of the items they needed in the store. Since he needed to pay before the pump would allow him to dispense the gas, he left the car parked by the pumps that were as far from the clerk's view as possible.

"Howdy," Kevin said as he approached the counter where the only person in the store sat reading.

The clerk looked up from his book and asked, "Cash or credit?"

"Cash," Kevin said, taking three $20's from his pocket. "This should be plenty. Are the pumps on?"

"As soon as I put the money in the cash register, I will turn one on," he answered. "Which one are you using?"

Kevin handed him the money and looked at him for a moment, smiling, and finally told him, "Well, son, I reckon it would be the one with the car beside it. What do you think?"

Finally, looking out of the window, the clerk glared back and punched a few keys on the cash register. As soon as he shut the drawer, he said, "You can now use pump 3. It will shut off if you try to put more than $60 in your car."

"Not a problem," Kevin said as he took the receipt from him. As he turned away and headed for the door, he glanced around the store to see if they had any diapers or blankets. He noticed a shelf with disposable diapers but very little else that would be useful.

Standing beside the car, holding the nozzle into the filler tube, he told Gene and Leslie, "Not much useful in there for us. I'd rather not buy the diapers here and still need to stop again. Unless you need them right now, I'd prefer to wait. Besides, I may have upset the towel-head running this place, and I sure don't want him remembering me buying diapers. I just don't look like the new papa sort, and it might be useful information if someone stops by and questions him later. I'd just as soon let him think I'm alone in the car anyway."

Leslie was sitting in the rear seat holding the baby while Gene sat in the front watching them. "I'm going to need them soon," she answered. "This little blanket they wrapped him in isn't going to last very long. How far is the next town?"

Kevin finished filling the tank and replaced the nozzle, telling her, "Well, Mineral Wells is about 30 or so miles down the road. I think there may be a store there that will have what we need. If not, we'll have to take a little detour or wait until we get to Stephenville, and that's another hour and a half past Mineral Wells."

Leslie looked at Gene and asked, "What do you think?"

Surprised, Gene asked, "Me? I don't know anything about that. You're going to have to make those decisions."

Leslie just smiled back and told him, "I know, but you need to start learning these things and helping me decide. Being a daddy will take more than just watching him, you know."

Gene looked chastised and mumbled, "I know I don't know anything. I'm sorry, and I'll try to learn. It seems so sudden, and although I read everything I could, it's just that I wasn't as ready as I thought I was."

"Don't worry," she told him. "I know you'll do fine once you get used to it. I just want you to help me make decisions about everything concerning our child."

"All right, children, I'll make this decision," Kevin said. "We head south and find the stuff down the road. If you two can't figure out the basics, it's going to be mighty tough if you're left alone."

Kevin walked back inside and waited for the clerk to put his book down. It was obvious that he was exacting some minor revenge for the previous insult, so Kevin stood quietly waiting.

Finally, he rang up the total and asked, "Will there be anything else?"

"None," Kevin replied. "That should do me until I reach either Springtown or Azle."

Kevin took his change, thanked him, and walked back to the car. As he got in and started it, he told Gene and Leslie to try to stay out of sight as they left. Obviously, the clerk hadn't paid any attention to them as they arrived, but he was certain that he would be watching them leave.

"Maybe I should learn not to be such an asshole," he said as he checked the road before pulling back onto 281. "It's just that I hate people that don't seem to care about customers. Probably some dislike of all the stores being run by turban-heads too."

About five miles south of Jacksboro, they passed State Road 199 that, went through Springtown and Azle into Ft Worth. If questioned, maybe the store clerk would at least remember that Kevin had mentioned heading in that direction. Any little subterfuge that would delay their discovery put them closer to what plans Butch was making.

The countryside south of Jacksboro was mainly rolling hills and rocky terrain, but at least the road was well maintained, and the only traffic they passed paid them no attention. The occasional truck would wave as they met, the way most of the people out in this area did. Kevin always returned the wave but watched them in his rearview mirror until he was certain that they continued in the opposite direction.

"I don't want you to think I'm paranoid," Kevin told them. "But I'm afraid that since Leslie has been seen and they will surely know about the baby now, we can't take any chances. We became almost too relaxed up there for so long and forgot that some very serious people are desperate to find us."

He waited for them to think about what he was telling them and then continued, "What I did back there was stupid. We have to be as unobtrusive as possible from now on. The level of intensity that went into the first hunt will pale in comparison to what they will do once they're sure of the baby."

"What else can we do?" Gene asked. "I'd go back and turn myself in if you thought it would do any good."

"No," Leslie screamed. "I won't let you do that. They can't have any of us."

"That wouldn't work anyway," Kevin told him. "Now they'll continue looking for each of us, especially the baby. The safest thing to do would be to split up and take separate directions."

"No, no, no," Leslie cried with tears running down her cheeks. "I don't care if they do take us, as long as we're together."

"I don't mean splitting up you three," Kevin quickly told her. "I mean getting you guys somewhere as safe as possible and for me to head somewhere else. Maybe they'd spend a lot of effort chasing me and give you a chance to disappear again."

"You mean you'd leave us?" Gene asked.

"I mean, it may come to that," Kevin acknowledged. "I don't want to, but when we meet Butch, he may be forced to split us up. I've known him for more years than you folks have been alive and sort of know how he thinks. I'd bet that when we meet in Stephenville, he'll have something in mind that would misdirect those people who are looking for you. I'm willing to bet that I'm the bait."

"He wouldn't do that, would he?" Gene replied. "He'll figure out how to keep us together; I just know it."

"I know he doesn't want to," Kevin said. "But he knows that the more people on their list, the more the chance that one of them will be seen, and that jeopardizes the rest. To his way of thinking, you folks are the things worth protecting. I'm the expendable one."

"He'd never let you get caught," Leslie said. "Just look at what he's done all this time when he could have turned us over and not worried about it."

"I know," Kevin said. "I also know he'd turn himself in before he'd give us up. But we've got to be prepared if he separates us when we get there. Even if it's just temporary and allows him to get us somewhere else."

"Well, if he does," Gene said, "I'm sure he'll figure out a way to get us back together somewhere."

Approaching the little town of Perrin, Kevin slowed slightly and watched closely for anything that looked unusual. Once out of town, he relaxed a little and wondered just what Butch was planning. What worried him most was the sudden change in direction. There must have been something that happened to cause him to deviate from whatever he had been planning for months. That was beginning to concern him.

Twenty minutes later, they were approaching Mineral Wells, and Kevin told them, "If I remember correctly, there's a Wal-Mart on the east side of town. They'll have everything we need, and I'll just be another fat man on a shopping spree in there."

Kevin turned left on FM 1821 and avoided the more congested route through the city. A couple of miles down the road, he came to the intersection with Highway 180 and saw that the store's parking lot was fairly crowded. Pulling into an empty slot several yards from the entrance, he said, "We'll just sit here a minute or so and watch the traffic."

He turned in his seat and looked at the small child held so lovingly in Leslie's arms. Just a glance at the two of them renewed his determination to do everything possible to protect them, and he knew Butch would do everything he could. If he had to be the sacrificial lamb, so be it.

"Say, do you know about the ghost that lives in the Baker Hotel here in Mineral Wells?" he asked.

Gene turned to face him and answered, "Ghost? What are you talking about?"

"Well," he began, "the story is that there's the ghost of a lady that lives on the 7th floor of the Baker Hotel. She's been heard repeatedly over the years but never seen. She is rumored to have been the mistress of the manager years ago and committed suicide when the love faded."

Leslie looked up and replied, "You don't believe that, do you?"

"Not saying yes or no," Kevin said. "Who knows what's real or imaginary these days? A year ago, I was sure there were no aliens, but now? All I'm telling you is what the tale is."

Gene's interest was mounting, and he asked, "How many ghosts live there, just her?"

Kevin smiled, knowing that he had taken their minds off the possibility of separation, even if just for a few minutes. "Oh, no," he continued. "There've been lots of things there. I think there was a story about a young boy, maybe 7 or 8, and his dog. I think he's the only one that's been seen. The others have just been heard, or they've done things like leaving a glass with lipstick on it. Once, a big party was heard by several people, but there was no party happening."

"I don't believe it," Leslie told him. "I think it's all a story to bring attention to the place and get visitors."

"Well, everyone has their opinion," Kevin said as he took a quick look around before opening the car door. "You can sit here and discuss it while I hit the store and do some power buying. Just remember to try and not be noticed. Don't do anything that would make people think you're hiding, but don't look at anybody that passes by. Just relax and tell ghost stories."

Kevin quietly closed the door and headed toward the entrance. As he walked, he pulled his billfold out and looked to see how much money he had left. It was getting pretty low, and he knew he couldn't use any credit cards without leaving an obvious trail. He counted just over $300 and figured that would be sufficient, but he had to be a little more cautious and just get the essentials.

CHAPTER 7

Butch left Benbrook, heading south on 377 at a rather leisurely pace. There was no real rush, and he knew that it would be very strange if he arrived too early and sat alone in the Hard Eight Restaurant. Although he did want to beat everyone else, he wanted to keep as low a profile as possible. Remaining in one location for too long would draw needless attention.

Just a few miles further down, he passed the small town of Cresson and started thinking about how much time one other element of his plan would take. Crossing over the Brazos River on the east side of Granbury, he pulled into a convenience store and parked in front. Entering the store, he went directly to the counter and bought another prepaid cell phone. *"My phone bill is getting out of hand,"* he thought as he recalled all of these 'one-use' phones he had bought over the last few months.

"Howdy," he said as he approached the counter. "I need one of those cell phones that have prepaid minutes. How much do I owe you?"

The clerk turned and looked at the display of phones on the wall behind him and asked, "How many minutes do you want? There are several different amounts of time available."

"Oh," Butch said, looking at the displayed phones. "I reckon about an hour or so will do."

"Well, this one has 90 minutes, the battery is pre-charged, and it only costs $25 dollars. Will that be sufficient?"

"That'll do," Butch told him, taking the money from his pocket. Sliding the Skoal money clip from the bills, he removed a $20 and a $10 and laid them on the counter.

"With tax, that'll be $27.19, sir. Will there be anything else?"

"Nope, that'll do it," Butch answered as he waited for the clerk to ring up his purchase and get his change before walking back to his car.

Sitting in the car watching traffic, he reevaluated the time schedule he believed they were all following. He wished he could call both Kevin and Sancudo to determine their exact location, but that was taking a chance that someone might hear them and be there as a very unwelcome greeting party. No, he decided, just get on down to Stephenville and give them time. If they weren't there within a few minutes of when he thought they should be, then he'd make the call.

What Butch really wanted to do was to give Tammy a quick call. Although he knew he ran the risk of having the call monitored and the location possibly known, he needed to let her know he was all right and to be prepared in case, she was taken in for an interview.

He had intentionally kept every detail of Gene, Leslie, Kevin, or any other aspect of the last nine months or so from her. He didn't worry about her revealing any details since she knew nothing about that portion of his life. But he wanted to let her know that there may be some questions that might portray him in a very unfavorable light. He hoped she had learned enough about him in the short time they had known each other that she wouldn't believe that he was the villainous character such as they would portray him.

Starting to dial her number from memory, he tried to think of the best way of breaking the disturbing news to her without frightening her too much. Finally deciding that regardless of what he told her, it couldn't lessen the reality of the problem. Hanging up just before he hit the last digit, he sat wondering how she would react to the interrogation she was sure to receive.

"I can't start letting my emotions dictate my actions now," he decided. Now certainly wasn't the time to start leaving even the slightest clue as to where he was or the direction he was headed. He knew they had monitored his trip to San Antonio and Del Rio several months ago and didn't want to appear to be heading even close to that direction.

Too much of his plan depended on getting Gene, Leslie, and the baby down to the border area, where he had a chance of getting them out of the jurisdiction of the US government. Although he doubted the mere existence of another country's border would completely stop them, it might make things a little more difficult. If Sancudo still maintained contact with his friends south of the Rio Grande, there were several isolated and remote locations where they could live while a permanent solution might be arranged.

During his assignment at Laughlin AFB, he had ridden his motorcycle all over that area of the country. Most of the trips were on the US side of the river, up to Langtry, where Judge Roy Bean made the law and dispensed his own brand of justice, and many of the small towns that held the history of early Texas.

Many miles of riding through the open country up toward the Big Bend area and across the border at little-known locations revealed an isolated land that held few people, and many of them wanted no contact with others. That seemed to be the perfect place to send someone that wanted no contact themselves. If anyone knew how to get lost in that part of the world, it was Sancudo.

With his help and the fact that Gene did have a faint resemblance to a mixed-origin Hispanic young man, it might provide the perfect approach to the problem. Although Butch had never seen the baby, the fact that Kevin hadn't posed it as a problem led him to believe that any abnormalities could be explained or covered up.

Back on the road, he passed through Tolar and Bluff Dale before reaching the outskirts of Stephenville. Turning left on 281, he saw the sign depicting the local airport on the left side of the road. He turned in and drove up to the operations office. He parked Renee's car there and walked across the ramp area, looking at the sparsely parked airplanes. There wasn't much activity, and the chance of being seen by anyone who knew any of them was extremely remote.

Butch headed back toward Highway 281 and down the road to the Hard Eight Restaurant. Checking his watch, he expected to see Kevin within the next 10 minutes or so. For now, he would stay on the east side of the road where he could watch arrivals. Not knowing what type of car Kevin was driving meant that he would have to pay attention to each one until he saw his friend.

Taking all of his purchases from the bags, he began addressing all of the envelopes. Most of the addresses were to people he knew at various universities, governmental offices, or other well-known individuals located throughout the state. Others were individuals that he knew from either the US Air Force or had met while flying for American Airlines.

Using the phone he had purchased in Benbrook, he called 18 people to confirm their address and advise them of a package they were to expect very shortly. Most importantly, he needed to get their assurance that they would adhere to the instructions he was providing. He gave them very explicit yet concise guidance as to the handling and security required. Each agreed to follow his directions and wait for further advice before taking any further actions.

Next, he labeled 20 of the quart zip lock bags with letters denoting whose samples were enclosed. There was a bag for each individual's fingernail cuttings and one for a lock of hair. Finally, he labeled three of the gallon-size bags with just the name of the donor who had supplied the samples.

He figured he would have almost an hour to take care of getting the samples and pictures before Sancudo arrived. Since he didn't want any of them seen with Gene and Leslie, he would have Kevin park his car over at the airport as far from the operations area as possible. While there, he would collect all of the material and have a chance to visit with Gene and Leslie.

Once Sancudo arrived, he could determine what the plan was regarding getting them headed toward the border. That part of the plan was going to be entirely in Sancudo's hands. He hated sending them off with a stranger, but there was no choice. And Kevin had been a stranger when he had picked them both up. And Leslie, in particular, had not viewed the initial meeting as the least bit friendly.

It had been well over two hours since they had started making the run south, and Butch was certain that the government wasn't sitting still. He was sure they would have teams heading to Ringgold within minutes of hearing about Leslie. Once there, they would soon know everything except where everyone had gone. The only thing he could do for now was cover their trail and try to mislead them as to where they were really headed.

If he could get everything he needed to accomplish before they left Stephenville, he had a chance. It was a slim one, and he didn't give it even odds of success, but for now, it was about the best he could do. The one thing that gave him some measure of hope was that there was at least one individual within the government's organization who seemed sympathetic to the situation. How much assistance he could provide, if any, was unknown. Even that man might have a change of heart if it came down to whose ass was on the line. But for now, he had some hope.

CHAPTER 8

Colonel Erickson was in the conference room, making sure all of the phones, television systems, and necessary accessories were sufficient. This would be the first time in several months they had met to review the current information and attempt to regain control of their product. Each time before, when they thought they had located Gene, they arrived only minutes too late.

Rick was well aware of the pressure that had been placed on General Nelson by the members of MJ12. This would probably be their last chance to redeem themselves and also the last chance to save their careers. Another failure would be the final nail in their coffins.

Jerry entered and began checking the coffee pot, cups, and amounts of cream and sugar. He needed to keep his hands busy and not say what was on his mind. He had said entirely too much when he had broached the subject of the group's disregard of Butch's privacy, that of his children, and that of Tammy Terbush.

"Did you get any more information from the Trooper?" Rick asked as he placed notepads in front of each chair.

"He agreed to get the doctor and nurse to talk to me," Jerry answered. "He'll have them call me after he clears the building. I don't think we'll have any problem with him."

"Well," Rick countered, "I can exert pressure on him through his bosses at their headquarters. I'm more concerned with the doctor and nurse. They saw the lady and her baby and have evidence that could make this very difficult for us. When do you think you can talk to them?"

"Thomas, the Trooper, was going in to talk to them just a minute ago," Jerry explained. "He had to hang up because his phone wouldn't have a signal within the building. They will either call when he comes back out, or he'll let me know otherwise."

"What about the material left inside?" Rick asked.

"He will treat the entire facility as a crime scene," Jerry answered. "If you don't need me in here right now, I'd like to return to the operations center and wait for his call."

"That's fine," Rick told him. "I'm waiting on a call about the helicopter support from the base. The rest of the group should be getting here any time now. Try to get some concrete answers from the doctor before the meeting starts if you can."

"Yes, sir," Jerry replied as he turned to leave the room.

Rick was still checking the final details when General Nelson walked in.

"Anything new?" Mike asked, walking over to the coffee pot.

"Not really, sir," Rick said. "Jerry is still talking to the Trooper and has gotten assurance that the facility will be vacated and secured."

"What about our transportation to the site?"

"I'm waiting for the Base Commander's call," Rick told him. "He said he would supply whatever we need; he just needs a little time to recall the pilots and reschedule the birds. I should be hearing back from him any time now."

As they were talking, Colonel Amy Moore, the laboratory commander, entered the room. "General Nelson, Colonel Erickson, I understand there have been some new developments regarding Gene," she said.

"Welcome, Amy," Mike told her. "Quite possibly, but until we verify the sighting, we'll proceed cautiously. Even if it was Leslie that was spotted, we have no positive connection with Gene. And it gets more interesting. But I'll cover that when the rest of the team arrives."

"Of course, sir," Amy said. "Is there anything I can do in the meantime?"

"Yes, although it may be premature, you need to direct your staff to be prepared to be flown up north and collect some samples that need to be treated as classified genetic material," Mike answered.

"Right away, General," Amy acknowledged. "How much material are we talking about?"

"About the amount you'd expect after a live birth," he told her. "Just phone down and advise them to start gathering their equipment. If you have any special requirements, let me know during the meeting."

"Yes, sir," Amy said as she stepped to one of the phones.

"Anything I can do to help?" Kathy Blevins asked as she walked in.

"Hello, Kathy," Mike said. "If you could retrieve any records you have regarding the people we identified as of interest during the search for Gene we conducted last September."

"Certainly, sir," she said as she turned to leave. "How many copies of each do you want? I only kept the originals of each."

"Just the originals will be fine for now," he told her. "If we determine that we have found one of the players, and if it proves to be connected with our project, we'll decide who needs copies at that point."

Leaving, she replied, "Yes, sir. I'll be back in about 10 minutes with them."

As she exited the room, Colonel Karyn Lynch greeted her and walked in. As the Communications Officer, she was responsible for all interfaces with outside agencies. This became extremely important during multi-force operations, and ensuring complete secrecy of classified material was paramount.

"General Nelson, Colonel Erickson," she said, approaching the conference table. "I assume from the urgency of the call that there is new information regarding Gene."

"Possibly," Mike told her. "I need you to be prepared to establish secure communications between our facility and base helicopters and get the remaining ground teams linked through us."

"Yes, sir," Karyn said. "Most of the equipment from the initial operation is still available and being used by the Suburban teams. There is adequate capacity for integration of the other systems."

"Fine," Mike said. "Please make a quick check in the operations room and let me know during the briefing if you need anything. We should be ready in about 10 minutes."

"I'll be ready," Karyn said as she departed the room.

Major Fleenor was talking on the phone when she entered. Making a rapid evaluation of each piece of equipment, Karyn made a few quick notes on a pad she picked up from Jerry's desk.

Jerry was busy writing as he held the phone against his head. "What was that you were telling me earlier about stopping her speeding car? Where is it now?"

He waited for the reply and then said, "Can you get someone out there to get the license plate numbers and remain with the car until we arrive? Have them report to you as soon as they determine the owner of the car. Consider it as part of the same crime scene as the clinic."

Scribbling as fast as he could, he asked, "What about the doctor and nurse? Will they talk to me?"

Hearing that they were standing there, he waited for either of them to take the phone from Thomas. As soon as he identified the speaker as the doctor, he said, "Doctor, I'm Major Jerry Fleenor from a facility down in Ft Worth. We are extremely interested in the young lady who gave birth in your clinic earlier today. What can you tell me?"

As the doctor began his story, Jerry interrupted him and told him, "Please, wait just a moment, sir. With your concurrence, I need to record this conversation so I don't miss anything or make a mistake when I report it to my Commander."

Jerry hit the record button on the phone and asked the doctor to begin again. As he listened to the tale of the birth of a strange-looking baby, he knew without a doubt that they had found the Leslie they were looking for and that the child most certainly was Gene's.

"Is there anything else you can think of?" Jerry asked when the doctor finished talking.

Hearing the negative reply, he asked, "May I speak to the nurse for a moment?"

As soon as Amber came on, he asked her, "Ma'am, do you mind if I record this conversation? I just need accuracy, and my memory isn't good enough to bet on, and my shorthand is horrible."

After she finished, Jerry asked to speak to the doctor again. Her version of the birth and then the rapid removal of both mother and child was nearly identical to the doctor's, and he felt he could rely on their stories. The next question he asked would be the most important, and he needed to approach the subject as delicately as possible.

"Doctor, do you think you could come down here and talk to our laboratory commander and describe what you saw? I'd also like for your nurse to accompany you. We'll make all the arrangements and try to have you back home later this evening."

When the doctor told him he would be glad to come and bring his nurse, Jerry smiled and said, "Thanks so much, doctor. If you'd just stay with Thomas, we'll let you know when to expect us.

"Good news?" Karyn asked as Jerry hung up the phone.

"Yes and no," he replied, reviewing his notes. "We may have more problems than we started with. However, I think we finally have a location for our missing man."

"Where do you think he is?" Karyn asked as she watched him taking the phone recording from the machine and replacing the small disk that could be downloaded to a computer.

Jerry stepped to the map, pointed to the small town of Ringgold, and told her, "Here's where we believe we've located Leslie."

"What about Gene?" she asked. "I thought we'd found him."

"I'm positive that he's with her," Jerry told her. "And there seems to be a baby involved, but you'll hear more about that during the meeting. Anything I can do to help you?"

"No, I don't think so," Karyn answered. "I'm just checking on the status of our communications links. Everything is still in place and operating. The only piece of equipment we don't have is the satellite for surveillance that we used before."

"Well, if you don't need me, I'll get back to the conference room and make sure this disk will play," Jerry told her as he gathered his material from the desk. "I'll see you in there, Colonel."

CHAPTER 9

"Good afternoon, sir," the elderly man told Kevin as he entered the store. "Welcome to Walmart. Do you need a cart?"

"Howdy," Kevin said, taking the shopping cart the man had pulled from the long line neatly arranged just inside the store. "How's your day going?"

"Just fine, and yours?" the man answered. Not waiting for an answer, the man turned to greet the next customer coming into the store.

Kevin headed straight to the infant section of the store and kept an eye out for anything he thought they might need. He wasn't sure exactly what Butch's plans were, but he knew he would have to get supplied for at least one day. It had been a long time since he had been shopping for a baby. Trying to recall the necessities blended in with the messages the television commercials had supplanted into his brain and had become one massive muddle of information overload.

Once within the section of the store that displayed all the necessary items for proper infant care, he was amazed by the amount of the various things available. The shelves were loaded with every sort of outerwear and in more colors and prints than imaginable.

He just stood there for a couple of minutes watching an obviously pregnant woman selecting a little from here, more from there, and something from the next shelf. Everywhere he looked, he saw sizes and styles that covered the entire spectrum of attire for the well-dressed toddler.

"Okay," he thought, *"let's just start naked and build our way out."*

Locating the shelves lined with several brands of disposable diapers, he searched until he found a group labeled for newborns. Since most of them were packaged in numbers of 30, he decided one would be sufficient.

Next came some sort of one-piece suit that snapped up the inner legs and middle to the neck. Since he didn't know the baby's weight, he picked up four pairs of four sizes ranging from 10 pounds to 15 pounds. If they were a little big, well, that just gave him some wiggle room. It's better than having the crotch cut into you.

Since the clothes had built-in feet, shoes wouldn't be necessary, but probably some socks just to keep his little feet warm. Oh yes, mittens, too. Since it was a boy, it wouldn't have to have too much of a frilly or feminine look. If this boy was going to be part of his family, he's gonna get jeans and boots. But that can wait for a year or two.

Wandering around the shelves and racks, Kevin spotted some small knitted caps and went over to inspect them. There was one with a picture of the Lone Ranger embossed on it; at least, that's what he thought looking at it. That had to be the one; at least, it was manly.

Having covered the little rascal from head to toe, Kevin decided to pick up a couple of blankets. Again, the number of styles, colors, and designs was staggering. He certainly wasn't going to stand there and hold up each one as he had seen so many of the women do. By now, most of the blankets were not quite folded correctly, but that didn't worry him.

Selecting one with the Dallas Cowboy emblem and another with the Texas A&M logo, he piled them on top of the diapers and clothes. Just down the aisle, he saw a collection of children's car seats and headed that way. As he arrived before the display, he couldn't believe what he saw. Again, the selection was overwhelming.

Settling on the simplest-looking model that appeared to be about the right size, he tossed it in. Next to the seats were what appeared to be 20 different types of baby strollers. They ranged from single-seat models to one that looked like it would hold four infants. The simplest folding version was selected, and on he went.

A vast array of bottles, liners, nipples, pacifiers, and items whose use he didn't recognize spread across the next layer of shelves. The one thing he didn't see was the old glass bottles he had used with his kid. Knowing they wouldn't have facilities for a while led him to select what appeared to be the most disposable type. Selection of nipples was easier; he just looked at what he thought he would enjoy and took 10.

Now to the formula, more critical decisions he was ill-equipped to make. Recognizing the familiar baby face on one batch, he took 12 cans. Of course, he had no clue as to how much the kid would require. Naturally, he had neglected to ask Leslie if she planned to nurse the baby. Oh well, these things probably had a shelf life of eons.

So far, it appeared that he had spent just under $100, and there was very little else he could think of that couldn't wait. About the only things left were some paper towels, wet wipes, and toilet paper. The bags the purchases were loaded in would suffice as waste containers and keep the mess to a minimum. It went against his nature to be using so many disposable items, but being on the run didn't allow much time to do laundry.

He figured another hour of road time, and they would see Butch. Maybe some snacks for the drive, but he was anxious to wrap his lips around one of those succulent ribs down at the Hard Eight. It had been over a year since he had tasted Bar-B-Q like that. It would be fun to watch Gene eat it since he didn't think the boy had ever eaten real Texas Bar-B-Q. The stuff they had grilled up by the Red River was no match for slow-cooked brisket or those juicy ribs.

A trip down the snack and chip aisle had netted him a bag of Doritos, tortilla chips, and a jar of Queso dip. Now standing in line to checkout, Kevin spotted a disposable camera with prepaid development. He grabbed a couple, smiling at how much fun it would be to look at their pictures over the years. Seeing the bottles of cold Dr Pepper, he took three.

The thought of the years ahead made him pause and wonder just how many years or even days; they may have if Butch didn't get them away from here. It had been a matter of luck and timing that had spared them from being captured when knowledge of Gene's disappearance had first occurred last September. Certainly, Butch had been instrumental in devising the plans that finally gave them a break from the ever-present threat, but luck had been on their side.

Well, never worry about what you can't control, Kevin thought as he waited for the rather obese woman in front of him to extract all of the high-calorie items she had piled into her shopping cart. *If you can control it, do so. If not, worrying never cures anything.*

Finally, Kevin got to start placing his items on the moving belt that carried them toward the cash register. Seeing him placing the first things on the belt, the lady in front turned and glared before slapping down the little square tube that separated the customer's purchases. Kevin just smiled and said, "Sorry, lady, I didn't think the cashier would believe you'd be buying baby things."

"Oh really," she retorted. "I happen to have two children myself."

"Twins?" he asked nonchalantly.

"Two girls, a three-year-old, and the baby is two," she huffed.

Still smiling, Kevin asked, "Different fathers?"

"No," she snorted, "what would make you think that?"

Kevin waited until she began pushing the overloaded shopping cart away and said, "I just didn't think any one man would have sex with you more than once."

He thought the lady was going to return and attack him! Seething, she stormed off as if she were trying to leave some foul smell behind her as quickly as possible. As Kevin turned his attention to the cashier, he could tell that she was doing everything possible to keep from laughing.

"Sorry, Miss," he told her. "Sometimes I just can't seem to keep my mouth shut. One of these days, it's going to get me into a lot of trouble. I just hope she doesn't have a husband her size waiting outside when I leave."

The girl kept smiling but refused to say anything until she had scanned each item and totaled the bill. "Cash or credit," she asked him, stifling her smile.

"I reckon I better pay cash," Kevin said. "She might come back here later tonight, go through all the old credit card receipts, find my name, and hunt me down like the sorry dog she thinks I am."

Seeing the total, he pulled the money from his billfold and handed it to her. As she put the money in the register and handed him his change, she said, "Thank you, sir. And have a very, very nice day. It was a real treat to wait on you; you've made my week."

"It was my pleasure," Kevin said as he took his change and grabbed all of the bags with his hands instead of using the cart. Turning to look back as he approached the door, he saw the girl smiling broadly as she was telling another one something that soon caused both of them to break out laughing.

Telling the greeter goodbye as he exited, he strolled across the parking lot, chuckling at himself and the ladies he left laughing within the store. Once again, he had opened his mouth and made someone certain to remember him. Hey, life's too short to watch every step. But there certainly was a need to be careful not to step into something you can't wash off your boots.

As he arrived at the car, he noticed Gene sitting in the back with Leslie and holding the baby. If there was ever a picture of a proud daddy, there it was. Kevin could hardly wait to get into the car and start taking pictures. His daughter was still single and not pregnant, thankfully. He envisioned being there with her when his first grandchild was born and the joy of seeing her and the baby's father together.

However, the opportunity was now, and these two were almost like they were his very own children. That made the baby almost his grandchild, and he would enjoy every second he could spend with them. Regardless of the ultimate outcome, the next day or so was going to be his and theirs.

Sliding behind the wheel, he pulled one of the small cameras out of the bag. "Look what I've got! Time for baby's first picture and shots of the proud parents, and then you get to take one of me and what is now my grandson."

Kevin took several of the baby lying on the blanket placed between Leslie and Gene. Then he took a few of each of them holding the baby separately and some of them with Gene's arm across Leslie's shoulders while she held the kid.

"Okay, my turn," he said as he handed Gene the camera. "Just get a couple of me holding this little rascal. By the way, have you decided what you're going to name him?"

Gene took the camera and started taking pictures of Kevin holding the baby in his arms. "We've decided to name him B K Grubbs," he said, watching for Kevin's reaction. That's for Butch, you, and the last name of the lady that was like a mother to me."

"Since I don't think I have a last name," he continued, "and I'm not even sure if *Gene* is my real name, we decided that if we get the chance to get married, those are the names we'll use."

If Kevin was ever sure he and Butch had done the right thing, it was now. He couldn't remember being this proud before in his life. Maybe he was seeing his baby daughter, but this was right up there. He lowered his head toward the baby so they couldn't see the moisture gathering in his eyes.

"You two have surely picked some sorry desperados to name that innocent child after," he mumbled desperately, sniffing and trying to be as gruff as possible.

"No," Leslie told him in a quiet, soft voice. "You two are the most sensitive and loyal men I have ever known. We're proud to have your names on our son. And we'll make sure he knows just how wonderful both of you are."

Kevin finally regained control and laughed, "You better not ever let Butch know you thought he was sensitive. He equates that with being light in your loafers, and I'd never even let him think there's the slightest homosexual thing about him."

"That's not what I mean, and you know it," Leslie laughed as she thought about Butch being the least bit gay. "Let's just change it and say you're the most 'caring' men I've ever met."

"Better, yep, definitely better," Kevin said as he passed little BK back across the seat to Leslie.

Taking the packages from the seat beside him, he handed them to Gene and told him, "Here, you sort this out and help the little missus take care of my grandson. Just stay back there while I drive; it shouldn't be much more than an hour, maybe less."

Kevin started the car and headed out of the parking lot. When he reached Highway 180, he made a right turn and proceeded straight ahead until he joined 281 going south.

"How about a Dr Pepper and a Doritos?" he asked as he sped south toward Stephenville. "And I want that second camera to be used to record BK's next couple of weeks. I don't need a bunch of naked kid pictures, and I know he'd rather not have them show up when he's a teenager. Especially when he brings his first girlfriend home."

They sped quickly down the road slowing only slightly passing through Morgan Mill. Each thinking their own thoughts but never dwelling on the fact that today might be the last one they spent together.

CHAPTER 10

Butch knew that there wasn't much to do now but wait for Kevin and the kids to arrive. He pulled his cell phone from his belt and checked the time. They should be here very shortly, and he will start getting his 'packages' ready for Kevin to send to the recipients.

Sitting there watching the traffic pass, Butch was suddenly very tired. The strain of getting Gene hidden back nine months ago had passed and was only a distant memory. It had been a hectic time, and the number of close calls was too many to count. Each time he had involved another person, he knew that it was a potential hole in the plans. But the main reason he tried to limit the number of people was the possible adverse impact on their lives.

Kevin had been his biggest ally and had become the prime player. He had been slightly reluctant at the beginning, but as time elapsed, he grew closer to Gene and Leslie until he would have sacrificed everything he owned to protect them. Without Kevin's involvement, they would have lost the battle long ago.

Butch still wanted to call Tammy and warn her. More than that, he wanted to tell her how much he missed her and wanted her with him. Maybe it was just the stress of orchestrating this current attempt to safeguard Gene and his 'family,' but a veil of loneliness was settling across his shoulders.

Thinking back to the years of living alone out on his ranch, he wondered if he was missing anything. Sure, there had been plenty of chances to be more involved romantically. But it seemed that the minute things got too close, he would find a way to distance himself once again.

During times when things were going smoothly, and his biggest worry had been when to sell the few roping steers or what time to head for the local cantina, he loved his private life. It was only when things began to get stressful that he wished for someone to talk to. The problem with that was he didn't think it fair to involve someone else in his problems. Especially one like this that could have very serious repercussions.

Very seldom did he just sit and think negative thoughts. Butch always held the philosophy that if you have a problem, you fix it. If you can't fix it, get help. If you can't get help, quit worrying about it and move on. Life has enough problems without wasting time on things you could do nothing about.

Thinking of things you could do nothing about, Butch wondered just how much time was available before the government would know exactly what had happened. He knew it would take them an hour or so to get people up north and begin their investigation. Certain that they would question the doctor, nurse, and trooper, he knew they would be aware of the child, and only an idiot couldn't add the pieces. And those folks were no idiots; they had been very clever but very unlucky.

Given the assets at their disposal, it would be only a matter of hours before they could have everyone's picture spread across the nation. It had been long enough since the first time they had shown Gene's face being tied to the atrocities of the World Trade Center disaster that few, if any, would tie the two events together.

No, now they would probably use some other ruse to portray the entire bunch of them as members of a radical party or terrorist cell. Even if they resurrected the old files, it would take very little time to embellish them with the current information.

If they could just remain undetected for the next couple of hours until Sancudo got here and headed back for the border. They stood a very good chance of saving Gene and the other two. As for Kevin and himself, there were slim odds to avoid being caught.

The only reason Kevin had avoided detection earlier was that he was never seen, and the truck that he had used was hidden in the barn at his ranch in Vashti. Since those first couple of days, he had remained well away from Butch, and their limited contact had been on disposable phones that were destroyed after only one use.

Although they had taken Butch and his daughters in for questioning immediately after learning of Gene's location in the Boyd area, they had left him alone since then. They had monitored his every move, tapped his phones, questioned everyone he contacted, and forced him to be very secretive in his actions. If it hadn't been for the one man from their organization who had provided him with the knowledge that Leslie had been spotted, they would probably all be in custody right now. When they placed you in custody, it wasn't in the local jail, and bail was not an option.

'*Tammy*,' he thought, *'you're the one I'm most concerned about.'* He knew that she was one of the most unique women he had ever met. And, he had placed her in very grave danger. The rest of them had more or less volunteered to play this game, but she was completely unaware of the risks and was entirely innocent.

Butch had dated numerous women since his divorce years ago. There had only been a couple that had lasted more than a few dates. As a matter of fact, there had been only two before her that had lasted more than a few months. Most of them had been wonderful and had remained friends with Butch after their 'mutual' separation. Smiling, he remembered what he had told his cousin about his *three-phase interview process* for selecting the new mother for his little girls. The first phase was to just spend the night, enjoy yourself, and be gone when he woke up. The second phase was the same, except that there should be a fresh pot of Folgers made for him before they left. Phase three included all the above: making breakfast, cleaning the house when he left, and, of course, being gone when he returned.

Although it was always meant to be a joke, he wondered if there wasn't some truth in the way he approached relationships. He always had difficulty in maintaining a relationship once it got past just going out and spending a night or two together. Either of the two he had dated for over two years each would have made any man happy. Both were very attractive, intelligent, motivated to succeed, and desirable in almost every fashion. Just why he had failed to close the deal was no great mystery to him.

Over a decade of being single and the bitter experience of his previous marriage made him cautious to the point of being a fault. It wasn't that he didn't really love those women; he just couldn't face things he knew would come with having someone else in his life permanently.

A very close friend had once told him that he lacked the capacity to express his feelings and emotions with women. Hell, he knew that! He didn't express his emotions to anyone. Maybe that was because he felt that if he didn't show vulnerability, he wouldn't be hurt. The cowboy rides away mentality. He had seen too many old Westerns when he was growing up. Hell, Matt didn't need Miss Kitty to move in, and he's the all-time cowboy hero!

Getting disgusted with all this self-pity, he reminded himself that he had set the rules, and if he didn't like the outcome, then he needed to do something about it. Like his great-grandfather had always told him, if you don't like the game, get out. Never worry about whether you're ahead or behind; just get out.

With that behind him, he decided to review what he would want to say when he gave himself up to those folks who really did want to talk to him. Mentally, he organized each point he should make, considered the responses he would likely get, and developed a counterargument.

They would be the ones setting the rules, and the only ace he had to play needed to be shown on the opening hand. He had never been a big fan of Texas Hold 'em, but he knew that having a high card showing meant a lot in the game that followed. Bluffing wasn't an option here; he had to let them know he had the winning hand. At least he had to let them know they couldn't win regardless of their strength.

As he sat considering and developing the play, a rather decrepit old Ford sedan pulled into the parking lot across the street at the Hard Eight. Noticing immediately that Kevin was behind the wheel, he started the Mustang and headed across the street as soon as traffic permitted. Pulling alongside, he said, "Hey, fat boy, taking the kids for a ride?"

Kevin smiled and replied, "Yep, got my boy, his wife, and little grandson. Would you like to meet them?"

"You bet," Butch answered. "I've heard a lot about them and would enjoy getting to know them. But, maybe you better follow me back across the street. Being a rather private fellow, I don't want to become emotional out here in public.

Butch wheeled the car around and headed back to the airport, with Kevin following closely. After getting back to the airport, they parked at the end of the lot, where only a couple of dusty vehicles sat, waiting for their owners to fly back in. Once parked, Butch exited his car and climbed into the front passenger seat carrying the packages he had been working on.

"Hello, Gene," he said, reaching his hand across the seat back. "It seems that a few things have changed since I last saw you."

Turning to Leslie, he said, "And I guess I owe you an apology and congratulations at the same time. Now, let me see that baby."

Leslie held the baby up and told him, "We've named him BK; that stands for Butch and Kevin."

Butch immediately noticed the abnormal eyes and other features that at first seemed strange, but given his heritage, it was to be expected. "He's beautiful," he told them. "I'm proud to have my name attached to this little rascal. But to pick such nefarious characters as Kevin and I shows poor judgment on your part, don't you think?"

They spent a few minutes talking before Butch finally said, "Well, now we have some work to do. First, I want pictures of each of you, individually and in groups that include Kevin and me."

They took turns facing the camera, standing side by side, holding the baby in different groups, and from each imaginable angle. Once Butch decided they had enough shots to depict every detail of each of them, he handed Kevin the camera and told him that he would need to get the photos transferred to several disks as soon as he could get to a photo shop.

Next, he pulled on a pair of sterile latex gloves and took the Q-tips from the box. Carefully, he swabbed the inside of Gene's, Leslie's, and the baby's mouths. Using two swabs per person, he then placed them in the quart zip-lock bags he had Kevin hold open. Once sealed, they were placed into separate gallon bags marked with their names.

Taking the nail clippers, he took a cut from the nail on each finger and toe, placing them into separate bags for each individual. These, too, went into the larger bags.

Finally, Butch took the scissors and cut a small lock of hair from each and bagged it as he had the other material. Once a bag containing all three samples was sealed, it was slid into one of the pre-addressed envelopes along with the written instructions and copies of the original DNA evaluation done in Lewisville that Butch had placed inside earlier.

"Once you get the packages assembled with the photos," Butch told Kevin, "you'll go to the Rhome Post Office. If you get there before they close, they'll guarantee delivery by noon tomorrow of the package going to the NAS/JRB. I'd like express delivery of the others, but make sure you ask for overnight on that one."

Butch paused while Kevin was looking at the packages, then told him, "There are no cameras in that post office, so you shouldn't be worried about recognition. And I don't believe they would expect you to be around that area anyway."

"One other thing," he told him. "I'll meet you there, and we'll drop the Mustang off at the Woodhaven Bank. I imagine Renee would like her car back."

"What's so important about this one?" Kevin asked, holding the envelope addressed to the NAS/JRB. "And, aren't you providing them the proof they need of our involvement?"

"To answer your last question first," Butch said, "they already know of our involvement. The car Leslie left behind, the doctor, the nurse, and the Trooper will give them all the proof they need. It can all be tied to you, and they already know about me. And any physical material left from the birth? They know, believe me, they know. They have all the proof they need as if they really need proof."

"As far as the importance of getting this envelope in their hands by noon tomorrow," Butch continued, "I plan on giving myself up at that time."

"What?" Gene and Leslie shouted from the back seat. "Why in the world would you do that?"

"Hold on a minute, folks," Butch replied. "First, this chase is over for me. Unless I'm willing to completely disappear, I have no choice. Second, if there's any chance of allowing y'all to live any sort of normal life, I've got to strike a bargain with those people."

"The one thing I haven't told any of you is that there is a man arriving shortly that will take you kids and the baby down south somewhere," Butch told them. "You'll stay with him until I can find some way to settle this thing."

"For now, you guys just sit here and discuss things while Kevin and I run across the street and get something to eat," Butch said as he got out of the car. "It's going to happen the way I've told you. There is no negotiating on your part. Your only options are to do as I say or turn yourselves in."

Pausing to let his words sink in, he finished, "Sancudo should be across the street in the next 30 minutes or so. When he arrives, I'll have him get take-out for all of y'all, and you can eat on the road."

"Now, if you don't like the way things are going to be done," Butch sternly told Gene and Leslie. "The keys are in the car. If you're not here when we come back with Sancudo, I guess you'll have made your decision."

With that, Butch turned and got in the Mustang. Kevin sat behind the wheel for a moment before turning to face Gene and Leslie. "Listen," he told them, "give me a few minutes to talk to Butch. I don't want you guys heading off somewhere without me. Just stay here until I get back, and we'll see if there isn't some other way to resolve this.

Getting out of the car, he pleaded, "Please, just give me a chance to change his mind." With that, he slid out of the car and got in with Butch for the short drive over to the Hard Eight.

CHAPTER 11

The conference room was filled when General Nelson walked in. As they all stood at attention, he motioned for them to sit and began, "Rick, let's have a quick overview and get started."

"Yes, sir," he replied, still standing. "First, I'll start with the known and proceed to what we are assuming."

Pausing while everyone looked on expectantly, he continued, "Major Fleenor received a call about an hour ago from a Texas Highway Patrol Trooper working up around Ringgold. He claimed he stopped a speeding car and took the obviously pregnant female driver to a local clinic."

"He was met at the clinic by the local doctor and nurse, who took the lady inside," he said. "When he headed back to where her car had been left, he thought he recognized her and looked through the wanted bulletins he carried."

"Finally finding the one we had published on Leslie, he called the FBI number listed. That call was immediately transferred to our operations center, and Major Fleenor, the on-duty officer, directed the Trooper to return to the clinic and observe but not approach."

"What about the car?" Mike asked. "Has anyone been sent to impound it?"

"Major Fleenor has been on the phone with the Trooper for the last few minutes before this meeting," Rick answered. "Jerry, have you gotten any information regarding that and the other personnel at the clinic?"

Jerry stood and referred to his notepad as he began, "Thomas, the State Trooper, is requesting assistance from his department to cover the car. I've asked for the license numbers to be processed and for us to be notified immediately."

"Additionally," he continued, "I've spoken with the doctor, Doctor Adams, I believe, and the nurse named Amber. They seem willing to talk with our people when we arrive and stated they will remain at the clinic until then."

"What about the clinic?" Colonel Amy Moore asked. "I need to obtain any material that may have evidence of the birth in case it is Gene's, as we're assuming."

"The clinic is currently being evacuated and sealed," Jerry told her. "I directed Thomas to treat the area as he would any crime scene, which included safeguarding any evidence within the clinic."

"Okay, what's the feeling on this thing," Mike finally asked. "Do we launch a full-scale investigation?"

Rick looked at Jerry and asked, "What's your take on this, Jerry? You've had almost all the contact and should have the best idea as to the probability of this being a chance to find Gene."

Jerry stood silently for just a second and then answered, "I believe that it was Leslie, and I believe that she has been with Gene this entire time. I think that if we can get there fast enough to find her, we'll find Gene."

Everyone in the room watched him as he looked General Nelson in the eyes and said, "The doctor and nurse both said something that leads me to believe that the child she delivered is the offspring of Gene. Of this, I have no doubt. I have the recordings of our conversations that should lead you to the same conclusion."

"Rick," General Nelson asked, "has the base got the helicopters ready?"

"Yes, sir," Rick answered. "I just got word before we started that the crews and choppers are standing by waiting for our instructions."

"Amy," Mike continued, "do you have the people from the lab ready to move out?"

"Yes, sir," Amy responded. "I'll be ready to go in 5 minutes. We've prepared containers for every bit of the material that may be present from the birth, and we can analyze it within 30 minutes of our return to verify if any of Gene's DNA is present."

"Okay, let's start the ball rolling," Mike said as he rose. "I'm going to call General Modelle and advise him of the sighting. He'll probably be on the next flight down from Washington."

Stopping at the door, he said, "Rick, get the cars and birds heading north. I don't need to tell any of you that if this ends up being a wild goose chase, we'll all be working as Wal-Mart greeters in Bumphuc, Egypt."

Mike left for his office, and Rick told the remaining officers, "All right, let's rebuild the entire system from the first search. Determine what support each of you requires and get it to me within the hour."

"Karyn," he said, "make sure you have sufficient encrypted radios and work on getting satellite coverage. If you need more, let me know."

"Amy, get your people together and meet me topside in 15 minutes. You'll have one of the choppers for your team and equipment."

"Jerry, get your contacts in Washington to start the process of loaning us one of their reconnaissance satellites. If you have trouble, let General Nelson know immediately."

All three acknowledged and rose to leave the room. "Jerry," Rick called as the rest departed, "get that Trooper back on the line. I'll talk to him when I get to operations."

Jerry acknowledged and left. Rick stood silently, hoping that this time things would work out. They were running almost an hour behind, but with any luck, they could start putting the pieces together. It was almost inconceivable that Leslie could disappear with the newborn baby and leave no trail. The evidence they left behind this time should be easy to follow.

Jerry entered the operations room and went directly to the phone. Dialing the number Thomas had left, he waited for him to answer. As soon as he heard his voice, he asked, "Do you have a name to go with that car you stopped?"

Holding his pen while he waited for the answer, he wrote *Won Dum Phuc* on the pad before him. As he listened to the Trooper recite the name and address from their search of the license plate, he scribbled directly below his previous notation: Kevin Knox, Vasthi, Texas.

Jerry took one look at the map and noticed the proximity of Ringgold, Vashti, and Bowie. 'Son of a bitch,' he thought. 'After all this time, we finally have you.'

Rick walked into the room as Jerry was finishing his conversation by asking Thomas to check for additional vehicles registered to the same name, and a physical address, if any, was on record.

"Got something?" Rick asked.

Jerry held one finger up and told Thomas, "Get me that information as soon as you can. I'll be standing by."

"Was that the Trooper I wanted to talk to?" Rick asked.

"Yes, sir," Jerry admitted hanging up. "I had to let him go; there's a crucial piece of information that we need right now."

"I think we've hit the jackpot," Jerry said, smiling as he finished his notes before looking up again. "Do you remember that red truck we couldn't identify?"

"Yeah, the one that kept showing up, but we never got enough information to tie it to anyone," Rick answered. "Have you found it?"

"No," Jerry admitted, "but I'll bet my next year's paycheck that it belongs to one Mr. Kevin Knox of Vashti, Texas."

"When will you know for sure?" Rick asked.

"They're searching for registered vehicles right now that match the name of the owner of the car the lady was driving," Jerry told him.

He walked over to the map and pointed to Vashti, telling Rick, "Here's the location of Knox's property. Every time we spotted the red truck, it was heading in this direction when it was moving. If he was involved with Gene, as we suspected, and now we know Leslie was driving one of his cars, then I'll still bet that check on finding the truck hidden there."

"Let's get a vehicle headed there right away," Rick directed. "With just the least bit of luck, that's where they'd head from the clinic. I'll take one of the choppers and some of our security people to that location. Amy's people can take a couple of the security folks with her, and you'll stay here and work with Karyn to run the operation."

"Yes, sir," Jerry acknowledged. "There's one other thing we ought to do while we're waiting to get things under control up there."

"What's that?" Rick asked.

"I don't believe that Mr. Knox would have kept Gene and Leslie at his house. I want to run a search for any additional property he may have."

"That's a good idea," Rick replied. "What about rentals? Do we have any way of finding out if he has rented or leased any other property?"

"My guess is that if he did, there's no public record," Jerry answered. "But I plan on accessing the postal records to see if there are any other locations that receive mail addressed to either Kevin Knox or Leslie Barber. I doubt if Gene had any mail sent from anyone."

"How long do you think that will take?" Rick asked.

"It shouldn't take long," Jerry told him. "I'll have Washington search the postal records and restrict it to a 100-mile radius of Bowie. I'd bet that there are less than ten names matching any combination of their names within that area."

"Okay," Rick said as he started to leave the room. "When Karyn gets here, make sure you pass any information to me personally. She'll have my discreet frequency, and I'll direct the ground vehicles from the air."

"One other thing," he said, stopping at the door, "Get the Texas Highway Patrol busy finding any other vehicle owned by our elusive Kevin Knox. I want that man to find every road blocked and every gate closed. If he is the man that's been hiding Gene all these months, I want him standing before me when I get back."

Then smiling menacingly, Rick said, "And get Butch North; I want to talk to him when I get back."

CHAPTER 12

Both Kevin and Butch were silent on the short drive across the street to the Hard Eight. For the first time in years, there was tension between the two. Never making eye contact, they parked and walked into the cooking area to select their meat before entering the restaurant.

Butch was first in line and looked at the various cuts sizzling on the large grills, the mesquite smoke rising around the ribs, brisket, chicken, and ham. Not only did everything look good, it smelled delicious.

Selecting four ribs and about ½ pound of sliced brisket, he took the tray and walked to the counter for an ear of corn, a bowl of potato salad, and a glass of tea. Kevin was sliding his tray right behind him when he arrived at the cashier. Paying for both of their meals, Butch went to one of the long picnic tables and sat his tray down. He took his glass to the ice dispenser and filled it before placing a slice of lemon on top. After he had let the tea run until the glass was almost full, he took a jalapeno and returned to the table.

Sitting there waiting for Kevin to return, he looked around the large dining area and all of the pictures and memorabilia on the walls. Although he had been there several times, he enjoyed looking at all the rodeo related pictures. In addition to hard eight, meaning two 4s on a pair of dice, it also referred to the rough 8 seconds a cowboy had to remain on the bull or horse to receive a score in the rodeo.

Kevin slid onto his seat and opened the napkin, holding his knife and fork. Finally looking at Butch, he said quietly but venomously, "Asshole!"

Surprised, Butch replied, "What did you say?"

"You heard me," Kevin answered. "I just said you're an asshole."

"And what do you mean by that?" Butch asked, picking up his glass and squeezing the lemon into the tea.

"Exactly what I said," Kevin said, staring at him. "Just who do you think you are to be doing this?"

"If you're referring to trying to get Gene and the others safely out of here," Butch said defiantly, "just who else do you expect to do it?"

"That's not what I'm talking about, asshole," Kevin told him. "I'm talking about splitting us up, sending them God knows where, and you are giving up."

"Well, slick, if you have a better idea, let's hear it," Butch argued, setting his glass down with such force that it slopped over onto the table.

"Maybe I should have some say in this; it's my life you're fucking with, too," Kevin said, almost shaking with fury.

"For the last few months," he continued, "you've sat down there on your ranch while I've had to be marriage counselor, father, errand boy, and whatever else needed to be done. I think I've earned the right to have some input on the decision that's going to affect the rest of my life."

"Fine," Butch told him. "Let's hear it."

"First," Kevin started, "I know you've worked hard at keeping those kids safe, and you've done a great job. But you've picked the notes and written the music while I've had to play the melody."

"It's like a lot of your sorry-assed life," he continued. "You seem to try to remain aloof and uninvolved personally. Just like you do regarding your attachment to women."

"Just what does my personal life have to do with this?" Butch almost shouted.

"Everything," Kevin replied. "When you start getting emotionally involved, you start building a wall around yourself. Remember that lady you started dating right after you got out of the Air Force? For almost three years, you went with her, and what happened?"

He paused for just a second and said, "I'll remind you, just in case you've erased that little phase of your life from your memory. You shut her out, not of your life, but of your emotions. That woman loved you; you could see it in her eyes every time she was around you."

"And you loved her too," he continued. "But you just wouldn't let it happen. Oh no, you can't let someone get so close. What is it that you're afraid of? Getting hurt?"

Butch had leaned back and crossed his arms as he listened to Kevin's delving into what he considered no-man's land.

"And what about that pretty little girl you were seeing a couple of years ago?" Kevin pushed on. "Same story, same result; you shut down when you know the next logical step."

"And now let's look at Tammy. This turning yourself in is just the extreme escape from another potentially great relationship."

"How the hell do you figure that?" Butch asked, his temper reaching critical mass.

"You know as well as I do," Kevin answered. "Once those people have you, they won't let you go. You'll never be seen again."

Watching Butch's eyes narrow menacingly, he said, "You think you can just walk into their offices, smile, and tell them they can't have their little boy?"

"You think they can't take you and pull every detail of what we've done and are doing out of that smug little brain of yours?"

Pausing, Kevin continued his lecture, "Well, you can't beat them. I know; I spent several years learning how to encourage people to tell me things. Give you a week without sleep, little to eat or drink, constant harassment, and you'll be giving them everything you know. And if you don't provide it quickly enough, there are numerous wonderful drugs that will encourage you."

"Even if you don't know the exact details of where Gene and I are, you'll slip, and they'll take every word and analyze it until they find a thread to follow. If they even hear the word 'Sancudo,' they'll figure it out. They have the most extensive data bank available to them that's ever been seen."

"They'll have FBI, CIA, Border Patrol, and every law enforcement computer spitting out anything that remotely sounds like Sancudo. Then they'll tie your little trip to San Antonio and Del Rio together with him, and they'll have a name and a location."

"And if you think being on the other side of the Rio Grande will stop them, you know better. Now let's talk about me," Kevin finished.

"Okay, what about you," Butch answered, still sitting motionless across the table.

"Your plan just leaves me wandering around the country trying to hide. As you said, they'll know who I am, where I live, what I drive, and soon, every aspect of my previous life. I'm out there running scared while you're vainly attempting to smooth the ruffled feathers of a gigantic pissed-off eagle."

Kevin took a sip of his tea and continued, "I want to go with them, wherever that is. They're my family now, and I care. I want to be there if that poor little baby needs something. I'm not sure your friends south of the border can take care of that potential problem."

"Not only that, what good can I do for either them or you if I can't contact either of you? I'm not going to be your postal clerk delivering the mail and then quit worrying because *'you're in control'*! No sir! I'm going with them! And, as you always say, there's no negotiating," Kevin finished emotionally.

Butch sat watching his oldest friend with tears about to start streaming down his face. He had never seen this much emotion from him in the years they had known each other, and it hurt him that he had caused such apparent pain for his friend.

Finally uncrossing his arms, Butch leaned over and put his elbows on the table, and quietly said, "Kevin, you're right, and I'm sorry. You've got more right to be in this decision than I do. Whatever you think you need to do, I'm willing to listen."

Kevin stiffened slightly and dabbed his eyes with one of the paper towels he had pulled from the roll on the table. "Let's just start over right now and re-plan this entire operation from here on. Can we do that?"

Butch had relaxed significantly and quietly said, "Sure, old friend, let's start over. How're the ribs?"

Kevin cracked a slight smile and said, "Asshole, why won't you let me stay mad at you? You're such an asshole, and that's about the kindest thing I can think of to say right now. The answer is I'll let you know when I finally get a chance to eat them; you haven't shut up long enough for me to have a single bite."

After each of them had managed to strip the meat from a couple of ribs and devoured almost half of the brisket, Kevin said, "Here's my idea."

"Go ahead, Señor Knox," Butch said as he took a bite of his jalapeno. "Since you're going to be living down there, get used to the name."

"Let's start with the envelopes," Kevin said, wiping his mouth with another paper towel. "Why don't you mail them from somewhere in Ft Worth yourself? Then go hide somewhere over in Grapevine or Lewisville with one of your old airline buddies. Most of them are gone most of the time, especially those that live here and fly out of another base; there's always a room available."

"Then, after a week or so of them having the things you're sending, you can figure some way of making contact without them knowing where you are. That will also allow us some time to get burrowed deep into our hole down in Mexico."

"Then what?" Butch asked, finishing the last of his potato salad.

"After they've had the information for a week or so," Kevin continued, "they'll have had time to realize that you have proof of what they've been doing. Once you contact them and let them know that there are several other identical packages out there, I think you'll be in a better bargaining position."

"I'm not saying it won't still be dicey," Kevin acknowledged as he sipped his tea. "But, once you explain where they can expect to find opposition to any further clandestine activities regarding us, you may have a chance."

"Sometimes letting your opponent stew with a piece of the puzzle gives you more leverage than letting him see your entire hand," he finished.

"One other thing," Kevin said quickly, "make sure you get someone you trust to video your initial meeting. It's got to be off the base and limit it to one or two high-ranking officers that'll have the highest profile and the most to lose if things turn to shit in the end."

"All right," Butch told him. "I'll agree to that with one caveat."

"And that is?" Kevin questioned.

"You never try to analyze my life again," Butch told him, smiling. "If you ever try that again, I'll expose every quirk or deviant behavior you've ever exhibited. And now, as you're so fond of saying, there's no negotiating, and you, sir, are dismissed."

CHAPTER 13

Kevin and Butch were smoothing over any remaining issues of their differences and discussing things that needed to be done in the near term and for potentially long-term protection of Gene, Leslie, and the baby. By now, they were both starting to call him BK, but Kevin had some reservations about the name.

"BK," he told Butch, "sounds like a hamburger. I kind of like KB."

"KB?" Butch questioned. "Not a chance. I knew a flight attendant whose initials were KB, and he was a flaming Democrat! Nice guy, but his politics would hair-lip the Pope."

Picking at the remaining food left on their plates, they continued to banter about why one name was better than the other when Butch looked up and saw the familiar figure of Mel Bailey walking into the restaurant. He stood up and watched him approach the table with wariness as his eyes swept the room.

Seeing nothing there that concerned him, Sancudo's crooked smile told Butch that he felt safe, seeing very few people sitting around the tables, and they had paid him no attention. If anything, they probably thought he was one of the kitchen staff or busboys who roamed the restaurant.

Approaching the table, Sancudo said, "Mr. North, it has been too long, my friend."

Butch came around the table and shook his hand before they gave each other a quick hug. Butch looked at him as he stepped back, his hands still resting on Mel's shoulders. "You've grown old, little mosquito," he said as he noticed the increased lines etched on Mel's face.

"And you still have the face of a boy?" Mel retorted. "I wouldn't tell just anyone this, but your face looks like it's already worn out at least two bodies."

Kevin had wiped his mouth and hands and was waiting for the familiar greeting of two friends to be finished. Watching Butch and Sancudo razzing each other reminded him so much of the relationship that existed between him and Butch. Regardless of the differences of opinions that may arise, they respected each other enough that any hurt feelings, such as the minor verbal skirmish that had taken place, would dissipate quickly.

Turning to Kevin, Butch said, "Kevin, I'd like for you to meet the infamous 'El Sancudo,' or just Sancudo for short. But maybe you should just call him Mel for now."

Looking back at Mel, he said, "Mel, meet Kevin Knox, a very, very good friend of mine."

Mel shook Kevin's hand and told him, "Con mucho gusto, Kevin. It is a pleasure to meet any friend of the villainous character with whom you seem to be so carelessly associated."

Kevin readily shook his hand and retorted, "Sir, the pleasure is all mine. And I'm afraid you'll have to overlook some of the people I am forced to befriend. Since you obviously know this one, you'll understand why I feel the need to apologize."

Mel laughed and said, "Well, you are obviously a shrewd judge of character if somewhat lacking in discretion. Shall we sit for a moment?"

As Butch returned to his seat, Kevin observed that Mel exhibited the characteristics of someone who is continuously aware of his surroundings. The same careful watching of everyone, never quite relaxed the way that he might seem to be to most observers. He had seen that look many times during his tours in Vietnam, especially of those who had been forced to live in the jungles and survive by learning to notice the slightest inconsistency.

Mel's physical appearance reminded him of people who had led a rather hard life. He was probably only five feet six or so inches tall and might weigh 120 pounds with a good meal in him. He was obviously of Hispanic descent, but the blue eyes denoted a Caucasian parent, and maybe more in the past generations.

The leathery skin and deep creases on his face showed a life lived out of doors and many hours in harsh sunlight. Still, he had a friendly demeanor and an obviously good sense of humor. He would probably be considered to be nondescript if surrounded by other Tex-Mex men of his age. Kevin imagined that Sancudo could blend into any town or city along either side of the Rio Grande.

"What do you say to getting some food?" Butch asked. "I'm afraid it needs to be carried because we're sort of pressed for time. How do ribs, sliced brisket, potato salad, jalapenos, onions, and pickles sound to you?"

"Sounds wonderful," Mel answered. "I haven't eaten since I had a small breakfast burrito in Del Rio this morning.

Since you sounded sort of anxious, I hurried here as fast as my little Bronco could go."

"And I appreciate it," Butch said as he rose to return to the array of meats just outside the seating area. "You and Kevin get acquainted while I gather the eats."

Kevin watched Butch heading for the door and said, "I'm not sure exactly what Butch told you, but there may have been a small change of plans."

Mel continued to monitor every movement within the restaurant while he asked, "What sort of change?"

"I'm going with you, with your approval, of course," Kevin said. "There will be four of us. Has Butch told you of our situation?"

"Just parts," Sancudo admitted. "We didn't have a lot of time when he came to Del Rio last year, and he just told me he might need some assistance in an area that I have some expertise in."

"What is your normal area of expertise?" Kevin asked.

Mel smiled back at him and answered, "Well, I guess you'd say I'm sort of in the import and export business."

Understanding his meaning, Kevin continued, "That must be a relatively secure vocation since there seems to be no end to the demand."

Mel laughed and replied, "Yes, there seems to be no end to the demand. It's been a family business for generations now. As a matter of fact, one of my great-grandfathers was in the business back when the government of the region was still rather uncertain. Of course, that little incident at the Alamo seemed to be the thing that resolved the issue."

Kevin smiled and said, "Well, it did seem to bring things to a conclusion. But I'm not sure whether or not it's really the end. I think Mexico's long-term plan is to peacefully occupy the state and then try for annexation."

"You could be right about that," Mel admitted. "I'm not sure where my allegiances would lie if that were to happen. I've got so much family on both sides. Most of my male ancestors were white, but not all. And conversely, the mothers were primarily Hispanic, but there were a few of the others."

"Well," Kevin nodded and told him. "That's about as normal as anything in this part of the world. Take Butch, a mix of Cherokee and Irish, I think."

"Whatever the mix is," Sancudo laughed, "the result is one seriously deranged hombre."

"You got that right," Kevin said. "What else do you do besides the import/export business?"

"Oh," Mel answered, "I'm sort of in the tourist industry as well."

"Really?" Kevin questioned. "Just what does that entail?"

"There's always a need to help vacationing travelers," Mel smiled. "There seems to always be someone that would like to visit somewhere south of the border. And, I try very hard to accommodate them, especially those that require certain, shall we say, privacy considerations?"

"It seems that we've met the perfect agent for our vacation plans," Kevin told him. "And, you come very highly recommended. Very highly indeed."

"Nothing like referrals from satisfied customers to help the business grow," Mel acknowledged. "I have two sons that will probably inherit my small but growing concern in the next few years."

They saw Butch reenter the seating area carrying a large tray piled with what appeared to be enough meat from at least half of a medium size cow. He proceeded to the line, and they watched as four containers of salad and other items were placed on another tray.

Kevin rose and said, "Excuse me, Mel. I think I need to help the gentleman with his purchases. What would you like to drink?"

"A large glass of tea, unsweetened, please," he replied. "And let's drop the formalities; just call me Sancudo. Most of my friends do."

"Sure thing, Sancudo," Kevin said as he walked over and took the four glasses from the tray while Butch paid the cashier. "I think we can handle it. The problem will come when we try to divide this up. I'm full right now, but the smell of that Bar-B-Q may tempt me to try another rib or two."

After the cashier had ensured that all of the food had been neatly packaged in Styrofoam boxes and bagged with the necessary plates and plastic utensils, Butch carried them over to the table and sat them down. Kevin had the to-go cups filled and a small cup of lemon with tops securely fastened, ready to go. Once he headed back to the table, Butch and Sancudo rose to leave.

"You better let Mel carry that food," Kevin said as he approached. "I've seen you ready for seconds 10 minutes after you've eaten like a hog. And I want to make sure there are no teeth marks on those fresh ribs. That is unless they're my teeth."

The three men took the packages of food and started out of the door. Once outside, Butch told Mel to follow them, and they separated for their cars. As soon as he knew Mel was ready, Butch started the Mustang and headed back across the street to the airport.

CHAPTER 14

General Mike Nelson entered his office after leaving the conference room, thinking that just maybe they had caught a break after all this time. The patience of his superiors in Washington had been stretched almost to the breaking point, and it was General Modelle's position on the staff of MJ12 that had prevented a full-scale revamping of the personnel here at the facility.

Passing his secretary's desk, he said, "Kathy, please get General Modelle on the phone for me. If necessary, have him called at home. Let his office know this is an emergency."

Continuing on into his office, he sat in the plush leather chair behind his desk and once again looked around the office that he had occupied for the last couple of years. All of the memorabilia on the walls recalled a very successful career but would be meaningless if this was truly a chance to capture Gene and was fumbled.

He recalled the countless assets and money spent during the first few days of searching and the humiliation he and his staff had felt after being outwitted by a bunch of country bumpkins. Granted, what he had learned about

Butch North proved that not everyone out there was a complete idiot, but the network of communication and cooperation between those people was truly amazing. Hell, he had seen less effective operations among some of the military's finest officers.

As much as he hated to admit it, that rag-tag group had always been one step ahead of him and all of the technology and assets he had at his disposal. Although he had met Mr. North on one short occasion, he knew they had vastly underestimated the man and his friends. He couldn't make that mistake again.

The entire previous operation reminded him of the US involvement in Vietnam. How could a country with such limited weaponry and sophistication ever have a chance against the might of our military? Well, the result of that underestimation is in the history books.

A group of ill-equipped conscripts led by a few brilliant tacticians had defeated the best we had to throw at them. The ingenuity of their methods, using hand-dug tunnels, walking barefoot along muddy trails in the dark, and melting into the dense forests that covered so much of the land, had defeated the United States of America. It's not so much that they defeated us; it's just that we couldn't defeat them.

Kathy Blevins stepped to the door and announced, "Sir, I have General Modelle on the phone. Shall I transfer him now?"

"Please, Kathy," Mike directed. "And thank you."

Kathy closed the door as she left and went to her desk to transfer the call. She had been Mike's secretary for all of his time at the facility, and they had known each other long enough that she knew the strain he was under. She didn't know all the details of the facility's function, but she knew it was one of the blackest programs being operated by the federal government. And, she knew not to even attempt to delve into speculation. But, still, she worried about what was going on and the impact on all of them. She just wished she could do more to assist the people she had grown so fond of and respected even more.

"General Modelle," Mike began, "I think we have a fortunate development regarding our missing product." Although it had long been the habit of using the name Gene, every precaution was always taken when using any potentially vulnerable method of communication.

"What is that?" Paul asked from his office in the Pentagon. Although his most important duty was as a ranking member of MJ12, he still kept an office for other routine military duties. It was also necessary to have an office for appearances and non-descript contacts with those outside either the function of the NAS/JRB facility or those relating to MJ12.

"We have a sighting of one of our suspected conspira-tors in the case," Mike answered. "A State Trooper reported a sighting of Leslie, the girl we believe is involved with Gene, in an area just north of here."

"What's the reliability of the information?" Paul asked.

"I believe it's reliable," Mike told him. "Colonel Erick-son and others are departing to determine the validity of the contact and we should have proof within an hour."

"The reason for my call is to inform you that it may be in the best interest of our group to have you prepared to travel if the evidence warrants your personal attention," he continued. "Additionally, we may require some assistance with procuring the necessary assets to fully exploit the situation."

"Fine," Paul told him. "I'm ready to assist you in any way I can. But, before I start any further activities on this end, I need absolute proof. Not only the sighting of Leslie but of her positive involvement with the main reason for the operation."

"I understand, sir," Mike replied. "As I said, I hope to have that information for you within the hour. Once I have it, we need to be ready to act immediately. I'd hate to be playing catch-up the way we did last time."

"I completely agree, Mike," Paul said. "Just let me know the second you have the proof. I'll be ready to come down the minute you have that. Good day."

"Good day, sir," Mike said as he heard the line go dead.

He rose from his chair and walked to the closed door wondering if the curtness of General Modelle's goodbye was indicative of future distancing of Paul from the on-going failure of their attempts to find Gene. Not only that, but the program had been unsuccessful in developing another being. Except for Gene, their work and efforts have been pretty dismal, considering the expense and time involved.

Opening the door, he told Kathy as he walked by her desk, "Please bring every record you have down to the operations center when you get a chance. I'll be there until we get a report from Rick, so please transfer any calls."

Mike left Kathy's office and headed down the hall to where Jerry was busy trying to get more information from the trooper and the others at the clinic. Not wanting to disturb either him or Karyn, he walked to the map and was amazed at the relatively small area that had encompassed their previous search. Ringgold, the most northern point of the area, was hardly a two hour's drive from where Gene had been produced.

Yet, much as it had been in Vietnam, the enemy had used every natural feature of the land and all the indigenous personnel to their advantage. More importantly, he decided, it's very hard to beat conviction. Even the most un-capable people can accomplish amazing feats with conviction and determination.

And the resourcefulness of motivated individuals was not to be underestimated. Their monitoring of Butch North had proven that he hadn't had contact with Gene or Leslie from almost the second day of Gene's escape. Yet, someone else had successfully evaded them. As much as he disliked what these people were doing, he still admired them.

During these months of vain attempts to locate either Gene or Leslie, he had begun to wonder if what they were doing was entirely legal or even ethical and what would happen if the truth was ever known. Much like some of the more publicized atrocities from previous wars, sometimes personal zeal clouds your judgment, and it's only in retrospect that you see the extent to which you've exceeded acceptable behavior.

However, now was not the time to have self-doubt. Mike turned from the map when he heard the sound of Jerry hanging up the phone. "Anything new," he asked as Jerry was busy writing notes for himself.

"Yes, sir," Jerry answered, rereading what he had just written.

Giving the General his full attention now, he said, "I believe that we have identified the unknown individual that we thought took Gene from Butch. As you recall, a certain red truck was all over the area after we questioned Butch, and we could never positively tie them together."

"Yes," Mike assured him. "I remember that truck all too well."

"We think we know his name and address," Jerry quickly said. "The car the lady was driving was registered to him and we have proof that he did own a red truck that matches the description of the one we were looking for."

"Colonel Erickson is currently headed for the ranch that Mr. Kevin Knox, the owner of the car and a red truck, owns," Jerry continued. "We should have positive proof of Mr. Knox's truck being the one we wanted within minutes of his landing up in Vashti."

"What about the clinic?" Mike asked as he turned and located Vashti on the map. Again, he was surprised at the relatively close proximity to Boyd, Bowie, and all of the other locations they had been monitoring.

"Colonel Moore is en route to that location also," Jerry answered. "She should arrive there about the same time Colonel Erickson gets to the Knox Ranch. She has a group of her staff and equipment to both retrieve evidence and to ensure complete sterilization of the clinic prior to leaving."

"Anything else?" Mike asked as he looked toward Karyn as she was checking each frequency on the encryption device.

"Not at this minute, sir," Jerry answered. "Is there anything else I can do for you?"

"Yes, as a matter of fact," Mike said, "I'd like to have a complete dossier on Kevin Knox as soon as you can get it. I prefer to have as much information as possible on the people we identify as involved with this operation."

"I'll notify Washington," Jerry told him. "They'll search all the FBI, CIA, military, federal, and state data banks for anything available. Anything else?"

"No," Mike told him. "Thanks; just let me know as soon as you get the information. And let me know when Rick or Amy has anything to report."

Turning to Karyn, he asked, "How's the communication end holding up?

"Fine, sir," she answered. "I've been able to re-open all of our discrete frequencies, and we'll have secure communications for the entire group, including the ground personnel that have been dispatched."

"Do we have adequate assets?" he asked.

"Honestly," she replied, "I'd like to have more on the ground. We can get by with what we have and the air support. But in the long term and to fully investigate the entire area, we've got to get more boots on the dirt."

"I agree," Mike said. "What do we have left from the first operation?"

"There's only two," Karyn answered. "We reduced our surveillance to just monitoring Butch North. Colonel Erickson directed Jerry to find Mr. North, and one of the two was on his way to get him. The other one is here, and we're getting him on his way to the clinic as soon as his vehicle is serviced."

"Okay," Mike told her, "I want you to determine how many more teams you think will be necessary and what communications systems will be required. Let me know what you think, and I'll coordinate with Rick when he returns."

"I would have preferred to have sent our ground team up to the area instead of getting Mr. North, but we'll still need more teams to adequately cover the area up there," Mike continued. "However, maybe Butch should be easier to catch, and he is undoubtedly involved to some extent."

"Yes, sir," Karyn acknowledged, "I still think he was, and still is, the main player in the effort to prevent our capture of Gene. He's had some extraordinary help, but he's the central point."

"I think we all agree with that," Mike said. "But, there's only so much we can do without drawing unwanted attention. There were just too many people that knew about us bringing him in the first time."

Jerry had been quietly listening to the discussion and finally decided to provide some insights of his own, saying, "I continue to think that if we'd solicited Mr. North's help instead of the confrontational approach we took, we'd have been better off."

Mike looked questioningly at Jerry and asked, "Are you saying that we made a mistake in questioning Mr. North?"

"No, sir," Jerry responded immediately. "It's just that given that man's background, I think that if he knew the importance of our operation, he might have been persuaded to help us regain Gene. I think the biggest mistake was in telling him the story about Gene being part of the group responsible for the World Trade Center and Pentagon attacks."

Hurrying to further explain, Jerry continued, "I've read everything we have about that man and I'd stake my life that he's as dedicated to the country's safety and security as anyone. But I also think that he knew from the minute we started questioning him that something wasn't kosher. You could see it in his face and eyes when he decided that we were lying to him."

"I've spent hours watching that interview with him and his kids," Jerry explained. "It's almost as if a switch was thrown, and it closed down his willingness to cooperate."

"You could be right about that," Mike said. "But the fact remains that he withheld information concerning a federal fugitive and may even be guilty of harboring him. That fact is indisputable and is the reason we're going to bring the full might of the US government to bear down until we get some answers."

"Yes, sir," Jerry said, realizing that he may have stepped too far. "I just thought that there may be a better way to approach the problem. I certainly agree that we need any information that man has. I'm just proposing a different method of trying to get it."

CHAPTER 15

Butch and Kevin drove the Mustang back across the street to the airport, with Mel following. As they rounded the corner that led them to the operations area, Butch was pleased to see the old Ford sedan still sitting where they had left it. Parking beside the sedan, Butch got out and waited for Mel to park his Bronco beside him. Kevin started carrying the bags of food to Gene and Leslie while Butch approached Mel as he exited his car.

"One quick point," Butch said as Mel closed his door. "You need to be aware that the baby boy has some, let's say, unusual features."

"What do you mean, unusual?" Sancudo asked.

"You'll see," Butch told him. "Just realize that the baby's appearance is somewhat different. Just consider it to be some slight irregularities and remember that Gene and Leslie are as aware of it as anyone, but it's still their baby, and just as any parent having a child with birth defects, they love him."

"I understand completely," Mel told him. "Thanks for telling me, but I know how new parents feel about their children. I'll make sure they continue to feel pride in the wee one."

"Hell," Mel said smiling, "I just wonder how your parents explained your 'abnormalities' when they saw you. I can just imagine their disappointment when the doctor held you up and said, *'Mr. and Mrs. North, here's you creature!'*"

"And your father said what when he saw you?" Butch retorted as they approached the sedan. "Mom, have you been sleeping with the Planter's Peanut Man? 'Cause that thing sure looks like a goober to me!"

"One other thing," Butch said, stopping Mel. "I don't want to know where you're going. I'll give you a phone number to call if you need me, but you must have someone else use a throw-away phone to relay your messages."

"And they need to be as far from your location as possible when they make the call," he continued. "I would prefer it if the call to me came from Oklahoma or somewhere else north of Ft Worth, but I know that may be impossible."

"Not at all," Sancudo told him. "In my business, I have associates all over the country. There are people living as far north as Michigan and on each coast that do business with me. I've become very popular in Chicago with my tourist vacation packages. I'm considered the 'go-to man' for arranging things for certain people who need extra privacy in some of their business dealings."

"That's just wonderful," Butch said. "But you're going to be facing more than gang rivalry in this case. There may be some governmental interest."

"Not a problem," Mel assured him. "I've dealt with them for years, and I know how to handle their methods. You've heard of Jimmy Hoffa?"

"You're not going to tell me that you arranged for Hoffa to take one of your vacations, are you?" Butch asked him incredulously.

"No," Mel smiled, "but I can hide anyone just as well. And for half the price, I might add."

"Speaking of price," Butch said, "I'll take care of it when this little problem is resolved. If you need something up-front, let me know."

"Amigo," Sancudo asked with a hurt look on his face, "why do you try to insult your poor little mosquito? Is there no trust between friends? Have I ever been unreasonable or demanding? No! Besides, I don't know what to charge you yet. But, rest assured that this is business, and I must make a profit, the shareholders, you know."

Butch laughed at the thought of shareholders in Mel's business and told him, "You must be referring to your espousa y ninos, amigo. And I'm pretty sure they're very demanding. I'll make sure they're satisfied with your profit margins."

They continued around to the sedan, where Kevin had just begun passing out the plates and food from the containers that now covered most of the front seat. Gene and Leslie sat with BK, sleeping quietly between them as they waited for Kevin to fill their plates with the ribs, brisket, and salad.

He had spent his time while Mel and Butch were talking to tell them that plans had changed, and he was accompanying them to wherever they were going. That, of course, had brought smiles to their faces and was a great relief to them.

"Gene, Leslie," Butch announced as he stood beside the open window, "I'd like for you to meet your tour guide."

Both of them looked at Mel as Butch continued, "Folks, this is Mr. Mel Bailey. His friends, and some that really don't like him, call him Sancudo."

Turning to face Mel, Butch said, "Mel, I'd like to introduce Gene, Leslie, and their beautiful baby boy, BK."

"Howdy, folks," Mel said as he nodded his head. "Con mucho gusto; that is to say, it's my pleasure."

"We're glad to meet you," Leslie replied anxiously. "I hope we're not causing you any trouble, but we do appreciate you helping us."

"No trouble at all," Mel quickly told her. "Your friend Butch told me months ago that you might want to take a short vacation to visit the wonderful country just south of the border. I've already made the arrangements for any length of stay you desire, and I'm pleased to provide any services that you may require."

"Yes, thank you," Gene parroted. "All of you people have been so kind and caring for Leslie and me. I can't begin to tell all of you how much we appreciate it."

"Don't be so quick to thank him until you see where you're staying," Butch said, smiling. "Some of his 'Five Star' accommodations have been rated on a rather loose scale. I think the five stars refer to how many you can see at night through holes in the ceiling."

Kevin had finished dividing the food for Leslie and Gene, saying, "Sancudo, I have left you a little bit, just in case you're hungry. I do think we need to get on the road, though. I know Butch has several things he needs to do, and all this standing around jawing is letting the ribs get cold."

"He's right," Butch said, "I have a lot to do, and some of our 'friends' from up north may be trying to interrupt our travel plans."

"Kevin, if you have a minute," Butch asked. "I need to have a private word with you before you folks leave."

Kevin stepped out of the car while Mel continued to talk to Gene and Leslie, telling them that he would take very good care of them and their wonderful son. Following Butch to the driver's side of the Mustang, Kevin glanced back and was pleased to see such easy rapport between Mel and the kids.

"What's next?" Kevin asked as soon as they were out of earshot of the others.

Butch reached inside the Mustang and pulled several bundles of money from beneath the seat. Handing it to Kevin, he said, "Here's about $22,000. That's all I could get on such short notice. I hope that it will last until we get this settled, but if you need something more, ask Mel. He'll just put it on the bill for me to settle later."

Kevin took the money and looked at it for a moment before saying, "And just how do you expect to get by? If this is all you could get, that's going to leave you sort of short on living funds yourself."

"Don't worry about that," Butch told him. "I kept a couple of thousand out; that should last me until I figure out the best way to convince our friends that we need to resolve this in a way that benefits all of us."

"So," he continued, "you just take care of your end, and I'll get by up here. Have Mel use my personal cell phone for any communications, and make sure he's passing the information to someone else as I told him."

Butch hung his head for a second and then said, "There's no need for elaborate conversations on this. Just a simple, things are good or that you need assistance will suffice."

"Won't that alert them to your location and involvement?" Kevin asked. "Why don't we keep using the other method with disposable phones?"

"First, I don't know who Sancudo will use as his relay man," Butch answered. "The logistics of providing all the phones and keeping track of who, or which phone is to be used, is too cumbersome."

"Besides," he continued, "it's time to bring some of this game out in the open. I want them to know that you're gone, and when I finally meet them, I can honestly say I don't know where you are and can only wait for you to contact me."

"What about when things get resolved?" Kevin asked. "How do we know when it's safe to reappear?"

"That's probably the simplest thing of all," Butch said. "If things work out as I hope, all I'll have to do is get word to Sancudo, and he'll arrange for your return."

"And if things don't work out for us," Butch told him, "then you guys just stay put and do the best you can. I'm sure you'll find a way to make a life for you and the kids. You've done quite a job so far, and there's nobody I'd trust more."

Putting his hand out, Butch said, "Now, you guys hit the road. You've got to trust Mel to take care of you. If you need medical attention, he'll know where to go. Don't worry about me; you've got enough to worry about."

Kevin took Butch's hand and told him, "I'll worry about what I want to, ass-hole. You take care."

Kevin quickly turned away and walked back to the sedan. He withdrew the envelopes and camera that they had left there before coming back to where Butch was waiting. "You'll need these, I believe," he told Butch as he handed him the material. With that, he returned to his car, where Mel was chatting with Gene and Leslie.

Butch watched as he and Mel talked for a moment before Kevin got into the sedan and began placing some of the food onto two plates. Once done, he closed the containers and handed a couple of sacks out of the window. Kevin then turned and said something to Gene and Leslie as he passed the filled plates across the back of the front seat.

Mel took the sacks and rounded the rear of the Mustang, walking to his car. He paused as he came to Butch and said, "Well, amigo, I guess this is it. I'll take good care of your friends."

Butch shook the extended hand and told him, "I know, and I'd trust no one else to do this. Kevin will let you know how to communicate with me and also if he needs any medical care. I'm sure you know some very discreet doctors that can assist that little boy if necessary or, Leslie, if complications arise."

"Not a problem at all," Mel said, placing his left hand on Butch's right shoulder. "You just take very good care of yourself. I'd hate to read about you in the papers unless it's announcing your upcoming wedding."

Butch laughed and said, "Those two events you're referring to are about the same, amigo. Being married is like being pecked to death by a chicken: a long, slow, painful process. Now, lead them south or wherever you're going, and don't look back. I hope I can call you in a week or so and tell you that summer's approaching and the birds can fly north."

With that, Mel climbed into his Bronco and headed out of the airport, with Kevin following close behind. Waving goodbye to Gene and Leslie looking at him from the back of the sedan, Butch couldn't help but worry if they would make it safely across the border and if he'd ever see any of them again.

CHAPTER 16

Butch watched as Sancudo led Kevin out of the airport and turned north on Highway 281. Knowing that they would soon be heading toward the border, he wondered if they were going to take US 377 all the way to Del Rio or if Sancudo would use some back road to cross somewhere north of Lake Amistad. He remembered a road crossing the dam that had been built across the Rio Grande to form the lake. He also knew that there were several places further up the river toward Langtry or south around Eagle Pass where crossings could be made, avoiding the usual border checkpoints.

Whichever way they went, he decided, it was once again out of his control. This time, even more so; once they disappeared from his sight, he had no idea where they would ultimately wind up. But Butch had faith in Kevin's resourcefulness and in Mel's ability to get them safely either across the border or to some other location where they wouldn't be found unless they wanted to be.

Kevin had watched Butch disappear in the rearview mirror as he followed Mel back north on 281. He saw Gene and Leslie looking backward and waving as Butch stood all alone, waving back. Again, he thought of how Butch brought people close to him and then watched them leave while he remained alone. This time, it was necessary for Gene, Leslie, little BK, and himself. But the pattern of running from permanent relationships remained.

Approaching the intersection with 377, he saw Mel turn on his signal for a left turn and saw the sign announcing that the next road led south toward Dublin, Texas. Seeing the name of the town made him smile, and he looked in the mirror at Gene and Leslie.

"Hey," he announced. "See that sign? The one that says Dublin is 12 miles down the road?"

Both Gene and Leslie looked up, and Gene said, "Yeah, what's Dublin? I thought that was somewhere in Ireland."

"Maybe so," Kevin said. "But this particular Dublin is the home of the last place where the original formula Dr Pepper is still made."

"Oh, I remember something about that," Gene said excitedly. "What was it that Butch always said about it? Something about how much more refreshing it was than the newer version."

"Yep," Kevin answered. "I remember the first time we stopped at the Chicken Express in Azle. They're one of the few places that serve the original formula as their fountain drink."

"Butch told me that their Dr Pepper was at least 15% more refreshing than the other versions," he continued. "I'm not sure if he was absolutely correct, but it did taste better to me."

"Funny," Gene replied, "Butch always seemed to have some little-known fact or observation to tell about almost anything."

"Yeah, that he did," Kevin reminisced. "Of course, I'm convinced that at least half of what he told you was something he had made up. The man was certainly full of ideas or opinions."

"Why did you say 'was'?" Leslie questioned. "You're acting as if he no longer exists. You don't think we'll ever see him again, do you?"

"No, that's not true," Kevin hurriedly explained. "That's not what I meant to imply. I guess it was just a slip of the tongue."

Gene leaned forward, rested his arms on the back of the front seat, and looked at Kevin. The worry was evident in his eyes as he searched Kevin's face for a clue to how Kevin really felt about their future and that of Butch.

"You don't think he has much of a chance, do you?" Gene asked.

Kevin glanced over at Gene for a second, wondering just how much he and Leslie knew about what Butch was planning. Although neither of them had had any contact with Butch after they moved to their home up north of Ringgold, he kept them aware of what Butch was doing.

Leslie, especially, didn't know much about the efforts that had taken place to get them to this point. She had only seen Butch once, when she met him at Red's Take 5 Sports Bar in Bridgeport. Other than that, all of her knowledge had come from either him or Gene.

Gene had only been around Butch for a couple of days but had personally seen how much Butch cared about his situation and the extent he would go to when doing what he thought was right. But that was the extent of his knowledge of the man. Just like most of the people that know who Butch was, few really knew him. *"Hell,"* Kevin thought, *"I don't really know him either, and I've known him for over 20 years."*

"Let me tell you something," Kevin said, trying to convince them that everything would work out for all of them. "I think Butch will come out of this just fine. We discussed what we thought would be the best thing to do for all of us, including him."

Trying to watch the road and maintain eye contact with both of them, Kevin continued, "He knows, as we all do, some permanent solution has to be found that we can live with. Butch is just as tired of playing games with the government as we are."

"We can't continue hiding up there any more than Butch can keep having to watch every step, worry about every word, or know that your every move is being scrutinized by someone," Kevin told them.

"That's especially true now that BK is here," he reminded them. "I know, and so do you, that by now, the government is aware of the child. And we all know that they want to get their hands on him as much, if not more than to get Gene back."

Kevin paused while he thought of how to phrase the next words, "And given BK's potential problems, as any newborn might have, we may need certain medical attention that we can't get from some rural facility."

Kevin waited while both Gene and Leslie looked lovingly at BK sleeping between them, cartons of untouched food still sitting on their laps. He knew that they recognized the abnormalities and realized that life in the outside world would be difficult.

"Now," Kevin said, "I don't know the full extent of Butch's plan, but I do know that he intends to confront the people that came looking for Gene and also for you, Leslie."

"He's aware of the potential problems with direct contact," he continued. "But, he's fairly certain that he can mitigate the danger by providing evidence of Gene's existence. And that fact is what the government has been trying to safeguard this entire time."

"Butch believes, as I do also," Kevin said, "that if he can demonstrate he has the ability to reveal the truth in a manner that people will believe, then maybe he can bargain for some sort of compromise for all of us."

"Now, you guys better eat that food before it gets cold," Kevin said as he saw Mel signaling to pull off the road. "We'll have plenty of time to talk about this when we get wherever Mel is taking us."

Mel had pulled into one of the numerous rest stops scattered along most of the roads throughout Texas and had parked well away from the restrooms. Although there were no other cars there at the time, he had selected a spot that would be as far as possible from the vending machines knowing that's where others would be going.

Kevin pulled into the open spot left at the end of the lot, keeping Mel's Bronco between him and any other arrivals. He killed the engine and stepped from the car, stretching as he stood. It had been a long drive so far, but most of the tension in his back came from other reasons. The argument with Butch, the uncertainty of their journey, and concern for all of them weighed heavily.

Mel was quietly sitting in his car, sipping from his glass of tea, when Kevin reached the passenger door. Seeing all of the containers resting on the passenger seat, he leaned through the open window and watched Mel select a rib from the box. Mel slowly bit into the side of the bone and easily pulled off a chunk of meat with his teeth.

Turning to look at Kevin while he chewed, he said, "Time we had a little talk, amigo."

Kevin became alarmed immediately at the words. "What do you have in mind?" he asked cautiously.

Sancudo kept his watchful eyes on Kevin's face as he said, "Where do you think we're going?"

"I assumed we were heading for Mexico," Kevin answered. "Isn't that what you and Butch had planned?"

"Butch and I planned nothing," Mel replied as he took a slice of brisket from the container. "I do all the planning on this end."

Kevin watched as Sancudo slowly savored every morsel of the Bar-B-Q and waited for some clue as to where the conversation was going. He knew that Butch trusted this man, but he also knew that it had been years since the two had actually been close. If things had changed, Butch might not know about it and may have grossly miscalculated where events were heading. Concern for their safety now became foremost in his mind as he watched Sancudo silently chewing his food.

CHAPTER 17

As Jerry and General Nelson were finishing their discussion regarding the previous handling of Butch's initial interrogation, Kathy entered the room carrying a box filled with the records of the first operation to find Gene. "Where would you like for me to put these?" she asked Mike.

"Please take them to the conference room," Mike answered. "Just sit them on the table, and we'll sort them out later. There's too much material to try to sort it out in here. Thanks, Kathy."

As she turned to go, Colonel Erickson's voice came over one of the speakers mounted above the communications console. "We've arrived at the Knox ranch," he said. "I'll get my team moving and call back when we find anything significant."

"Thanks," Karyn replied, "General Nelson is here and needs your initial appraisal of the situation."

"I'll have it in a couple of minutes," Rick responded. "As soon as we make a quick search of the area, I'll get back to you."

Just outside of Vashti, Rick had directed the helicopter to land on the gravel road that led from the front gate toward the house and other buildings. They had first completed a cursory aerial surveillance of the property and noted that there was only one road providing access to the house from the public roads. It was almost a quarter of a mile from the gate to the house, and the chopper's location would prevent any vehicle from exiting the property in that direction.

As they had been ordered just prior to landing, the five members of Rick's team sprinted toward the buildings they had been assigned to search. Rick had one Airman with him as he approached the house. As he went to the front door, the other man circled toward the back.

Rick walked onto the porch, where three cats were lounging on a couple of wicker chairs, watching his every move. Opening the screen door, Rick knocked very loudly and rapidly. At the sudden interruption of their leisurely rest, the cats jumped from the chairs and scrambled toward the barn about 100 yards down a well-worn dirt road. As they disappeared, Rick again beat on the door and waited for an answer from within the house.

When he heard no noise indicating movement or occupancy, he tried the doorknob. The knob turned easily in his hand, and the door swung open, revealing an empty living room visible through a short hall where a couple of coats, a well-worn black hat, and a pair of boots were resting.

Rick cautiously continued on into the room and loudly announced his presence. Hearing no response, he saw a kitchen to the right and walked toward it. As he was passing by a sink that contained several dirty plates that looked as if they had been there for several days, he heard the other team member announcing his entry through a door in the rear of the house.

"I'm in here," Rick said loudly as he passed through the kitchen and into a hallway that appeared to connect to the bedrooms. As he started down the hall, he noticed a door that appeared to provide access to the garage.

"Take the other side of the house," he told his companion. "I'll check out the bedrooms on this side. If you don't find anything, meet me back over here in the garage."

After hearing that his directions were being followed, Rick conducted a rapid search of the three bedrooms and bathrooms off of the hall. Seeing only rooms with normal beds, chairs, and tables but no obvious recent use, he returned to the door that apparently led into the garage.

That door was also unlocked, and Rick had just entered when the other member arrived. "Anything?" Rick asked as he looked at a very familiar red truck parked in the garage.

"Nothing, sir," he responded, "just the master bedroom and a connecting bathroom. What would you like for me to do now?"

"Head down to the barn and see if the rest of the men have found anything," Rick told him as he circled the truck.

"Yes, sir," he said as he turned and exited through the door back into the house.

Rick looked at the wall beside the door and found the switch for the garage door. Pressing the plastic button, the door began to roll up, and sunlight poured through beneath it as it climbed toward the ceiling. As the interior became brighter, Rick grimly smiled and said, "I've found you, you son of a bitch."

Taking a video camera from one of the pockets of his flight suit, Rick began walking around the truck, making sure to cover every inch of the familiar vehicle. Once he had ensured that he had each side and end fully recorded, he headed toward the resting chopper.

As he entered the sliding door on the right side of the helicopter, he reached for the radios temporarily mounted inside for their use. After checking the frequency and ensuring it was still on the secure channel they had been assigned, he made a terse call back to the operations room.

"Colonel Lynch, are you still there?" he asked.

"Right here," Karyn replied. "Do you have something?"

"Oh yes," Rick told her. "Is General Nelson still in the room?"

"Yes," Karyn told him. "Would you like to speak with him?"

"That won't be necessary," Rick answered, "as long as he can hear me."

"He can," Karyn said. "What do you have?"

"I've found our mysterious truck," Rick told her. "I'm almost positive, but I'm going to download the video, and you can have it verified against our previous pictures."

Mike picked up the microphone and asked, "What about personnel? Is there anyone at the location?"

"I don't think so," Rick answered. "The house is empty, and it appears that nobody has lived in it for several days. The master bedroom's bed was unmade, dirty dishes were in the sink with dried food still on them, and none of the other rooms appeared to have been used."

"We're still searching the other buildings," he continued, "but I don't think there's anyone here."

"Any hint as to how long the place has been empty, other than the dishes?" Mike asked.

"Well," Rick said, "it's impossible to tell from the interior, but the grass around the house appears as if it hasn't been cut for over a week or so. My guess is that Mr. Knox rarely stayed here but returned occasionally to take care of a few chores."

As he was talking, he noticed the remaining members of his team walking up from the barn, shaking their heads. Glancing around and seeing no livestock close by, he continued, "Sir, the only animals that appear to be here are three cats that may or may not be his. The others are almost back from the barn, and I'll have their report shortly."

"I'd like to transmit the video data now if that's all right with you," Rick told Karyn and Mike. "I'll have the rest of the team's information for you as soon as the download is complete."

"Go ahead," Karyn said. "I've got a monitor connected to the recorder, and we can see the pictures while you're sending them."

The video of the truck was streaming across the monitor. Jerry joined them and stood quietly as they watched the emerging images. When the camera passed behind the truck, Karyn excitedly cried, "There, right there! See that bow in the tailgate? I know I saw that same thing in the truck we were looking for."

"I think you're correct about that being the truck," Jerry announced. "But I'd bet that 90% of the trucks out there have that identical bow."

"What do you mean?" Mike asked.

"Well," Jerry continued, "just about every truck that's used on ranches has a trailer ball in the bed of the truck. It's used to pull what's called a gooseneck trailer."

"What's so different about that instead of one that hooks on the bumper?" Karyn asked.

"To start with," Jerry told her, "a gooseneck trailer has a tube from the front that extends down into the bed of the truck. That's what causes the problems. They provide a much better turning radius and more stability when pulling them, but if you ever forget to lower the tailgate after you disconnect and try to drive off, that tube hits the tailgate and bends it before it drops down.”

“Just about everyone that has pulled a gooseneck long enough has forgotten to lower the tailgate at one time or another,” he continued. “It doesn’t necessarily ruin the tailgate, but it does leave that telltale bend in it.”

“I guess we’ll have to wait for the computer to match the rest of the scratches and marks before we’re positive,” Mike replied. “But, based on Rick’s assessment and both of yours, I’m sure we’ve found our man.”

The video had finished downloading, and Rick called them back, saying, “There’s not much more to report here, other than they found a 50-pound bag of cat food down in the barn that looks fairly new. At least only a few pounds appear to have been removed. There’s an automatic feeder that probably holds 20 or so pounds, and it still has a little bit of food left. I’d guess that if there are only three cats, the feeder would last them two or three weeks. Given the remaining food, I’d say the last visitor out here was about ten or so days ago.”

“With your permission, sir,” he continued, “I’ll load up and head back. I’d like to send some forensic people up here later to do a more thorough analysis of the house, but I don’t think we can get much more right now.”

“That’s fine,” Mike told him. “Just be prepared to go assist Amy if she calls. I especially want that clinic scrubbed clean and every molecule of evidence secured as soon as possible.”

“Very good, sir,” Rick acknowledged as he directed his team back into the chopper. “We’ll be airborne in a couple of minutes and heading back. Just call if you want us to meet Amy.”

"Have you heard from Colonel Moore?" Mike asked, looking at Karyn.

"No, sir," Karyn answered. "She should be landing any minute now."

General Nelson turned and told Jerry, "Now we really need that information on Kevin Knox. I'm very interested in learning about the man who appears to have had as much to do with Gene's disappearance as Mr. North."

Deep in thought, Mike looked back at the map, wondering just how many other players there were in this game. At least now they could put a name and a face on another one of them. Without taking his eyes from the area around Boyd, Bowie, and Ringgold, he asked, "Major Fleenor, I want Mr. North and Ms. Terbush brought in here immediately. And keep them separated. It's time we started comparing stories and confronting these people with each falsehood they try to provide."

He turned and headed for the door, telling Karyn, "I'll be in the conference room reviewing the information we have on Butch North and Tammy Terbush. Have Jerry bring me anything we can get on Kevin Knox as soon as it arrives."

"Yes, sir," Karyn replied.

"And come get me if you hear from Colonel Moore," Mike said, pausing before the open door. "Let her know she can have Colonel Erickson and his team if she needs them. Also, you and Jerry get busy getting us some more ground units. It's going to take several teams to cover the area and find all the people we need to bring in."

CHAPTER 18

Butch climbed into the Mustang and looked at all of the things he had collected from Gene, Leslie, and BK. Carefully, he opened each of the envelopes and double-checked each Ziplock bag again to ensure it had the correct information written on it and the material sealed inside. Then he reread each of the pages of instructions, making minor additions to each one before returning everything to its original envelope.

Holding the camera, he tried to remember where there was a photo shop in Stephenville that could transfer the images to a CD and also provide prints. If he wasn't mistaken, there was a Walmart Super Center just on the west side of town on Highway 377. The only problem, he decided, was that each store would probably imprint something that would identify the store that processed the pictures.

That would provide information about the direction they were traveling through, and he needed to withhold any clues of the ultimate destination as long as possible. He finally decided that the safest place to get everything together and also mail it was to head back north toward Decatur. He also needed to get Renee's car back to her. The trick would be getting another vehicle, processing the photos, and mailing everything to the recipients before he was discovered.

That decided, he started the car and pulled back onto 281, heading north toward the same area he knew was being watched. This time, he followed the same route that Kevin had taken as he drove down from Ringgold. It was about an hour and a half to get up to Jacksboro and then another hour or so east on 380 into Decatur. With any luck, he could make it before the photo shop in the Wal-Mart closed. Otherwise, he would need to find someplace and spend the night while the government continued to intensify its search and possibly disrupt all of his plans.

Driving as fast as he could without attracting attention, he sped through Mineral Wells, Perrin, and Jacksboro. The open countryside from there to Decatur would probably be the most hazardous since he was getting closer to every area he and Kevin had been seen in during the first manhunt. It would take more than good planning if this was going to work. Major luck was needed.

As Butch crossed the Runaway Bay Bridge over Lake Bridgeport, he decided that he would take one more chance on contacting an additional person that could provide at least a car and maybe a place to stay, if necessary. Although he had seen no suspicious activity along any of the roads, he knew that by now, the Texas Highway Patrol and Sheriffs' offices would be in on the hunt. Now that he was back in Wise County, he also knew that his chances of being recognized were dramatically increased.

As he passed through the east side of Bridgeport, he realized that time was running out for him in more ways than one. First, he had to get to Decatur and make a quick stop at David's Western Wear to talk to Ted, an old friend who had shaped almost every hat he had owned for several years, including the one he was currently wearing.

Then, either make it to the photo shop at Wal-Mart or find a hiding place for the night. If he could convince Ted to help him, then he could gain a little more time, and Ted might also be able to loan him a car so he could keep Renee's ire down somewhat. Butch decided that he was certainly asking a lot of several of his closest friends, and some might even take offense at what he was doing.

Butch pulled into David's Western Wear and parked as far from the entrance as possible. As he walked from the car toward the doors, he saw a helicopter speeding southward. Although it was certainly not a rare event to see choppers flying around the area, each one caused a moment of concern.

Once inside the store, Butch walked to the counter, where he was glad to see Ted assisting a man in getting his new hat creased to his personal specifications. Watching, Butch thought of how many times he had asked Ted to make some minor adjustments to each hat he had bought here. Such changes may seem slight to people who don't wear cowboy hats, but subtle things distinguish everyone's particular look.

Waiting for Ted to finish, Butch walked into the rear of the store and looked at some of the things displayed in the National Ropers' Supply section. Seeing a ball cap with *NRS* embroidered above the bill, he selected a maroon one with white lettering. Next, he took a pair of mirror-surfaced sunglasses from the rack on the counter.

Holding the items in his hand, Butch returned to the front of the store. Just as he was passing a room filled with part of their saddle inventory, Ted met him, saying, "Hey, Butch. What're you up to today, need a new saddle?"

"Afternoon, Teddie," Butch replied. "Nope, I haven't worn out the ones I have."

"Well," Ted smiled, "you have to use them to wear them out. If I can't help you find a saddle, how about a new hat? That one you're wearing looks like it needs to be replaced."

"What do you mean replaced?" Butch asked incredulously. "You sold me this hat less than six months ago, and I only wear it when I go out dancing."

"Yeah, but you seem to spend a lot more time dancing than you do roping," Ted chided. "Now, what can I do for you, or are you just in here trying to ogle some pretty cowgirls?"

"No, not looking for the ladies today," Butch answered. "But I do need a huge favor."

"And what's that?" Ted asked.

"First, I need this to be very private," Butch said seriously. "I need to return a car to a friend down in Rhome, borrow another one, and sort of hide out for a day or so."

"What's it this time?" Ted asked him. "Somebody's husband after you?"

"More or less," Butch lied. "I swear I had no idea; she had no rings, never mentioned even a boyfriend, let alone a husband."

"And just how did you get into this mess?" Ted said with a slight smile still on his face.

"I was out at Red's in Bridgeport," Butch told him. "And there was this sort of cute little thing sitting with a couple of other ladies. Well, naturally, I asked her to dance, being a gentleman and all."

"Of course, you being so concerned about her enjoying her evening, I suppose," Ted retorted.

"Exactly," Butch said. "Anyway, later, we were sort of discussing things in my truck when this pickup came sliding to a stop right in front of us. Then, this wild-eyed truck driver-looking character comes running up to us shouting something about her lack of certain moral values."

"Yeah," Ted laughed. "I can certainly see that."

"Well, the jerk opens her door and drags her out," Butch explained. "And then he tells me he's fixing to get his gun from his truck and demonstrate the folly of conversing with another man's wife. That's when I decided that discretion was the better part of valor and got my ass out of there."

"And I'm sure that's exactly the way it happened," Ted said, stifling a laugh. "So, just how can I assist you in this predicament?"

"Since you asked," Butch told him, "the man is obviously deranged, but by now probably knows my name, where I live, and the cars I drive. So, to avoid any unnecessary confrontations, I just need to be unobserved for a day or so."

"I reckon I can appreciate your circumstances," Ted admitted. "Before I got married a few years back, I fell into unfortunate positions myself once or twice. We're closing in about 30 minutes, so if you can wait until then, I believe I can take care of you for a few days."

"That's great," Butch told him, greatly relieved. "I need to run down to Wal-Mart for a couple of things, and I'll meet you back here as soon as I'm done. If you close before I get back, just wait around a couple of minutes for me, if you don't mind."

"Not a problem," Ted answered. "If the store's closed, just knock on the door. I'll be working on a couple of hats that are supposed to be picked up tomorrow."

Butch shook his hand and said, "Thanks, Teddie. I'll just pay for these on my way out and see you when I get back."

Ted looked at the ball cap and glasses, remarking, "Not much of a disguise there, Butch, but better than that well-known hat."

Agreeing with him as he walked away, Butch stood in front of the cashier as she rang up his purchases. Once they had been placed in a plastic sack, he left the store and walked back to the Mustang.

The short drive to Walmart was quickly done, and Butch parked in the closest spot he saw. After laying his black hat on the seat, he pulled the tags from the ball cap and sunglasses before putting them on. Grabbing the camera, he hurried into the front entrance and went directly to the photo processing area.

One of the salespeople smiled as he walked up, asking what she could do for him today. Telling her that he needed 20 CDs made from the disk in the camera, she then asked if he also wanted pictures. Thinking about it for a second, Butch told her to make 20 copies of each photo as well.

He handed her the camera and waited while she extracted the disk and slid it into a computer behind the counter. When she asked what size photos he needed, he told her to just make a composite of all of them on a single sheet if it was possible. Then, he explained, the people getting the photos could select which ones they wanted enlarged and do it themselves.

Once the disk had been inserted, it was very few minutes before the CDs were processed, and sheets of the images began sliding out of the machine. Butch took a quick look at the pictures and nodded his head in satisfaction. Once completed, he paid for everything and took the camera with the disk reinserted.

After driving to the Decatur Post Office, he began placing a CD and a sheet of the pictures into each envelope with the other material. After a final review of the contents, he sealed them and carried them in. The postal employee informed him that they did have guaranteed next-day delivery and that the package addressed to the NAS/JRB would arrive there before noon tomorrow. He sent the others via regular mail and paid the postage.

After taking the receipt, he drove back to David's and parked to wait for the store to close. Finally seeing Ted walking out, he relaxed a little and sat and wondered where Sancudo and Kevin were right now. Not knowing what was happening with them felt strange and disconcerting to him. Resigning himself to being out of control of the situation, Butch climbed out of the car and went to meet him.

"Where are we headed?" Ted asked as he approached.

"Rhome," Butch answered. "I need to drop off this car at the Woodhaven National Bank. Think you can follow me down there?"

"Sure," Ted told him. "Do you need to go by your house?"

"That's the last place I need to be right now," Butch smiled. "I wouldn't be surprised if the gentleman in question isn't sitting at Kountry Korner watching for me to pull into my driveway. Nope, let's just stay well clear of anywhere he might think I would be."

"Okay," Ted said. "You lead the way; I'll be right behind you. I've already called home, and my little sweetie has got your room ready, and a pot roast is waiting for dinner. Not to mention, there's a fresh bottle of Jack Daniel's sitting on the table that has our name on it."

"Excellent, mi amigo," Butch said as he climbed back into the Mustang. I'll meet you at the bank if you get too far behind." Taking a quick look at Ted walking to his ancient pickup, Butch pulled onto 380 and headed toward 287. Once he arrived in Rhome, he would be within a couple of miles of where he was certain that the hunting party was not so patiently waiting for his return.

CHAPTER 19

As Kevin waited for Sancudo to finish chewing the meat from the rib, his level of concern skyrocketed. It wasn't so much what Mel had asked or said; it was more the tone of his voice that had Kevin worried.

"All right, "Kevin finally said. "I understand that you're doing the planning. Butch only told me that you would take care of us and implied that we would be going somewhere down around Del Rio. I may have assumed that we would be on the Mexico side of the border from your conversation."

Mel placed the stripped bone down into the container and selected a slice of brisket from the diminishing pile of meat. "What we are doing is a serious matter, amigo," he said, licking his fingers. "I hope you are not taking this lightly. Regardless of the careless manner in which Butch and I seem to behave, I do not place myself or my friends into dangerous situations without everyone knowing the risks and certain rules."

Kevin nodded his head and replied, "I fully understand the consequences of any mistakes, Mel. And I can assure you that we all know the potential results of any miscalculation.

Whatever rules you think necessary will be followed as best we can."

"First," Mel told him, "you do not need to know where you are going. You don't even need to know where you are once we arrive. I realize that you can read the signs along the road and will generally know the locations, but once we get off the main roads, never question anyone about where you are."

"That's not a problem," Kevin said. "My only concern is for potential medical assistance should we need it. I'm sure you have considered that when you decided where we were to be taken."

"I consider everything," Sancudo told him. "In my business, nothing is left to chance. But I will not compromise any aspect of my operation for either you or those with you."

"Now, second," he continued. "This is going to be an expensive operation, and I need to collect some cash before we go any further. Since I do not know how long we will need to remain unobserved, I can only guess that it will be a minimum of a week."

"That's probably the least amount of time," Kevin acknowledged. "How much do you need for the first week?"

"I require $5,000 to cover the initial costs of getting you safely hidden," Mel said. "Then, it will be $100 per day for the length of time required. So, before we go any further, I would like for you to provide me with that amount. Better yet, let's just make it $6,000; that will cover the first ten days."

Kevin thought that the amount was much more than anticipated, but also knew that there weren't too many options at this point. "Okay," he told Mel, "I have that amount available right now. What else do you need before we get going?"

"I forgot to mention," Mel said, "all transactions are to be in cash, and there are no refunds. So, if you will kindly make the first payment, we can continue our discussion."

Kevin turned and walked back to the sedan as Sancudo pulled a jalapeno from the container and bit off half of it. Reaching the car, he opened the door and slid inside. He had stashed the money beneath the front seat and bent slightly to retrieve one of the bundles that Butch had provided.

"Any problems?" Leslie asked from the rear seat.

"No," Kevin answered as he counted out 60 $100 bills from the first stack. "I just need to pay Sancudo for the first part of our trip."

Gene was watching as Kevin took the money and then replaced the remainder back beneath the seat. "How much is this going to cost?" he asked.

Kevin recounted the money and said, "It's a little more than I originally thought, but we don't need to worry about that right now. We just need to get this settled and on our way."

"I hate that you and Butch are going to such expense for us," Gene complained. "Isn't there something else we can do?"

"Not at the moment," Kevin told him as he opened the door again. "We'll have time to debate this when we're safe. For now, just let me take care of things."

As he shut the door, he leaned through the window and said, "Hey, maybe you'll win the lottery later and can take care of Butch and me for the rest of our lives!"

Watching the traffic passing as he returned to Mel's Bronco, he decided that he needed to be extra cautious working with Sancudo. He was certain that he had been observed as he took the money from beneath the seat, so he needed to find another place to safely hide the cash in case things got dicey.

Mel wiped his hands on a napkin and said, "Mucho gracias, amigo," as Kevin handed the money through the open window.

Pulling out the fake front of the radio, Sancudo placed the stack of cash into a tray behind it. "Now, let's discuss a few procedures," Mel said as he slid it back into position.

"You will follow me no closer than one mile when we are on the open road," he directed. "If I pull over for any reason, you will continue along the same road for at least two miles, find a place to park, and wait for me to pass you."

"Now," Mel continued, "if you need to stop for any reason, you can flash your lights as long as there are no other cars within sight. If there are other cars around, you will pass me and then pull over wherever you need to. I never drive over the posted speed limit, so use your discretion as to your own speed."

"Then," Mel said as he sipped his tea, "I will be waiting a mile or so down the road. If we are getting close to where I need to change roads, I will be waiting at least a mile before the intersection."

He sat his tea down and continued, "I will tell you that unless circumstances change, we will stay on 377 all the way to Rocksprings. If we do get separated and either of us has spent more than 15 minutes waiting, that is where we will rendezvous. Specifically, about three miles west of town, you will see Highway 674 and a sign saying that Brackettville is 60 miles ahead on that road."

"Turn left on 674, and after about a mile or so, you will come to a gravel road on your left that leads into some ranch land," Mel said. "There is a cattle guard with a metal sign that reads 'Southwestern Cattle Raisers Association' attached to the fence. That particular sign has three bullet holes through the o's."

"If you arrive before I do, drive in until you come to a small corral about a mile or so from the road and wait," he continued. "I will, of course, do the same. Now, if either of us waits there for more than 30 minutes, we must assume that there's a problem."

"What do I do if you're not there after that?" Kevin asked.

"In that case," Mel said smiling, "you're on your own."

"You've got to have something else in mind," Kevin told him. "You can't just leave us out in the middle of nowhere."

"Oh, but I can," Sancudo replied. "I can and I will if it means compromising my operation."

Kevin stared at Mel and tried to decide if this was just a way of ditching them and running off with the money. He just couldn't believe that Butch would have placed them in such a situation, and there had to be some way of reestablishing contact if things got so out of hand.

"How do I contact you if this should happen?" Kevin questioned.

"Listen, my friend," Sancudo answered. "You are never to contact me or attempt to do so anywhere. If you even try, you will find me unavailable. However, if you do not think you can comply with the directions I have given, maybe we should part company right here."

"I can follow your instructions all right," Kevin said, "but if we do get separated, I need to know what the rest of the plan is."

"And that is just why you will never know my plans," Mel said. "If you are the one caught, and that is much more probable than them catching me, I will not have our identities or locations known. This is not a game, senor! From here on, the risks mount, and I must take precautions to protect myself and my people.”

“Unfortunately, you are expendable to me,” he continued. “You must understand that my people and I have been doing this for many, many years and have learned the hard way that too many of you ‘*turistas*’ are willing to sacrifice us for your own selfish reasons.”

“Now,” Mel concluded, “I think we need to start south again. I would suggest that if a true emergency develops, then you try to contact Butch. He and he alone will make contact with me. And if your contact with him results in difficulties on my part, I will toss you to the dogs that are hounding you faster than a Tijuana whore sends you from the room when you’re done. Comprender?”

Without waiting for his reply, Mel started the Bronco and began backing up. Kevin returned to his car and quickly started it, waiting for Sancudo to head south before he put the car in reverse. Shaking his head in frustration, he entered the road with Mel already at least a mile away. Accelerating to slightly above the speed limit, he soon closed the distance and slowed to match the Bronco’s speed.

“Are we in trouble?” Leslie asked as she picked up BK and prepared to nurse him.

“No,” Kevin told her. “But we’ve got to be sure we don’t cross that friend of Butch’s. From here on, if you are talking to him, be nice and polite. But do not reveal anything unnecessary. I would prefer that you let me handle him myself.”

Looking down, Kevin saw that they would need to stop for gas pretty soon. From the road signs, he knew they were about 60 miles from Brownwood, and they could certainly make that. *“Heaven help us if we should run out of gas,”*

Kevin thought. *"That man would probably keep driving and be laughing at us poor gringos as he spent our money!"*

CHAPTER 20

Amy and her team landed just across the road from the clinic, and she immediately climbed down from the helicopter, hurrying to where the doctor, nurse, and Trooper were standing. As she approached them, she noticed a couple of cars stopped beside the road watching them, apparently only interested in the excitement of having some new happenings in the small town.

"Hello," she said, walking up to the Trooper and the rest of the group. "I'm Colonel Amy Moore, and the folks behind me are here to assist in securing the clinic."

The Trooper took his hat off and told her, "Yes, ma'am, I'm Thomas, and this is Doctor Adams and his nurse, Amber."

Amy shook the doctor's hand and said, "Doctor Adams, I'm pleased to meet you. If you and Amber would be so kind as to assist us, we need to start gathering all the material available from the delivery of the child."

"We'd be glad to help you," Doctor Adams replied hesitantly. "But, I would like to know just why you need all of it?"

"We think the baby is the son of a fugitive we have been trying to find," Amy explained. "I plan on taking everything back to my laboratory, and we'll run DNA analysis to either prove or disprove his paternity."

"Then, assuming the DNA matches the samples we have on file," she continued, "we'll know that it's his child. That will confirm either he or an acquaintance has been in this area, and we can focus our search efforts up here."

"I understand," the doctor told her as he turned and walked toward the clinic. "Amber and I left everything just as it was when Thomas asked us to close."

The doctor unlocked the door, and Amy followed them into the waiting area. As the rest of the team began bringing in the containers to transport the material back to the base, Amy took a sealed bag of lab clothing and told them to wait there while she inspected the area where the delivery had taken place.

As the doctor started into the examination room, Amy stopped him and said, "Doctor, I'd prefer to keep the room from any further contamination. If you and Amber would please wait here, I'll put on my things and take a look around."

Taking a sterile paper gown and booties from the bag, she quickly slipped them on and walked into the room. Seeing that the examination table still had a blood-stained covering in place and the tray of surgical instruments lay scattered on the floor, she stepped back out and told her team to suit up. "Are there any other things you used, such as gloves or towels?" she asked Doctor Adams.

"Why yes," he replied. "I used a pair of latex gloves, as did Amber, and there were a couple of white cotton towels."

"What did you do with them?" Amy asked.

"They were put in the receptacle just inside the door," the doctor told her. "As soon as the lady took her son and left with the man who arrived shortly after the birth, I told Amber to start cleaning the room. I tossed my gloves and a couple of towels away and tried to follow them, but they were already getting into a pickup."

"What about you, Amber?" Amy asked. "Did you put everything you used into the container as well?"

"Yes," she answered, "I think I did. There wasn't very much time from when they left until Thomas came back and told us to close the clinic."

"I need you to be certain," Amy told her. "I've got to take everything that might have been used back for analysis.

"Well," Amber said after thinking for a second, "I'm sure I didn't take anything from the room. I had started to pick up the things I dropped from the tray when Doctor Adams came back and said we were leaving. Then, I just pulled my gloves off, dropped them in with the other things, and walked out."

"What about any after-birth or other fluids?" Amy asked.

"Anything of that nature is still on the table," Doctor Adams replied. "As I said, we didn't have time to clean anything."

"Why is it so important to get all of that?" he continued. "If all you need is a sample of the child's DNA, the rest of it would undoubtedly belong to the mother."

"In addition to the child's DNA," Amy explained, "we need to identify the mother as well. Every piece of evidence will be necessary to determine who she is and also to help isolate the father's DNA."

"I have her name," Doctor Adams told her. "She's been here before, and I've got records of every visit."

"I'll need copies of those," Amy said. "If you can get them while we get to work in here, I'd appreciate it."

Amy walked to where the team had finished donning their sterile clothing and told them to start gathering everything that had any possibility of containing evidence. As the team started collecting anything that could be removed, the doctor motioned for Amy to follow him.

When they were standing by his office door, he told her, "I'm not sure I can just hand medical records over to you, ma'am. Privacy regulations prevent me from disclosing that information."

"Doctor," Amy said sternly, "I'm fully aware of the regulations. I am also a licensed medical professional, in addition to being a US Air Force officer. What I'm asking for must be considered as necessary for potential treatment of the mother and the child."

"Now," she continued, "if you were to refer a patient to another doctor, you'd provide that information. Wouldn't you? And since the child isn't technically a patient, you wouldn't be violating any rights there."

"So," Amy concluded, "as the doctor of record for any future medical procedures regarding either the mother or child, I am entitled to all of their records."

"I suppose that would be correct," Doctor Adams replied. "If you can provide me with documentation that you are her new physician, then I will gladly transfer all of the records to you. It'll take me a couple of minutes to gather all of them, so if you'd get me some authorization, you may take them."

"Gladly," Amy said. "Do you have a fax machine or computer where I can have it sent?"

"I'm afraid not," he answered, closing the door to his office. "You'll have to bring me a letter before I can release anything. Until then, I'm afraid I can't give you anything regarding the mother's treatment."

Amy was becoming very frustrated as she realized that the doctor wasn't going to be as willing to cooperate as she had hoped. "Well," she tried, "can you just give me her name and address?"

"I'm afraid I can't do that either," Doctor Adams told her. "The names and addresses of my patients are not to be released without their consent. You still need some sort of authorization to get that information."

"Now," he said as he locked his office door, "I've done about all I can do for you right now. If there's nothing else, I need to get back home. Thomas has my home phone number, and you may call when you have the documents authorizing you to have the records."

He walked toward the front of the clinic while Amy tried to decide whether or not to stop him. Her orders were to gather all of the evidence and return it for examination. She could do that. But she also knew that any record of Leslie and the birth of a son needed to be destroyed, especially if that son belonged to Gene.

Having no real options right now, she returned to supervise the sterilization of the examination room. As she arrived, she saw that the room was completely stripped of every piece of cloth, plastic, or item that wasn't permanently attached.

The team placed each article in separate bags and loaded them into the containers for transfer back to the base. Additionally, they had scrubbed every surface with a disinfecting solvent that would ensure every particle of remaining evidence was removed.

Amy watched as they loaded all of the material onto the helicopter and then told Amber that they were finished and she could lock up whenever she wanted. Thanking Thomas for his help, Amy climbed aboard the chopper and directed the pilot to take them back to the base.

After they were almost halfway back to the NAS/JRB, she suddenly realized that they hadn't gotten everything. All the time she had been talking to the doctor, he had been wearing a pair of operating scrubs. On the sleeves and front there had been some stains that must have come from the delivery. And the nurse was still wearing hers also.

"Oh, shit," she thought. *"Now I've got to figure out how to get those clothes as well as the medical records. General Nelson will have my ass over this, and there's no way to go back now."*

As the helicopter continued southbound, Doctor Adams arrived back at his house. As he stepped from his car he realized that he was still wearing his scrubs. Not only that, there was a clamp holding a piece of umbilical cord in one of the pockets. Not realizing that what he had could provide proof of things he couldn't possibly imagine, he removed them and tossed them into the trunk of the car, intending to return them to the clinic tomorrow. For now, he just wanted to sit and sip a little of the new bottle of Gentleman Jack, his wife had brought home from the Wise Liquor Store in Bridgeport after visiting their grandson.

Sitting on the porch with the glass of Jack in his hand, he began wondering why the US Air Force was so interested in that particular lady. Why hadn't the FBI or someone else come to do the investigation? Why had they wanted every bit of bodily material? And, even more, he had worked several crime scenes earlier in his career before he became the local country doctor, and never, ever, had he seen any member of a law enforcement organization clean the scene as they had done.

The more he thought about it and remembered the sight of that newborn boy, the more he believed that something else was going on. *"No,"* he decided, *"I think I'll just keep that little piece of umbilical cord. It may be the only thing I can save of those folks."* Old Doc Adams sat the glass down and went into the house where his wife of almost 60 years was setting the table. After getting a Ziplock bag, he removed the cord and clamp from the trunk of his car and dropped them into the bag.

Back in the house, he placed the sealed bag in the back of the freezer beneath several sacks of frozen corn and then took a handful of ice cubes from the tray before shutting the door. As he walked through the kitchen back toward the porch, he told his wife how good dinner smelled and how pretty he thought she was. Smiling, he returned to his drink and thought, *"I may be getting along in years, but I can still smell a skunk. And I do believe there's a polecat loose out there somewhere!"*

CHAPTER 21

Butch continued south on 287 into Rhome with Ted close behind. They went beneath the crossover where Highway 114 went west through Aurora into Boyd and passed within yards of Butch's house. Taking the next exit, Butch turned left at the stop sign and drove the short distance to the parking lot of the bank. After checking to make sure he didn't leave anything in the car, he locked it and put the keys in one of the envelopes available for after-hours deposits. Once he had scribbled a thank you note on the envelope, he dropped it into the slot and headed to where Ted was parked.

"You about ready to head for the house?" Ted asked as Butch put his suitcase in the bed of the truck and shut the door.

"As ready as I'll ever be," Butch answered, latching his seat belt. "You wouldn't happen to have a cold beer in this relic of a truck, would you?"

"I'm afraid not," Ted said as he started to drive away. "I used to keep a cooler in the bed, but once everyone found out it was there, it was always empty before I could get one.

I finally got tired of supplying beer for that bunch of deadbeat cowboys that come into the store."

"I know what you mean," Butch said. "I've taken a cooler to a roping and swear that I might get two beers out of the 12 or so I put in it. Hell, those guys are worse about drinking my beer than my daughters."

"But," he continued, "If you just pull over there to the liquor store beside Subway, I'll run in and grab a cold six-pack. Old Creed keeps a few cold ones ready for the thirsty traveler."

"I reckon a frosty beverage would make the drive home a little more pleasant," Ted replied. "It's certainly a dusty trail we've got to ride, and I'm practically parched right now."

Ted pulled into an empty spot and waited for Butch to get the beer. As he waited, he watched two black Suburbans with dark-tinted windows speeding north on 287 and a low-flying helicopter heading west over 114. Seeing the Suburbans turn west on 114 also, he wondered what was going on in that direction.

Butch came out carrying a six-pack of cold Budweiser longnecks and climbed into the truck. "Better wait until we at least get out of the parking lot before I open them," Butch said as he sat the beer on the bench seat between them. "I'd hate to be seen drinking this close to the Baptist church. Might ruin my reputation, you know."

"Yeah, I know how you worry about what the Baptists think," Ted said. "And if they ever found out that you danced, I guess they'd picket your house night and day until you repented and confessed all of your sins."

"I don't believe they have that much time," Butch smiled. "If I was to confess all of my many sins, it'd take years. And it just might embarrass a few of those Bible thumpers as well. Hell, I've even seen one or two of them drinking and dancing down at the Stagecoach Ballroom in Ft Worth occasionally."

"You don't mean you've actually seen a Baptist dance?" Ted joked as he pulled onto 287, heading back north.

"Oh, yes," Butch said as he twisted the top from one of the bottles.

Handing it to Ted, he continued, "I've even seen a few skulking around the liquor store, waiting for everyone else to leave before they buy their beer."

Ted took a long pull from the beer and said, "Do you know there are three things that the major religions refuse to recognize?"

Butch opened another beer and took a sip, answering, "Really? What's that?"

"Well," Ted told him, "Catholics don't recognize contraceptives as a means of birth control, Jews don't recognize Jesus as the son of God, and Baptists don't recognize each other in the liquor store!"

Butch almost spit his beer out as he laughed. "Yep, I certainly understand that. Bless their little hypocritical hearts. Some of the sorriest folks I've ever met were Deacons in their churches."

"Now," he continued, "that's not to say they're all bad. Most of them are good people, but I just can't understand why they put up with some of the crap the bad ones do. I think it gives religion a bad name, like those priests that molest the choirboys. And the church covers it up; that's what really pisses me off."

"I agree," Ted said, "But without religion, I think the world would be a hell of a mess. At least the church tries to teach folks the right way to live, and there're always a few rotten apples in any barrel."

"I know," Butch agreed. "It's just so frustrating that so many of them cloak themselves in religious robes while trying to screw their fellow man. I'd hate to go back to the Puritan days, but I would like to see a scarlet letter on the thieves, liars, and cheats."

"I suppose you'd like to see the scarlet 'A' on the adulterers also," Ted remarked.

"Well, it'd make it easier to know the ladies that were somewhat available," Butch answered. "Not to mention the ones to avoid!"

"Sort of like that one you're avoiding up in Bridgeport?" Ted chuckled.

"Exactly," Butch agreed. "If that lady had been wearing a big 'A' on the front of her shirt, I might not have to hide from that ill-tempered husband of hers."

"I'd bet that if it wasn't him, it'd be someone else," Ted said. "You just seem to be attracted to married ladies."

"Of course," Butch said as he finished his beer. "I always figure that I can dance with them a couple of times, and they won't try to follow me home. I'd be glad to ask their husband's permission if I know they have one."

He pulled another beer from the box and continued, "The problem comes when they don't tell you and try to get you to do more than just dance. I've come to believe that dance halls are filled with succuba."

"Sucu-what's?" Ted asked, laughing. "What are you talking about?"

"Succuba, a succubus," Butch explained. "Evil women sent from hell to mislead us, poor innocent cowboys. If you'd watch South Park, you'd learn these things."

"Amazing, just simply amazing," Ted said, shaking his head. "With your education and world travels, you reference a cartoon to explain things. I'd have thought you'd quote one of the classics, like Dante's Inferno or something."

"Nope," Butch explained. "Sometimes wisdom comes in the simplest ways. And my simple mind finds relevance in the strangest of places."

"Simple and strange do fit your warped little brain," Ted agreed. "Not to change the subject, but did you notice those black cars and the helicopter that were heading west when we were leaving the liquor store?"

"Nope," Butch lied. "What'd they look like?"

"Just a couple of black Suburbans with dark windows driving pretty fast and one chopper just above the tree level," Ted answered. "It looked like they were heading toward Boyd or somewhere in that area."

"Probably some DEA raid over in Aurora Vista," Butch said. "I've heard that there are a few meth labs in those big houses."

"You gotta be shitting me," Ted replied. "I thought that was one of the premier housing areas around here."

"It is," Butch told him. "But just because you live in a nice neighborhood doesn't mean there aren't some scumbags living a few doors down. I just think we need to have an area where they can all be placed and do whatever they want with their pathetic lives."

"And where would you suggest?" Ted asked as they approached the turn that would take them to his house.

"How about Newark?" Butch answered. "I think at least half of the dealers in the county live down there anyway. The only problem is that it would probably triple their population if all of the dealers in Wise County moved there."

"Why not move them to Aurora?" Ted asked. "Too close to home?"

"Nope, can't do that," Butch said. "Because we've already got the first known UFO that ever crashed on Earth, and you can't go mixing drugs and aliens together. Besides, they've already done that down in Marfa. I think that's why so many UFO sightings happen down there: a little too much whiskey and pharmaceuticals."

Despite the light banter they were having, Butch had realized where the helicopter and cars were heading and knew the trouble Ted would be in if they were caught together. It had been risky to come back down to Rhome, but since no one had seen them leave Decatur together, it was worth taking the chance just to return Renee's car and have nobody know what vehicle he was in.

The only person who had a chance to see them together was inside the liquor store and couldn't have seen Ted's pickup. The government would find his Corvette still parked inside the garage and either catch Steve driving his truck, or it would be parked back at the stables.

And now that every vehicle he had borrowed was back where it belonged, and since he hadn't been seen driving any of them by the government, those owners wouldn't be questioned about why he had borrowed them. One more car change, and he should be unnoticeable as he moved about completing his plan.

Now, Butch felt that if he could stay at Ted's for a couple of days, those two Air Force officers that had been at his first interrogation would have time to consider the ramifications of the letter and material he had sent. Maybe when they realized all the evidence Butch had compiled and the fact that numerous others were in possession of the same thing, they might be willing to discuss some alternative to their current plans.

If not, Butch had no doubt as to his future. Knowing that Kevin would take care of Gene and the others was comforting, but he hated that none of them could probably ever return to their homes or families. The uncertainty surrounding the rest of their lives weighed heavily on his mind. That and knowing that he was responsible for the difficulties the others were enduring.

He sat quietly, sipping his beer as they drove, and hoped that Ted and others who had helped would never be discovered and considered conspirators in his plans. Butch really worried about Tammy, knowing that she would be suspected of aiding him. The fact that she knew absolutely nothing didn't mean they wouldn't make her life extremely difficult. Just hearing that she was suspected of these things would be tough enough for her. But to be told that her current lover was considered a fugitive and a traitor would be devastating.

CHAPTER 22

Kevin kept a close eye on Sancudo's Bronco and did his best to stay one mile behind him as he had been directed. Since they were driving slightly under the speed limit, occasionally, another car would pass him and block his view of what Mel was doing. Finding himself getting nervous when there were cars between them, he fought the urge to speed up and get closer.

Knowing that Sancudo could pull over at any time or take an exit unobserved continued to worry him until each car that had passed him went around Mel. The relief at seeing the Bronco still there every time did little to quiet his nerves. Being this tense for the next couple of hours was going to be difficult, but he couldn't let Gene or Leslie know of his doubts.

They passed through Dublin and entered Comanche County just before coming to Proctor. As they hit the outskirts of the small town, Kevin saw Mel signaling to pull into a small convenience store. Slowing to the reduced speed limit within the city limits, Kevin continued on by and saw Mel carrying the remains of his Bar-B-Q to a trash can located beside the store's door. Having not seen any road signs showing any intersecting roads until they approached the city of Comanche, he was fairly certain that Mel wouldn't disappear here.

Kevin checked his watch and continued on out of town before finding a place to wait. As he pulled over, he told Gene and Leslie that if they needed to use the restroom, they'd have to wait until they reached Brownwood. Saying they could wait, they sat there making idle conversation for several minutes while Kevin kept a close watch on the time that had passed. This would be the first test of Sancudo's trustworthiness, and as the 15-minute mark approached, Kevin started to think he needed to start making plans in case Mel did try to ditch them.

Just as he was about to say something about leaving, he saw Sancudo's Bronco coming down the road. As it passed, Mel gave no hint of recognition of them and appeared to be talking on a cell phone. Kevin started the old sedan and rejoined 377 after a couple of other cars had passed him.

Leslie had finally finished nursing BK and was rocking him slightly as he slept. Gene leaned across the front seat and watched the countryside sliding past the windows. As they crossed the Leon River, he asked if he could sit in front for a while. Kevin told him that would be fine, and he climbed over the seat, giving Leslie more room to relax and let little BK sleep on the seat beside her.

"Is Comanche named for the Indians?" Gene asked as they came to a sign showing they were only 5 miles from the town.

"I believe so," Kevin answered. "This part of Texas was supposedly their territory before either the Mexicans or the white men arrived. They started out up in Nebraska and started migrating down here back in the late 1600s.

"They normally lived in small bands, and the first of them arrived in the early 1700s," he continued. "Each band lived more or less autonomous from the others unless they needed to join to fight a common enemy or go on a large raid."

"Were they the ones that attacked the covered wagons?" Gene asked.

"Probably," Kevin answered. "But they were more likely to raid settlements where they could capture people or steal horses and cattle. Then they would try to trade the captives or other things they had stolen."

"Wow," Gene said. "That sounds like they were pretty bad people."

"They were tough," Kevin told him as he noticed Leslie becoming interested in the story. "They were probably the best horsemen around and could outfight just about anybody when they were mounted. But, not so good on the ground."

"Couldn't the army stop them?" Leslie asked.

"You have to remember that Texas sort of belonged to the Spanish back then," Kevin said. "The main reason the Spanish didn't get much further north was because they couldn't beat the Comanche."

"And," he continued, "the white man wasn't so nice to them either. Once, when several Comanche Chiefs came to San Antonio to work out a peace agreement, they were slaughtered because they didn't immediately turn over all of the captives. What made this especially bad was that the Indians had come under a white flag of truce, and the white man dishonored it."

"I'll bet that really made the Indians mad," Gene remarked.

"Certainly did," Kevin said. "A Chief named Buffalo Hump got a band together, and they headed south, raiding all the way to the Gulf coast. When they got there, they burned a couple of towns and stole hundreds of horses and other things."

"Then, about six years later, Chief Buffalo Hump signed a peace treaty and was finally sent to Oklahoma to settle the tribe, I think," Kevin finished.

"Is Butch a Comanche, and that's why he hates Oklahoma?" Gene asked. "He's always saying something bad about Okies."

"No," Kevin laughed, "Butch is part Cherokee and all the things he says about Okies are more or less jokes with him. He may not tell you, but his grandfather was one of the early settlers in Oklahoma and lived in what's called a half-dugout. Then his father was raised there also."

"What's a half-dugout?" Gene asked as they were approaching the little town of Blanket.

"I know that one," Leslie answered. "It's where they dig a hole about four or five feet deep and then put up short walls and a roof. I've seen some pictures of them. And if that's what is meant by the 'good ol' days,' then I'm glad I didn't live back then."

"Yeah, it was pretty rough for the early settlers," Kevin agreed. "It took a lot of determination and intestinal fortitude to live in those days. I'll just keep my central heat and air and my satellite television, of course."

Approaching Early, Texas, Kevin sped up and passed Mel. When he saw the first gas station that had restrooms and a chance to get some drinks, he pulled in. Leaving Gene in the car, he headed in to prepay for the gas while Leslie went to the ladies' room. He saw Mel drive by seconds before he opened the door for Leslie and glanced at his watch. After reminding her that they only had a few minutes, he returned to fill the car with gas.

When Gene asked if he could go to the restrooms when Leslie returned, Kevin told him they didn't have enough time, and unless he could wait, then he'd have to use one of the Styrofoam cups that littered the floor. Kevin said he wasn't about to take a chance on being late and kept watch while Gene unzipped and filled almost half of the cup.

"Now," Kevin directed as he replaced the nozzle and closed the gas cap, "just open the door slightly and pour it out on the ground."

Leslie was leaving the store as Kevin headed back in to get his change from prepaying for the gas. "Toss Gene's cup in the trash before you get in, please," he asked her as they passed.

Kevin quickly took his money and hurried back to the car as he noticed that they had already used 13 minutes. That gave him just two minutes to get back on the road and catch Mel. Here they were, slightly less than an hour from when Sancudo had made the rules, and Kevin was rapidly getting tired of jumping through the hoops.

He just hoped he could find Mel before they came to where highways 377, 67, 84, and 183 mixed and separated in the downtown area of Brownwood. Once they got south of there, the towns got smaller and further apart. Then, it wouldn't be so hard to keep track of the Bronco. Wishing he had grabbed a Texas road map while in the store, Kevin checked the traffic and sped back onto the road.

He had gone less than a mile when he noticed Mel's car parked about half a block past a traffic light. Just as the light was turning yellow, Sancudo pulled back onto the road, and Kevin accelerated to make it through the intersection before the light changed to red. Once safely through, Kevin let Mel get further ahead but still kept closer than the mile Sancudo had directed.

With Brownwood being the last fairly large town until they reached Junction, Kevin hoped he wouldn't have to press the limits of Mel's tolerance for violating his rules again. Now that they were just a little over two hours from reaching Rocksprings, he didn't want to give Sancudo any reason to abandon him before he learned where they were headed from there.

Kevin still thought they were going to Mexico but knew they wouldn't be taking the normal route across the Rio Grande between Del Rio and Ciudad Acuna. Just where and how they were to cross the river without being stopped by either the US Border Patrol or their Mexican counterparts, he wasn't sure. But he hoped they would get somewhere safe before dark.

Once clear of the town, Kevin slowed slightly and let Mel get a little more distance before resuming the speed limit. Leslie was busy changing the diaper while Gene leaned back across the seat and talked to her. Knowing that they trusted him to keep them safe while he had no control was infuriating him.

Worse yet, the further they went, the less he knew about the area. At least he knew people and places back around Bowie and thought he'd have a better chance at hiding than down here in this unknown country. Kevin decided that if anything happened before they reached Rocksprings, he'd turn around and head back north. He still had about $16,000, and they could hide somewhere in one of the many small towns along the Red River. Or, he thought, they could try to make it to Missouri, where he had some distant relatives.

Right now, anything that gave him a little control over their destinies seemed better than heading into the desolate country with a man he didn't really trust.

CHAPTER 23

Major Fleenor heard Colonel Moore calling in, telling them that she was inbound with the material found at the clinic and advising Karyn that a team of ground personnel would be required later that day. When Colonel Lynch asked what the ground team needed to do, Amy just said she would provide the information when she finished her preliminary examination of the confiscated material.

Karyn told Jerry to notify General Nelson that Amy was returning and requesting the ground team. She then picked up one of the microphones and called the team that had headed toward Ringgold. Once she made contact, she told them to proceed to the clinic and standby for further instructions. Colonel Erickson had just reported that he would be landing in about five minutes, so she switched frequencies and called the Suburban that had been sent to Butch's house.

Mike walked into the room just as the team was acknowledging Karyn's call. "Colonel Erickson back?" he asked looking at the map where the location of each vehicle was supposed to be.

"In less than five minutes," Karyn answered. "And Colonel Lynch should be back in 15 to 20 minutes."

"Did she get everything?" Mike asked.

"I'm not sure," Karyn replied. "She requested a ground team at the clinic when she called in, and I've notified the one up there to wait for further instructions."

"What about Mr. North?" Mike asked. "Have we picked him up?"

"Not that I know of, sir," Karyn told him. "I've just made contact with the team we sent for him."

Karyn turned and keyed the microphone again, asking, "What is your exact location?"

Hearing that they were at Butch's house, she asked, "Is he there?"

The speakers carried their negative reply and the team informed her that the Corvette was in the garage, but the truck was gone.

"All right," she said. "Head over to the stables and see if he's there. Call back when you arrive."

As she was replacing the microphone on the desk, Colonel Erickson came into the room looking both disappointed and very angry. He went directly to the map, pointed to the location of Kevin's ranch, and began his report.

"That damn truck has been right there all the time," he informed them. "Have you run the photos I sent?"

Jerry removed a folder from his desk and answered, "Yes, sir. I've just gotten the results of the computer matching of the previous truck and the one at the Knox ranch. They are practically identical, almost a 100% match."

"Why not a 100% match?' Mike asked.

"Not sure, sir," Jerry answered. "It could be because of a scratch we didn't previously see or something that happened to the truck after our last surveillance photo. I think it would be impossible to ever get 100%, but the computer geeks say it's as close as anything they've ever seen."

"Okay," Mike said. "Now we're sure that he was involved with the lady that delivered the baby. When will we know if that was Leslie and if the child is Gene's?"

"Colonel Moore should be here within 10 minutes," Karyn answered. "It shouldn't take her more than half an hour to get preliminary DNA results. That will tell us the answer to both questions."

"What about Mr. North?" Rick asked. "I want his ass in here yesterday."

"I've just heard from the team," Karyn told him. "He's not at his house and his truck is missing. The team is headed to the stables right now."

"General Nelson," Rick said turning to face Mike. "I think we need to get a team to pick up Ms. Tammy Terbush. If Butch isn't at home or the stables, he may have gone to see her."

"You're right," Mike agreed. Turning to Karyn, he said, "Get another car to find Ms. Terbush. And if Butch is there, bring them both in."

"Yes, sir," Karyn answered. "I just got word from the base that they could let us use a couple of their staff cars until we can get some of our own."

"What about using their security people also?" Jerry asked. "If all they're going to do is locate Ms. Terbush, then we can hold our people until we get the Suburbans and their communication gear ready."

"No," Mike said. "I don't want to take a chance on having them find Butch with her and possibly screw it up. I want our teams. And, I would prefer that we send at least two cars and separate those two as soon as possible."

"I agree," Rick responded. "I want to avoid any collusion between them and I'd just as soon they not know where the other one is after we separate them."

"What justification are you going to use to pick up Ms. Terbush?" Jerry asked.

Both Mike and Rick turned to stare at him. "She's a material witness to an ongoing investigation," Rick said. "And I'm beginning to wonder if you're still able to perform your duties with the dedication we need."

"Let's settle down a bit," Mike directed. "Jerry, do you feel you are going to have a problem with the way we're running this operation?"

"No, sir," Jerry explained. "I just want to make sure we've covered our asses if Ms. Terbush wants to make a stink. I believe we need to pursue getting a warrant if we're involving citizens with no apparent connection to Gene."

Quickly continuing he said, "Butch has some direct contact and involvement, so does Kevin Knox. But we have no evidence that Ms. Terbush even knows of Gene's existence. I just don't want this to be the thing that blows up in our faces."

Mike stood quietly for a moment and then said, "You're probably right, Jerry. See if you can get a quick warrant from the local FBI folks. Just tell them that it's as we discussed, a material witness or whatever they think would be best."

"But, regardless of how we proceed," Mike finished, "we will have her in here for an intimate little conversation. Either willingly or not, I want her to tell us what she knows about Mr. North's and Mr. Knox's activities."

Jerry slowly released the breath he had been holding and said, "Yes, sir. I'll have the warrant issued immediately. Will there be anything else?"

General Nelson was telling him to proceed when Colonel Moore walked in. "General, I'll have you some results in just a few minutes," she said. "The material is on its way to the lab and I can determine if Gene is involved or not pretty quickly since his DNA is so unique. Leslie may take slightly longer."

"I'm not really interested in Leslie's if Gene isn't the father," Mike said. "Just rush that to me if you determine that he is."

"Yes, sir," Amy said as she turned to leave.

"What about that ground team you wanted?" Karyn asked.

Amy turned back and said, "I need them to enter the clinic as clandestinely as possible and get me every record of the lady, presumably Leslie, and anything that would show she was pregnant."

Amy thought for a second and then confessed, "I also need them to confiscate the scrubs both the doctor and the nurse were wearing."

"What?" Rick asked astonished. "How did you miss getting those?"

"I screwed up, sir," Amy admitted. "They were wearing them and I just forgot to get them when we were cleaning the clinic. I actually didn't notice them since it's such a normal thing for them to be wearing. It was after we were headed back that I remembered seeing some stains on them, probably from the delivery."

"Damn it," Rick shouted. "We can't be having these mistakes. It only takes one sample of that DNA to jeopardize this operation. What do you plan to do about this little situation, Colonel Moore?"

Amy accepted the chastisement and said, "I plan on having the team stop by Dr. Adams' house and just tell him that we neglected to get it earlier. And, do the same with the nurse. If we make it seem routine, and tell him that I forgot to get them, it shouldn't arouse any suspicions."

"I hope you're right, Amy," Mike said. "If anyone, anywhere, gets hold of that DNA, we've got a major security leak and the potential for public disclosure would condemn us."

"I'm sorry, sir," Amy said. "With your permission, I'll run those samples and find out if Gene's DNA is present. If it's not, we don't really have a problem."

"No, Amy, go ahead," Mike said. "I guess now it would be better if that lady had someone else's child instead of Gene's. I'm almost positive it's his, but it would be better for us at this point if it wasn't."

Karyn picked up the microphone as the team looking for Butch called in saying they had found Butch's truck at the stables, but he wasn't there. "Is anyone there that can tell you where he is?" she asked.

Hearing that the stable hand, Steve, was the only person around, she asked, "Does he know anything about where he went or who he went with?"

A couple of minutes later, the team told her that Steve didn't know anything except Butch had asked him to take the truck to Boyd for an oil change and that Butch was still at the stables when he left an hour or so ago. Then they told her that Butch had asked Steve to wear his hat when he left the stables, but Steve didn't know why.

"All right," Karyn told them. "I want you to search every inch of the stables and Butch's house. See if you can find anything that might suggest where he may have gone. Specifically look for any clue that would lead you to believe that he's planning an extended absence."

She replaced the microphone and looked at Mike and Rick. "Looks like everybody decided to make a run for it. Having Steve wear his hat must mean Butch was trying to sneak away unnoticed and wanted anyone seeing the truck to think he was in it."

Mike slowly shook his head and agreed, "Looks like it, now where do we start trying to find them?"

"The only one we think we can lay our hands on right now is the Terbush woman," Rick said. "Now, it's even more important to get her in here. Jerry, where's that warrant?"

Major Fleenor hung up the phone and told him, "It's on the computer now. I'll print a couple of copies and they'll be ready when the team gets here."

CHAPTER 24

Butch and Ted continued north on 287 toward Decatur. Butch sat watching the road slide past as he thought about what he was going to do when he did make contact with the people at the NAS/JRB. He remembered the General and the Colonel but didn't know their names. Then there was the officer that had provided him with the phone and warned him about their discovery of Leslie.

"What's your wife going to say about me hanging out for a few days?" Butch asked as he put the empty beer bottle into the container and pulled out another one.

"Oh," Ted answered as he pulled into the left lane avoiding the debris falling from the rock truck several yards ahead of them, "Mildred's excited to have you over. For some strange reason, she thinks you're a pretty nice guy."

"She's certainly disillusioned," Butch said. "I just hope I don't shatter her idea of me being the perfect gentleman she got when I met her with you down in Ft Worth. By the way, you guys still going to the Stagecoach?"

"Not as much as she'd like," Ted admitted. "We sort of started seeing each other because we both enjoyed dancing, but I just don't seem to have the time anymore."

"Don't have the time or don't make the time?" Butch asked taking a sip of beer after checking to make sure there weren't any cops that could see it.

"Probably the latter," Ted admitted as he finished his beer. "Yeah, I reckon I still have the time to take her out a little more often. I just don't enjoy going down there as much as I used to."

"Not getting old, are we?" Butch chided.

"Of course not," Ted said. "It's just that the crowd down there is getting younger. And I dread the drive back home after a couple of drinks."

"I understand that," Butch agreed. "I pretty much stick close to home. There're more Highway Patrol cars on that little stretch of 114 between Rhome and Bridgeport than anywhere else in the entire state of Texas."

"Same with 287 from Ft Worth to Decatur," Ted agreed. "And they'll pull you over if you have as little as a burnt-out bulb in one of your license plate lights."

"I know," Butch agreed. "And they're just looking for an excuse to have you blow in their little machine. I certainly don't need one of those expensive tickets, just think of how many beers that would buy."

"Well, Mildred would be pretty mad if I spent that much because of a couple of drinks," Ted told him. "She's been after me to trade in this truck and get something a little nicer, and that money would go a long way toward buying it."

"I never meant to ask," Butch said as they saw another of the helicopters flying south just a little way from the road. "Why do you keep driving this old thing?"

"It was the truck my dad gave me when he bought his last new one," Ted answered as he watched the chopper pass from view. "I just hate to give it up, but it's just about as worn out as you are."

"Wasn't that the same chopper I saw when we left Rhome?" he continued.

"Probably not," Butch replied. "Most of them look a lot alike unless you really know the differences. And if it belongs to the same company or organization, it's most likely the same model."

"I don't think I've ever seen more than one every few days," Ted said. "It's just sort of strange to see so many of them in this area at one time."

"Like I said," Butch said as they approached the exit for FM 51 South, "I'd guess it's some coordinated drug operation down in Aurora Vista. I'm pretty sure it's those damn Yankees that have moved down here. Or maybe it's the Okies!"

Ted laughed and made a left turn off the access road and headed toward the neighborhood where he lived. "You like to blame everything on either the Yankees or the Okies, don't you?"

"Hey, don't forget the Democrats," Butch said smiling. "They're responsible for most of the mess we're in right now. And the worst thing is that most of the Yankees are also Democrats. Not to mention those that have relatives in Oklahoma. Sort of a triad of evil."

They had just passed the rodeo arena when Ted made a right turn and headed for the house. "Don't be telling Mildred how you feel about Okies," he said. "She really likes going up across the river to do a little gambling. When she's winning, she's pretty happy having a casino close by."

"What about when she loses?" Butch asked as they pulled into the driveway and parked.

"Then she blames it on the Indians," Ted said smiling. "And trust me; she loses more than she wins."

Butch grabbed the remaining beer and followed Ted to the front door. Looking back toward where they had seen the helicopter, he didn't see anything unusual and felt relatively safe that he had arrived unnoticed.

"Honey, I'm home," Ted shouted as he closed the door behind Butch. "Come look what followed me into the house."

Mildred came in from the kitchen and said, "Butch, so nice to see you again. Ted tells me you're going to be staying with us for a couple of days. What's happening, do you have to fumigate your house after one of your dates?"

"That's so wrong," Butch said as he gave her a quick hug. "That's about as wrong as two men sleeping together. So very, very wrong."

"Oh, you know I'm just teasing," Mildred said smiling. "You're welcome anytime. Now, you two better take a seat and enjoy your Jack while I finish dinner."

"There's a new bottle on the table by Ted's chair and a couple of glasses just anxious to be filled," she said returning to the kitchen. "Dinner will be ready in about 20 minutes."

"Thanks honey," Ted replied as he led Butch into the living room. "Anything we can do to help?"

"No," Mildred answered. "I'll call you when it's ready."

Ted pointed to a chair for Butch as he poured a couple inches of Jack Daniel's into both glasses. "Take a seat, Butch."

He handed Butch a glass and they raised them in a toast saying, "To long life and pretty women."

"Don't forget fast horses and more money," Butch replied as he lowered his glass. "And to our boys and girls overseas that make it possible for us to enjoy all of the above."

They sat down and set their glasses on the table between them. "So," Ted began, "when do you plan on telling me the real reason you can't go home."

Butch had known he hadn't fooled Ted but also knew he couldn't tell him the truth. "Let's just pretend it's like I told you, Teddie. That's the best story you can tell anyone if ever asked."

Ted watched Butch's eyes as he listened to what he had said. Finally nodding he replied, "Okay, have it your way. You know neither me nor Mildred really believe you. But, we'll play along until you decide to tell us, if you ever do."

"I appreciate that Teddie," Butch said thanking him. "I promise I'll be gone in a couple of days, maybe sooner. It's just that I don't want anyone involved in something I've gotten into."

"Well, knowing you," Ted said as he took another sip of his drink, "it certainly isn't illegal. Immoral maybe, that I'd believe."

Butch laughed and told him, "Just don't be thinking I'm running from the father of some cute little jail bait. I do have limits as to how depraved I can be."

"I'm sure," Ted said as Mildred called them to dinner. "What about that young thing you bought that black felt hat for? Sort of young, wasn't she?"

Butch got up and followed Ted into the dining room saying, "Yeah, but definitely over 21. Hell, she was almost 30 and you know I can't keep running around with a woman that old!"

"I heard that," Mildred said as she placed a plate of corn on the cob on the table. "You men and your obsession for younger women! When will you learn that real beauty takes time to blossom? Now, have a seat and see what a real beauty can do."

Everyone sat down and Butch told her, "Mildred, if every woman over 30 looked as good as you do, I'd have a hard time picking the prettiest one. And if she could cook like this, I'd marry her tomorrow!"

"Like hell," she answered. "You'll never settle down, you've lived alone so long you can't take having anyone around for more than a couple of days. Now, let's eat."

They began filling their plates with the pot roast, potatoes, and corn while commenting on the events of the day. Butch admired the easy relationship between Ted and Mildred wondering if he and Tammy would ever be able to try to match it. First, he knew he had to resolve the problem that had caused such a disruption in his life for the last nine months.

"Hey, Teddie," Butch said as he finished chewing a bite of roast, "do you think you could do me another favor? And this one wouldn't be much of an imposition."

"Probably," Ted answered as he placed the remnants of the corn cob on his plate. "What do you have in mind?"

"Well," Butch explained. "I need to rent a car, but I can't have my name on the rental agreement. I'll give you the cash to cover it for a week or so, but you'll probably need to give them a credit card or something. We can settle it when I'm ready to return it."

"I guess I can do that," Ted said. "I've rented cars from James Wood's before when they were working on my truck. I'll just get one from them tomorrow and you can use it as long as you need."

"Great," Butch said. "I'd prefer some little white car that isn't too noticeable."

"Don't you always drive maroon cars?" Mildred asked raising her eyebrows. "Is this part of your disguise? Don't think I didn't notice the baseball cap instead of the usual black hat. And those sunglasses you were wearing when you came in, I've never seen you use shades."

Ted sternly looked at her and said, "Honey, let's just let that dog lay. Butch has his reasons for this and I'm sure he'll tell us when he can. For now, we'll help as much as we can and pretend he's running from some crazed rock truck driver. Okay?"

Mildred frowned for a second and then said, "Fine, I just want you to know that I'm not convinced about that first story. But, if it'll make it easier, I'll go along with it for now."

"Thanks, Mildred," Butch said solemnly. "I promise to square things when I can."

After they finished dinner, they sat in the living room and chatted about everything from the cost of hay to how fast the country was filling with new housing developments. Finally, Ted showed Butch to his room and they closed their doors for the night.

Butch lay awake a long time wondering about Kevin, Gene, and Tammy, and how tired he was of this game. Finding no real answers, he finally fell into a fitful sleep and hoped for a better day tomorrow.

CHAPTER 25

Kevin followed Sancudo south on 377 down through Winchell while Leslie slept in the back seat with BK and Gene sitting up front watching the scenery. After they passed the small town, Gene noticed a sign advising them that they were approaching the Colorado River.

"I thought the Colorado River ran through Arizona," Gene remarked. "How does it end up passing back through Texas?"

"Different river," Kevin told him. "The one everybody knows about does run through Arizona and by California. It's at the bottom of the Grand Canyon and empties into the Gulf of California."

"This one starts up just south of Lubbock and passes through Austin," he continued. "Then it winds its way down to the Gulf of Mexico west of Houston."

"I've noticed a lot of places in Texas that have the same names as other places," Gene said, "like Rhome, Paris, and this river."

"Maybe the people that founded the towns or discovered the rivers named them after something they left behind when they came to Texas," Kevin ventured. "Of maybe they just made up the names. Who knows how things get their names?"

Kevin was growing more concerned with where they were going than explaining the odd names of every place they were passing. He could tell that they only had a couple of hours of sunlight and he didn't relish the thought of following Mel through back roads in the dark.

The best he could figure, they would hit Del Rio about sunset and if they were going across the border, it would definitely be dark. Crossing the bridge into Ciudad Acuna would be the easiest way, but also the riskiest. If Sancudo was planning on some other place, doing it at night meant he had even less ability to see where they were going and have a chance to go back safely.

It was about an hour drive to Junction, where Interstate 10 crossed and could take him either to San Antonio or El Paso depending on which way he wanted to go. After that, there were nothing but small towns spread further and further from each other. After Rocksprings, there was little chance of going anywhere except on across the almost barren country into Del Rio.

True to his statement, Mel was keeping his speed just below the posted limit and as fewer and fewer cars or trucks were on the road, it was easy to maintain visual contact. The land sped past as they wound their way past Brady and Mason on into Junction. Gene had finally tired of asking questions and was dozing with his head resting on the window.

"Where are we now?" Leslie asked waking and stretching her arms over her head.

"Just about to pass through London," Kevin told her. "And not London, England either."

"I know that," Leslie said. "What would make you think I thought we were in England?"

"Sorry about that," Kevin explained. "It's just that Gene didn't know how many Texas towns had the same names as European towns."

"He's got a lot to learn about Texas," Leslie replied as she picked BK up and checked his diaper.

"Looks like little BK's system is working just fine," she said as she wrinkled her nose. "I just hope we have enough diapers to get through this little trip."

She started changing BK and asked, "Do you know where we're going or how long we have to be gone?"

"I'm not sure," Kevin admitted. "I still think we're headed into Mexico, but Mel won't tell me where."

"As to how long," he continued, "I'm not sure about that either. Butch seems to believe he can work out some compromise within a week or so. But I wouldn't bet on it."

"You don't think he's going to get caught or something, do you?" Leslie asked.

"Caught? No, he's going to turn himself in," Kevin explained.

Gene had woken up as Kevin was talking and exclaimed, "He doesn't know those people! They'll make sure he disappears and is never heard from again! You've got to stop him, please."

"There's nothing I can do," Kevin said. "We discussed everything back in Stephenville and if there's any chance for all of us, it's what Butch is planning."

"Remember all those pictures and the other things he put into those baggies?"

Kevin asked. "Well, he thinks that if he can show it would be impossible for them to keep you and BK a secret any longer, then he may be able to find a way to protect their secret and let you guys stay free. And Butch and I also, of course."

"Isn't there some other way?" Gene asked.

"No, I don't think so," Kevin answered. "If we're to be left alone, then Butch has to convince them that there's another solution that benefits all of us. Otherwise, we'll all be running and hiding for the rest of our lives. Or, we'll be caught and we certainly don't want that."

"I hope he's right," Leslie said. "I'd love to be back home where my mother can see her grandson and we could have a true family without worrying every time some strange car comes up the road."

"I know," Kevin told her. "I want to be able to go as I please and I know Butch is tired of having to watch his every move. I even think he may want to settle down with Tammy one of these days."

"Butch settle down?" Leslie said. "From what you've told me about him, he's about as likely to settle down as an old coyote on the prairie."

"I think this time he's about ready," Kevin told them. "These last few months have shown him that he needs somebody around to confide in, sort of share his problems. I know he's getting tired and worries about all of us. He needs someone close to him, whether or not he knows it."

They were just coming upon Junction and Kevin had to make a quick decision. If he kept the mile space he had been staying behind Sancudo, he could turn either way on I-10 and be gone before Mel knew it. Even if he knew it, he might not care. After all, Sancudo had his money and may be planning on ditching them later anyway.

But he still had to trust Butch's instincts and continue. Not only that, if he disappeared and Butch made some arrangement with the government, Butch would be left hung out to dry. No, abandoning the plan right now would place Butch in jeopardy and he couldn't do that. Besides, he had no better plan.

Kevin sped up slightly, and as they passed I-10, he resolved to let Sancudo lead them to wherever he had in mind. If he didn't think it would work after they got to their destination, then he'd do something and try to get word to Butch. For now, just try to quit worrying and do as he was told.

Once out of town, Leslie sat back and began nursing BK again. Gene watched as the baby boy attached himself to her breast and closed his eyes in contentment. Just watching Leslie and the baby made him so proud and strengthened his resolve to be the best father and husband possible. As much as he hated to think it, Gene decided that regardless of what happened to any of them, he'd protect Leslie and BK, even if it meant that he had to turn himself in and go back to the facility.

As they crossed the South Llano River just past Telegraph, Kevin noticed how low the sun was on the horizon. He knew that Rocksprings was only about 30 miles further, and it would be getting pretty dark by then. He was still concerned about crossing the border after sunset, but that may have been Sancudo's plan. He also realized that once south of the Rio Grande, he'd have no idea about where they were anyway.

About 30 minutes later, Kevin watched Mel pull off the road and stop. As he neared the Bronco, he saw Mel waving his arm out of the window, signaling him to pull over. Parking behind Mel, Kevin told Gene and Leslie to wait while he went to talk to Sancudo. There were no cars in sight as Kevin approached the Bronco, and Mel was talking in Spanish on his phone.

Mel hung up and looked at Kevin standing beside the door. "We need to fill our cars in Rocksprings," Sancudo told him. "There may not be any gas stations open for several miles now."

"You will also need to get something to eat for this evening and tomorrow morning," he continued. "You will be spending the night at the place where I told you we would meet if we got separated."

"Will you be with us?" Kevin asked.

"No, you will be alone," Sancudo tersely replied.

"Are you telling me that we will spend the night in the car in the middle of nowhere?" Kevin asked.

"It could be worse," Sancudo told him. "You could be spending more than one night behind bars. I have already told you that I'm making the plans, and you are to simply follow them. Do you think you know what is best? Do you have contacts on both sides of the border telling you when things are safe?"

Mel paused for a second and continued, "I didn't think so. Now, you will be spending the night in a small cabin a few miles from the corrals I told you about. There's no electricity or water, but there is an outhouse. I suggest you make sure you have toilet paper also because there may be none there."

"How long will we be there?" Kevin asked, still worried about being dumped with no means of contact.

"You will be there until I come to get you or send someone else to do it," Sancudo answered. "It could be only for the night, but it could also be a couple of days. If it is longer than noon tomorrow, someone will bring food and water. If at any time you decide you no longer wish to wait, the road out is the same one you took in. I strongly suggest you wait."

Kevin stood quietly, listening to Mel tell them that they were going to be spending an indeterminate amount of time in the middle of some ranch with no facilities. He already knew that his cell phone would be useless in this remote area since he hadn't had a signal for the last 50 miles. This was quickly becoming a nightmare for him. But he had no choice right now other than running, and that was no real option.

If Sancudo knew something that was making it necessary to stop for the night, anything he did contrary to his plans could be running them into more danger. Finally nodding, Kevin said, "Fine, we'll get what we need and do as you ask. Will you at least take us to the cabin?"

"Of course, my friend," Mel replied, smiling. "You don't think I would turn you loose to wander about the countryside, do you? Now, get what you need and meet me where I told you to."

Mel started his Bronco and headed on toward Rocksprings. Kevin returned to his car, telling Gene and Leslie to figure out what they would need for a couple of days as he started the car. Fuming at the way things were happening, he took off, slinging gravel behind him as he hit the road.

CHAPTER 26

Major Fleenor hung up his phone and told General Nelson and Colonel Erickson, "You wanted proof that Butch North was planning an extended absence? Well, I think I have it."

"What have you got?" Rick asked still somewhat suspicious that Jerry wasn't as deeply involved as he would like.

"I just heard from our contacts within the banking industry," Jerry said. "It seems that Mr. North has withdrawn about $25,000 from his accounts at the Woodhaven National Bank in Rhome."

"When did he do that?" Mike asked.

"Today," Jerry answered. "It had to have been while his truck was being taken in for the oil change. He must have borrowed someone else's car, and that's what he's driving now."

As they were discussing whose car he may have taken, Amy came in with a stack of papers and announced, "The baby is definitely Gene's. I've run comparisons of several samples, and they match his DNA in every case."

"All right, that settles it," Mike said. "I'm going to inform General Modelle and get him down here. We're going to need his influence in Washington to speed up getting the equipment we'll require. Rick, get Ms. Terbush in here immediately. I want to know if she's involved in Butch's disappearance."

"Yes, sir," Rick answered as Mike left the room.

Turning to Karyn, he asked. "What's the status of a team to arrest Ms. Terbush?"

"I just got off the phone with the Ft Worth office of the FBI, and they're on their way," she answered.

"I thought we decided to use our own assets," Rick told her. "Why are we going outside our own resources?"

"I can't get another team here for at least another day," Karyn answered. "I didn't think we should wait that long. If you'd like to cancel the request, I'll be glad to do it."

"No," Rick acknowledged, "we can't wait. Each day Butch and the rest of them are gone means a wider search area. Just make sure the agents understand that they are operating under Department of Defense authority and Tammy is not to be questioned before being brought to the base for incarceration."

"Not a problem," she said. "The warrants specify that she is to be held on the base for disposition. We just need Jerry to take the warrants over to the Base Commander's office and ensure they know to hold her in isolation until we can question her."

"Go ahead and have the stables and Butch's house checked for anything that might give us a clue where he may have gone," Rick directed. "And let's get a run of every number he has called in the last few days from either his home phone or his cell."

"I'll get that right now," Jerry told him as he picked up his phone. "I'd bet that he's still using those throwaway phones for anything other than routine calls. I just wish we had some way of voice-matching in every conversation across the United States. Then we'd be able to monitor him regardless of what phone he was using."

"What about your concern over personal rights?" Rick asked sarcastically. "Wouldn't that cause you a problem?"

"No, sir," Jerry said. "As long as we have proof that an individual is involved with any actions that are illegal or concerning national security, I think we have the right to monitor their activity."

"I'm just surprised to hear you say that," Rick countered.

Jerry held the phone in his hand, looked Colonel Erickson directly in the eyes, and said, "Colonel Erickson, you may have some doubts about my abilities to do my duty. But, I assure you, I'm as interested in solving this problem as anyone."

"But," he continued, "I don't want to jeopardize any part of it because we crossed a line needlessly. With the baby out there, some unrecovered tissue samples, Gene still missing, and all of the other things that could become disclosed, I think we need to avoid any potential civil issue when we can easily avoid it."

"And, speaking of that," Jerry said as he looked away and started dialing, "I think we need to get authorization from the Base Hospital to force Doctor Adams to turn over the medical records. If we just break in and take them, he'll know who did it and become suspicious, potentially making him an adversary."

Rick stood watching Jerry dial as he tried to decide if Jerry was right in his concerns or if he was just reluctant to follow the orders that both General Nelson and he were giving. He listened while Jerry informed the people on the other end of the phone call what he wanted and told them to expedite the results.

"The information on the phone calls should be sent in the next few minutes," Jerry said as he hung up the phone. "I'll take the warrants for Terbush's arrest over to Colonel Brown, and he can give them to the FBI agents."

"And don't forget to make sure the Colonel knows to put her in solitary confinement when she gets here, and no one is to question her or talk to her," Rick directed as he decided to forget the previous differences of opinion.

"I understand, sir," Jerry said as he placed the warrants in a briefcase and left.

Rick watched him go and turned to where Amy was standing with the DNA test results still in her hands. "Do we have anything to prove that the lady in question is definitely our Leslie?"

"No, sir," Amy replied. "I have no samples of her DNA to compare with what I took from the clinic. However, I can use what I found to verify the mother, and I believe that the testimony of the Trooper is good enough to confirm her identity."

"When we do get her," Amy continued, "we will have proof of her involvement with Gene and hold her the same as we can Mr. Knox and Mr. North."

"Proving their involvement is the least of our worries," Rick said, watching Karyn monitor the various communications of the teams. "Unless we find them, having all the proof in the world isn't doing us any good."

Back in his office, Mike was on the phone with General Modelle, telling him, "We can confirm the relationship between the child and our product. I think you need to be here to make sure we get all the support from the state and all national agencies."

"We can't afford the time it takes to make calls back and forth when we finally get a location of the fugitives," he concluded.

Hearing that Paul would arrange to fly into the NAS/JRB as soon as he could schedule a plane, Mike told him that a room would be prepared for him. Once the call was concluded, Mike told his secretary to get the General's room ready and to notify the Base Commander of the estimated time of arrival. "Also," he directed her, "make sure his aircraft is brought immediately to our hanger and not to publicize the arrival as having a General on board."

Kathy told him she would take care of it and began dialing. Mike sat back in his chair and thought of all the things that could now go wrong with the program. It would only take one credible person finding out what they had been doing to spell disaster for the entire operation and possibly force the release of information that had been guarded closer and for longer than anything else the government had ever kept secret.

He wished he could present an alternative to finding Gene and his son, but at this point there was nothing that seemed feasible. Absolute containment appeared to be the only solution. And to do that, they had to gather every person that had made contact with Gene or the baby. At least those who potentially knew the origins of both.

Mike rose from his desk and made his way to the operations center, hoping there would be some shred of good news. Right now, anything that pointed to discovering any of the major players would be welcome.

As he entered the room, Karyn was talking to the team that had been sent to Butch's house, and he listened to them telling her that there was absolutely nothing in the house that even hinted at him being gone. It was impossible for them to know if any clothes were missing since the closets still had several shirts and jeans hanging inside.

Everything appeared to be as if he was coming back at any time. Food was still on the shelves of the refrigerator, and the thermostat was still set to 70 degrees. The only odd thing they reported was that there were two bags of bite-sized Butterfinger candy bars in the freezer. But nothing pointed to either a rapid departure or prolonged absence.

Karyn told them to come back to the facility and be ready to get their next orders. "Well," she said as she set the microphone down, "they've found nothing that helps us. It's as if Butch just went out for the day as usual and planned on coming back this evening."

"Well," Mike said, "I think his withdrawing all of that money is proof enough of his intentions. He's running, and so is Kevin. I'd bet that they are all heading somewhere together. I'm not sure how they knew that we were closing in, but they definitely coordinated their actions."

"I don't know how they could have found out so quickly," Rick told him. "We had a helicopter headed to the clinic minutes after the Trooper reported in. And the Trooper was only gone from the clinic for less than an hour."

"During that short period, Leslie had the baby, and Knox showed up immediately to take them away," he concluded. "There just doesn't seem to be enough time for that to happen and for North to find out, gather all the cash, and everyone completely disappear."

"Mr. North must have made some sort of arrangements ahead of time," Mike said. "And when Knox called about the baby, he implemented his plan. Now, if we can reconstruct any calls he made between when Gene disappeared and the birth, maybe we'll have a clue as to where they went."

"I've got a list of every number he called from any known phone for the entire time," Rick said as he grabbed the printout Jerry had requested. "It'll take days to analyze every call. And, as we already know, he's had some alternative method of maintaining contact with Kevin all of this time."

"Well, if all we have are the phone calls on that list, let's get busy eliminating those that are to local businesses, friends other than Kevin or Tammy, or what appear to be routine calls," Mike said. "When Jerry gets back, have him pass it to the computer folks and break it down into blocks of matching numbers. Anything that appears only randomly needs to be scrutinized."

When Major Fleenor came back in telling them that the FBI had met him at General Brown's office, he said, "I personally instructed them to deliver Tammy to General Brown, and he will have her taken to the conference room to wait for us to talk to her."

"I also told them not to question her or discuss anything about where they were going," he continued. "The only information they were to provide was exactly what was within the warrant. And General Brown knows to keep her isolated until we get there."

"Good," Mike told him. "Now, I need for you to get all those phone numbers organized. Rick will tell you what I want, and you three will analyze the results to see if there are any numbers that might provide a clue as to where Butch went, or Kevin Knox may have gone."

"I can have that in a couple of minutes," Jerry said as he picked up his phone. "I'll have them organized and provide the registered owners; also, I'll have them search for any calls made to Butch in the same format. We can then tell if a specific number was returning any calls that we think may be suspicious."

"Good idea," Mike said as he prepared to leave. "Let me know when Tammy's picked up. Rick, you and I will do the interrogation ourselves. Make sure you have your dress blues on, and I'll be ready when you come for me."

"Yes, sir," Rick said as Mike left. Turning to Jerry, he said, "I'm going to change uniforms. Call me when you get those lists."

"Karyn," he asked as he started for his office, "can you contact those FBI agents and have them call you the minute they find Ms. Terbush?"

"Yes, sir," she answered. "I have their discreet frequency, and we've already established contact. They'll advise me the minute they head back here." "If that list of numbers comes in before I get back," Rick told them, "get busy eliminating everything you think doesn't pertain to the situation."

"Yes, sir," both Jerry and Karyn responded as Rick left.

When Mike entered his secretary's office, he asked, "Is General Modelle's room ready?"

"Yes, sir," Kathy told him. "And the base just called to say he's already in the air headed here. They estimate that he'll be here just after dark."

"Yeah," Mike said as he entered his office. "It looks like we're running out of time in more ways than one. Now, I need you to prepare a room for Ms. Terbush, and it needs to be coordinated with Lieutenant Colonel Mallory for absolute privacy and security. I'm afraid she'll be our guest for a couple of days."

Mike grabbed a bottle of Gentleman Jack and a glass from the table inside his office and sat behind his desk. After pouring an inch of it into the glass, he sipped it and picked up the phone.

Dialing the number he had stored in the directory of the phone, he waited for it to be answered. On the second ring, he heard General Brown's voice, and Mike said, "Gary, I need you to do me a favor."

Hearing that it would be granted, he continued, "Colonel Erickson and I will be over there to greet the lady the FBI is bringing in. Since you've already agreed to us using your conference room, we'll meet her there, and we'll do our initial questioning. However, since it's getting late, we'll transfer her to our facility for the night and plan on resuming the interrogation tomorrow morning at your place."

"Maybe a little time under uncomfortable circumstances will help her decide to cooperate with us," Mike concluded.

Mike thanked General Brown for his cooperation and hung up the phone. Just as he was finishing the drink, his phone rang, and Colonel Lynch informed him that Tammy was in custody and on her way. The agents had estimated it would take about 30 minutes to get back to the base. Mike thanked her and told her to send Colonel Erickson to his office.

Mike really didn't think Butch would have told Tammy anything about Gene, but he needed to know if she had knowledge of Kevin or of where Butch had gone. Not expecting much, he began to understand Jerry's hesitation in arresting civilians with no direct ties to their project.

A few minutes later, Rick arrived, and they left for the Base Commander's headquarters. Once there, they waited in

General Brown's office until they were notified that Tammy was being brought to the conference room. Thanking Gary for his hospitality, they headed for their first personal contact with Ms. Terbush.

After initial introductions, Mike told her why they were searching for Butch and why she had been brought in. Tammy was surprised that Butch would have done anything that was contrary to government security and proclaimed no knowledge of his disappearance.

Not surprised, Mike told her that she would be remaining overnight with them at a secure facility. And that she should use the time to search her memory for anything Butch had said about either Kevin or Leslie. And especially of the fugitive from the World Trade Center attacks that had been made public during their initial search.

After almost an hour of getting no further useful information, Mike and Rick took Tammy back across the base to their facility. Once there, Tammy was escorted to a room just inside the guarded entrance on the top floor. She was told she would have food and water delivered and that they would resume their discussion in the morning; Rick and Mike watched as the room was locked.

They took the elevator down to Mike's office and headed for the operations room. Finding Karyn and Jerry poring over the list of phone numbers, they joined in until everyone was becoming numb from trying to find the needle in the haystack. Finally telling everyone to break for the night, Mike returned to his office to wait for General Modelle's arrival.

CHAPTER 27

Butch woke up early the next morning. He slipped quietly down the hall and into the kitchen, trying not to wake Ted or Mildred. The sun was just peeking above the horizon and barely lit the room. The first thing to do was to find the coffee and start a pot.

He hated searching someone's cabinets but knew Mildred wouldn't mind. It wasn't as if he were sneaking around prying into their belongings. He found a large can of Folgers Classic Roast behind the second door. He opened it and set it on the counter.

The coffee maker was easy to figure out; Mildred had emptied the grounds from the last time it had been used, and all Butch needed to do was fill it with water and put fresh coffee into the mesh filter. Not knowing how strong they liked theirs, he doubled the amount he normally used. You can always add water if it's too strong, but it's very difficult to strengthen a weak brew.

The coffee had just begun to percolate and drip into the glass pot when Ted came into the kitchen wearing a pair of wranglers, a long-sleeved shirt buttoned but hanging outside of his pants, and white socks showing beneath the legs of the jeans.

"Good morning," Ted said as he saw the coffee dripping. "Find everything you need?"

"Morning," Butch replied. "Yep, found the coffee, and that's about all I need to start the day."

Ted went to the refrigerator and took a carton of orange juice from the shelf. "OJ?" he asked as he took a couple of glasses from the cabinet.

"Sure," Butch replied. "I wasn't sure about how strong to make the coffee, so I hope it's all right."

Ted poured two glasses of juice and handed one to Butch, saying, "Looks fine to me, I'm not too picky. Too many years of drinking coffee at the store or on the road have made me just thankful that someone makes it for me."

They took their glasses and sat at the table, waiting for the coffee to finish brewing. "How'd you sleep?" Ted asked.

"Just fine," Butch said. "I hope I didn't disturb you and Mildred too much yesterday. I wish I could tell you the whole story, but I just can't right now."

"I hate having to be deceitful to anyone," Butch explained, "especially my friends."

"I understand," Ted told him. "And so does Mildred. We had a little discussion last night after we went to bed, and she's convinced that you're trying to help someone out of a jam of some kind."

"She's convinced that you're helping some lady get away from an abusive husband or something," Ted continued. "She knows you wouldn't be doing this unless you needed to keep it quiet."

"Well, she's a sharp lady," Butch said. "If that's the story she needs to believe to make it all right, then that's the story we'll let her believe."

"But it's not true, is it?" Ted questioned.

"No," Butch admitted. "And like I said, I'll fess up when it's over. For now, pick your version of the truth and keep that secret."

Ted finished his juice and carried his glass to the sink. Opening another cabinet, he took three cups down and set them on the counter beside the coffee pot. As he poured one full, he asked, "How do you take yours?"

"Just like most of the women I've met these last few years," Butch replied, "bitter with no sweetness at all."

Laughing, Ted poured a second cup and brought them to the table. "What about that Tammy woman you've been seeing? She seems to be pretty nice."

"Yeah, she's an exception," Butch agreed. "But that's one out of a thousand."

"What do you think makes the rest of them so bitter?" Ted asked, sipping his coffee.

"Lots of things, I guess," Butch said as he blew across the steaming cup. "Mostly, they seem to blame men for the way their lives have turned out."

"Since the majority of the ones I meet are divorced," Butch continued, "they seem to want to dwell on everything bad their exes have done. Of course, they want to tell you every detail of how sorry all the men are that they've met since the divorce."

"What're you men talking about?" Mildred said, walking into the kitchen. "What's this divorce and sorry men discussion about?"

"Good morning, Mildred," Butch said, looking up. "I'm just doing what men do when women can't hear us, or so we think. Mainly griping about how all the good women are taken."

Mildred filled her cup and sat down at the table with them. "I could say the same thing about men, you know."

"I know," Butch acknowledged. "But I hope you'll make an exception for a couple of us."

"Maybe," Mildred said, smiling. "There might be one or possibly two that aren't pure snakes. I might even put you on the short list of salvageable men if you'd just hurry up and let some good woman start to work on you."

Ted laughed and told her, "I'm not sure there's a woman that would want to tackle that problem. Too much effort for too little return."

"I'm starting to feel unwanted here," Butch said, trying to put on a sad face. "I just don't think you fine folks understand how sensitive I really am and how desperate I am to make a perfect husband for a wonderful woman."

"Don't start telling lies this early in the morning," Mildred chastised. "I haven't known you as long as Ted, but I haven't seen a sensitive bone in your body."

"I keep it well hidden," Butch said as he finished his coffee. "If it was well known, I'd be irresistible."

Butch got up and took his cup to the sink, and said, "Well, I'll go brush my teeth and try to shine up a bit before we go. I'll get my bag from the truck and see if I can't be presentable before we leave."

"I put out clean towels for you in the bathroom across the hall from your bedroom," Mildred said, holding her cup between her hands. "Let me know if there's anything else you need."

"Thanks, Mildred," Butch said as he headed for the front door. "I think I've got everything else I need in my bag. Sort of like when I'm flying, plan on having everything for a week even if it's only scheduled for one day."

As Butch came back in, Ted was rinsing his cup in the sink and said, "I'll be ready to go when you've showered. We'll run by James Wood's and find you a car before I go to work."

"That'll be great," Butch replied, heading for the bedroom with his suitcase. "This won't take me long. I'll be ready in about 15 minutes."

While Butch was showering, Mildred put her cup in the sink and asked, "Still not telling what he's up to?"

"Not really," Ted told her as he headed toward their bedroom. "He'll tell us when he's ready. Now, I've got to get ready for work."

A few minutes later, Ted came out fully dressed, fastening his belt buckle. Taking his cup out of the sink, he poured it full and sat to wait for Butch to finish cleaning up. He had drunk less than half of it when Butch came out carrying his suitcase.

When Ted saw the suitcase, he said, "You can leave that if you want. I'll give you a key to the house, and you can stay here while Mildred and I are at work."

"I might need to go somewhere later today," Butch explained. "I'd rather have everything with me in case I get rushed. But, thanks for the offer."

"Just let me know," Ted told him. "Mi casa es su casa."

Ted yelled goodbye to Mildred as they headed out the door. Butch threw his suitcase back into the truck and said, "Better let me drive; I'll drop you off at James Wood's and meet you somewhere to swap cars."

"That'll work," Ted replied as he threw Butch the keys. "Where do you want to meet?"

"How about Wal-Mart?" Butch asked. "It's on the way to David's, and we won't be noticed swapping keys as we shake hands. I can do a little shopping while I wait for you to get there.”

“Okay,” Ted said as he got into the passenger side of his truck. “I’ll park beside this old truck and come in to find you.”

“Sounds fine to me,” Butch said as he started the truck and backed into the street. “If I’m done shopping when you get there, just look for me in the magazine section.”

Butch drove north on 51 past David’s and Wal-Mart, then turned south on 287. After taking the exit for 730 towards Boyd, he turned left and pulled into the parking lot of James Wood’s. Ted quickly got out, and Butch headed back to Wal-Mart to wait.

After parking Ted’s truck in a conspicuous spot, Butch entered the store and walked around killing time. The only item he thought he might need was another cell phone. Finding one with 90 minutes of pre-paid time, he picked it up and wandered over to the magazine section. Looking through the rack, he picked up a copy of Western Horseman and glanced at the pictures. He had almost finished the entire magazine when Ted came up beside him.

Trying to appear as if they had just run into each other, they shook hands, and Butch took the keys from Ted. He dropped them into his shirt pocket and stood talking before he pulled the truck keys from his jeans. Holding them in his hand, he told Ted goodbye and passed them as they shook again.

Butch waited, still reading, until Ted was out of sight, and then headed for the checkout area. Using the self-checkout, he paid for the phone and headed back to where he had left the truck. When he got there, he saw a white four-door sedan with a tag hanging from the mirror.

Using the remote to unlock the doors, Butch could see the lights flash as he pushed it. Assured that he wasn't taking someone else's car, he opened the door and saw that Ted had already set his suitcase and hat in the rear seat. He climbed in and started the car while he figured out where the various controls were located.

Finally satisfied that he knew where the turn signals, lights, and steering wheel tilt control were, he pulled out of the parking lot and headed south on 287 toward Rhome. Not exactly positive where he would spend the night, he pulled the tag from the mirror and placed it on the seat with the cell phone he had just bought.

Butch knew that the package he had sent to the base wouldn't get there until around noon, so he needed to find someplace to hide until he decided how much time to give the government to verify the things he had sent them. Then, he had to figure out how to approach them with the least danger to himself.

Finally deciding to get as close to the base as he could, he joined the morning traffic that would merge with the crowd of commuters driving down I-35 into Ft Worth. He knew there were several small motels in White Settlement, and that would place him mere minutes from the base.

Most of the motels in that area were fairly old, and anyone with cash was never questioned. He planned on providing a false tag number when he registered, so even the car he was driving wouldn't be recorded if anyone found out he was the one that had it.

That settled, he tuned the radio to his favorite country station and relaxed as the traffic merged and separated for the various exits or on-ramps for the next ten or so miles until he could take loop 820 around the north side of Ft Worth.

With a little luck, he'd be settled in unobserved less than five miles from his adversary.

CHAPTER 28

The sun wasn't quite up when Kevin heard the pounding on the wooden door of the one-room cabin they had spent the night in. All of them had slept in the same clothes they had worn the day before, and they were beginning to get a little smelly. Between that and the soiled diapers that Leslie had tossed in the plastic bags from yesterday's lunch, the small room was rather rank.

He slid off the cot and pulled his boots on as the pounding continued. Both Gene and Leslie were awake and fearful of who was at the door. Kevin crossed the room and opened the door, wondering who would be standing there.

"Good morning, my friends," Sancudo announced, holding two paper sacks in his hands. "I have brought your breakfast. Aren't you going to invite me in?"

Kevin stood rubbing his eyes, trying to make out the figure standing in front of him. Finally, he stepped back and nodded for Mel to enter. "I'm a little surprised to see you this early," Kevin said. "Actually, I didn't expect to see you until late this afternoon."

Mel walked in, looked around the room, and wrinkled his nose, saying, "Smells like a herd of coyotes have been living here."

He held the bags out to Kevin and said, "There's coffee and burritos in the bags. You guys need to get up and be ready to go as quickly as possible."

Kevin took the bags and pulled a cup of coffee with a lid from one while handing the others to Gene. Tearing the lid off, he took a tentative sip to see how hot it would be, but it was barely warm.

"There have been some changes," Mel said as Gene passed the burritos around. "Late yesterday afternoon, some new information was sent that makes this a little more risky than I originally assumed."

Kevin had taken one of the burritos and was unwrapping it while sitting on the edge of his bed. "What do you mean?" he asked as he took a bite.

"All of the manned border crossings have new pictures of Leslie and Gene," Mel told him. "It is not unexpected to have photos of people the government is searching for, but these are new, and the guards will be sure to be looking closely for anyone matching their general description."

"I can work around that with no problem," Mel continued. "A few minor changes in clothes, a wig, and maybe a little more grime on the faces, and I can waltz them across almost anywhere."

"What's the problem then?" Kevin asked as he finished his food.

"You are the problem, Senor," Mel answered. "They now have a picture of you, and with your size and obvious American looks, I am running into difficulty in finding a way to get you across."

"So, what's your plan?" Kevin asked, wondering if this was a way to split them up and make it easier to deal with him.

"First," Mel said, "I'll get the clothes for Gene and Leslie to wear. With an old wig and worn clothes, Leslie can pass for a Mexican if we use a little shoe polish on her face."

"Gene looks enough like one of the mixed breeds that all he needs are the clothes and a hat," Mel continued.

"And if the child is kept wrapped and remains completely covered as we cross, there should be little problem," Mel concluded.

"And me?" Kevin asked.

"Ah, that is the second thing," Mel said, smiling. "I will be taking the others across with me. You will be riding in the trunk of your car while a friend of mine drives it."

"That way," Mel told him, "if you run into trouble, my friend can leave the car, and you may do as you can to join us."

Gene stood and tossed his empty cup and wrapper into the trash, saying, "I want to stay with Kevin, and I want Leslie and BK with us."

"I really do not care what you want, little one," Sancudo told him. "I have told Kevin, and now I'm telling the rest of you. You have a choice: do as I say or find your own way home. Or, wherever you want to go, I do not really care."

Leslie was holding BK and told Gene, "I agree with you, but we have no choice right now. Butch and Kevin paid this man to get us somewhere safely, and we have to let him do it the best way he knows."

"You seem to be the only one with sense," Mel told her. "Now, I will go get the clothes and things. Please put your trash in the trunk of your car when you finish; there are others that must use this place later this evening."

Leslie quickly checked BK's diaper and decided that she would wait until it was a little lighter, and she could see better to change him. She busied herself, picking up everything and putting it into the rapidly filling sack with all of their trash.

Gene and Kevin stood watching as Mel opened the door of the Bronco and took out a large plastic sack. Although the dome light didn't come on, they could see that there was another person in the car.

Mel came back in and started pulling the stained and worn clothes from the bag and passing them to Gene and Leslie. "Put these on," he directed. "Put your other clothes in this bag, and Kevin can put it in the trunk of his car."

While they were changing clothes, Mel held two dark wigs in his hand and told Kevin, "These may look like they are in need of a good shampoo, but they are very clean. Once they have them on, it will be much more difficult to recognize them if we are stopped."

As soon as Leslie had her clothes on, Mel took a small can of brown shoe polish and gently rubbed a little across her neck and face. Taking his time to make sure it covered every inch of her skin that would be visible, including the inside of her ears, he told her to put her wig on.

"You can do your arms and hands in the car," he told her as he handed her the can and a scarf. "Now, put this on and keep it as far forward to hide your face as much as possible."

He handed Gene a dirty baseball cap and his wig, saying, "Get used to wearing this while we're moving. And keep the hat pulled down as low as you can without looking like you're trying to hide your face."

Once everyone was ready, he said, "Now pay attention. I will do all the talking if we are stopped. You just sit in the back and hold the baby as if it's a normal day driving around the country."

"And you," he said, pointing at Leslie. "If you have to feed the baby, make sure there is no one around. Even if you don't see anyone, use the blanket to conceal your breast. Not only would it be considered indecent, it would expose the part of you that has not been colored."

Turning to Kevin, he said, "You will be riding in the trunk for a little over an hour and a half. The road will be pretty smooth until we hit the border, but it will not be a comfortable journey. Although I have been assured that most of the Border Patrol agents will be up around Del Rio and Lake Amistad, you can never count on things to go as planned."

"I will tell you that if your car appears to be drawing attention," Sancudo continued, "the driver will try to avoid being stopped and will signal you that it may happen. I suggest that if it happens, you get away any way you can."

"What then?" Kevin asked.

"Make your way to Quemado," Mel answered. "If you get there, you will find a couple of men wearing checkered shirts sitting in front of a cafe along Highway 277."

"The man in the blue shirt will start walking north along the road when they see you arrive," Mel continued. "Watch him, and when he gets off the road, see where it was and follow a few minutes later."

"The man in the red shirt will let you know if anything is wrong after the other one leaves," Mel told him. "He will also follow you after you leave the road to make sure no one else is interested in you."

"About a half of a mile after you cross the Rio Grande, you will come to a dirt road that runs north and south," Mel said. "Go north for a few hundred yards, and you will come to another dirt road that heads west. There is a cross at that intersection, and if everything is going well, a red ribbon will be tied to it."

"Head west along that road, and someone will pick you up in a couple of miles," Mel continued. "He will be driving a flatbed truck with a 55-gallon barrel tied to the bed. He will either open the door for you to get in, or he will stop and wait for you to get into the barrel."

"Do as he says," Mel finished. "If luck is with us, we will simply drive across the border, and you will disappear until Butch is ready for you to return. All of these precautions are just in case things don't go as planned."

Mel turned and started for the door as the sky was finally beginning to brighten. "Let's just get started, and by tonight, maybe you'll be safely hidden on a comfortable little ranch my family owns deep inside Mexico."

"Let's go," Kevin told them as he picked up the bag with their clothes inside and the bag of trash. "You can take the things you need from the car, and I'll see if I can make the trunk a little more comfortable for my ride."

Mel was talking to another man beside the Bronco as they started gathering the diapers and other things from the rear of the sedan. Kevin slipped his hand beneath the seat and pulled out the remaining cash, sliding it into his shirt. He then went to the trunk and opened it, removing the keys as soon as it was unlocked.

Throwing the smelly bag inside, along with the clothing bag he planned to use as a cushion, he walked back to the rear door of the car and helped Gene and Leslie carry things to Mel's Bronco. Once everything had been stored, he handed his keys to Mel and said, "I hope you know what you're doing and that you aren't trying to pull anything. I'd hate to have to try to find you if you aren't being straight with us, but I will."

Mel just smiled and handed the keys to his partner, saying, "Be careful with this one, amigo. He has problems with following orders. Maybe a couple of hours sweating in the trunk with some smelly diapers will improve his attitude."

Kevin was fuming as he turned and got into the trunk. The last thing he saw before the lid closed was the face of a smiling Mexican with a greasy ponytail and one gold tooth shining among the rest.

CHAPTER 29

During the night, General Paul Modelle arrived and had been escorted to his quarters by General Nelson. Mike had briefed him quickly and made sure everything Paul needed was available. After almost an hour of discussion, Mike excused himself and went home for the evening.

The head of the facility's security department, Lieutenant Colonel Mark Mallory, had finished the evening by making sure Tammy was safely confined and cared for. He briefed the oncoming shift that they were not to talk to their prisoner except in the event of an emergency.

The additional teams borrowed from the CIA and FBI had been placed in a motel located a few miles from the base on Loop 820 for the night while their assigned vehicles were equipped with secure radios and computers to allow instant communication with the operations center. Karyn had spent most of the night making sure everything would be ready to begin the hunt the next day.

General Modelle woke early and started the small coffee pot with its single cup of prepackaged Folgers. As he thought back over the briefing from Mike, he pulled one of the orange juice containers from the refrigerator and drank it to wash down the numerous pills his doctor had prescribed.

He was still in the shower when he heard his phone ringing. Shutting off the water, he wrapped a towel around his waist and walked into the room, dripping water across the floor.

"General Modelle," he said as he answered the phone.

"Good morning, Paul," Mike greeted him. "I hope I'm not waking you."

"Not at all," Paul replied. "Matter of fact, I'm trying to get a quick shower before we meet."

"I'll let you get back to that right now," Mike told him. "I just wanted to tell you that Kathy will have coffee, juice, and some donuts in my office whenever you can make it."

"I'll be there in about 10 minutes, Mike," Paul said. "When do you expect the rest of the team to be ready to brief the operation?"

"They'll be ready in about 30 minutes, sir," Mike answered. "Most of them are already here, and Colonel Erickson is setting up the conference room."

"Fine," Paul told him. "If there's nothing else pressing, I'll finish my shower and see you in a few minutes."

"Yes, sir," Mike said. "I'll be waiting in my office."

Mike hung up his phone and headed out of his office. As he closed his door, he told his secretary, "Kathy, General Modelle will be here in about 10 minutes, maybe less."

"Yes, sir," she replied. "I'll have everything ready in about five minutes. Is there anything else you'll need?"

"No, not that I can think of," Mike told her. "But, please call General Brown and tell him we'll be using his conference room at about 8:00. And if you'd ask him to meet us at the Officer's Club for lunch, I'd appreciate it."

"Of course, sir," Kathy acknowledged. "How many will be attending?"

"Just him, Paul, and I," Mike replied. "Make it for 11:00 if that fits his schedule."

"I'll take care of it," Kathy said, making a note on her day planner. "If there's any problem on General Brown's end, I'll let you know."

"Thanks," Mike said as he left her office.

Mike walked to the conference room to see how the preparations were coming for their briefing. Rick was talking to Amy about her portion and making sure each seat had copies of all relevant material.

"Morning, folks," Mike said as he entered the room. "Will everything be ready as scheduled?"

"Good morning, General," Rick and Amy said in unison as they came to attention.

"Definitely, sir," Rick answered as Mike motioned for them to relax. "I'm just finishing checking Amy's part, and everything's fine."

"What about Karyn?" Mike asked.

"I spoke to her a few minutes ago, and she's making a few revisions based on the last team's arrival," Rick answered. "She assured me that she'll be ready in plenty of time for me to recheck it."

"And Major Fleenor?" Mike queried.

"Jerry's briefing will be ready as well," Rick said. "He's making a few revisions based on the data he just received regarding the final phone number review."

"And how's our unhappy guest?" Mike finally asked.

"Mark just called and said they took her a tray for breakfast," Rick told him. "She's not too happy, as you said, and keeps asking for a lawyer."

"Maybe Jerry was right about the warrant," Mike said. "I know we can't hold her indefinitely, but if she makes a fuss after we release her, it's good to have some legal protection on our side."

"Yes, sir," Rick acknowledged. "Jerry seems to be thinking ahead of us in some respects. But I'd still like to see him a little more aggressive in some other areas."

"Well, we'll discuss that later," Mike said, turning to leave. "I'll be back in about 20 minutes with General Modelle. Make sure everyone's here when we arrive."

"Yes, sir," Rick said, coming to attention again.

Mike returned to his office and asked Kathy to have Mark come in for a moment before Paul arrived. As she started dialing, he continued on in checking the coffee and other refreshments. Satisfied that everything was ready, he sat behind his desk and waited for his head of security to arrive.

"Good morning, sir," Mark said as he entered and saluted.

Mike returned his salute and said, "Have a seat, Mark. Is everything going okay with Ms. Terbush?"

Mark remained standing and answered, "As well as can be expected, sir. She's eaten her breakfast and just asked when she'll be released."

"When you get back," Mike directed, "have her escorted to one of the restrooms that have a shower and let her clean up if she wants to. Just make sure she understands that we're not finished talking to her."

"I'll take her myself," Mark told him. "When do you want to start the next interrogation?"

"In about an hour or so," Mike answered. "You'll be escorting her to General Brown's conference room a few minutes before General Modelle and I leave. We've scheduled the room for 8:00, so make your plans based on that."

"She'll be there," Mark said. "Will there be anything else?"

"Just try not to ruffle her feathers any more than necessary," Mike told him.

Mark saluted and left just as Kathy announced that General Modelle was waiting in her office. Mike told her to send him in and came from behind his desk to meet Paul.

"General," Mike said, welcoming Paul into the room. "Care for some juice or coffee?"

"Hello, Mike," Paul said. "Just coffee will be fine."

Paul walked to the table, started pouring himself a cup, and remarked, "You still eating these fat pills?"

Mike looked at the donuts and said, "Every now and then, sir. But I've got to watch what I eat these days. It seems that my waist just about explodes with every candy bar or sweet thing I eat."

"I understand," Paul said, walking to a chair facing Mike's desk. "My doctor has put me on so many pills for blood pressure, pulse rate, cholesterol level, or some other malady that I'm a walking drugstore."

"This getting old is certainly not what I planned," Mike said as he carried a cup of coffee and sat behind his desk.

"Speaking of getting old," Paul said, sitting his cup on Mike's desk. "This operation is drawing way too much-unwanted attention back in Washington."

"I don't see any way of protecting any of you if we don't get a satisfactory conclusion rather quickly," he continued. "Not only are your jobs at risk, as is mine, but the entire program is under intense scrutiny because of the meager results of late."

Mike nodded somberly and agreed, saying, "I completely understand, sir. We all know that this is our last opportunity to contain this disaster. Our only hope right now is getting information from Ms. Terbush that helps us narrow our search or just plain assed luck."

"Luck is one thing we haven't had for any of this mess," Paul replied, "unless it's been bad luck. And we can't afford to make any more bets that our butts can't cover."

"Yes, sir," Mike nodded, putting his cup down and standing. "I believe the rest of the folks are ready in the conference room now. If you're ready, we'll head down there."

Paul stood and said, "Let's hope they have some good news. I'd like to report anything positive to my boss by noon today, if at all possible."

As they passed through Kathy's office, she told them that the Base Commander's conference room was ready, and he had agreed to an 11:00 lunch. Mike thanked her, and they headed down the hall.

Colonel Erickson and the others came to attention as Paul and Mike entered for the briefing. "Good morning, sir," Rick said as they waited for Paul to tell them to be seated.

"Good morning, folks," Paul responded. "Please have a seat, and let's get this going."

Paul took his chair at the end of the long table, and Mike sat on his right. Rick remained standing as the rest of them took their seats. Once everyone had relaxed slightly, he began, "Sir, as a quick overview, we've verified that the child born up in Ringgold is definitely Gene's. The man we couldn't identify back in the initial hunt is Mr. Kevin Knox, and we've acquired every piece of information available on him. Butch North disappeared sometime yesterday morning, and we've had no information as to where he may be."

Rick paused for a second and then said, "Colonel Amy Moore, the laboratory commander, will give you her assessment of the DNA used to verify the paternity of the baby boy."

Paul nodded, and Amy stood, saying, "Sir, the top folder in front of you shows the comparison of Gene's DNA and that of the material we took from the clinic where the baby was delivered."

She paused while Paul and Mike opened the folders and pulled the loose sheets out. "There is no chance that the child isn't Gene's. We cannot verify the genetic data on the mother, but my conversation with the doctor, nurse, and trooper that saw her made me positive that she is the 'Leslie' woman that we were looking for."

Waiting for the information to be considered, Amy continued, "My team and I removed everything from the clinic that could possibly contain evidence leading to Gene or Leslie."

"I need to tell you that there was a piece of evidence that escaped our initial operation," she admitted. "The scrubs the doctor and nurse were wearing were not collected. However, I sent a team back later with authorization to get the medical records, and Doctor Adams gave them a bag containing both sets of scrubs."

"Are you certain that there is no further evidence up there?" Paul asked.

"As sure as I can be," Amy answered. "I can think of nothing else that wasn't collected."

"And the doctor had no problems giving us the medical records once we provided him with authorization," she continued. "I think we're safe on those issues."

"Thanks, Amy," Paul said as he returned the papers to their folder.

Rick stood again and said, "Now, Major Fleenor will bring you up to date on Mr. Kevin Knox and a search of Mr. North's phone records."

As Rick sat down, Jerry rose and said, "Good morning, sir. The second folder has a complete history of Mr. Knox and our analysis of the phone records of both him and Mr. North."

Pausing while everyone opened their folders, he continued, "Mr. Knox is a former Marine with three tours in Vietnam, numerous decorations that include four Purple Hearts, a Meritorious Service Medal, the Bronze Star, and others as listed."

"He also served as a drill instructor for Marine Basic Training and taught advanced hand-to-hand combat as well as other martial arts. Since leaving the service, he has lived on a small ranch very close to Ringgold, where the baby was born."

Jerry waited for them to review Kevin's military records and then said, "The records show him to be the owner of the car Leslie was driving and also the truck we couldn't previously identify. There is no doubt as to his involvement with Gene and Leslie. And one final piece of evidence."

He paused as each of them looked at him expectantly, "Kevin and Butch have a history of association that goes back to Vietnam when Butch was in Naval Intelligence and Kevin was involved in some clandestine work eliminating some village leaders that were suspected of being aligned with the Viet Cong."

"There is very little information available since most of those records were expunged, but there's enough to know that Mr. North was partially responsible for covering some of Mr. Knox's less-than-conventional methods," Jerry concluded.

"Do you have any proof of their conspiracy in our operation?" Paul asked.

"No, sir," Jerry answered. "The only thing we have that does tie them together is the sign-in record from the VFW in Avondale. We have photos of the truck Mr. Knox owned being there at the same time Mr. North was followed there."

"Mr. North signed in first, and a 'Won Dum Phuc' signed in later. It is our conclusion that Mr. Phuc is actually Mr. Knox," Jerry concluded.

"Quite a pair," Paul said, laying the papers aside. "Anything else?"

"Not really, sir," Jerry finished. "We've spent hours trying to find something in Mr. North's phone records that may give us any clues but have come up empty-handed. The same goes for Mr. Knox's phones. The consensus is that they were using prepaid cell phones for any direct communication, and we have no method of tracking them."

"Pretty ingenious of them," Paul remarked. "And I suppose we're the ones that gave them the training to beat us at our own game and using readily available assets, just pure low-tech smarts. What's next?"

Rick introduced Karyn, and she stood saying, "General Modelle, I have nothing good to tell you. I'm afraid that all of our efforts in locating any of the people have been unproductive. We've searched every piece of property owned by both North and Knox, located every vehicle North owned, and are only missing an old truck Mr. Knox owned several years ago that hasn't been registered in over five years."

"Why haven't you located that truck?" Paul asked.

"It may not even be around now," Karyn told him. "Even though we have no record of his disposing of the truck, he may have sent it to a wrecking yard, or sold it to some rancher who never registered it. There's just no record of what happened to it. We only know it wasn't on his property, and we can't verify its current existence."

"Any other good news?" Paul asked sarcastically.

Rick stood and said, "No, sir. That concludes everything we have except for Ms. Terbush and her initial interview. She gave us no insight as to where Butch may have gone, and she says she's never heard of Gene or Leslie."

"What about her knowledge of Kevin Knox?" Paul asked.

"Just that she's heard Butch speak of him," Rick answered. "But she says she's never met him, and Butch rarely mentions him except to relate something they did or some people they met at a bar."

Mike thanked Rick and said, "General, we'll be meeting with Ms. Terbush in a few minutes, and you can determine if we need to pursue any further questioning."

Paul thanked everyone and told Mike, "Not much good news here; let's see if we can improve our luck with Ms. Terbush."

Everyone stood as Paul and Mike left the room. Rick looked around at the resigned faces and said, "That certainly didn't give General Modelle any warm fuzzies. Unless Tammy gives us something, we're depending on a miracle to find any of these people we have to bring in. And I don't believe in miracles."

CHAPTER 30

Butch continued south on I-35 and finally came to the exit for Loop 820 West. Sliding into the right-hand lane, he joined the flow of traffic and continued around until he crossed Lake Worth and came down to where I-30 intersected. The Holiday Inn Express had several cars in the parking lot, and he knew that he could park the nondescript little white sedan unnoticed while he stayed.

Although there were a few old motels scattered around, Butch decided that sometimes it was better to hide in plain sight. Besides, parking a fairly new car among the usual clunkers you find at the lower end of the spectrum of cheap motels might draw unwanted attention, not to mention the fact that he'd rather have clean sheets and a phone.

As he pulled in and started toward the lobby area, he noticed a familiar black Suburban parked there. There was also a blue van with the distinctive markings of an Air Force vehicle. Butch continued to a more remote area of the parking lot and sat waiting to see who was coming out to those vehicles.

He hadn't been waiting long when he saw four men wearing dark suits come out of the door and get into the cars.

Now, he was beginning to have second thoughts about his choice of accommodations. This was apparently where at least one or two of the teams from the base were staying.

Finally, he got out of the sedan, locked it, and walked into the lobby. Wearing the baseball cap and pulling his shirt tail out of his jeans made a huge difference in the way he normally looked, and the sunglasses hid his eyes enough that most people wouldn't recognize him unless they really knew him.

He remembered the times when he had been places and just not wearing his hat had caused some of the people he knew to take a second look before they realized that it was him. Also, sometimes you never look in your own backyard for the missing dog.

Maybe being this close to the team members would be the best place to hide. They would probably never think he was living right next door, and this was certainly one of the last places anyone would suspect him to be.

That decided, he walked up to the counter and waited for the young lady working there to come help him. Looking around, Butch noticed a few people busy with laptop computers and talking on cell phones. Obviously, business people from out of town and unobservant to their surroundings, they blended together and paid no attention to anyone. If he had been wearing a suit, he would have melted into that crowd with little effort.

The young lady finally came over and said, "Good morning, sir, my name is Ann. How can I help you?"

Butch smiled and said, "I'd like a room for a few days, ma'am. I'm not entirely sure how long I'll be in town, but I'm sure I'll be here for three or four."

"That's fine, sir," Ann said, sliding a form across the countertop. "If you'll just fill this out, I'll get you registered. How will you be paying?"

Butch kept his head down while he filled in the blanks and asked, "Is cash acceptable?"

"We'd prefer a major credit card, sir," Ann answered, "just in case there are supplemental charges, like the phone or restaurant."

"How about if I leave a deposit," Butch asked. "I'll be glad to prepay for the room and leave a reasonable deposit in case I use the phone, although any calls will be local."

"I'll have to ask the manager, sir," Ann told him. "We normally need a credit card."

"I understand," Butch replied. "If you'd get him, I'll finish filling this out."

As Ann went to find the manager, Butch continued putting the information on the registration form. Since he couldn't use his own name, address, or car license plate numbers, and he didn't want to use any friend's name, he wrote one of the false names he had used back in the Air Force.

It had been common when deployed to another base to wear a name tag with a nickname or something that seemed normal but was considered humorous if you paid attention. Smiling, he wrote Hugh G. Wrexion for his name and Happy, Texas, as his home.

When Ann and the manager came back, he handed her the form and said good morning to the manager. Ann accepted the completed form and began making sure every space was filled before she handed it to her boss.

He took it and said, "Good morning, Mr. *Rexun?*"

"That's close enough," Butch said, smiling. "Dad was an old Greek descendant."

"Sir," the manager said, "we normally don't take cash in advance. Our policy is to use credit cards, but if you want to close the account with cash when you check out, that will be fine."

"Yes, sir," Butch lied, "but the only problem is that I lost my wallet yesterday, and it had all of my credit cards, driver's license, and everything else in it. It's just lucky that I carry my cash in a money clip in my front pocket. Otherwise, I don't know what I'd do."

"Well," the manager said, "I think we can work something out. How many days did you say you'd be staying with us?"

"Three or four, at least," Butch answered. "I'll be glad to make any arrangements for paying that suit your needs."

The manager turned to Ann and said, "Charge him for one day at a time and add $100 as a deposit. Mr. Rexun can check back in each morning and make up any of the deposit he uses."

"Will that be satisfactory?" the manager asked Butch as Ann began entering the information into her computer.

"That'll work for me," Butch said, pulling his money clip from his pocket. "I'm sorry to put you to so much trouble, but I've got to finish some business here in Ft Worth before I head back to Happy. I really appreciate your assistance."

"We're glad to help," the manager said as he turned to leave. "Just let us know if there's anything else you need."

Ann finished and asked if Butch wanted just a single bed or maybe a suite. Telling her that anything with a king size would be fine and to please try to find a room as far from the highway as possible. After a few more keystrokes, Ann gave him his key and told him how much he needed to pay.

Butch glanced at the charges and gave her two $100 bills. "Just use what's left from the room amount as an additional deposit," he told her.

Ann entered the amount into her computer and waited for the printer to finish before saying, "Thank you, sir; here's your room key and receipt. Have a nice day."

Butch took them and thanked her as he turned to go. Now, all he had to do was get his bag and make it to the room without drawing any more attention. The unusual method of getting the room would definitely stick in their minds, but by tomorrow, they'd probably forget it. Hopefully, he wouldn't have to deal with any new shift workers and re-explain the problem.

Butch left the car parked several rows from the front and carried his suitcase through the lobby to the elevators. Hoping he wouldn't have to share the ride with anyone, he made sure there was nobody waiting before pushing the 'up' button. If he hadn't been carrying the suitcase, he'd have taken the stairs, but it would have looked strange if he hadn't used the elevator.

Butch found his room at the end of the hall, opened the door, and took a quick look around as he set his bag on the bed. It was pretty much a standard, medium-priced, clean traveler's accommodation with a bed, phone, TV, bath, sink just inside the door, and a closet. He had spent countless nights in such rooms all over the United States working for American Airlines.

After he hung his few shirts in the closet and put his shaving kit in the bathroom, he picked up the phone directory and began looking for the number of an old acquaintance he hoped would be a key to his plan. He was not really expecting to find it; he was surprised when it was listed. Taking the pen from the desk, he jotted the number down on the pad inscribed with the motel's name.

Getting hungry, Butch locked the room and took the stairs back down to the lobby. Keeping his head slightly down and the glasses on, he strode to the doors without glancing at any of the people sitting around. As he passed the counter, he happily noticed that Ann didn't even glance up.

He remembered a What-A-Burger just north of the motel up by where White Settlement Road crossed Loop 820. Heading up the access road from the motel, he tried to determine just how he was going to present his case to the one person he thought could help him. And more importantly, probably would if he could just get a chance to tell the story, or at least the part that would interest him.

Pulling into the What-A-Burger, Butch parked and walked in. It was still a little early for lunch, but a few people were sitting around drinking coffee or eating. He looked at the menu behind the cashier and decided that a double-meat cheeseburger with jalapenos would be just about perfect.

When the cashier asked him for his order, he told him that the double-meat what-a-meal combo with cheese, French fries, and strawberry malt, with extra malt, would be wonderful. Paying and taking his plastic order number, Butch went to a seat by the window where he could watch the passing traffic on the highway. The base was located just a couple of miles down the road, and he knew they were using White Settlement Road to leave or go there.

They may be looking for him, but now he was watching them and waiting for his chance to stop the interruption to everyone's life. Checking his watch, he figured the package he had sent would be arriving at the Base Commander's office within the next hour or so.

The cashier brought a tray with Butch's order and placed it in front of him. Taking a couple of packages of catsup from the offered assortment of condiments, Butch sat back to enjoy his meal. As much as he enjoyed What-A-Burger, what he wanted right now was to pick Tammy up and have a 16 oz prime rib at Outback. And a Jack and Coke. And spend the night with her. And not be worrying about all this crap.

CHAPTER 31

Mel led the way, driving from the cabin toward Highway 674. The Bronco bumped along a little faster than he normally drove, and he smiled, thinking of how the ride in the trunk of the sedan felt to Kevin. He glanced in the mirror repeatedly and watched the car bouncing along in the dust he was leaving as they sped down the dirt road.

Leslie was having difficulty holding BK to her breast, trying to feed him, and Gene was doing his best to keep from yelling at Mel to slow down. He was getting frustrated at being kept in the dark and worried that they might be leaving Kevin behind.

Kevin's head slammed into the lid of the trunk several times, and the dust from the road filtered in and mixed with the foul air from the bag of trash he had tried to shove as far as possible from his face. The bag of clothes provided little cushion under his body, and the spare tire made it extremely cramped.

Finally, after what seemed like hours of choking, Kevin felt the car slow and make a left turn. Immediately, the bouncing stopped as the cars headed south on 674. Kevin remembered that the next town along the road was

Brackettville, and the sign had informed them that it was about 50 miles past where they had spent the night.

From Brackettville, it was at least another hour down to Eagle Pass, where the bridge across the Rio Grande went into Piedras Negras. At least two hours in the trunk seemed to be the best case, but if they were separated, Kevin had no idea how much time would pass before he could get out. Finally able to relax and rest his head on the bag, he tried not to think of the difficulties that awaited him if he was forced to try to make it across the border alone.

In the Bronco, Sancudo kept his speed just below the limit and watched the sedan slowly separate until it was several miles behind him. Occasionally, he would lose sight of it in the rolling hills. He also noticed that Gene would look back every few minutes, trying to see where Kevin was.

Leslie finished feeding BK and laid him on the seat to change his diaper. As soon as the tabs were pulled loose, everyone knew it was certainly time for a change. She pulled a wet wipe from the container and began cleaning him as she held his legs up while Gene took the soiled diaper and tried to roll it up and refasten the tabs.

"Please roll your windows down," Mel said as he lowered his. "I don't think having the smell in the car will facilitate our journey."

"However," he continued, "I want you to leave the diaper on the floor, and we will use it when we approach the crossing."

"How will we use a dirty diaper?" Leslie asked as she finished putting a new one on BK.

"That is simple, little lady," Sancudo told her. "When we get close to the border, we will roll our windows up and open the smelly diaper. Then, if one of the guards decides to look in the car, the smell will keep him from looking in for very long and will probably make him look at the baby instead of you two.”

Gene was still trying to keep track of Kevin and hadn’t seen the sedan for four or five minutes and finally asked, “Is Kevin coming across at the same place we do?”

“If all goes well,” Mel answered. “However, he will be several minutes behind us.”

“If there is trouble,” he continued, “it may be an hour or more before he gets to us.”

Mel reached beneath his seat and pulled a CB radio out. Placing it beside him, he plugged the cord into the cigarette lighter receptacle and turned it on. Selecting a frequency, he made a short call in Spanish. A few seconds later an answer was heard, two quick words also in Spanish.

“You will be glad to know that for now, our way is clear,” Mel told Gene and Leslie. “A minor issue just north of Del Rio has resulted in several of the Border Patrol people moving up there for a day or so.”

Mel switched frequencies again and spoke a single word into the microphone. Immediately, he got a single-word reply. Smiling, he switched to English and said, “Try weaving side to side and tap your brakes hard a couple of times.”

“Who are you talking to?” Gene asked.

“My friend behind us,” Mel answered. “It seems that he is hearing some unusual sounds from the trunk of his car. I think maybe he needs to adjust the load; maybe it will stop the noise.”

The ride on into Brackettville continued uneventful with Gene and Leslie talking softly while she held BK as he slept. Gene hadn’t seen the sedan for the last 15 minutes or so and finally asked. “How far behind us is Kevin?”

Mel looked at Gene in the mirror and answered, "I don't know, and you shouldn't worry about him right now. You probably will not be seeing him again until we are safely across the border."

"My friend driving his car knows what to do," Mel continued. "My job is to get you three over; his job is to get Kevin over. Your job is to try and not look nervous, keep your mouths shut, and do exactly what I tell you immediately without question."

Mel continued to stare at Gene and Leslie while he waited for their answer, "Do you understand?"

"Yes, sir," Leslie answered, staring back at Mel. "We understand, but you could be a little more courteous about it. We're not criminals."

Mel laughed and told her, "Oh, yes, you are. There is probably more interest in you right now than any of my previous customers."

Just then, the radio came alive with a few words in Spanish. Mel picked up the microphone and replied tersely. Neither Gene nor Leslie could understand the short conversation, but they could tell from Sancudo's tone that something had changed.

Mel switched frequencies again and called. When he was answered, he spoke rapidly and waited for the response. Nodding his head when he heard it, he switched frequencies again and spoke. Several seconds later, he got a response and spoke a single word.

Shaking his head slightly, he focused his attention on the road as they approached Brackettville. When he came to the intersection of US 90, he made a right turn, and Gene saw the sign informing him that they were headed toward Del Rio.

In the trunk of the sedan, Kevin had been cramped so long that he had begun moving around, trying to adjust his body into a more comfortable position. He estimated that they had been on the road for almost an hour and should be coming to Brackettville any time now. Sure enough, the car slowed and finally stopped. Immediately, he felt panic, thinking that the driver was about to abandon him. The car remained stopped for only a couple of seconds, and Kevin felt it make a right turn.

About two minutes later, he felt it slow again and made a left turn. For the next ten minutes they seemed to be going straight. Having made the turns, Kevin had no idea which way they were going. He knew they had been going south, and the combination of a right turn and a left one should mean they were still headed in that direction.

He didn't know very much about the country down here and could only guess at their destination. His biggest worry right now was what to do if the car stopped and the driver got out. Although he had been told to head for Quemado, he had no idea of what direction or how far it was.

At first, he had wondered how to get the trunk open, but he had found a lug wrench while trying to adjust the bags. The end would fit into the lip of the lid, and he could pry the latch open if he had to. The wrench would also make a weapon if he needed it, and he placed it between himself and the rear, where he could grab it quickly if necessary.

Several minutes later, he felt the car slow again and turn right. The roughness of the road meant they had left the paved road and were again on dirt or gravel. Less than a minute later, the car stopped, and he heard the engine quit. As the door opened, he placed his hand on the wrench and waited to see what was happening.

The sound of footsteps coming toward him beside the car stopped at the trunk. He heard the key being slid in and watched the lid rise. Still gripping the wrench, he waited to see who would be standing there. As the trunk opened, he saw the same smiling face he had seen when it had last closed.

"Please get out, Senor," the man said. "We will take a short break while some minor repairs are made to the car."

Kevin slowly crawled out and tried to stretch the kinks out of his back. "What repairs?" he asked as he held his arms over his head.

"Just minor," the man with the gold tooth said, stepping back. "Now, if you would please put the wrench back into the car."

Kevin was surprised to find that he still had it in his hand and was holding it over his head. The look on Gold tooth's face told him that the unintentionally threatening stance was not appreciated.

"Sorry," he said as he lowered his arms and threw the wrench back into the trunk.

"You do not need a weapon, Senor," the man said. "And that one would not save you if there was truly any danger."

"You may go into the house there," Gold tooth told him, pointing at a small adobe building. "There is a restroom and water. The repairs will only take a few minutes."

Kevin headed toward the house as he saw three men carrying what appeared to be buckets of paint toward the car. The man with the gold tooth spoke rapidly in Spanish, and they began to lay newspaper across the hood and started taping it to the metal.

An elderly woman was sitting in a wooden rocking chair as Kevin entered. She smiled, showing very few remaining teeth, and pointed toward a door at the rear of the room. Nodding her head, she kept pointing and saying, "Bano."

Thankful he could relieve himself somewhere other than the trunk of the car, Kevin said, "Gracia," and went into the bathroom. The bouncing of the car and the coffee he drank had placed an enormous strain on his kidneys, and the discomfort had become almost unbearable.

As he came out, the woman was standing at a small sink, running water into a glass that she held out as he walked over. Taking it, Kevin again thanked her and swallowed half of it. Not wanting to fill his bladder again, he handed her the glass and nodded.

As soon as he walked out of the house, he saw that the men had painted the left front fender a rusty red with primer. They had also smeared what looked like mud along the bottom of the entire car. With the dust that had settled on it from the dirt roads, the car no longer looked as it had when Kevin had taken it.

Gold tooth was thanking the men as Kevin walked up. As soon as he finished shaking their hands, he motioned for Kevin to follow him to the rear of the car. As the trunk was opened, Kevin saw that there were now Mexico license plates on the car. Climbing in as directed, he also saw some dirty tarps, paint cans, and brushes inside.

Once Kevin had lain down in the trunk, the tarps were placed over him, and the brushes thrown on top. The man with the gold tooth smiled as he started to close the trunk, saying, "Please try not to move too much, Senor. And you should make no noise until I open this again."

With that, the lid slammed, and Kevin was again in the dark with the smell of dirty diapers, some undetermined odors, and the fumes from the paint cans. Resigning himself to discomfort and uncertainty, he tried to find a position that wouldn't be too bad and waited for the car to start.

CHAPTER 32

As they walked down the hall, General Modelle said, "Mike, I've got to make a quick call to Washington. I'll meet you in your office in about five minutes."

"Yes, sir," Mike said. "I'll make sure Mark has taken Ms. Terbush over to the base conference room and has my car ready to go when you are."

Mike continued to his office as Paul opened the door to his room. Once inside, Paul opened the metal case holding his encrypted phone and connected it to the outlet beside the desk. Waiting for it to connect and run a check for security, he dreaded the call.

Finally hearing the familiar clicks that confirmed everything had been checked, he dialed the number for the head of MJ12. When it was answered, he said, "Good morning, sir. I'm afraid that I have no real good news. There's definitely a child carrying Gene's DNA, and still no information as to where any of our players are. I'm interviewing Ms. Terbush in a few minutes, and I'll call back after that, but I just wanted to let you know that unless she knows something that will help us, our chance of success is very slim."

Paul listened to his boss for a second and then said, "I know this is potentially a national disaster, and I'll do everything possible to find a solution, but we need to be prepared for complete disclosure. I'm recommending that the folks in public relations come up with a plan to try and put this in a favorable light if we can't locate Gene and the child."

Paul nodded as he listened and then said, "Yes, sir. I'll call as soon as the interview is finished. Thanks."

Paul hung up, disconnected the phone, and closed the metal case. Getting his dress blue jacket from the closet, he checked to make sure the Command Pilot Wings were straight, and the vast array of ribbons was secure above the left breast pocket. Slipping the jacket on, he picked up his hat and left the room.

Mike was waiting in his office with his dress jacket on and talking to his secretary when Paul arrived. "Ready to go?" Paul asked as he entered.

"Yes, sir," Mike answered. "Ms. Terbush was taken over a few minutes ago, and Kathy cleared everything with General Brown."

"Fine," Paul replied. "Let's hope the lady has some answers that may help us get control of this disaster."

Although Kathy didn't know the full extent of the problem, she shook her head slowly as the Generals left the room. Having been Mike's secretary for several years, she knew that something was jeopardizing his career, and she felt sorry for all of them.

Mike drove them to the Base Commander's headquarters, and they parked the sedan in one of the parking spots reserved for staff cars with a star on the license plate. Both he and Paul checked that their jackets were buttoned and hats perfectly straight before they entered the building.

Passing General Brown's office, they went directly to the conference room where Lieutenant Colonel Mallory was waiting by the closed door. "Good morning, General Modelle," Mark said, standing at attention. "Ms. Terbush is waiting inside, and General Brown's secretary left coffee and water for all of you."

"Thanks, Mark," Paul said as he shook his hand. "I'd appreciate it if you'd hang around while we talk with Ms. Terbush. Why don't you see if General Brown's secretary can't find you a comfortable place to wait? This may take a couple of hours."

"Yes, sir," Mark answered. "I've already taken care of that, and the phone in the conference room is connected to the secretary's office. She can let me know the minute you need me."

Mark opened the door and held it for Paul and Mike to enter the room. As they walked in, they saw Tammy standing on one side, looking at the pictures along the wall and holding a cup of coffee.

"Good morning, Ms. Terbush," Paul announced. "I'm General Paul Modelle, and you've already met General Mike Nelson."

Tammy turned as she heard him speak and angrily asked, "Why am I being kept here? I've already told you everything I know last night. When are you going to let me go home?"

Paul removed his hat and sat it on the long polished oak table and told her, "I'm very sorry about all of this, Ms. Terbush, but we've got to make sure we've got every possible thing that may pertain to our problem. Please have a seat."

Mike had laid his hat on the table in front of a leather chair just to the left of Paul's chair at the head of the table.

Both men stood as Paul motioned for Tammy to take the chair to his right. Tammy stood quietly, looking at them before she finally walked over. Paul pulled her chair out and stood behind it as she took her seat. Once she sat, Paul and Mike took their seats and waited for her to relax before Paul started the conversation.

Crossing his hands on the table, Paul explained, "Ms. Terbush, I know Mike has already asked you most of the questions, but I'd like to hear your answers myself."

Pausing while Tammy looked from Mike back to him, he continued, "What is your relationship with Mr. North?"

Tammy thought about it for a second and replied, "We've been dating for about six months or so. I guess you'd say that we're involved in a romantic relationship."

Paul nodded and asked, "During this time, have you ever heard of a lady named Leslie Barber?"

"As I said last night, no," Tammy answered. "And I have not heard of anyone named Gene, except for a guy Butch knows who works on lawnmowers or something."

"Have you met that man?" Paul asked.

"Once," Tammy answered. "Butch took a weed eater or something to him for repairs."

"What did he look like?" Paul questioned.

"Kind of short with a scar on the right side of his face," Tammy answered.

"How old did you think this man was?" Paul asked.

"Probably about 50 or so, maybe older," Tammy said. "I think Butch said they had been friends for several years."

"All right," Paul replied, knowing that the Gene she had met couldn't possibly be the one they were interested in.

"What about Mr. Kevin Knox?" Paul asked.

"Again, I've heard Butch talk about him, but I've never met him," Tammy answered.

Paul studied her face for a moment and then asked, "Are you aware that Mr. North and Mr. Knox have conspired to help a terrorist to avoid capture? One suspect in the attempted hijacking of an aircraft like during the World Trade Center attack?"

"That's not true," Tammy shouted. "I know Butch too well to think he'd do something like that. He'd be the first one to help you catch him if he knew anything."

"I know how he feels about the attack on the World Trade Center," she emotionally continued. "He hates those people and constantly makes remarks about Muslims and how cowardly he thinks they are. No, he wouldn't help any of them; you're wrong!"

Paul looked at Mike and thought about what he could say that might make a difference in how much Tammy would reveal about Butch. Finally, he said, "We know that you went to San Antonio with Mr. North a few months ago. We also know that you went to Del Rio and over to Ciudad Acuna. What was the purpose of your visit?"

Tammy's eyes were beginning to water, and she softly said, "Butch just wanted to get away from the stables for a few days and take a vacation. He wanted me to meet a good friend of his in San Antonio and just relax for a while."

"Who was the man in San Antonio?" Paul asked, already knowing the answer.

"John Freeman and his wife Margaret," Tammy said. "They were friends of his from the Air Force."

"What about Del Rio?" Paul asked. "Who did you meet there?"

"I don't remember their names," Tammy answered. "Just some people Butch had flown with at Laughlin or people that lived around there."

"Who were the people he knew that lived around there?" Paul continued questioning.

"I told you that I don't remember," Tammy said. "Just some people that ran a restaurant, some others at some of the bars, I don't remember!"

"All right," Paul continued, "what about when you went to Mexico? Who did you meet over there?"

Tears began running down Tammy's face as she lowered her head and said, "I don't remember. It was just people that Butch had known. I don't remember, can't you understand? It was just people!"

Paul looked at Mike and shook his head. Mike nodded and said, "Ms. Terbush, we're very sorry to be putting you through this, but it is vital that we know where Butch is right now."

Tammy just sat sobbing as they waited for an answer. It was becoming obvious that she didn't know anything that would help them, but they kept trying to find the smallest clue as they continued.

Finally, after over an hour of changing tactics and ensuring her that they believed her, Paul told her, "I'm sure Butch wouldn't knowingly help someone like the man we're hunting. But he may have unwittingly gotten involved with these people. It may even be that they have him, and he's in danger."

"For his sake," Paul tried to convince her, "you need to make sure there's nothing you can think of that you haven't told us."

Tammy just sat sobbing as the phone rang on the desk. Paul picked it up as he watched her, "Yes?"

He listened for a couple of seconds and said, "We'll be right there, could you send Mark down?"

Replacing the phone, he said, "Ms. Terbush, we've got to leave for a few minutes. Is there anything you need?"

Tears running down her face, she softly answered, "Yes, I need to go home. Please let me go home. I just want to go home."

"Soon, very soon," Paul said as he rose from his chair. "We're almost finished. Mike, we're needed in General Brown's office."

They both took their hats and headed for the door as Tammy lay her head down on the table, sobbing. As they opened the door, Mark whispered to them and glanced inside at Tammy.

"Just let her relax," Paul said as he and Mike walked away. "We'll be back as soon as we can."

General Brown was waiting in his secretary's office as they walked in. "I think this package is for you, General Nelson," he said as he held out the envelope Butch had mailed the day before. "It's addressed to the General of the Project and was mailed by Butch North from Rhome, Texas. That's got to be you."

Mike took the envelope and stepped to the side while he opened it. A quick glance inside showed several filled baggies and a CD, as well as numerous photos. He stared at the images of Gene, Leslie, Butch, the baby, and Kevin as he pulled them out.

Quickly scanning the letter Butch had placed inside, he said, "General Modelle, we need to get back."

Slipping everything back into the envelope, he said, "Gary, I'm afraid our lunch will have to wait. Please have Lieutenant Colonel Mallory escort Ms. Terbush back to our facility."

Shaking his head slowly, Mike looked at Paul and continued, "Sir, we've got to get this back to my office immediately."

CHAPTER 33

Butch finished his hamburger and sat enjoying the strawberry malt while he watched the traffic on Loop 820. He hadn't seen any suspicious vehicles since he had first checked into his motel room. He didn't know exactly how many cars the people looking for him were using, but at least he thought he would recognize any of them.

Smiling to himself, he wondered why they thought they had to use those obvious black Suburbans. And why were they all dressed in dark suits that made them stand out just about anywhere they went? If they'd just use white pickups and dress in jeans and T-shirts, they could be just about anywhere and not be noticed.

Pulling the lid off of the malt, Butch tipped the glass up and waited for the last of the sweet red liquid to slide from the bottom into his mouth. As much as he enjoyed the huge meal and drink, his stomach told him that if he kept eating that way, he'd need to start buying bigger pants, especially if he sat around his room and couldn't get out to do any work for the next week or so.

After carrying his trash to the receptacle, he went out and climbed into the little white car. Now, he needed to make a call to a man that he had only met once several years ago. The then Senator had come to Laughlin Air Force Base, and Butch had been assigned to set up a tour for him and his entourage.

The tour included a flight in the T-38 with one of the young instructors flying them into the local training area and demonstrating the versatility of the aircraft. Before the visitors could climb into the supersonic airplane, they had to undergo demonstrations of the ejection seat, parachute, and G-suit (which helped counter the high G forces the maneuvers required) and be fitted with a flight suit, boots, gloves, and helmets.

Since Senator Larry Burklow and his people had arrived the day before the official tour began, Butch was tasked with arranging lodging, and meals and making sure all of the items required for the flight were the correct size and placed in each of the people's rooms. Additionally, he had custom name tags for all of them on their flight suits.

The Senator had proven to be a very nice man and appreciated everything that had been done to accommodate them. The morning before the flight, Butch sat with him at breakfast, and they had talked about growing up in Texas, the ranches their fathers had owned, and joked about Oklahoma and the other states. Butch hadn't been able to see him much after they had eaten since an instructor had been assigned to each of the men to get them ready for the flight.

Later in the afternoon, when the official tour was over, Butch had a chance to visit with him a little more at the Officer's Club during lunch. The Senator had given Butch a card and told him to give him a call if there was anything he could ever do to help him. Butch had thought that it was really a meaningless gesture and had just placed the card in with other memorabilia that he had accumulated.

Over the years he had spent in the Air Force, Butch had been given the opportunity to meet two Presidents, a Governor, and numerous other elected officials. He had found them to be generally pleasant and enjoyed talking to them. Their assistants were normally a different issue; they seemed to think they were of great importance and were often rude and overbearing.

Once whatever event that brought them together was over, Butch had usually never seen them again, except on the news. The only one he had talked to again had been the Senator from Texas. Butch had flown a General he worked for to a meeting at the Pentagon and stopped by the Senator's office while he waited for the General to finish his business.

Not really expecting to get an audience with the Senator, Butch had really just wanted to see the buildings and offices his tax dollars were buying. He had been talking to some assistant just outside of the office when the Senator stepped out. Surprised at seeing him, Butch had just said hello, not expecting the Senator to remember him.

The Senator looked at Butch in his flight suit and immediately remembered the trip to Laughlin. It may have just been the name tag that had Butch's name on it, but the Senator extended his hand and called him by name. As busy as the Senator must have been, he did take a couple of minutes to reminisce about the flight.

Now retired, the Senator had moved back to Ft Worth and rarely made the news except when he came out to support some issue or attend social functions. Butch just hoped he would be remembered and could have a chance to talk to him. The first step would be to call the number Butch assumed would be a clearing office for the people attempting to contact the Senator.

Leaving the What-A-Burger, Butch drove north on Loop 820 until he came to a convenience store that had a pay phone inside. He parked and walked in, keeping his head lowered to prevent the always-present camera from capturing his face. Needing change, he bought a Butterfinger and stepped to the phone.

As he waited for the call to be answered, Butch kept his back to the cashier and watched the large circular wide-view mirrors attached to the corners of the inside of the store. Finally, a voice answered and told Butch he had reached the public affairs office of Senator Burklow.

Unsure of his chances of success, Butch told the lady on the phone who he was and asked her if she would pass a message to the Senator. He tried to emphasize his previous contacts with the Senator and hoped he could at least get through on the phone or find where the Senator would be so that he could meet him.

After being assured that she would pass the message on, Butch had no choice except to give her a number where he could be reached. The only safe number he could give was the one in his room back at the motel. That meant he would have to sit around waiting, maybe for days. Having no choice, Butch gave her his room number and asked when he could expect a call.

The lady told him she would pass the information on right away, normally having an answer within a couple of hours. Thanking her, Butch hung up and went to the cooler for a couple of bottles of Dr. Pepper. Taking the drinks and a bag of Doritos from a rack of chips, he paid the bill and returned to his car.

When he got back to the motel, he picked up a newspaper that had been left in the lobby and climbed the stairs to his room. Once inside, he put the drinks in the mini-refrigerator and turned the TV on. Listening to the unbiased commentator from the Fox News station, he thumbed through the paper while waiting for the call he hoped would come soon.

Dozing in the chair, Butch was somewhat startled when the phone rang. Quickly clearing his head, he answered it and heard the lady from the Senator's office asking for him. Assuring her that he was speaking, she told him that the Senator had 15 minutes later that afternoon before he had a dinner engagement. He would be glad to meet him in the lobby of the restaurant if Butch could make it.

Surprised to hear that the restaurant was one of the best Mexican food places in Ft Worth, Butch told her he'd be there waiting. After thanking her and hanging up, Butch checked the clock beside the bed and saw that he had about three hours before he needed to leave.

He also knew that he needed to be dressed a little better than a T-shirt and baseball cap. The restaurant certainly had no dress codes, but meeting the Senator required more appropriate attire. If he expected the Senator to help him, Butch needed to be presentable and articulate in stating his request.

Butch figured it would take less than an hour to reach the restaurant in the traffic, and 30 minutes to shower and shave, giving him an hour and a half to figure out how to get the Senator's interest and not seem like some nut case with paranoia. The best he could hope for was that the Senator would have some interest in hearing his problem.

Even if Butch could convince the Senator that he had a real problem, he didn't know how much assistance the Senator could provide, and what Butch really needed was for the Senator to go with him to the base. Then the Senator could let the people from the facility know that unless they changed their methods of dealing with Gene, Leslie, BK, and Kevin, he would use all of his contacts still in Washington to bring unwanted attention to their operations.

Butch didn't know if the Senator was aware of the facility and its programs or not. If he wasn't aware, Butch didn't want to provide unnecessary information to him. But, if Senator Burklow was one of the people that were aware of the program, Butch certainly didn't want to be seen as a threat to it. He just wanted to show that there were other options, and he was willing to cooperate as necessary.

He finally decided that he would take the package of evidence with him and let the Senator know he had it and that it would be handed over to him if necessary. However, he had to make it clear to the Senator that if something wasn't done, other packages that had been mailed would be opened by the recipients as directed. And those directions would be followed on a certain day if Butch did not counter the instructions ahead of the designated date.

Now having a reasonable plan in mind, Butch took a nicely starched shirt and fresh pair of jeans from the closet. He planned on carrying the shirt to the car and putting it on over the T-shirt so that he kept his 'incognito' appearance as he went through the lobby. Now, it was time for a shower.

CHAPTER 34

After about two miles of driving west on US 90 heading toward Del Rio, Sancudo made a left turn onto Farm Road 693. From the back seat, Gene sat forward and watched the narrow road winding through the mesquite and sagebrush that covered the countryside.

"Does the other driver know where to turn?" Gene asked.

"He knows," Sancudo replied. "He knows not to follow us down this road."

"What do you mean? Isn't he following us?" Leslie asked.

"No, he is not," Sancudo told her. "It became necessary for us to take different routes."

"Why?" Gene asked. "I thought you said the Border Patrol had gone up to Del Rio. Are you sending Kevin up there?"

Mel turned to look directly at Gene and replied, "First, I told you not to question my decisions. Second, I told you that my job is taking care of you, not Kevin."

"And finally," he said as he turned back to watch the road, "I will tell you for the last time, sit back and keep your mouth shut. The Border Patrol is not stupid enough to send everybody up there. There are still many of them in this area."

Gene sat back and looked at Leslie with worry in his eyes. Even though Mel had seemed to be taking them toward Mexico, he had always known that Kevin was right behind them. Now, it seemed that they were going to be separated, and he didn't know when or if they would ever see him again.

Leslie leaned over and put her hand on his arm, trying to comfort him. Although she was just as worried as he, she realized that with no money and no friends down here, Mel was their only hope. She whispered in his ear and reminded him that they were still safe and that she was sure Kevin would be with them soon.

Gene finally settled down and picked up BK. Watching the baby wrap his little hands around his fingers brought a slight smile to his face. He turned to Leslie and said, "All right, I'll try to understand. I've just never been without either Butch or Kevin telling me what to do. I'm not sure I can take care of you and BK on my own if something were to happen."

Leslie squeezed his arm and said, "You're not on your own, I'm here and so is your son. I know we'll be just fine, even if it's just us."

The sedan with Kevin had gone south from Brackettville and had stopped in Spofford for the 'repairs'. Now continuing south on State Road 131, Kevin was unaware that Mel had taken another route and was planning on crossing at a different location. Since Mel had told them that many of the Border Patrol agents were being sent to Del Rio, he assumed that they were going to cross somewhere south of there.

He knew that the Texas/Mexico border was thousands of miles long from El Paso down to Brownsville, and that there weren't too many 'official' crossings. He also knew that hundreds of people crossed illegally every day along the sparsely populated areas that stretched along the border.

There were several sections of the Rio Grande where you could easily walk or drive across. Before Texas became a state, people had flowed back and forth bringing cattle or horses they had bought or stolen. It wasn't uncommon for people from both sides to raid their neighbors across the river and steal their livestock. Although the Rio Grande River was a natural boundary, it by no means was a deterrent to anyone wanting to be on the other side or take something from there.

The problem down here now wasn't so much the ones that just wanted to come into the states for work, it was the smuggling of drugs or trafficking in humans. Those people were well armed and very dangerous. Kevin just hoped that Sancudo knew the areas to avoid and wasn't involved with those individuals.

He had heard that some people paid as much as $10,000 to be carried across and taken almost anywhere in the United States. With so much money at stake, it was no wonder that the border land had become almost a battlefield between the law and the lawless. And then, competition for the illegal trade resulted in turf wars that were even more dangerous than encounters with law enforcement on either side.

About ten minutes later, Kevin felt the car slow and pull to the side of the road. When it stopped, he heard a voice ask, "Senor, can you hear me?"

Not sure if anyone was talking to him, Kevin kept quiet and waited. Again, the question was asked, "Senor, in the trunk, can you hear me?"

"Yes," Kevin answered. "I can hear you."

"Fine," came the reply. "We will be crossing the border in about 15 minutes. I will have to stop at the toll bridge on the Mexico side and pay. There should be no other stops. If there seems to be trouble ahead, I will tap the brakes hard two or three times and then stop."

"Then, if you hear me open my door, you need to get out of the trunk as quietly and as fast as you can. I will be far enough away from the problem for you to sneak away from the car. Do you understand?"

"Yes," Kevin answered.

"Quemado will be about 15 miles north on 277 and you must do as Sancudo directed at that point. Now, just stay quiet and hope that the people on the Piedras Negras side have been taken care of and there are no problems until we get there."

Without waiting for a reply, the car accelerated back onto the road and made a left turn about two minutes later. Kevin realized that they were very close to the border and he hoped there would be no more stops until he felt the distinctive rumble of the bridge as they crossed. Making sure he had the tire wrench beside him, he tried to remain absolutely still and quiet.

Only about 20 miles further north, Mel had made a left turn onto 277 and headed south toward Quemado. As they drove along the road paralleling the Rio Grande, Gene and Leslie could see where the river ran because of the trees and shrubs that grew along its banks. The rest of the country was barren and dry with very little vegetation.

Mel was busy plugging his CB radio in and watching the road. Finally, he checked the frequency and picked up the microphone. Saying just one word, he waited for a reply. Hearing nothing after waiting for a minute or so, he rechecked the frequency and tried to make contact again. This time, he was answered and seemed pleased with the response.

Unplugging the CB and returning it to beneath the seat, Mel turned to Gene and Leslie saying, "We have been blessed, my children. It seems that there are no Border Patrol agents within ten miles of the town."

Smiling at them in the mirror as he looked back at the road, he said, "In about five minutes, you should be in Mexico. But you must now make sure your faces are hidden and the baby is covered."

Gene adjusted his wig slightly and pulled the brim of his hat lower and looked at Leslie for her approval. She checked his appearance and nodded that it was all right. Leslie then picked up BK and made sure the blanket completely covered him.

As she was doing that, Gene pulled her scarf slightly forward and rubbed his fingers across the tan polish that darkened her appearance. Mel had been watching as they tried to make themselves look as Hispanic as possible and nodded his head.

"You two look like returning workers," he told them. "Even though I don't expect any problems on this side, I would like to get several miles into Mexico before we relax."

Shortly he slowed and checked both directions of the road before he made a right turn onto an almost unnoticeable trail that led toward the river. A small town was still a mile or so further south and there were no other vehicles or people visible anywhere.

The trail led through increasingly taller grass and shrubs until they could see the shimmering water running across a bed of rock and gravel. Just before they reached the edge, they saw a man wearing a blue checkered shirt leaning against a small tree holding an old bicycle at his side. Mel looked at him and nodded as they entered the water.

Twenty miles further south Kevin felt the car slow, making several turns and stops. Thinking that they were probably in Eagle Pass, he hoped that they would be crossing the border within the next 15 minutes or so. Although he had somewhat gotten used to the smell of the diapers and trash, the fumes from the paint had given him a massive headache.

A few minutes later, he felt the car almost stop and then inch its way forward. This continued as he heard cars passing going the opposite direction. Assuming that they were almost to the bridge, he knew that one of the most dangerous parts of their journey was about to take place. Although initially he had little trust in either Sancudo or this driver, he knew that if the police on either side of the border discovered him, things would be very difficult for him.

There was nothing he could do now but wait, and worry about Gene, Leslie, and BK. He recalled the number of times he had needed to sit absolutely quiet in some insect infested jungle in Vietnam waiting for a certain person to either arrive or go to sleep. Even knowing that discovery back then would have probably meant torture and death, it was better than being trapped in this smelly trunk with little chance of escape once they were on the bridge.

CHAPTER 35

Mike carried the envelope as he led Paul back to the car. Handing it to Paul as he started the engine, he backed from the parking space. Paul opened the envelope and glanced inside. Taking out the letter, he scanned it and then looked at the photos.

"I think we have a problem here," Paul said as he replaced everything. "I think we have a very real problem."

Mike nodded as he hurried back across the base to their facility. "No shit," he said. "This is about as bad as it can get, if what's in those baggies is what Mr. North says."

"That won't take long to verify," Paul said as they parked inside the hanger above their facilities.

Passing through the security check point, Mike told the guard to have Lieutenant Colonel Mallory come to the conference room as soon as he finished locking Tammy back in her room.

Neither man spoke as they rode the elevator down to the first floor. With Mike leading the way, they went straight to his office and he told Kathy to call Colonel Erickson. Paul sat in front of Mike's desk, placing the envelope on top of it.

Mike took his seat and looked at Paul as he stared at the envelope. "What do you think of what Butch says about other packages?"

"I sincerely hope he's bluffing," Paul answered. "But I don't think he is. We really need to talk to that man."

Rick knocked on the door and said, "General Nelson, you asked for me?"

"Come in Rick," Mike said. "I need for you to get everyone into the conference room as quickly as you can. Paul and I will be there in a couple of minutes."

"Yes, sir," Rick acknowledged as he turned and left.

"Do you need to call Washington?" Mike asked Paul as they both continued looking at the envelope they wished would disappear.

"Yes," Paul said. "But I'll wait until we verify the contents of the package. Maybe we can even have some suggestions as to how we plan to proceed. Let's go on down to the conference room and try to sort this out."

Mike stood and waited for Paul to pick up the damning envelope. As he followed Paul through Kathy's office, Mike told her to call General Brown and cancel their lunch and hold any calls unless they were from Washington.

Walking into the conference room, Paul laid the envelope on the table and took his seat at the end. Mike sat to his right and leaned forward with his arms resting on the table.

"Unbelievable," Paul said. "Yesterday we think that Gene is the father of a child. This morning we confirm it. Now we learn that all of our attempts to keep his identity a secret have been in vain."

"Let me see that letter again, please," Mike asked reaching out his hand.

Paul pulled it from the envelope and handed it to him. "How do we verify that he actually took the photos? And, can we determine where they were taken?"

Mike held the letter and sat back in his chair. "I don't know, sir. Maybe Rick or Karyn will have an idea."

As Mike was reading, Rick came in with Amy and said, "The rest of the team will be here in about five minutes. Did you learn anything from Ms. Terbush?"

"No," Mike answered tersely. "But we've learned something from Mr. North."

Surprised, Rick asked, "How did you manage that?"

"We didn't manage anything," Paul said. "Mr. North managed it. I think that man has been managing just about everything since he became involved."

Mark Mallory stepped into the room and asked, "Did you want to see me, sir?"

"Yes, I did," Mike told him. "Did you get Ms. Terbush back to her quarters?"

"Yes, sir," Mark answered. "And she still wants to know when she can go home."

"Probably very soon," Mike said. "Please have a seat while we wait for the rest of the people to get here."

Mike finished reading the letter and handed it to Rick saying, "Take a quick look at this. I think you'll understand what I meant about 'managing'."

Rick remained standing as he read the letter as Amy waited knowing she would have a chance to see it as soon as he was finished. Both Karyn and Jerry came in as Rick looked up and silently passed the letter to Amy.

"Everyone, please have a seat," Mike said. "I'm afraid we have some very bad news."

As the rest of the team began to take their seats, Mike continued, "We've just heard from Mr. North. It appears that he has been in contact with Gene, Leslie, their child, and Mr. Knox."

He waited for them to consider the implications of what he had just said. "Now, we need to verify the contents of the envelope Mr. North mailed yesterday, but I have no doubts about the authenticity of them," Mike finished.

Mike took the envelope and removed its contents and spread them across the table in front of him. He sorted the photos into one stack and passed the large baggie to Colonel Moore.

"Amy, you need to get your folks to run an analysis on everything in these bags as soon as you can," Mike told her.

Mike passed the CD to Jerry and told him, "Major Fleenor, this needs to be run on your computer and see exactly what's on it. Also, find out where it was processed."

"Colonel Erickson," he continued. "I want these photos analyzed to see if we can determine where they were taken as well as where they were copied."

"Karyn," he finished, "I want you to send your teams up to Rhome and see if they can find anything at the Post Office that might give us a clue about how he's moving around the country."

Paul looked around the table and told them, "This is potentially a disaster for all of us. We don't know exactly what Mr. North has in mind, but for now we need to make damn sure everything he sent is authentic."

Looking at Colonel Moore, Paul told her, "Amy, get me your results as quickly as possible. Make sure you compare everything with what we have from the clinic. I don't need iron clad proof right now, but I do need your professional opinion. Basically, are the samples from Gene, Leslie, and the baby?"

"Yes, sir," Amy said as she handed the letter back to Rick and gathered the baggies. "I'll have an answer in about half an hour that will confirm any genetic matches."

As she was leaving, Mike looked at Paul and asked, "Do you think we need to keep Ms. Terbush any longer?"

Paul thought about it and said, "No, unless anyone here thinks she's withholding anything."

Mike looked around the table and as everyone shook their heads, he said, "Mark, please have someone from the FBI take Ms. Terbush home as soon as you can arrange it. But, advise her to be prepared to return if we determine it's necessary."

"Yes, sir," Mark said standing. "Will there be anything else?"

"No, I don't think so," Mike answered as Mark left. "Just thank her for her cooperation and apologize for any inconvenience we may have caused her."

Mike took the letter from Rick handing it and the envelope to Colonel Lynch saying, "Take a look at this and you'll understand more of our difficulties. When your teams reach Rhome, they can narrow their search to the time frame based on the date and time stamp on the envelope."

"While they are up there," he continued, "have them stop by the bank where Butch withdrew the money and see if anyone there has seen him since yesterday."

"Rick," Mike said, "I want you and Jerry to get busy on those photos. If Colonel Moore confirms what we suspect, the only possible clue as to where they are, or where they were, is in those photos."

Both Rick and Jerry stood holding the material they had been given. "I'll get these pictures scanned and sent to the photo intelligence division in Washington immediately," Rick said as he turned to leave. "Major Fleenor can check the disk, and if it's the same photos, he can send the contents electronically."

"Fine," Mike told them. "General Modelle and I will be down there in a few minutes. Let's just hope there's a clue on one of those pictures."

"What do you think now?" Mike asked Paul as Rick and Jerry left.

"I think that Mr. North has us by the short hairs," Paul said, leaning back. "I'd like to know just exactly to whom he has mailed those other envelopes. Without direct communication with him, I can think of no way to find out."

"Maybe the Rhome Post Office can give us an answer," Mike said hopefully. "Maybe there are cameras that can give us a view of the addresses, or maybe they have some record of where they were sent."

"I think that if they were sent as either registered or certified," Paul said, "there'd be a record. But, if it's just plain mail as ours was, a camera is going to be our only hope. And it has to be at just the right angle to see anything."

"What do you think Mr. North is trying to do?" Mike asked.

"I think he's telling us that he knows, or at least suspects, who Gene really is," Paul said. "And more importantly, I think he's telling us that without his cooperation, we've got no chance of finding any of them."

"What's the next step?" Mike asked as he stood.

Paul slowly got out of his chair and replied, "Get the verification and wait for Mr. North to make his move. I doubt very seriously that he'll wait too long. And, given his past record, I doubt if we'll find any clues in the pictures. He's been too careful so far. I just don't see him making any mistakes."

Mike followed Paul out of the room and agreed, "I think we've grossly underestimated that man. Maybe Jerry was right. Maybe we should have been a little more direct when we talked to him and his daughters last year." "Well," Paul said as they headed down the hall, "we may get a second chance if he's willing to give it to us."

CHAPTER 36

Butch stepped from the shower and checked the clock. Although he knew he had plenty of time, the habit of making sure he was never late had been instilled when he was in the Air Force. Back then, if a briefing was scheduled for eight o'clock, that meant the doors were locked at eight o'clock. If you were one minute late, you missed the briefing and, therefore, the flight.

Even with the airlines, if you missed the sign-in time, you could be removed from the flight. They were a little more lenient, but unless you called the scheduler and told him you were running late and assured him you would make the flight, you were removed. Since your pay depended on each flight, it could cost you a lot of money. Repeated offenses would cost you your job.

After drying and shaving, Butch pulled on a clean pair of well-starched jeans and a fresh T-shirt. Using the soiled towel, he wiped the dust from his boots and tried to make them shine a little brighter. At least he hadn't been wearing his old work boots that would take more than a wiping to make them presentable.

After a final glance in the mirror, Butch took the clean shirt from its hanger and picked up his baseball cap and sunglasses from the desk. With the cap and sunglasses on, he opened the door and checked the hall, hoping that it would be empty. Although he thought he wouldn't be recognized, he didn't want to press his luck.

The self-locking door snapped shut, and he headed for the stairs, keeping his gaze lowered so that the bill of his cap covered most of his face unless you were much shorter and looking up at him. He wished he knew which rooms the people from the base were using, but finding out that information wasn't worth the risk.

Having encountered no one in the hall, he took the stairs down to the lobby and surveyed it before opening the door. Seeing nobody sitting around or at the counter, he headed for the front doors and left without being noticed. Outside, there were no cars moving, and he went straight to his rental and climbed in.

After laying the shirt on the front seat, Butch reached under the seat and pulled the envelope he had kept beneath it. Although he really didn't want to give it to Senator Burklow, he checked the contents to make sure everything was there if it became necessary. Satisfied that each of the items was still inside, he slid it back beneath the seat and started the car.

Exiting the parking lot, Butch drove south to the intersection of Loop 820 and I-30. Heading east on I-30, the traffic was fairly light, and he made it to Highway 183 with no delays. Driving north on 183, he knew he would again be passing very close to the south entrance to the NAS/JRB. There were other routes he could have taken that would have kept him further away, but the chances of being spotted among the other cars seemed to be very slim, and he hadn't allowed time for any other route.

About 15 minutes later, Butch turned south on Main Street and drove toward the Stockyard area. The road passed through the main tourist attraction part of Ft Worth as it crossed Exchange Avenue. He had spent many hours at the saloons and dance halls there over the years, and his first memory of the area was when his father had taken him to the Cattleman's Steak House. The pictures of many previous years' Grand Champion Bulls on the walls had fascinated him, and he still looked at them when dining there.

There weren't too many tourists walking the street as he drove across the old brick surface of Exchange Avenue. On weekends, the streets could be packed as they shopped for something 'authentic' to take back to wherever they had come from. Butch usually enjoyed the area, but it had gotten too crowded lately. He especially disliked seeing people trying to dress Western when they didn't even know the front of their hats from the rear.

A couple of blocks past Exchange, Butch turned left on North Commerce and headed for Joe T Garcia's Mexican Restaurant. He had eaten there several times and especially liked their fajitas and margaritas. But today would not be the day to drink many of them. Pulling into an empty slot toward the rear of the parking lot, he checked the clock on the dash of the car.

He still had about 15 minutes before the Senator was due to arrive, but he certainly didn't want to take a chance on him being early and already seated. Butch removed his cap and glasses, pulled the T-shirt off over his head, and put the clean shirt on. Sliding down and forward in the seat, he unfastened his belt and pants so he could get the shirttail stuffed in.

After locking the car, Butch walked to the entrance and stepped inside. The aroma of the cooking food made him wish he hadn't eaten so much earlier. Glancing around the restaurant, he walked to the bar where he would have a view of anyone coming in. As he took a seat, he asked the bartender for a bottle of Negro Modello and some chips with their special salsa.

Butch wasn't sure if the Senator was going to be seated in the main dining room or one of the private areas. Taking his beer, he went back to the entrance and asked the lady standing by the door if Senator Burklow had made reservations for a table or a room. Hearing that he had reserved a private room for 10, Butch thanked her and returned to the bar.

The restaurant was slowly filling up, and several new patrons were sitting at the bar while waiting for their tables or for other members of their party to arrive. Butch quietly watched as each person came and went looking for the telltale marks of the government people. So far, everyone had looked like locals or one of the tourists that had been told about the food.

He had almost finished his beer when he saw Senator Burklow enter with several people. Leaving the bottle on the bar, Butch waited until the group was about to be escorted to their tables. Just as the young lady with an armload of menus asked them to follow her, he walked up to the Senator.

"Good evening, Senator," Butch said as he approached. "I hope you remember me."

Senator Burklow stuck his hand out and said, "Of course I do, Butch. It's good to see you again."

Butch shook his hand and replied, "You have an outstanding memory, sir. It's been a few years, and although you haven't changed, I've lost a little hair and wrinkled around the edges somewhat."

Senator Burklow laughed and told him, "To be honest, I had my secretary do a little research. She's the one that keeps my memory working. I do remember the flight in that T-38, though; that was something pretty special. Now, what can I do for you?"

"Sir, if there's somewhere private, I need to explain a problem I'm having with a government program," Butch answered.

"Sure," the Senator said. "Why don't we step outside for a couple of minutes?"

He turned to his aide and told him to take the rest of the group and go on in. Turning back to Butch, he said, "What program are you talking about?"

Stepping out into the warm air, Butch looked around to make sure they weren't being overheard and told him, "I have proof of a project that has been taking place at the NAS/JRB involving genetic research."

"And how is that causing you a problem?" the Senator asked.

"I happened to become aware of their program last year when I picked up a young man that I thought was one of the many Mexican day workers from around the area," Butch explained.

"I took him to my stables that morning to help while my normal man was on a couple days of vacation," he continued. "I'm sure you remember the day, September 11, 2001."

"Of course," the Senator answered. "But what does that have to do with this program or the young man you picked up?"

"Well," Butch answered, "I didn't think much about this kid; he just seemed to be an average guy looking for work. It wasn't until the next day when I saw a news bulletin showing the very same man as one of the terrorists involved in the attacks."

"Then, that morning," he continued, "I was at home with my kids when a man came up telling me that he was with the FBI. He asked about the man I had hired, saying that they were looking for him."

"I explained that Gene, the young man I'd hired, was at the stables," Butch said. "Then he took me and my kids over there and we looked for Gene, but he wasn't there."

"I also need to tell you that there were several vehicles, along with the one I and my kids were in, as well as a helicopter. When we couldn't find Gene, we were flown down to the base and questioned by someone there."

"Now, a couple of strange things happened while this was taking place. First, the people who had come to find Gene weren't what I'd consider to be the type of force that meant to arrest a dangerous terrorist. There were no usual law enforcement officers from the state, county, or other normally marked vehicles."

"Second, the officer that seemed to be in control was an Air Force nurse, not a security person."

"That does sound strange," the Senator said. "I do remember seeing the news about how a group was supposed to attempt to hijack an aircraft at the DFW airport. And how one of them was denied entrance or something, and that prevented them from accomplishing their plan."

"Yes, sir," Butch replied. "Well, the pictures I saw that morning were definitely Gene. However, the news showed him dressed as a Middle Easterner with a beard and other things that made him appear just like the ones from the other hijackings."

"Then," he continued, "they showed him as he really looked when I found him. But I'm sure the photos were doctored to portray him as one of the terrorists, not as he really was. To start with, I don't think the boy could grow a beard if he had to. And, his English was as good as mine with no noticeable accent."

"But the interview at the base was what really made me believe that the government was hiding something," Butch said emphatically. "There was an Air Force General and a Colonel monitoring our interview. After I had explained everything we had done with Gene, where we had gone, and who we had met, my daughters and I were taken back home."

"Did either of the officers talk to you?" the Senator asked.

"No, sir," Butch answered. "They just listened. But, after we were taken home, I went over to the stables to feed the horses. That's when I found Gene hiding behind some bales of hay."

"Did you notify anyone of this?" Senator Burklow asked.

"No, sir," Butch replied. "I did lock him in the cage where the hay was stored and told him to explain who he was and where he was from. That's when I determined that he was from the base and part of some secret program."

"What exactly did he tell you?" the Senator asked.

"That he had spent his entire life in some underground facility," Butch answered. "The only time he was out of it was to be flown somewhere to look at machinery or other things and questioned about their uses."

"From that day on, I've been followed, my phones have been tapped, and my every move has been monitored," Butch emphasized.

"Where is this Gene now?" Senator Burklow asked.

"I really don't know," Butch answered. "I initially had him hidden by a friend of mine while I tried to figure out exactly what to do."

"Then, I found out that Gene had met a girl the night we went out," Butch said. "And I had my friend get her since I believed that the government would also try to find her. It turned out that she and Gene had engaged in a little, shall we say, pre-marital activities?"

"You're telling me that this lady and the supposed terrorist had a sexual relationship?" the Senator asked.

"Yes, sir," Butch said, "and with the not unexpected result. As a matter of fact, the lady had Gene's child yesterday. And, the government found out."

"I suppose you managed to get them all hidden again," Senator Burklow said.

"Yes, sir, I did. Now, I also need to tell you that there is someone within their organization that gave me a call warning me of their discovery," Butch admitted.

"I had previously met him in Decatur at David's Western Wear, and he gave me a phone to use if he ever needed to tell me anything," Butch continued.

"Who was this man?" the Senator asked.

"I don't know his name," Butch answered. "I really can't prove he's from the facility. But he certainly knew what they were doing. If it hadn't been for him, Gene, Leslie, their baby, my friend Kevin, and I would have been taken in by now."

"Just what do you suspect is happening at the base that would make this such an unusual program? You and I both know that military or governmental programs require varying levels of secrecy," Senator Burklow told him.

"Yes, sir," Butch said. "And I'm fully aware of the need for it. But, in this case, I truly think the research at that facility involves genetic material that has been combined with human material."

"Are you implying that we, the United States of America, are doing unlawful genetic research on humans?" the Senator asked incredulously.

"Yes, sir," Butch answered. "I have samples taken from Gene, Leslie, and the baby that I can provide if necessary. I also had a DNA analysis of Gene's blood done last year that showed some very abnormal things."

Senator Burklow paused, thinking for a moment, and then said, "All right, what do you want me to do?"

"All I want is for you to accompany me to the base," Butch told him. "I plan on meeting with the General I saw at my interview and see if we can't come to some solution to our problem."

"When do you want to do this?" Senator Burklow asked. "I would very much like to know what is going on over there. If we are involved in illegal research, I want to know about it."

"I'd like to meet with them as soon as possible," Butch explained. "Although I don't know exactly where Gene and the rest of them are at the moment, I would like to get them back here as quickly as we can. One of my main considerations is the child. Having seen him, I can tell you that he will need medical attention. Maybe not for his immediate health, but I think some major cosmetic work will need to be done if he's to live a normal life."

Senator Burklow checked his watch and said, "All right, you've got my attention. I need to get inside and join my group, but I'll have my secretary give you a call to set up an appointment in the next day or two."

"Sir," Butch asked, "I'd rather call your office if you don't mind. I'm not exactly sure where I'll be. Would it be okay if I just call the same number I used this afternoon?"

Senator Burklow put his hand out and said, "That'll be fine, Butch. Call tomorrow morning, and you'll get an answer. Is there anything else?"

"No, sir," Butch answered. "But if you don't hear from me by noon tomorrow, would you please contact the Base Commander over there and let him know you're looking for me?"

Laughing, the Senator said, "Sure, I'll check to make sure they haven't kidnapped you. I really don't think they'd want any of your genes. One of you is certainly more than enough. Take care."

Butch headed for his car as he watched the Senator go into the restaurant. Now, to stay hidden for another day or so, and maybe this nightmare would be over soon, he hoped. It's time for life to get back to its normal boring routine. And time to be with Tammy.

Butch started his car and headed back to his room. Feeling some relief about the situation, he stopped at the first liquor store he came to and bought a six-pack of Coke and a large bottle of Jack Daniel's. *"Might as well relax and watch some reruns of Gunsmoke,"* he thought as he continued to the motel.

CHAPTER 37

The Bronco splashed its way across the shallow water of the Rio Grande and entered Mexico. The trail through the brush and shrubs beside the river continued up a gradual slope until it topped the ridge. Gene and Leslie had sat quietly, holding their breath, as they crossed the border. Now, as Mel looked at them in the mirror and smiled, they relaxed.

"Welcome to Mexico," Mel told them. "Now we have only a few more miles until most of the danger is behind us."

"However," he continued as he came to a paved road that paralleled the river, "I would not assume that we are completely free. There are still many '*Policia*' on this side that may know of your problems."

"That is not necessarily our worst worry," Sancudo finished. "There are many of those who would stop any 'Norte Americano' and try to get any money they are carrying. So, keep your disguises as they are until I tell you it is safe."

"Where is Kevin?" Gene asked as he scratched his head beneath the wig.

"I do not know," Mel answered. "He may be on this side of the border; he may not."

"When will we know?" Leslie asked as she pulled the blanket from BK's face and looked into his dark eyes.

"Maybe an hour, maybe a day," Sancudo told her. "Maybe never; I do not know right now."

"Why would you say we may never see him again?" Gene demanded, leaning forward.

Mel shrugged his shoulders and replied, "Maybe he was stopped at the border and taken. Maybe he got nervous and tried to get away. Maybe one of the many groups that prowl the borders looking for easy money found him. I am telling you that for right now, I do not know where he is or when he may get to us."

"Can't you do something to help him?" Leslie asked as she noticed that BK's diaper needed changing.

"No, I can do nothing right now," Mel said, wrinkling his nose. "But you can do something."

"What?" Gene asked quickly.

"You can open your windows and let some of the smell out," Sancudo said. "From here on, if someone stops us, the odor will not prevent them from looking into the car."

Gene rolled his window down and leaned across to roll Leslie's down. As he looked out of the window, he noticed a road sign showing that they were on Mexico Highway 2, and Piedras Negras was only about 15 miles away.

"Can we stop when we get to the next town?" Gene asked as he sat back in his seat. "I would like to get Leslie and me something to drink."

"No, we will not stop," Sancudo replied. "The next town is on the border, and we can't take a chance being seen there. Maybe in an hour or so."

In the trunk of the sedan, Kevin was still trying to make no noise as he felt the car inching forward. Now, the fumes of the exhaust were mixing with that of the paint and the odors from the trash bag. Slowly pulling one of their old shirts from the bag beneath his head, he tried to use it as a filter to minimize the pungent air.

Finally, after what seemed an eternity, he felt the car stop and heard the driver talking. He couldn't understand what was being said but knew that they must have finally reached the toll booth on the Mexico side of the border. He wasn't sure exactly where they were, but he had been told that it was south of the place he was supposed to find if things got out of hand. The only place he could think of that had an official crossing in this area was Eagle Pass.

Hearing the driver thank someone, Kevin felt the car begin to move again. Still not positive they had cleared the checkpoint into Mexico, he moved his legs slowly beneath the smelly tarp that covered him. His legs and back were beginning to cramp, and the hard floor of the trunk was becoming unbearable.

Traffic was now moving faster and Kevin hoped that very soon they would stop and he could get out of the trunk. If they were now in Mexico, he thought that the next stop wouldn't be because of some danger to them. As the car continued to accelerate, he took a chance and changed positions to provide some relief to his aching body.

For the next few minutes, he continued to feel the car slow, stop, or turn as it wound its way through the traffic. Finally, he knew they had left the busy road and had turned into a less congested area. As the car slowed and turned onto a gravel road, he felt it come to a stop. Hearing the front door open but the motor still running, Kevin waited anxiously for some clue as to what was happening.

The trunk opened, and he heard a voice quietly whisper, "Stay quiet; we are not clear yet." Then he felt the tarp lift down by his feet and the trash bag being pulled from the trunk. As the trunk slammed closed, he realized that the driver was trying to make his ride a little more comfortable.

Without the smelly bag and the brief time of fresh air coming in when the trunk opened, Kevin felt much better. It wasn't just the physical change; the small gesture had shown him that maybe Butch had been correct. He was being taken care of by professionals. Now, his main worry returned to where Gene, Leslie, and BK were and if they had made it over the border safely.

Mel drove into Piedras Negras as Gene and Leslie quietly watched the scenery pass. This side of the border did not appear to be any different than the other side. Although the signs were in Spanish, Leslie could read most of them and told Gene that they were in Coahuila.

"I thought we were in Mexico," Gene said when she told him.

"We are," she answered. "Coahuila is a state, like Texas is a state."

"Oh," he replied. "I didn't know they had states."

"What did you think they had?" Mel asked from the front.

"I don't know," Gene admitted. "I guess I never thought about it. It's just Mexico."

"That is the problem with you gringos," Sancudo chastised him. "You only think of Mexico as one of the border towns. A place to come and party while you toss money around like you were the emperor. Mexico has been around longer than the United States and its history is tied to Texas closer than Texas is to the rest of your states."

"I didn't mean to say anything bad," Gene apologized. "I just didn't know."

"Maybe you will know a little more before you leave," Mel told him. "Mexico isn't just some place for you to hide or celebrate. My family has lived around here for generations. We have as much love of our country as you do yours."

"I'm sorry if I offended you," Gene said. "I guess it's that I finally know how it feels to belong to something, whether it's a country or a family."

He looked at Leslie and continued, "Until just a few months ago, I never realized what that meant."

"What do you mean?" Mel asked suspiciously as he approached an intersection where Mexico 57 headed southwest.

"He just means that he's never had a chance to be around people that identify with a particular place, like Texas," Leslie answered as she frowned at Gene. "Unless you're from Texas, you just don't understand the pride we take in our heritage."

"Oh, but I do," Mel told her as they passed a sign showing that Morelos was about 40 miles down the road. "I am fortunate to have ties to Texas and Mexico, and I am proud to be both a Texan and a Mexican."

"As a matter of fact," he continued, "I think my grandmother was the first person to make Tex-Mex food."

"You're joking," Leslie said.

"Oh, no," Mel laughed. "No more than when your friend Butch North says the entire continent of North America was named after his grandfather."

It was obvious to Gene and Leslie that Mel had finally relaxed since they were now miles from the border. Each mile they traveled seemed to bring out more of the personality they had seen back in Stephenville when they had first met.

"We will stop in Morelos," Mel told them. "I have made arrangements for us to get some supplies at the home of a friend. And I hope you will get rid of that smelly bunch of diapers! And you may use the restroom if you need to."

"Can't we go to a store?" Gene asked.

"No, that would not be wise," Mel answered. "We can't risk having any of you seen. One wrong person knowing that you are here can destroy all of the plans I have made."

Mel made a right turn onto a narrow paved road following the sign showing Morelos was just ahead. "Maybe we will have some news on Kevin when we arrive."

Kevin could tell from the smoothness of the road and the sound of the tires on the pavement that they were on a major road again. Taking a chance, he pulled the tarp from his face and took a deep breath of air that hadn't been saturated with paint fumes. Even though they were moving much faster, he had no clue as to when they would stop, and he could climb out of the trunk and stretch. Each minute that passed made him relax and look forward to seeing Gene and Leslie.

Almost half an hour passed when the car slowed and made a right turn. The crunch of gravel was distinct beneath the wheels as Kevin felt them leave the paved road they had been on for the last hour or so. Finally coming to a stop, he heard the driver kill the engine and open his door. As the footsteps approached the rear of the car, he slowly pulled the tarp back over his face.

As the trunk opened and fresh air rushed in, Kevin heard the driver say, "Senor, you may come out now. Unless you are enjoying lying around in that smelly mess."

Kevin felt the tarp being pulled off of him and looked up to see the same gold tooth and ponytail framed in the bright light, causing him to squint. As the driver stepped back, Kevin's eyes adjusted to the light, and he could see Mel's Bronco parked in front of a small adobe building.

He climbed out of the trunk and stretched, asking, "Is that Sancudo's car?"

"Yes, it is," the driver replied. "I think he is inside. Shall we go in?"

The driver walked across the barren yard as Kevin followed him, wondering if he would find Gene and Leslie inside. As Kevin looked around, he could see no other buildings close by. Again, a small spark of fear surfaced in his mind. Here he was, far from home, with no clue as to where. And the remoteness of the house made it a perfect place for just about anything.

Kevin followed the driver into the semi-darkness of the house and looked around. Suddenly, he heard a voice from a corner of the room, "Kevin, I'm so glad to see you!"

Turning his head, Kevin saw Gene come running toward him. Acting completely nonchalant, Kevin said, "Well, little man. Looks like you made it here in one piece. Where's the little lady? And where's my godson?"

CHAPTER 38

Paul and Mike walked into the operations room as Rick was scanning the last photo into his computer. "Well," Rick said as he looked up, "I guess it's up to the photo intelligence folks now to do their magic."

Jerry had been taking each picture Rick had scanned and comparing it to those from the disk. "There are a couple of photos here that weren't made into copies," he said as he looked at the last one Rick handed him.

"I've already sent the contents of the disc to Washington," he continued. "They should have a preliminary report within an hour or so."

"Colonel Lynch, have you sent a team to Rhome?" Mike asked.

"Yes, sir," Karyn answered. "They should be arriving at the Post Office within 30 minutes to see if there's a camera in the area that may have gotten a picture of Mr. North's addressees or of the vehicle he was driving."

"Then," she continued, "they will go to the Woodhaven National Bank and see what they can find out about his withdrawal."

"Make sure they check on any cameras at the bank as well," Rick said. "I know they have them all over the area."

"That's correct," Mike agreed. "Just make sure they look at the ones in the drive-up areas. They may have a picture of his vehicle."

"I'll call them right away and take care of it," Karyn said as she picked up her microphone.

Colonel Amy Moore came in carrying a folder and announced, "It all matches; there's no doubt that the samples came from Gene, Leslie, and their child."

"Are you absolutely positive?" Paul asked as he took the folder from her hands.

"I'm positive," Amy said. "I don't know how he did it without contaminating any of the samples, but it's as good as I've seen from our own field investigators."

Paul scanned the results and could easily see that the analysis of the material Butch had sent matched exactly the ones from the samples they had collected at the clinic in Ringgold.

Paul handed Mike the folder and said, "Well, I guess I'd better call my boss. He's not going to be very happy about this."

Dreading the answer, he asked, "What's our plan at this point?"

Mike and Rick looked at each other, and finally, Mike answered, "Unless we get something from the folks at Rhome, we have to depend on someone spotting one of them from the pictures we sent."

"Colonel Lynch sent the information yesterday," Rick explained. "Every branch of any law enforcement organization has the latest photos, which include Mr. Kevin Knox and Mr. North. We've also asked every news station to broadcast the new information and pictures of Butch,

Kevin, Gene, and Leslie. But, as General Nelson said, for now, we're just waiting for somebody to see them."

"We were lucky with that Trooper up at Ringgold," Paul told them. "Unless one of them is stopped, our chances of having any of them recognized are slim."

"Okay," Paul said as he turned to leave, "I better break the bad news now. If you hear anything that provides even a glimmer of hope, get it to me right away."

"Yes, sir," Mike answered as they all stood to attention.

Paul walked to his room, pulled his dress jacket off, and tossed it on the bed. As he unlocked the metal case holding his secure phone, he tried to think of some way to lessen the impact of the news he was obligated to report. There appeared to be no way to put a positive spin on it; it was all damning.

Once the connection had been made and the encryption device activated, Paul said, "Sir, I'm afraid it's as bad as I first told you, maybe even worse."

He waited for the question he knew was coming and answered, "No, sir, there have been no reports of their locations. The real bad news is that Mr. North has collected samples of our project, his lady friend, and their child."

After hearing the response, he clarified his answer, "Colonel Moore verified the genetics of the child as being from our project. She compared previous lab data from him with the samples from the clinic where the child was born. It's a definite match."

"She also compared the clinic material with that sent by Mr. North," he explained. "We have perfect matches with all of them," Paul told him.

"Now for the worst part of it," Paul said, "Mr. North has also sent duplicates of the samples and a number of photos to several unknown people."

Shaking his head as he listened, Paul finally said, "No, sir. We don't have any clue as to who he mailed them to. We have a team up in Rhome checking for any cameras at the Post Office to see if we can determine any of the addressees."

"And," he continued, "they will also go to the local bank where Mr. North withdrew the money and check their cameras."

Following another series of questions from his boss, Paul admitted, "Our only real hope is for any of them to be spotted. I still believe that Mr. North is in the local area, and hopefully so are the others."

"They remained hidden around here for nine months," Paul explained. "I don't think they will stray too far from where they have friends and know where there are places to hide."

Again, after pausing for a response, Paul said, "General Nelson and I also believe that Mr. North sent the material to us for only one reason. He wants us to know he has the information and will use it. We think he may contact us, possibly to work out some agreement."

Finally, Paul finished by saying, "Yes, sir. I'll call if there are any further developments. But I think our real solution is in dealing with Mr. North."

He hung up his phone and locked the case, shaking his head very slowly. It had been a long time since there had been a security leak as potentially bad as this. To have information like this leaked to the public, especially if it came from credible people, would doom their project. And the public outcry would be unstoppable.

Paul left and walked back to the operations room, wondering what the response from MJ12 was going to be. He could think of no way for them to come up with a viable plan to negate the negative impact of program disclosure.

As he entered the room, he heard the report from the team at the Post Office saying that there were no cameras and that no records of the addressees had been made. Although the clerk knew Mr. North, she hadn't looked at the envelopes, just weighed them and affixed the postage. The only information on their computer was the destination city, and they were all largely populated areas. She did remember that a couple of them had been to universities but couldn't say which ones. And that at least one of them had been addressed to some doctor, but she didn't remember which city it had been sent to.

Meanwhile, the team had arrived at the bank and was looking at the location of the cameras. The leader walked to one of the teller's locations and asked, "Could I speak with your supervisor?"

"Of course, sir," she replied. "If you'll just have a seat, I'll get her."

The agent stood to the side and looked around the lobby as he waited for someone to talk to him. Finally, a tall lady came from down the hall and asked, "Is there something I can help you with, sir?"

"Yes, ma'am," he said. "Are you the manager?"

"Yes, sir," she replied. "I'm Renee Bailey, the branch manager."

"I'm FBI agent Larry Dendy," he said, holding out his identification. "Is there somewhere we can talk privately?"

"Of course," Renee told him as she looked at the badge and photo. "We can use my office. Would you like something to drink? We have soft drinks and coffee."

"No, ma'am," Larry answered as they walked to Renee's office. "I just have a few questions, and I'll get out of your hair."

"Please have a seat," Renee said as she closed the door and sat behind her desk. "Just what can I do for you this afternoon?"

"Are you familiar with Mr. Butch North?" Larry asked.

"Of course," she answered. "He's been a customer for several years."

"And are you aware that he made a substantial withdrawal yesterday?" Larry asked, watching for her expression.

"Yes," she said. "What business is that of yours?"

"We are investigating some of Mr. North's activities," he told her. "And we were notified that he had taken a large sum of cash from his accounts."

Larry paused while he let her consider just how they were aware of the transaction. Then he said, "I want the data from all of your cameras, including the ones outside, that was taken during Mr. North's time here yesterday. I also need to see any information you have of his banking activities and determine if you know what he planned to do with the money you gave him."

Renee leaned back and placed her hands on her desk, saying, "First, I need to see a warrant for information regarding any of our clients or to get access to our cameras. Second, I will tell you that I have no idea what Mr. North intended to do with the money. That was none of my business."

Larry stared at her and reminded her, "Ma'am, I'm with the Federal Bureau of Investigation and have the authority to examine any of the records of this bank that I believe to be pertinent to our investigation. Now, I'm asking again: will you give me the records? And what did he tell you he intended to do with the money?"

Renee stood and said, "Sir, with all due respect, I cannot divulge information regarding our customers. If you do not have a warrant or some other official authorization, I can't help you."

She walked around her desk to the door and opened it, saying, "Now, until that time, I'm asking for you to leave."

Larry stood up and said, "Ms. Bailey, I don't want this to be confrontational, but if you refuse to comply with my requests, you may be facing charges of impeding a federal investigation."

"Agent Dendy," Renee said, standing by the open door. "I will comply with any official authorization as required by law now if you would please leave. If you continue to interrupt my business, I will be forced to call the authorities."

"Very well," Larry said as he walked through the door. "You can expect authorization this afternoon. And I'd advise you not to tamper with any of the cameras or the data regarding Mr. North's financial records. Do you under-stand?"

"Certainly," Renee said as she followed him down the hall toward the lobby. "I'll make sure that everything is kept as it should be."

She stopped in the lobby and watched Larry exit the bank. Shaking her head, she wondered what Butch had done and if she was now in trouble. What he had done with the money wasn't her concern. But, by lending him her car, she could inadvertently be involved.

Larry walked to his car and picked up the microphone to contact the base. When he told them that the bank wasn't cooperating and that he needed a warrant for the cameras and

Butch's financial records, Colonel Lynch asked him if he thought the cameras would be of any benefit.

He told her that the only one that might have information regarding Butch's vehicle was in the drive-through, and it didn't appear to cover the parking area. Since Butch had done his business within the bank, the cameras inside would show what they already knew. The only benefit would be seeing what he had been wearing.

Karyn finally told him to wait for a warrant confiscating the exterior camera and to forget getting the financial records. She then asked for him to get the fax number of the bank and she would send the warrant directly to the bank manager. Larry acknowledged his instructions and returned to the bank.

Renee was talking to the two tellers about the strange requests when Larry walked back in. She turned to him and asked sarcastically, "Well, is there something else we can do to help you?"

"Yes, ma'am," Larry said as he approached her. "I need your fax number for the warrant you requested. And, if you don't mind, I'll wait here for it to be sent."

Renee picked up one of the business cards from the counter and handed it to him. "Now, please have a seat over there," she said as she pointed to the chairs at the side of the lobby. "I'll let you know when your warrant gets here. Until then, please try not to interfere with our business."

Renee turned and walked away as Larry watched her. Shaking his head at her attitude, he went back to his car and gave the number to Karyn. After she repeated it, he told her, "I don't think we can expect much cooperation from the people up here. I'm not exactly sure why there's such resistance, but I'm beginning to believe that these small-town folks don't like me."

CHAPTER 39

When Butch got back to the motel, he drove through the parking lot looking for any suspicious vehicles. Once satisfied that none of the familiar black Suburbans or marked Air Force cars was there, he pulled into an empty spot in the middle of the lot where his rental car would be surrounded by other lodgers' cars. Killing the motor and sitting there, he unsnapped the wrangler shirt and took it off. Donning the T-shirt and ball cap, he took his bottle of Jack along with the Coke and headed for the front entrance.

As he entered, he saw that Ann was back on duty at the desk. Still wearing his sunglasses, he checked the lobby for unusual activity and then walked up to greet her. "Evening," he said as he sat the paper sack with his bottle of Jack Daniel's and the Cokes on the counter before pulling the money clip from his pocket.

"Good evening," Ann replied as she looked up.

"I need to pay for another night," Butch told her as he took a $100 bill from his dwindling funds.

"Yes, sir," Ann replied as she pulled up his account.

After making a few entries on the computer, she said, "Your initial deposit of $100 is still available, plus the difference left from the cost of the room for tonight."

Butch laid the money on the counter and told her, "Just use the rest of this as part of the deposit also, please. I know I'll need to stay here another couple of nights, so we'll use it toward the third one."

"Certainly," Ann said. "If you wait just a second, I'll have your receipt, and it'll show another night's lodging and the balance of the increased deposit."

Butch glanced around as he waited and noticed a small bar just off to the side of the lobby. There were several men and women sitting inside at the small tables having drinks. Most of them were engaged in conversation and paying no attention to what was happening in the lobby. Although they were dressed casually, he knew that any of the government folks staying here wouldn't come down in their suits, so it was impossible to tell if they were in there.

Ann finished her task and handed him a single sheet showing that he had paid for one more night and the increased deposit, saying, "I hope you're enjoying your stay with us, Mr. Wrexion. Please let us know if we can do anything else for you."

Butch took the receipt and said, "I appreciate y'all helping me out, ma'am. If I need anything else, I'll let you know. Thanks."

As he picked up his sack and headed toward the stairs, he noticed a black Suburban pulling up to the front doors. Keeping his pace slow, he had just opened the door to the stairs as three men in dark suits came in. Once in the stairwell, he looked back through the small window and watched them stop momentarily at the desk. Watching Ann shake her head at some question they must have asked,

Butch waited to see if he could determine whether or not they were staying here.

The black Suburban had already pulled away as the three headed for the elevator. Now assured that they were indeed staying here, Butch headed up the stairs to the next level and waited by the door to watch the elevator. Guessing how much time it would take the elevator to make it to that floor, he watched to see if it would stop. After sufficient time elapsed, he took the stairs two at a time to the next level.

Looking through the window, he saw the three men heading down the hall toward their rooms. Satisfied that he knew where the men were staying, Butch walked up the next flight of stairs and checked the hall before he opened the door and went to his room. After putting the 'Do Not Disturb' sign on the outside of the door, he locked it and sat the bag on the small desk.

With nothing to do but relax, he pulled off his boots and used the remote to turn on the television. Flipping through the channels, he settled on Fox News and checked the market closing numbers. Keeping the volume low, he walked to the small refrigerator and put the Cokes inside. Although he knew the ice machine was just down the hall, he didn't want to take a chance on running into anyone just for ice.

Maybe later, he would check the floor below him to see if there was an ice machine there, but sometimes they weren't on every floor, and the lodgers would need to go either up or down a flight for the refreshment machines. After pulling the cellophane wrapper from one of the glasses, he poured it half full of Jack Daniel's and retrieved a Coke to top it off.

After testing the mixture for just the right amount of Jack, he put both of the bottles in the refrigerator and sat down in the stuffed chair in front of the TV. It had been a long day, and he was satisfied that his meeting with the Senator had gone well. Knowing that he could depend on the man to help him if necessary was very comforting. And, if something did happen before Butch could arrange a meeting at the base, he thought he could count on him to check with the Base Commander as to Butch's status.

The only problem with the plan was if the people looking for him found him. First, they could still deny any knowledge of his capture, and the Base Commander wouldn't have any idea of what had happened. And Butch had no doubt that whatever those people did, the rest of the base would never know about it.

Tired of watching repeats of the day's events, Butch switched to one of the local channels to get the local news. After seeing several minutes of information about traffic jams, collisions, and problems with local governmental issues, he saw a news flash bulletin on the screen. The commentator stared at the camera and started describing the ongoing search for Gene and those conspiring to help him evade capture.

Bolting upright, he watched as pictures of himself, Kevin, Gene, and Leslie were displayed behind the newscaster's head. He had seen all of the pictures of Gene portrayed as a terrorist before. The photos of Kevin showed him in his Marine uniform and what was obviously a picture taken from his driver's license.

Those of Leslie were also from her driver's license, her high school yearbook, and one from a newspaper article. Although they were fairly clear, she had changed enough since they had been taken that it would be difficult to spot her without very close scrutiny.

The pictures of Butch showed his driver's license photo, one with him normally dressed in his black hat and one that had obviously been taken while they were watching him.

Along with the photos, the commentator discussed where the individuals lived, their vehicles, and where they were thought to have been hiding. There was no information about Leslie having given birth at Ringgold, but the fact that there was a baby involved was made clear. Then he began to list the charges against Butch, Kevin, and Leslie and reiterated those against Gene.

Immediately Butch wondered just how many of his friends would be watching and believe this misinformation. Those who were close to him would know that it wasn't true, but many people who just knew who he was might believe it. That worried him; just reports of being associated with any criminal activity would make it impossible to ever clear his name.

Regardless of whether or not some news program was correct in defaming someone, they never spent the same effort when that individual was eventually cleared of the charges. Butch had always prided himself in his reputation and had spent his life trying to be a good citizen. Now, here, he was portrayed as helping someone who was *known* to be a terrorist.

Of all the things to be accused of and to have the country think he was traitorous, Butch was furious. Sitting his drink on the table, he jerked his boots back on and started to leave. He definitely wasn't going to sit still and let this go unanswered. Pulling the phone directory from the nightstand beside the bed, he found the number for the television station he had been watching. He wrote it on the pad beside the phone and headed for the door ready to try to present his side of the story.

Putting his ball cap and sunglasses back on, he ran down the stairs and headed for the lobby. Seeing no one around, he strode across to the doors and left, still fuming as he walked to his car and jumped in. Now, he had to find a phone far enough from the motel that it wouldn't provide any clue as to where he really was.

Pulling onto Loop 820, he headed north and drove to the intersection with the Jacksboro Highway. Once there, he saw a convenience store where a pickup was dropping off two Mexicans who must have been day laborers. Not realizing that this was the same location where Vicki Grubbs had first set Gene free, he pulled into the front of the store and looked for a pay phone.

It was getting late, and the phone wasn't too well-lit by the store's lights since it was on the side of the building. Pulling over to the phone, Butch killed the engine and stepped out. Lifting his sunglasses, he reread the number for the station and dropped the coins into the phone.

After several rings, the phone was answered by a switchboard operator. Butch started by saying, "Hello, this is Butch North. Your newscaster is talking about me right now, and I'd like to speak to him."

He waited for a couple of minutes and finally heard a man answering him, saying, "This is the control room; who did you say you are?"

"I'm Butch North, sir," Butch said. "And I want you to patch me through to whoever is telling the world that I'm assisting a terrorist to avoid capture. If you're going to announce that I'm guilty of something to the world, I'd like a chance to say I'm not."

"Just a moment, please," the man said, and Butch heard the phone transfer to a recorded voice saying how important it was to wait for the station to answer and how interested they were in your call.

Seconds later, Butch heard a man say, "This is Jim Burch. I'm the man you've asked for."

"Are we on the air?" Butch asked.

"No," Jim answered. "I need to verify that you are Mr. North first. Can you do that?"

"What do you need to know?" Butch asked.

"Where do you live?" Jim asked.

"I live in Aurora, Texas, and I also have stables there. I retired from the Air Force and am currently a pilot for American Airlines," Butch told him. "And I will not stay on the phone much longer. If you want to hear from me, you will put us on the air right now. If not, I'll call another station."

"Hold on just a second," Jim said.

Less than a second later, Butch heard Jim say, "We've just received a breaking story regarding the effort to capture the people you just saw on the screen. We have a man on the phone with us that says he's Butch North. Sir, would you tell us why you've called us?"

"Yes," Butch answered. "You're broadcasting a story concerning me, Kevin Knox, and Leslie Barber. It is not true. The individual you have been portraying as a suspected terrorist is also not true."

"Why do you think this isn't true?" Jim asked.

Wishing he could be watching television right now, Butch answered, "Because the young man you've been saying is using an alias as Gene; is really named Gene. And he is definitely not a terrorist. He isn't some sort of radical

Muslim and couldn't look like the pictures of him dressed as a rag-head if he tried."

"And," Butch continued, "Kevin Knox certainly wouldn't help any of those people if his life depended on it. The man is a Vietnam veteran and risked his life for this country. Hell, he'd be more likely to hunt those people down and kill them himself than to help them."

"And Leslie Barber is just a young lady from Bowie that got involved with Gene," Butch told him. "She had nothing to do with whatever the reason is that the US Government wants with Gene."

"Although I don't know the real reason the government is trying to capture Gene, I can state categorically that none of the facts you so causally toss about are remotely close to being the truth," Butch continued trying to emphasize that he was rational and lucid.

"Now," Butch finished, "I'm getting off this phone since I know it's being traced. But this is not the last time this issue will be discussed. And, if the people behind this want to meet with me and discuss it instead of hearing from me on some news broadcast, I will be glad to arrange that in the very near future."

Butch quickly hung up the phone and got back into the car. As soon as the car was running, he sped out of the parking lot and back onto Loop 820. He hadn't gone more than a mile when he saw two speeding black Suburbans exiting the loop headed for the convenience store. Not really surprised at the rapid response, Butch headed back to the motel, ready to finish the Jack and Coke he had left sitting on the table. He was still extremely upset, but venting some of it had settled his rage enough that he could make it through the night. He hoped.

CHAPTER 40

Sancudo came into the room from a back door carrying a set of desert camouflage clothes. Walking up to Kevin, he said, "Here, Senor, put these on. Those clothes you're wearing have an odor that I find offensive."

"You should have been in the car with him," Gold tooth said as he pulled off his ball cap. Then he removed the ponytail that had been attached to his hair and tossed it and the cap into a suitcase sitting on the floor by the wall.

Kevin watched as his driver proceeded to pull the gold cap from one of his front teeth and stick it in a small container he had been carrying in his pocket. Without the ponytail, ball cap, and gold tooth, the man was hardly recognizable.

Leslie came into the room carrying BK, who was wearing nothing but a clean diaper, smiling as she saw Kevin. She had obviously washed but still wore the same clothes Sancudo had given her earlier.

"Oh, Kevin," she said as she hurried to him. "I was worried that I'd never see you again. I'm so happy that you're here."

Kevin hugged her and told her, "You're too young to worry about an old fart like me. How's BK?"

Leslie looked down and smiled, "He doesn't seem to have a care in the world, but I know he's happy to see you too."

Kevin was letting little BK hold his finger as he looked to see if he could tell if there was anything wrong with the baby. BK still looked the same, and Kevin could see no obvious problems. That was one worry he could drop for now.

As Kevin and Leslie were playing with BK, Sancudo told Gene to go wash and use the restroom if he needed to. He then turned to Kevin's driver and asked, "Gil, have you fixed the car?"

"Not yet," Gil answered. "The truck isn't here with the things we will need. I'll take the car over there, and we'll get it taken care of."

As Gil was leaving, Kevin asked, "What are you doing to my car?"

"Just changing it back to the way it was before we crossed the border," Sancudo told him. "And we need to clean it, check everything, and get it ready for the trip."

"What trip?" Kevin asked. "Aren't we staying here?"

"Of course not," Mel replied. "This is not suitable for you to remain in for so long. And, it is much too close to the border."

"How far is it to where we will be staying?" Leslie asked as she rocked BK in her arms. "I will need to feed my baby in a little while, and would like to know how long it will be before we will stop."

"Oh, it is only about 100 miles or so," Mel told her. "But it will take two or three hours."

"Why so long?" Kevin asked.

"You will be traveling on mostly gravel or dirt roads," Mel answered. "Now, as soon as Gene gets out of the restroom, I suggest you go wash the stink from your body and put on the other clothes. A rich Americano down here with his family to do a little hunting would not smell as you do."

As Mel was finishing telling Kevin about the hunting, Gene returned, trying to dry his hair with a small towel. "Are we going to be hunting?"

"If you desire," Mel told him. "But that is not the real reason for going where you will be staying. It just makes more sense for you to be there if you came to hunt, not to hide."

"Now," Sancudo told Kevin, "you need to get changed. You will be leaving as soon as Gil returns, and I want everything out of here as soon as possible."

"Are you telling us that you won't be going with us?" Kevin asked.

"That is correct," Mel answered. "I have other clients waiting. Do you think Butch purchased me to be your babysitter? Even *he* could not afford that."

Pausing while they listened, Mel continued, "Gil will be taking all of you the rest of the way. Once you are there, he will also leave."

"Who will take care of us then?" Leslie asked.

"I have people to do that," Mel told her. "I am like a large corporation; I have teams that specialize in different areas and locations. Now, Kevin, I have asked you to get changed. I do not have time to waste explaining my business, nor do I have the desire. Now go!"

As Kevin carried the new clothes toward the small restroom, Sancudo walked out to his Bronco, leaving Gene, Leslie, and BK standing in the room. Leslie told Gene that she would try to get BK to nurse and asked him to bring her a small blanket from the back of Mel's car.

When Gene got to the car, Sancudo was removing all of their belongings and placing them on the dirt beside the Bronco. Seeing Gene, he said, "You will need to put all of this in Kevin's car when Gil returns."

"I just need a blanket for Leslie," Gene replied. "Are we all going to be in Kevin's car?"

"That is correct, little man," Mel told him as he pulled the last of the items out and laid them on the ground. "I will be leaving as soon as Gil gets back, and you can help him load everything."

Gene found the blanket and started back toward the house as Mel told him to make sure Kevin was hurrying up. Gene walked back in and handed Leslie the blanket and told her that he thought they would be leaving very soon.

"Kevin," Gene yelled through the closed door. "Mel says we must hurry; I think he is getting ready to leave."

"Just another minute or two," Kevin said, "and I'll be out. Is my car back?"

"No," Gene answered as he watched Leslie holding BK to her breast with the blanket covering him.

When Kevin finally opened the door and came back into the room, Sancudo was standing inside watching Leslie and BK. "Reminds me of my youngest daughter," he told Kevin. "She just had her second child and finally gave me another grandson."

"Can I speak with you alone?" Kevin asked as he dropped his old clothes on the floor.

"Certainly," Mel said. "Let's leave these two alone with their baby, but I only have a few minutes."

"This won't take long," Kevin told him as they walked from the room.

Outside, standing by the Bronco, Sancudo asked, "What is it you want to talk about?"

"I want to apologize for causing you any problems," Kevin began. "I must admit that I was worried about you when we left Stephenville."

"I understand," Mel said, looking at Kevin's downcast face. "You must also understand that I do not know you and do not know what troubles you face."

"I find it much simpler to be very strict and stern, to begin with," he continued. "Once everyone understands the rules and readily complies, I can be a little more agreeable."

"And you," he finished, "did not seem to want to follow my instructions without questioning them. I hope you understand that strict obedience is absolutely necessary if we are to be successful. The risks are much too great to take chances on some mistake, no matter how slight."

"No, I understand completely," Kevin continued to apologize. "I was just concerned because I didn't know you and worried about those kids in there."

"My friend," Sancudo explained, "I have been friends with Butch for several years and would do nothing to jeopardize that relationship. Not to mention, if I failed to get you safely over here, my reputation would suffer. And that would cost me future business."

Kevin extended his hand and said, "You've done a wonderful job, and we appreciate it. Thanks."

Mel shook his hand and replied, "It has been my pleasure, but I sincerely hope I never have to do this again for you. I don't care what you are running from or why. But those kids need to be where that baby can be cared for."

As they were shaking hands, Kevin's car came into the dirt driveway, now white and clean. Gil came to a stop and jumped out, saying, "Let's get everything loaded. I need to be at the ranch before it gets dark."

As they were putting everything into the backseat or the trunk, Kevin saw three rifle cases sitting where the tarp and paint cans had been. There were also several boxes of shotgun ammunition and some hunting vests inside. Just as they were finishing, Gene and Leslie came out with her carrying BK.

"All right, folks," Sancudo told them. "Gil has cleaned the car, provided some refreshments, and loaded your belongings. It is time for you to leave."

Leslie went to the rear door and climbed in putting BK in the car seat beside her as Gene walked around to the other side of the car and got in. Gil checked the ground around the Bronco for any missed items and got into the driver's seat, satisfied that they were leaving nothing behind.

Kevin stood looking at Sancudo for the last time and said, "Again, thanks. I'll let Butch know how well you've done. And, if you hear from him, tell him I owe him a trip in the back of my car with a load of crappy diapers."

Sancudo laughed and told him, "I will do that, and I would expect him to know you will never forget the misery you have endured. He will be watching for some trick from you, though. You have to be very sneaky around that man; he seems to know when something is up."

Shaking Mel's hand and turning to get into the car, Kevin said, "Sounds like you know him too well yourself. Again, thanks."

Mel stood watching as Gil backed the car from the house and headed west onto a gravel road that led into what appeared to be the only thing that was going into the barren countryside. As the dust billowed from the back of the departing car, he stepped into his Bronco and pulled the CB radio from beneath the seat. After speaking a few words and hearing the reply, he started the car and headed back toward Piedras Negras.

Gil drove cautiously along the rough road that switched from gravel to dirt and back again as they headed toward the mountains west of Morelos. The scenery consisted mostly of scrub brush, mesquite, and sage, with several shallow gullies crossing the road. The dust of the road had settled on the vegetation along the sides and gave them a grayish-brown appearance, and it looked like it had been months since the rain had washed the dirt from the leaves or flowed through where the small streams had left their marks.

For the next hour or so, they drove through low hills as they wound their way toward a mountain range that seemed to be forever in the distance. Finally, after crossing an occasional stream, other unimproved roads, and a few small clusters of houses, they came to the foothills of the range. A fairly large riverbed ran to the north as they entered the valley between two ranges of high mountains.

Following the riverbed, they continued into the valley as it widened. Although the sun was getting close to the tops of the mountains to the west, they could see many more trees on the slopes and along the almost dry riverbed. Finally, after another hour of going deeper into the valley, Kevin saw a small group of houses in the distance.

"Is that where we're going?" he asked.

"Si, Senor," Gil told him. "That is the ranch of Sancudo's uncle Pablo and his wife, Rosita. You may call them Paul and Rosy if you wish."

Almost to the buildings, Kevin looked to the right of the road and said, "Is that a runway over there?"

Gil looked and answered, "Yes, it comes in handy sometimes if we need to get someone out quickly or for Sancudo to bring supplies."

"Why didn't we just fly here," Kevin asked. "That would have been a lot faster and probably safer."

"It was considered," Gil told him. "Sancudo and Butch had discussed it; that is why you met him at Stephenville. But our airplane was suddenly not available, and Señor North could not quickly arrange for one himself."

"Well," Kevin said, "I just hope one is available to take us out when the time comes. I don't relish the thought of two days driving back."

"You do not like our pretty country?" Gil said as they came closer to the houses.

"This is very pretty," Kevin told him, looking at the mountains on both sides of the car. "I just don't want to drive back."

"Especially if it's in the trunk covered with a tarp," he said, smiling.

As they came to a stop a few yards from a fairly large adobe building, Kevin noticed that the ranch was built on the lower slope of where the two mountain ranges joined at the north end of the valley. As Gil climbed out of the car, a short lady wearing an apron came walking out of the large house.

"Tia Rosita," Gil said as he walked to meet his aunt.

The rest of them got out of the car and stretched their arms and legs as they watched Gil and Rosy hug. Gene walked around the rear of the car and put his arm around Leslie's shoulder as she stood holding BK.

"Come, meet Aunt Rosy," Gil said, coming toward them. "Tia Rosy, I'd like for you to meet Señor Kevin Knox."

Kevin stepped forward and took her outstretched hand, saying, "I'm glad to meet you, ma'am.

"And this is Gene, his esposa Leslie, and their child BK," Gil said, introducing them.

"I am pleased to meet all of you," Rosy said. "I know you've had a hard journey, and I have rooms prepared for you."

Turning away, she said, "If you will just follow me, I'll show you where you will be staying. There are clean towels in the rooms, and the bathroom is just down the hall from either of your rooms."

Entering the house, she walked across a large sitting area with a massive fireplace at one end, saying, "I will have a meal prepared in about 30 minutes or so. My husband Pablo will be here by then, so you will have time to clean up before we eat."

She led them to a long hall with rooms to either side and said, "Señor Knox, your room is the second door on the right. Señor Gene, you and your wife will be in the room across from his."

Walking down the hall, she continued, "There is a crib for the baby in your room, and the bathroom is at the end of the hall. Gil and I will bring your things in if you'd like to use the restroom and get acquainted with your new rooms."

They went into their rooms as Rosy and Gil returned to the car to bring everything in. Kevin's room was fairly small, with an old four-poster bed made from what appeared to be cedar posts. The double bed was covered with a faded quilt that was probably made by Rosy or some other member of the family.

He sat on the bed and tested the softness as he looked around at the small table with a lamp and wooden chair sitting beside it. Besides those, there were no other furnishings in the room. Standing, he walked over and opened the door to a very small closet. Satisfied with the accommodations and very surprised that it was so neat and clean after the other two places Sancudo had taken them, he went to check the bathroom.

Gene and Leslie went into their room with BK and looked around. Their room was furnished exactly as Kevin's, with the addition of an oblong basket suspended between two poles that held it off of the floor. Gene looked into the closet and checked the bed while Leslie pushed the side of the crib and watched it swing slowly between the poles.

Kevin stepped into their room just as Gil and Rosita were bringing in the few items they had brought, asking, "Everything all right?"

"It's very nice," Leslie said as she watched Gil set their belongings on the small desk.

"I like it," Gene announced. "It looks like one of the rooms I've seen in some old westerns."

"I'm glad you're satisfied," Rosita said as she turned to leave. "Please be ready to eat in a few minutes. Gil, will you be staying?"

Following her out of the room, he replied, "No, Tia Rosita. Mel is sending the plane for me, and he cannot land or take off after dark. I have to leave as soon as he arrives."

Just as Kevin was walking out behind them, they heard the sound of an aircraft engine roaring over the house. "That'll be him," Gil said, hurrying down the hall. "I hope you folks have a nice vacation. Adios, Tia Rosita, I'll see you next time."

CHAPTER 41

General Modelle walked into the operations room just as FBI agent Larry Dendy was calling and telling Karyn about his problems getting cooperation from the bank. "What's that all about?" he asked. "Are we going to have problems getting what we need?"

"Let's just say that those folks aren't as easy to manipulate as we'd like," Mike said.

"Well," Paul told them, getting frustrated, "let's get them their damned warrants. I'll put so much pressure on them that they'll wish they'd never pushed us."

"Sir," Jerry said, interrupting the conversation. "If I may offer a suggestion, I think we're going about this the wrong way."

Stunned, Paul looked at him and asked, "Just what would that be, Major?"

Taking his time to phrase his proposal as well as he could, he said, "Sir, I grew up in a small town up in the Panhandle of Texas. I know how these people think."

"What does that have to do with anything?" Mike asked.

Trying not to irritate either of them, he explained, "Sir, growing up in Muleshoe, I understand the resistance to any outside authority these folks have."

"You have to remember that most of the people in small communities like Muleshoe or Rhome can usually trace their families back to the start of the towns. Some of them have ancestors that helped settle the area, and some were here before Texas became a state," he continued.

"They have more of a pioneer attitude than people that live in large cities. They're more self-reliant, and they usually distrust most outsiders. They'll readily help a neighbor or even a stranger. But they'll resist anything they think is being forced on them. They also view government as the big city types trying to dictate their actions," Jerry explained.

"That's especially true when it comes to some outside agency digging into the lives of one of their tight-knit group of people that are well respected within the community. I think we'd be better off walking a little more softly," he finished.

"What exactly do you have in mind," Rick asked, watching both of the Generals' tempers rising. "You've always said that we need to pursue the legal side; now, are you trying to say something different?"

"No, sir," Jerry quickly said. "What I mean is that instead of walking in, slapping a warrant down, and demanding something, we need to approach these people as if we were trying to help them."

"For example," he continued, "if we'd ask for their assistance in finding Mr. North because he was supposed to be helping us, but he hadn't contacted us when he said he would. Then we could say that he was on our side, and we were worried about him."

"Anything else?" Mike asked.

"Yes, sir," Jerry told him. "I think we'd have better results if our people would dress a little less formal. I believe they'd be more receptive to someone dressed like they do. Maybe not boots, jeans, and hats because they'd know they weren't used to wearing them. But at least lose the dark suits, maybe wear slacks and a knit shirt, or even a sport coat."

Mike and Paul looked at each other, wondering if maybe Jerry was right. The frustration of having no information was wearing on them and possibly a change of tactics would produce some results. At this point, they were willing to try just about anything. And Jerry did make some sense.

Just as they were trying to decide if they should try Jerry's suggestion, Rick noticed the screen flashing on the computer. Walking over to take a look, he saw there was an incoming message from the photographic intelligence section in Washington.

Scanning it quickly, he announced, "Well, the photo folks have come up empty on the pictures."

Mike moved over to the desk and read the dismal report. None of the material they had sent provided any information as to an identifiable location. Even the most sophisticated equipment had been unable to determine where the pictures had been taken.

"So," Mike said. "We still have no clue as to where any of them are. We don't know what they're driving, if they've adopted disguises or anything. All we know is that they aren't anywhere we've looked."

"What about the cameras at the bank?" Rick asked.

Looking at Karyn, Mike asked, "Do you have a warrant for them?"

"Yes, sir," she replied. "The agent gave me the bank's fax number, and I'm sending it right now."

"It's probably too late to change tactics with the people at the bank," Mike said. "Just tell the agent to get the data from the cameras and send it as quickly as he can. If the folks in Washington can't find anything from that, we're still looking for the proverbial needle in a haystack."

"What about that guy we had up in Bridgeport?" Rick asked. "You remember the agent that met Butch at Red's and was supposed to get to know him. Maybe we could use him as Jerry suggested. He'd fit in around there."

"Sorry, sir," Karyn told him. "He was transferred months ago when that operation failed. I know I can locate him, but it would probably take several days to get him here."

"See what you can do," Mike directed. "In the meantime, does anyone have any new ideas?"

Jerry was reluctant to bring it up again, but he finally said, "Sir, I think I can help."

"What do you have in mind, Major," Mike asked, resigned to trying anything.

"Sir, I'd like to go up there and ask around," Jerry told him. "I believe that I could find out more from the people up there than any of our current agents."

"I know the guy Butch met would be the best choice," he continued. "But until he can be brought in, I think I can relate to those folks better than anyone else we have."

"What do you think?" Mike asked Paul.

"Well, we haven't many other options, do we?" Paul answered. "If we don't get something soon, none of us will have a job. My boss as much as told me that unless there's some progress in the next 24 hours, I may as well look for a new career."

"All right, Jerry," Mike said. "What do you need?"

"Nothing, really," he answered. "I've always worn jeans and boots when I'm off duty, so all that's necessary is to go up there and just ask around. I can even tell them that Butch and I flew together in the Air Force and that I'm looking for a place to retire and like the area around there."

"You might be closer to retirement than you'd like to think," Mike said. "As General Modelle just said, we may all be looking for a retirement home soon."

"All right, Jerry," Mike continued, "instead of coming in tomorrow morning, you head up there and see what you can find."

"Didn't Mr. North spend time at that little bar in Boyd?" Karyn asked. "I remember the agents following him there and to Tater Junction."

"The good thing about this," Jerry told them, "is that there aren't many places to visit. Probably a couple of restaurants, the bar, and the liquor store in Rhome. I can hit all of them within a day. If I strike out, it only cost us 10 or 12 hours."

"If nothing else," he concluded, "it will let me know if anyone has seen him around the area lately."

Just as they were discussing who would take over his duties, Karyn's phone rang. Answering it, she listened for a second and thanked the caller before hanging up.

"You're not going to believe this," she said, dialing the phone. "Butch North is on the phone, not two miles from here."

As soon as her call to the team was answered, she gave them the address of the phone Butch was using. After telling them to get there as quickly as they could, she hung up and walked to the map of the Ft Worth area.

Pointing to the intersection of Loop 820 and Highway 199, she said, "The bastard is right there."

Paul rushed to her side and asked, "How do you know that?"

"The FBI got a call just a few moments ago from one of the local television stations," she explained. "The station told them that someone claiming to be Butch North had called them about their broadcast showing his picture."

Rick quickly turned on the TV and started flipping through the local channels until they saw a commentator with Butch's picture on the screen behind him. As they listened, they heard Butch denying involvement in aiding a terrorist and that Gene wasn't guilty of anything.

Riveted to the screen, they watched as the station broadcast every word Butch was saying. They heard him talking about Gene, Kevin, and Leslie, telling the audience that the government was wrong and none of them were guilty of any of the things that were being claimed.

When Butch finally announced that he was planning to make contact with them and abruptly hung up, Mike and Paul stood staring at the screen. Everyone was silent as the impact of Butch's announcement sank in. Finally, Rick spoke, "I don't believe it. The son-of-a-bitch is right here and threatening us."

Mike shook his head and said, "And he's doing a pretty damn good job of it. First the pictures, now this, what's he going to do next?"

"Where's your team?" Paul asked Karyn. "Have they gotten there?"

Karyn sat listening to the speakers as the team reported arriving but didn't see anyone on the phone. She told them to go into the store and see if the clerk had seen anything and to check for security cameras.

Turning to General Modelle, she said, "I guess you heard, sir. If Butch was there, he's gone now."

"All right," Mike said. "Let's get the data from the cameras here as quick as we can. Maybe we'll find out what he's driving, get a license plate number, or something."

"Do you think that was really him on the program?" Paul asked.

"We'll run a voice match," Rick answered. "But I've listened to him so many times in the past that I'm positive it was."

"What do we do about this?" Paul asked.

"We'll have the FBI deny any knowledge regarding the truth of Mr. North's statements," Mike said. "We also have them issue a statement when asked, and I'm sure it will be very soon that the FBI has proof of the allegations against all of them."

"I mean, what do we do about Mr. North?" Paul said.

"I think we wait," Mike told him. "We have no idea where he is or how to find him. Our only hope is in the cameras from the bank or where he made the call. If there's nothing there, we're back to hoping they get spotted. And we know the odds of that aren't very good."

"At least we know he's close," Rick said.

"Close," Mike disgustingly said. "Hell, he might as well be in Bum F'in Egypt for all the good him being close has done us. We've looked everywhere we can think of, and he pops up right next door."

"Where's he going to be next? Sitting in the Base Commander's office?" Mike said as he stomped to the map. "I swear, I'd like to have him back in the conference room right now. This time, I'd do the questioning instead of just standing there listening to that smart-ass bastard. Just thinking of how smug he was even back then really pisses me off.”

“I don’t think now is the time to lose our tempers,” Paul said, trying to calm him. “Mr. North may be smug, but he’s proven that with all of our resources, we can’t touch him. What’s the old saying? Something about you’re not bragging when you prove you can do it, then it’s a fact. Well, we better face facts.”

“One thing I think we can count on,” Rick told them. “If he says he’s going to contact us, he will.”

“I agree,” Mike said. “All of the material he sent was just putting us on notice. That little tirade on the news wasn’t planned. I’m betting he hadn’t seen it before and just reacted. If anything, he seems to have plans for every contingency.”

“I’m sure you’re right,” Paul agreed. “I’ll bet he’s already got a plan for contacting us. And, given his record of success on his other plans, I’d bet he’s just getting the final pieces together before he lets us know.”

“So,” Mike said, “I guess the only things we can still do are to wait for the camera results and send Jerry up there tomorrow to see if he can learn anything.”

“I’m ready to call it a day,” Paul said, suddenly feeling very tired. “Mike, let’s head to your office for a moment before I retire for the night.”

“Yes, sir,” Mike agreed as he turned from the map where he’d been looking at exactly how close Butch had been to where they were standing.

Following Paul out of the room, Mike told the rest of them, “Whoever’s on duty can send the camera data to Washington and call me with the results when they get in. Everyone else, take off.”

Turning at the door, he said, "Jerry, let us know when you get up there. And remember, you may be our only hope right now."

CHAPTER 42

Butch woke up the next morning with a slight headache. He wasn't sure if it was from Jack and Coke or something else, probably the *'something else'* he decided. Either way, he'd take a couple of aspirins before he went out. Still in bed, he reached for the remote and turned the television on. It was still on the station where he had seen himself last night.

Listening to the station as he climbed out of bed and went into the bathroom, he waited to see if they would rerun segments of last night's broadcast. He had stayed up long enough after he got back from making the phone call to hear parts of the program and was glad they had at least told the public that he was denying the allegations about him and Kevin.

He turned on the shower and started the courtesy coffee pot while he waited for the water to get hot. As he stood in front of the mirror, he shook his head at the image that was looking back at him. *'I must be getting old,'* he thought. *"I look like death warmed over.'*

With steam rising above the shower curtain, he reached in, adjusted the temperature to his liking, and stepped into the tub. The hot water pounding against the back of his head and neck slowly drove some of the pain away but couldn't rid him of the tension he felt.

After almost 20 minutes of letting the heated water soothe him all it was capable of doing, he climbed out and dried while he kept one ear tuned to the local news. Finished with shaving and brushing his teeth, he wrapped the towel around his waist, poured a cup of coffee, and went in to watch the news.

When they finally began showing segments of last night's program, the lady anchor told how someone had called claiming to be Mr. North, but there was no positive verification. She then offered to allow whoever it was to call again and provide proof to the listeners that he was indeed who he said he was.

"Bullshit!" Butch said to no one in particular. "You just want to try to get me on the phone and be ready to turn me in. Hell, I'd bet that you've already made arrangements with the FBI or whoever to be there with your microphones and cameras ready to show the capture. They are a bunch of jackals, ready to feed on the bones of whoever you can. Well, sweetheart, this ain't my first rodeo, and I ain't biting."

For the next hour, Butch switched from station to station catching parts of several variations of the first one. Even the national stations were playing some segments of the program. At least they were giving him some air time, although they all questioned the identity of the caller.

Tired of watching the same old thing over and over, Butch rinsed his cup out in the sink, tossed the towel on the floor beside the tub, and got dressed. He wasn't sure how the day was going to go, but he knew he couldn't just sit around the room. Grabbing his ball cap and sunglasses, he walked to the door and peeked into the empty hall. Since he had already paid for this day's stay, he turned the 'Do Not Disturb' sign over as he closed the door behind him.

He stopped on the next floor down and looked through the small window to see if any of the team members were in the hall. Seeing no one, he went to the lobby floor and checked before opening the door. Again, as yesterday, the lobby held a few casually dressed people just sitting around or busy typing on their laptop computers.

Pulling his cap down and putting the sunglasses on, he strolled across the lobby and went out into the bright sunlight. By now, the coffee was causing his stomach to start rumbling, and he needed to get something in it. He figured he needed to give the Senator until at least noon before calling. That gave him a few hours to kill, and he had no idea of where to go.

Starting his car, he pulled onto Loop 820 and headed south. He definitely wasn't going anywhere close to where he had made the call last night. Not only was it probably under surveillance, but any teams heading for Rhome or Boyd would drive right by there.

At the intersection of I-30, he headed east toward downtown Ft Worth. There were several decent eating places a mile or so from the loop, and he turned right onto Camp Bowie Boulevard West. Seeing a small restaurant in an almost vacant strip mall, Butch pulled in and parked. The only store that looked like it had any customers besides the restaurant was the Hide Crafter Leather store, and he remembered it from when he had been making a pair of chaps and needed some fancy Conchos for decorations.

As he got out of the car and headed toward the restaurant, Butch saw a man he knew from Decatur. "Hey, Jim," he called as he walked toward the leather store. "What brings you down to Cowtown?"

"Hello, Butch," Jim said. "I just needed some leather for the shop. What about you? Did you wind up staying too late at one of the bars down here and not make it home last night?"

"Nope, just some early morning business downtown," Butch replied. "You still fixin' boots up at the Rafter R?"

"Yep," Jim said. "But my son Chuck needs some pink leather for the tops of a pair of boots he's making for some ol' hide that came in the other day. She's gotta have big pink hearts inset into the tops and real pointy toes tipped in pink."

"She's not the one that bought that awful saddle with the pink ostrich seat you had setting out front, is she?" Butch asked.

Jim laughed and said, "No, I don't think this gal could get on a horse, at least not without hurting the horse."

"She must be a local," Butch chuckled. "We've got more pounds of female flesh than any two counties around; it's just packed on fewer women."

"Well," Jim continued, "this one fits the average. Not only that, I swear if you put her brains on a pin head, they'd have as much room to roll around as a bowling ball on a four-lane highway."

"Don't tell me she's blond," Butch laughed.

"I couldn't tell. She had colored streaks all through her hair and a god-awful hat with pink feathers," Jim admitted. "And she must use a concrete trowel to put on her makeup. Bless her little ol' heart; there's at least 10 pounds of colored goo on that lady's face."

"Dare I ask if any of it's pink?" Butch asked, smiling.

"Oh, yes," Jim admitted. "Pink, purple, green, blue, gold, you name it. Her face looked like a peacock's tail fanned out in the sunlight."

"Oh, yea," Butch replied, grinning. "I've seen a few of those myself. It makes you wonder just what they're covering up, doesn't it?"

"I'd be afraid to look," Jim said. "But, if I don't get my shopping done, the good ol' Rafter R Boot and Shoe Repair will go unattended, and I won't get to meet any more of those charming ladies."

Jim turned, waved, and headed for the door to the leather store, saying, "Come visit sometime."

"I'll do it," Butch said as he watched Jim leave.

When he walked into the small restaurant, there were only two other customers sitting at the tables. He went to the very back table and sat facing the door so he could watch the parking lot and see anyone coming in.

The waiter was standing by the door to the kitchen and came over immediately with a glass of iced water and handed him a menu. "Would you care for coffee or orange juice, sir?" he asked.

"You bet," Butch answered. "Black coffee and a glass of OJ will be fine."

"I'll have it right away," the waiter told him and returned to the kitchen.

After reading the menu, Butch settled on what he wanted for breakfast. He had just set the menu on the table when the waiter appeared with a large glass of OJ and a small carafe of coffee.

"Ready to order, sir?" the waiter asked.

"Yes, sir," Butch answered. "I'd like the Spanish omelet with jalapenos, hash browns, crispy on the outside, and an English muffin."

"Fine, sir," the waiter said, scribbling on his pad. "It'll just take a few minutes. If you need more coffee, just wave."

"Thanks," Butch said, picking up the glass of juice.

Sitting there waiting for his breakfast, Butch realized that running into Jim next door could have caused a problem for him. Obviously, Jim hadn't seen the news, or he would have said something. Butch didn't worry about Jim running for a phone, but when he finally saw the news later today in his shop, he'd probably mention it to anyone that came in.

Can't worry about that now, he thought. Even if he does tell someone, it'll be too late for them to find him here. And the more locations where he's been seen and they find out, it'll just spread their problem. And maybe the Senator can meet him at the base this afternoon and it would all be over.

Minutes later, the waiter brought his food and asked if he needed anything else. Telling him no, Butch splashed some Tabasco sauce on his hash browns and started eating. Very surprised at the quality of the food, Butch took his time and enjoyed every bite. Munching on the muffin, he poured a final cup of coffee and sat back. In another hour or so, he'd have his answer from the Senator's office. He certainly hoped they could make it today, but he also realized that the Senator probably had a very busy schedule. Even retired Senators stay pretty active, Butch thought, with speaking engagements, writing their memoirs, or something.

Noticing that Butch was finished, the waiter came over and asked if he wanted anything else. "No, thanks," Butch told him. "Just the check, please."

The waiter pulled the check from his apron and placed it on the table. After picking up the plate and utensils, he walked away with the dishes and went into the kitchen.

Butch sat a couple of minutes longer drinking the coffee, mainly just killing time. Finally unable to sit any longer, he put his cup down and left the restaurant. There was a large mall on the east side of Ft Worth, and Butch figured that he could waste a few hours wandering around looking at all the things he didn't want. And there were several pay phones all over the place.

Back in his car, Butch joined the I-30 traffic heading east. It was only 15 miles or so to where he could get back on Loop 820 and go north to the Northeast Mall. He turned on the radio and dialed in 92.1 to listen to the old country music he had always enjoyed. He didn't care for much of the newer songs; he could never identify most of the singers, except Garth Brooks, and he didn't like him anyway. The newer guys tended to all sound the same, unlike when Merle Haggard, Ray Price, Hank Thompson, Mo Bandy, and Willie Nelson dominated the radio.

When he finally got to the loop, he pulled off I-30 on the northbound exit and drove another few miles to the mall. As he pulled in, he saw the parking lot crowded with cars. That was good, he thought, lots of folks to blend in with. He just hoped he wouldn't run into anyone else he knew. He might not be so lucky next time.

Butch cruised in and out of the stores, looking at shoes, socks, sheets, and shirts. The men's areas of the stores were practically vacant, except for a few women shopping for their husbands, kids, or maybe fathers. However, the ladies' areas were constant hubs of activity as the women pulled every item off the rack and held them up for inspection.

Checking the clock on his cell phone, Butch finally decided to try to contact the Senator. He still had plenty of change, so he walked down the broad hall between the shops lining the sides of the mall. Spotting a phone by the restrooms, Butch decided to use the facilities before making his call; he certainly didn't want to need to go while on the phone, and all the coffee that he had drunk was rapidly becoming uncomfortable.

Once through with that, he rechecked the number and dialed. It was answered after only two rings, and Butch said, "Hello, this is Butch North for Senator Burklow. Is he available?"

Hearing that he was, Butch waited for the operator to pass the call into the Senator's office. Seconds later, he heard, "Hello, Butch, this is Larry Burklow. I've been expecting your call."

"I'm sorry if I've kept you waiting, sir," Butch apologized. "I wanted to give your secretary plenty of time to coordinate your schedule if you decided we could visit the base today."

"I can't make it today, Butch," Larry said. "But I've blocked the entire morning tomorrow."

Pausing, Larry continued, "Are you someplace where you can tell me what's going on with your 'situation'?"

"As good as anywhere, sir," Butch told him. "I guess you saw the news last night."

"You're damned right I did," Larry said. "And I want to hear your side of the story. How much of what they're saying is true?"

"None of it, sir," Butch replied. "As I told you at the restaurant, the person they're accusing of being a terrorist is the very same person I told you was probably the result of their program at the base."

"Kevin Knox," Butch continued, "is an old friend of mine, and he helped me hide Gene until I could find out what was going on."

"And Leslie Barber," Butch finished, "just got caught up in the mess. But, as I said last night to the TV station, neither of them have done anything wrong. Okay, Kevin and I hid the *suspected* terrorist. But, I'm absolutely positive he had nothing to do with the 9-11 attacks."

"All right," Larry told him. "I believe you. I did a little checking this morning myself. You wouldn't be surprised to hear that there is no information regarding any facility at the NAS/JRB doing genetic research, would you?"

"No, sir," Butch agreed. "That doesn't surprise me in the least."

"And those people that were supposedly trying to get on an airplane at DFW?" Larry said. "There happens to be no real information about them either. Oh, there's some chatter about a couple of them being caught up in New Hampshire or something. But there's no record of where they were taken or of any charges naming them as defendants. Sort of strange, don't you think?"

"I understand what you're telling me, sir," Butch agreed. "As I told you last night, just too many things don't add up. That's why I decided to hide the kid."

"All right, Butch," Larry concluded. "Just tell me where you're staying, and I'll come pick you up in the morning."

"I can't do that, sir," Butch told him. "I may have to leave there later today or tonight. How about meeting me at the What-A-Burger on West Loop 820 just north of I-30? It's only a couple of miles from there to the base."

"You're not worried about me knowing where you're staying, are you?" Larry asked.

"Not at all, sir," Butch lied. "But if I'm spotted there, which I may very well be after being plastered all over the news, I may end up sleeping in my truck in some cornfield."

"All right, Butch," Larry said. "I'll be there at eight o'clock tomorrow morning. If you're not there by 8:30, I'll go to the Base Commander's office and meet you there or try to find out what's happened to you."

"Thank you, sir," Butch said. "I'll either be there at eight, or they have me. Thanks again, Senator. I really do appreciate your help."

"Well, if you're right, I may owe *you* much more than simply thanks," Larry told him. "I'll see you tomorrow."

Butch hung up and slowly walked through the mall, still having too much time on his hands and really nowhere to go that he really wanted to be. It would be nice to spend the afternoon with Tammy. That would be really nice.

CHAPTER 43

Kevin woke early the next morning as the sun was beginning to cast its rays over the mountains to the east. The house was still quiet, and he just lay there enjoying the comfort of the bed. After spending two days on the road, and half of one of them in the smelly trunk of the car, it felt really good to sleep in a soft bed and relax.

Now that things seemed to be safe for him and the kids, most of the worries of the last couple of days had disappeared. That night in the cabin south of Rocksprings had really been a low point for him. Concern over Sancudo's behavior and not knowing whether or not they would ever leave there alive was reminiscent of some of those nights back in Vietnam. At least back then, he had more control over his actions and had the weapons to ensure he wouldn't die alone.

Kevin tossed the covers aside, slipped out of the bed, and put on his camouflage pants. After he eased the door open, he looked across the hall and listened for any sounds coming from Gene and Leslie's room. Hearing nothing, he crept softly down to the bathroom and washed his face. Looking in the mirror, he saw that he really needed a shave, and his mouth tasted like a herd of elephants had used it for a latrine.

Next, he wandered down the hall toward the large room just inside the entryway and looked around. As he was inspecting the massive fireplace, Rosy came in from an adjoining room and said, "Good morning, Senor. How did you sleep?"

Kevin turned around and smiled, "Just fine, ma'am. I haven't slept that well in several days."

"Yes, I know getting here is sometimes difficult," she acknowledged as she returned his smile. "Would you like some juice and coffee?"

"I certainly would," Kevin replied. "But, is there a chance that you would have a spare razor and toothbrush handy?"

Rosy walked over to a cupboard that was sitting against the wall and said, "Of course, senor. We keep a supply of disposable razors and toothbrushes for our guests. Sometimes, they arrive with nothing but the clothes on their backs."

She opened a drawer and pulled out a package of razors, a can of shaving cream, a tube of toothpaste, and a toothbrush still sealed in its original wrapper. Handing them to Kevin, she said, "These should last you until you leave. My nephew Mel tells me that you might only be here for a week, but if you need more, I'll get them for you."

Kevin thanked her, saying, "I really appreciate it. Now, if you don't mind, I'll go put these to good use. I'd hate to be around nice people looking like this, and I'm almost afraid to talk with my breath as bad as it must be."

"It is not a problem, Senor," Rosy replied. "I'll have coffee, juice, and breakfast on the table when you return."

Kevin thanked her again and headed back toward the bathroom. As he passed Gene's room, he heard BK fussing and knew that Leslie would soon be up to take care of whatever problems the little boy had. Knowing that they might want to use the bathroom before he could finish shaving and brushing his teeth, he knocked on the door to let them know he was up.

Leslie called out, "Come in."

When Kevin cracked the door open and looked in, he saw her sitting on the side of the bed holding BK. "Good morning, sunshine," he said.

"Good morning, Kevin," she replied.

"Is Gene awake?" Kevin asked, looking at Gene's head resting on the pillow.

"I'm awake," Gene answered, rolling over and looking at Kevin. "I'm surprised that you're up this early."

Kevin walked into the room and said, "I'm an early riser; you already know that. I just wanted to see if either of you need to use the bathroom before I go shave."

Gene sat up in the bed, stretching, and replied, "I'm fine, and it looks like Leslie will be busy feeding BK for the next few minutes. Just let me know when you're done."

"Okay," Kevin said, walking back toward the door. "If you need a toothbrush, Aunt Rosy will take care of you. I know you don't have enough beard to need a razor, but if you want to practice, I'll leave you one in the bathroom."

Kevin smiled at the exaggerated hurt expression on Gene's face and heard Leslie say, "I'm glad he doesn't get all hairy and scratchy like most of you men. He's perfect just as he is."

"Well, maybe he'll grow up someday and hair over," Kevin said, laughing as he left the room and shut the door.

"How's BK?" Gene asked, stretching and watching Leslie nurse him.

"He seems fine," she said, holding him to her breast. "I don't think I've ever seen such a cute little boy."

"I'm kind of worried about him," Gene told her. "He just looks so strange that I'm afraid that he won't fit in."

"Nonsense," Leslie said, looking into BK's dark eyes. "I think all the girls will think he's handsome when he grows up. Just look at those big dark eyes; he seems to be aware of everything. And they look so kind, so thoughtful. No, he'll be just fine."

"I'm sure you're right," Gene told her. "I just never had a chance to grow up around other kids, but I've heard that they can be really tough on anyone that looks different."

Leslie finished feeding BK and laid him on the bed, saying, "Oh, they can be. But we'll make sure he's somewhere that won't matter if he's just a little different."

As they were talking, Kevin knocked on the door again and asked, "Are you guys about ready for breakfast? I think Aunt Rosy has juice and coffee on the table."

"I'll be right there," Gene replied. "I just have to get dressed and use the bathroom. Did you get us some toothbrushes?"

"No, but I'll go get them now," Kevin said as he heard Gene crawl out of bed. "I'll have them back in just a minute and bring them to the bathroom."

Gene pulled his pants on and headed for the door, asking Leslie, "Do you need to go before me?"

"No," she replied, "you go ahead. I've got to change BK and get dressed. Just let me know when you're done."

Kevin walked down the hall and called, "Aunt Rosy?" as he entered the front room.

Rosy came in from where she had been setting the table and asked, "Yes, do you need something?"

"Yes, ma'am," Kevin answered. "Gene and Leslie need toothbrushes."

"If you don't mind," Rosy said, "just get them from the cupboard. You know where they are."

Kevin walked over,

 opened the drawer, and said, "Yes, ma'am. I'll take care of it, thanks."

After taking two toothbrushes out, Kevin headed back down the hall to the bathroom and handed them to Gene, saying, "I'll see you in front when you're done."

Their door was open as he passed, and he told Leslie, "I gave Gene your toothbrush. Come on down when you guys get ready; I'll be having coffee with Aunt Rosy."

Passing through the large front room, Kevin went into the room that he had seen Rosy coming from. Inside, there was a large wooden table in the center of the room and 12 slatted wooden chairs with leather seats sitting around it. Kevin could see through the open door into the kitchen, where Rosy was busy gathering plates and cups.

He walked in and asked, "Can I give you a hand with anything?"

Rosy turned to him and said, "Oh, no, senor. You just go sit; I'll have these on the table in just a second."

As Kevin started to turn, the door going outside from the kitchen opened, and an elderly man stepped in saying, "Good morning, Senor."

Rosy smiled and said, "Pablo, this is Señor Kevin. He's one of the guests I told you about last night."

Pablo walked over and shook Kevin's hand, saying, "Con mucho gusto, Señor Kevin. You may call me Paul if you wish."

Kevin shook his hand and said, "Very nice to meet you also, Señor Pablo. You have a very pretty place here."

"Gracias," Pablo replied, nodding his head. "We are very proud of our little rancho; I hope you will enjoy your stay with us. Just let me know if there's anything you need or want to do."

"You men, get out of my kitchen and sit down," Rosy said sternly. "That's all men are good for; get in the way and wonder why we women can't get the food on the table fast enough. Now go!"

Laughing, Pablo said, "Let's get out of here; that old woman can get real mean when she doesn't get her way."

Leading the way back to the dining room, Pablo asked, "How was your trip?"

"Not what I'd call a luxury," Kevin replied. "But Mel got us all here safely, and that's what counts."

"Si, Si," Pablo said, nodding. "Our family has been providing services for many generations. Sometimes, it is necessary to take certain measures that are less than desirable, and we apologize."

"No apology necessary," Kevin said as he took a seat on one side of the table. "I completely understand."

As Pablo sat down across the table from Kevin, Gene came into the room smiling and rubbing his face as he said, "Man, it feels so good to get a close shave early in the morning."

"Right," Kevin retorted. "Gene, this is Señor Pablo, Aunt Rosy's husband."

Gene walked over to Pablo, who was getting up, and said, "Sir, it is my pleasure to meet you. Thank you for letting us stay with you and your wife."

"No, thank you," Pablo replied as he shook Gene's hand. "It is always our pleasure to have guests of my nephew, Mel. You are always welcome."

Rosita came in carrying a tray with glasses, cups, plates, a pitcher of orange juice, and a carafe of coffee, saying, "Talk, talk, talk, that's all you men do. Why couldn't you lend a poor old woman a hand with the things around here?"

"Pay her no mind," Pablo said as he reached for a cup and the coffee. "She is always cranky in the mornings, and I've had to suffer with her attitude for over 40 years. And believe me, this is her good side!"

"Oh, hush, old man, and pour our guests some juice and coffee while I go get the rest of the things," Rosy said as she gently slapped Pablo on the top of his head.

Leslie walked in carrying BK just as Rosy was leaving and said, "Good morning, sir," when she saw Pablo.

Pablo rose and said, "Good morning, Senora. I am Pablo, poor unfortunate husband of Rosita, and I am pleased to meet you and your child."

Kevin smiled at the practiced graciousness of Pablo and said, "Señor Pablo, this is Leslie, the wife of the poor unfortunate Gene. And the little one is called BK. Leslie; please say hello to Pablo."

"Please sit," Pablo said, still standing. "My wife will be back shortly with our breakfast. I hope you have found our accommodations satisfactory."

Leslie sat beside Kevin while Gene held her chair, saying, "It's very nice, sir. I can't wait to see the country around here. It looked so pretty driving in."

As Gene sat beside Leslie, Rosy came in with a tray of toast, rolls, butter, and several jars of jelly and some honey, saying, "Good morning, Ms. Leslie; I suggest you hurry and take some of the food before these men get it all."

Taking a chair beside Pablo, Rosy sat and told Leslie, "Now, let's eat. You'll have all day to see the country but only seconds to get a roll before the vultures circle the breakfast I've worked so hard to prepare."

"Breakfast," Pablo snorted. "Where are my eggs, my bacon, and some fresh tortillas? I swear, old woman, if it wasn't so much trouble, I'd find a new woman."

"And what, old man?" Rosy joked as she passed the plate of rolls across to Gene. "You think you can teach her to cook, clean your house, and put up with your laziness?"

Kevin smiled as he watched the two teasing each other and hoped that someday Gene and Leslie could look back on their lives and take pleasure in each other's company the way Rosy and Pablo did. Right now, he just wanted to hear from Butch and that he had found a way for them to return to Texas and have that chance.

CHAPTER 44

Major Jerry Fleenor left early the next morning and drove north on I-35 until he reached the intersection with Highway 287. Once there, he took 287 north for another 15 miles or so into Rhome. Having driven this same road back when he went to Decatur to make his first contact with Butch North, he knew to take the Highway 114 West exit toward Butch's house.

It was just getting light as he came to the stoplight in front of Tater Junction Restaurant. Not quite seven o'clock, there were only a few cars parked there waiting for the restaurant to open. Jerry cut through the parking lot and crossed FM 718 into Kountry Korner. He could see a couple of trucks at the diesel pumps filling their tanks as he drove to the gas pumps in front of the store. Parking, he went inside and told the lady behind the cash register that he wanted to fill his truck.

As she took three $20's from him, he asked, "Excuse me, but has Butch North been in this morning?"

"Not that I know of," she said as she reset one of the gas pumps so he could dispense the fuel. "You can ask Marshall if he's seen him."

"Who's Marshall?" Jerry asked.

"He's in the back loading some feed," she replied. "When you finish filling your truck, you can park on the side and go see if he knows where Butch is."

"Thanks," Jerry said as he went back out to fill his gas tank.

After putting $52 of gas into his truck, Jerry backed from the pumps and moved to the side of the red building where he could see the large roll-up doors open and a pickup loaded with sacks of horse feed.

After parking and waiting for the pickup to leave, Jerry walked in and followed the man who had loaded the feedback toward the front of the store. "Excuse me," he said as he followed him to the cashier's counter. "I'm looking for Butch North. Have you seen him this morning?"

Marshall turned and said, "No, I haven't seen him in a couple of days. I think he was in here yesterday or the day before and got gas, but I'm not sure which day it was. Can I help you with something?"

"No," Jerry said as he took the change from his gas purchase. "He and I were in the Air Force together, and he asked me to come up so he can show me around. I'm looking for some property up around here when I retire later this year."

"Well, he lives just across the road," Marshall told him. "You might try over there. If he's not home, he might be at Tater Junction having breakfast or over at the stables on Old Base Road."

"Okay," Jerry said, putting his change back in his pocket, "I'll look around. If you see him, please tell him that Major Jerry Fleenor from down at the base would like to talk to him. He has my number, and I'd like for him to call me so we can arrange a meeting today if possible."

"I'll let him know," Marshall told him. "Like I said, if he's not at his house, he's probably eating or at the stables."

"Thanks," Jerry said as he turned to leave. "I'll be looking around most of the morning. If he isn't at the stables or his house, I'll be having breakfast at Tater Junction and be there for an hour or so."

Jerry was positive that Butch wasn't at either of the places Marshall had suggested but knew that several of Butch's friends ate breakfast at Tater Junction, so he drove back across the street and parked. He could see Butch's house across the pasture and debated climbing the fence and walking to the house. But that would really serve no purpose and would definitely arouse suspicion if he was seen.

He locked his pickup and followed the two men who had parked their pickup beside his into the restaurant. Inside, he watched them wave to some other men sitting at one of the tables and go to join them. Standing by the cash register, Jerry waited for someone to notice him.

Almost immediately, one of the employees saw him and walked up, saying, "Good morning; if you'd like breakfast, just have a seat anywhere, and we'll take care of you."

"Yes, ma'am," Jerry said as he went into the same section he had seen the other men enter. Finding an empty booth, he sat down and waited for a waiter to arrive.

A lady walked up smiling, carrying a glass of water and a menu asking, "Breakfast, sir?"

Jerry smiled back and said, "Yes, ma'am."

"Coffee?" she asked, setting the water and menu on the table.

"Yes, thanks," Jerry answered, picking up the menu.

As she left, Jerry looked around at the people sitting at the other tables. They looked the same as he was used to seeing back home in Muleshoe, a combination of cowboy hats and ball caps, some in overalls and others in long sleeve shirts and jeans, and predominately middle-aged or older men.

When his coffee was brought, he asked, "Have you seen Butch North this morning?"

"No," the waitress replied. "I'll ask Teddy if he's seen him. He lives just behind the stables and would know if he's over there."

Moments after she left, a slightly built older man came over to the table carrying a pot of coffee, asking, "Are you the guy looking for Butch North?"

"Yes, sir, I am," Jerry replied. "Have you seen him this morning?"

"Nope," Teddy answered. "I haven't seen him in a couple of days, I think. He did borrow my van two days ago, but it was back that afternoon."

"You say he borrowed your van?" Jerry asked. "Why did he need your van?"

"I don't know," Teddy answered as he topped the half-full cup of coffee. "I actually didn't see him. He just left a note that morning saying he needed it, and later that afternoon, it was back."

"Anything else?" Teddy asked suspiciously.

"No, I reckon not," Jerry said. "But if you see him, please ask him to give me a call. Just tell him that Major Jerry Fleenor from down at the base was here and would like to talk to him."

The waitress was walking up as Teddy asked, "Does he have your number, or do you want to leave it?"

Jerry pulled a ballpoint pen from his shirt pocket and said, "He had it, but if you'll let me have a piece of paper, I'll leave it just in case he's lost it."

The waitress tore a ticket from her pad and handed it to him, saying, "Here, use this. Are you ready to order?"

Jerry scribbled the number of the cell phone he had used to call Butch two days ago, handed it to Teddy, and said, "Yes, ma'am. I'd like the Spanish omelet with jalapenos, hash browns, crispy on the outside, and an English muffin."

After Jerry finished his breakfast, he sat drinking coffee and watching the people come and go. Most of them seemed to know each other or at least be casually acquainted. It brought back a lot of memories of sitting with his dad at the Dinner Bell Cafe back in Muleshoe. Finally, he left a generous tip and took his ticket back to the cashier.

The waitress who had first met him at the door was ringing up another man's bill while he waited. Finally, when she asked him if everything was all right, he jokingly told her it was the best breakfast he'd had all day and handed her his money. After taking his change and thanking her, he went out and called the base to report in and to see if there had been any progress.

After hearing that nothing had changed, Jerry drove over to the stables and asked about Butch. Finally, after spending a couple of hours stopping at every place where he thought Butch might be known, he drove into Boyd and bought a prepaid cell phone at the Dollar General Store. Back in his pickup, he opened his briefcase, found Butch's cell phone number, and began a text message to him. As soon as it was sent, he wondered if his superiors back at the base would approve of what he'd just done.

Back at the base, General Modelle was up early, showering before making another call to Washington to give them the latest report. After shaving and brushing his teeth, he started a pot of coffee and opened the metal case holding his phone. Once the system was activated and the security systems verified, he called his boss.

"Good morning, sir," he said as it was answered. "I just wanted to give you a quick update on the progress here. I'm sure you already know about the broadcast that Mr. North interrupted last night, and regardless of the question of it being him by the media, we are convinced it was Mr. North."

After waiting for his boss to comment, Paul continued, "We've run voice analysis, and there's no doubt. We are currently checking any security cameras from his bank in Rhome and those where the call originated. I honestly don't expect anything from them to help us, but it's about all we have right now."

"I understand, sir," Paul said into the phone a second later. "I expect Mr. North to follow through with his promise to contact us. We all believe that the package was his first notice that he was going to take some sort of action. I don't believe that he's ready to expose our project because he'd have already done so if that was his intent."

Paul listened for a moment and replied, "To be honest, I don't know what he's up to. But, since there has been nothing regarding the other envelopes he sent, I can only assume that they haven't been opened. That leads me to think that he's instructed the recipients to hold them."

Paul took a deep breath and said, "Sir, if I was a betting man, I'd bet that Mr. North is doing his best to keep our secret but isn't going to stand for any more activity on our part that's causing him distress. He has plenty of information, but he hasn't made it public. That tells me he's not interested in exposing us."

Paul listened again and then replied, "No, sir, I haven't discussed this with the rest of the folks down here. But one of them, Major Jerry Fleenor, seems to think that we've approached Mr. North the wrong way and has an idea that Mr. North can be convinced to cooperate with us. Major Fleenor left this morning to visit the area around Mr. North's house to see if he could find some information that would help him contact Mr. North. I expect him to call us within the next couple of hours and let us know what he's found."

"To be completely honest, sir," Paul concluded, "until Mr. North contacts us, I think we're out of ideas. Nothing we've done has provided any clue as to where our project went and the fact that North's operating just outside the gates of the base proves that we're practically powerless to control the situation. The only things we have left are those cameras, and they can't tell us where he is, just where he's been. And I'm convinced that Mr. North is so far ahead of us that by the time we're where he was, he's disappeared and is working on his next move."

Paul listened again as he was chastised and finally said, "Yes, sir. I'll call as soon as I get anything."

He hung up the phone and locked it back in its case, feeling the full weight of their failure to accomplish the directives they had been given. Paul had been in the military too long to think that a lack of progress would be tolerated for much longer.

He left his room and headed for the operations room, hoping to hear that some small piece of information would help them find any of the people they were so desperately trying to find.

As he walked in, Colonel Erickson was talking to General Nelson about the information that had just arrived from the cameras at the bank. "Good morning, gentlemen," Paul said, approaching them.

"Good morning, General," Mike said as they came to attention.

"What're you looking at?" Paul asked, seeing the slightly grainy black-and-white images of what looked like a bank drive-through.

"We just received the data from Woodhaven Bank," Mike explained. "This is from the exterior camera that monitored the night deposit and ATM machine area.

As they watched, there was a good view of a man rounding the corner and walking toward the night deposit box. They watched him put some keys into an envelope, write something on it, and drop it into the box. Then he turned and went back out of view as he returned around the corner.

"That doesn't look exactly like Mr. North," Paul said. "Have you had it analyzed?"

"Yes, sir," Mike answered. "It was checked against every photo of Mr. North we had, and the facial recognition program gave us a 100% match. Although he's wearing a ball cap and sunglasses and kept his head down, there was enough information as he came around the corner to prove his identity."

"Can we get those shots of his face enhanced?" Paul asked.

"Yes, sir," Rick answered. "It's already being done in Washington. We hope to have a good quality photo of Mr. North's face as it appears in the first few frames."

"We'll have this on the news as soon as we get it," Rick continued. "It appears that Mr. North has hung up his hat. He's trying to change his appearance by wearing a ball cap and T-shirt instead of the usual long-sleeved shirt."

Paul watched as the scene was replayed and said, "Well, it seems to be working. I'd never have given him a second look, and it appears that no one else has either. Hell, he could be sitting in the lobby of a motel, and our agents probably would walk right by him."

Paul turned to Mike and asked, "Mike, what do you and Rick think about how Mr. North's handling this? What I mean is, why hasn't he made any of this public? He certainly has enough proof of our activities, and if he's given them to reputable people as he says, what's he waiting for?"

Waiting for them to consider his question, Paul continued, "I'm beginning to believe that he doesn't want to expose us. As Major Fleenor said, Mr. North appears to want to safeguard our secret but won't stand for any further intrusion or being lied to. What are your opinions?"

Mike nodded his head and said, "You may be right, sir. He hasn't acted as if he wants the information known, but he certainly let us know without a doubt that he has it and will use it."

"Do you remember when we were initially questioning him and his daughters?" Rick asked Mike. "I swear that initially, he seemed to be cooperative. Then, all of a sudden, it's like a veil dropped over his eyes. You could almost see the look of disdain when our agent started telling him the story we had concocted."

"I think Jerry was right," he continued. "I think we need to reevaluate the man and see if we can't convince him of the importance of our program and the impact of disclosure. Everything in his records points to him being capable of being trusted with information that would shock most of the civilian population."

"All right," Paul said. "Let's start thinking of a strategy that incorporates this line of reasoning to use when Mr. North contacts us. I believe we all know now that this is the only way we'll ever catch him. And, even if we get him, I don't think that by itself will result in the return of our project."

CHAPTER 45

Butch wandered about the mall for a few more minutes, spending some time in a couple of the stores that really had nothing that interested him. It was getting close to lunchtime, but he wasn't really hungry. Wasting time was one thing he wasn't used to, and it irritated him that he wasn't free to do the things he wanted to.

Almost to the doors leading outside, he suddenly turned around and walked briskly back to the phone. Digging a couple of coins out of his pocket, he checked the phone directory in his cell phone and dialed the number for Tammy's office. Maybe he was taking a chance, but the government already knew he was still in the area, and he wanted to tell Tammy that what he knew she would have seen on the news wasn't true.

Waiting for it to be answered, Butch thought about the odds of there being a tap on her office phone. Possible, but not very likely, he decided. Another possibility was some voice recognition program that scanned the entire spectrum of phone calls, searching for a match. That also seemed very remote.

When the phone was finally answered, Butch asked, "Is Tammy Terbush in?"

Holding it while it was transferred to her desk, Butch watched the people flowing up and down the hall between the stores. *'Looks like a bunch of salmon swimming up and down the stream trying to figure out where they want to spawn but lost in the currents,'* Butch thought. He also had no doubt that the women got more pleasure out of shopping than they did spawning.

Hearing her voice, Butch asked, "Tammy, can you get away for an hour or so?"

As soon as she said yes, he told her, "TM in TC."

Tammy replied, "Okay," and Butch hung up the phone. Several months ago, he had taken her to Cristina's Mexican Restaurant in Trophy Club, and they had started referring to eating there as 'Tex-Mex in Trophy Club' or just 'TM in TC.'

Just hearing her voice lifted his spirits, and he was smiling as he headed for the door. As quick as he could get the car started, he pulled out of the parking lot and back onto Loop 820. Merging with the northbound traffic, Butch followed the loop as it started going west. About five miles later, he came to Highway 377 and made the exit north toward Watauga and Keller. Although the traffic was fairly light, Butch seemed to hit every signal just as it turned red.

It took almost 20 minutes to drive the seven or eight miles from the mall to where 377 crossed Highway 114. Getting on the access road, Butch continued until he came to Cristina's and parked. Locking his car, he looked for Tammy's but didn't see it parked among the others.

The minute he walked in, the aroma of the cooking food hit him and brought on a hunger that hadn't been there just moments before. Looking around at the tables, he spotted Tammy sitting off to the side by herself, reading a menu. Leaving his ball cap and sunglasses on, he went to her table.

Tammy looked up momentarily as he approached but quickly resumed reading. When he remained standing, she frowned as she looked at him again until she recognized who he was. She dropped the menu on the table and started to get up, smiling.

"Please," Butch said, putting his hand on her shoulder, "keep your seat."

When Tammy sat back down, Butch slid into a chair beside her and asked, "Surprised?"

Tammy's expression changed from happy to one of supreme irritation, and she said, "Do you know what you've put me through? Do you have any idea at all?"

"No," Butch replied, "but I'm sure you're about to tell me."

"You're damned right I am," Tammy said as she roughly toyed with the napkin on her lap. "Not only do you leave me in the dark about what you've been doing these last few months, but you get me involved without my consent."

"And," Tammy cried with tears running down her cheeks, "you've caused me to be arrested because of what you've done. And I had nothing to do with any of it. How could you do this to me?"

"What do you mean?" Butch asked incredulously. "Who arrested you?"

"The frigging FBI!" Tammy almost shouted. "They took me out to the base and interrogated me for several hours, and then they locked me up for the night."

"Sshh," Butch said quietly, putting his finger against his lips. "There are other people here, you know."

"Then, they started again the next morning," she continued. "Hours of questions about you, someone named Gene, and your friend Kevin! Whom, I may say, I have *never* met."

Tammy pulled the napkin from her lap, dabbed her eyes, and started again, "I just can't believe that you'd do the things they said you did. And I really can't believe that you care so little for me that you'd keep secrets from me. That's what really hurts! You just don't care!"

Butch sat back and waited for Tammy to vent all of her frustration before asking, "May I speak now?"

Tammy went from weeping to being mad again in mere seconds, saying, "Yes, and it better be good. Otherwise, you can just pick your skinny ass up and get the hell out of my life!"

Just as Butch started to talk, a waitress came up and asked if they were ready to order. Butch looked at the chips and salsa already on the table and said, "If it's all right with the lady here, I'd like the beef fajitas for two."

Tammy just stared at him, finally nodding, and said, "Fine, give the man whatever he wants."

The waitress looked questioningly at Butch as if to ask if everything was okay, and he just nodded, saying, "I'd like a glass of unsweetened tea also, ma'am."

Tammy shoved the menu to the edge of the table and crossed her arms as she turned her face away from Butch. The waitress made a face that meant that she didn't want to hang around their table any longer than necessary and left.

"Are you ready to listen?" Butch said as soon as the waitress was gone.

"What? Are you going to tell me it was for my own good?" Tammy asked, glaring at Butch.

"No," Butch said quietly. "I'm going to tell you the truth as much as I can."

"Oh," Tammy exclaimed, "don't forget to explain the news either. Everyone in the country thinks I'm involved with a fugitive that's involved with terrorists."

"First," Butch told her, "this isn't about you! It's not about me, either. It's about trying to help someone who has been accused of something that he hasn't done."

Stunned that Butch would be so quick to dismiss her hurt feelings and chastise her, Tammy crossed her arms again, sullying up, and said, "Go ahead, make me the one that's done something wrong."

"I didn't say you've done anything wrong," Butch said. "I'm just saying that the whole issue is about trying to prevent an innocent person from suffering for a crime he didn't commit."

"Just how do you know he didn't do it?" Tammy asked, still angry.

"I just know," Butch told her. "The man called Gene is just a boy, and if you had ever seen him yourself, you'd know that he couldn't possibly look like those pictures of him dressed as a rag-head."

"Just how long have you known this Gene?" Tammy demanded.

"Since the government first started looking for him after the 9-11 World Trade Center attack," Butch said. "I found him that morning walking up 730 toward Boyd and took him to the stables."

"I never saw him over there," Tammy said, doubting his story.

"No, you wouldn't have," Butch explained. "The next morning, the 12th, some people claiming to be FBI agents and an Air Force Colonel came to my house looking for him and then took me and the kids to the base for questioning after we couldn't find him."

Watching Tammy's expression, he continued, "We listened to a bunch of bullshit from some jerk in a dark suit while a Colonel and a General stood watching us like judges in some bizarre trial. When they finally took us back to the house, I went over to the stables to feed the horses since Gene wasn't there when we had searched the place with the first Colonel."

"I found Gene hiding in the haystack, scared out of his wits," Butch told her. "I listened to his story, and what he told me made much more sense than the government's story."

"What did he tell you?" Tammy asked, almost over her anger.

"He said he had been raised in a laboratory beneath one of the hangers on the base," Butch said. "And, he had never known his mother, only a nurse named Vicki Grubbs. He never left the facility except at night and was flown somewhere and asked questions about things he had never seen."

"And you believed him?" Tammy asked.

"Yes, I did," Butch answered. "Now, here's the part that really convinced me. From that day on, including now, all of my phones have been tapped. Every move I make has been watched, including our trip to San Antonio and Mexico. Even my kids were followed, and most of my friends were. Don't you think they'd spend their time looking for their suspect instead of watching me?"

"Maybe they thought you'd lead them to him," Tammy reasoned.

"Maybe," Butch countered. "But, after months of me not having any contact with Gene, don't you think they'd shift their focus? And why did it all disappear from the news?"

"Okay, what about Kevin?" Tammy asked.

"He hid Gene," Butch answered. "And Leslie, and now he's with them and the baby."

"What baby?" Tammy asked, showing her first real interest. "Who's baby?"

"Gene and Leslie's baby," Butch told her. "The birth of their son is the real reason that the government is back in full swing trying to find Gene. It's not just him they're looking for; it's the child also."

"Why would they want the baby?" Tammy asked. "He didn't do anything wrong."

Butch paused and finally confessed, "It's his genes. I think Gene is the result of some genetic experiments, and the baby will have some of the same DNA. It's really the DNA that the government doesn't want the public to know about." "What makes you think there's some experiments with DNA going on at the base?" Tammy asked, very interested now.

"I had an analysis of Gene's DNA performed last year at a lab I know of in Lewisville," Butch explained. "I told them I was trying to determine the parents of the donor."

"And did you?" Tammy asked as she leaned forward.

"No," Butch answered. "But there were some very abnormal characteristics of the sample. The lab tried to explain it as a possible contamination, but I've done enough sample collection with the horses to know how to avoid that. No, there's something very strange with Gene's DNA."

"And," he finished, "it's very evident with the baby boy. And that's why I think the government is so interested in finding them. They hold the key to something they don't want to be made public."

"What's wrong with the baby?" Tammy asked anxiously.

"Some rather strange facial features," Butch told her.

Just as he was about to elaborate, the waitress arrived carrying a steaming plate of fajitas with sautéed onions and peppers. As she placed it on the table along with two plates half-covered with Mexican rice, two bowls of borracho beans, and a warmer full of tortillas, Butch looked up at Tammy seeing her smile for the first time since they'd started talking.

When the waitress left, Tammy asked, "What about the baby? What do you think caused him to look strange?"

"I have no idea," Butch lied. "But, I'm positive there's something going on down there, and I've enlisted someone with a little more horsepower to help me resolve this little 'inconvenience.'

Taking a hot tortilla and laying two slices of the fajita meat, some sautéed onion, and a little Pico-de-Gallo on it, Butch said, "Enough for now, I promise to tell you the full story when I can. But for now, just trust me that I'm doing everything I can to clear this up. If I ever find out what's really going on, I'll tell you."

Tammy started loading her tortilla with meat, onion, guacamole, salsa, Pico, and sour cream, saying, "Okay, but I want to meet them and the baby. Promise me I can meet them, all right?"

"I'll try," Butch said, getting a spoonful of his borracho beans. "But I never promise something I can't be sure of. And I don't know how this is going to end. But I'll do my best."

"That's good enough for me," Tammy said, looking like she'd like to take the rest of the day off and spend it in bed with Butch as she slid her foot up against his leg under the table.

Butch looked at her over the table, smiling, and said, "Not now, you know I'd love to spend the rest of the day with you, but I've got other things to do."

"The rest of the day?" Tammy replied. "I'm thinking about the rest of our lives. And today is the perfect time to get started. Don't you think so?"

Butch shook his head, smiling, and said, "I've always told you that I need to find a new mother for my poor lil' orphaned kids. But I promised my dear sainted mother that any future wife would have large hooters, a double-cab dually, and a four-horse slant-load trailer with living quarters. You got none, and I do mean *none*, of the requirements. Sorry!"

Tammy kicked him beneath the table, frowning, and said, "Jerk!"

Butch just smiled and replied, "Reckon so, but damn sure a charming one! How can you not just love me?"

Just then, Butch heard the tone on his cell phone that told him he had a text message. Glancing at it, he got up and laid two $20 bills on the table, telling Tammy, "I've got to take care of something. If you'd take care of the waitress and the check, I'll try to call you later. And, please, don't worry."

CHAPTER 46

After breakfast, Pablo took Kevin on a tour of the area around the house, showing him the corrals, barns, and livestock. Kevin asked if they could use one of the Jeeps and take a drive up into the mountains that surrounded the ranch. Pablo agreed to take them for a trip later in the afternoon, but he had a few things he needed to do that morning.

As Pablo talked about the size of the ranch, Kevin was surprised to learn that it encompassed thousands of acres and included most of the mountain ranges on either side. Pablo explained how his family had gotten the land generations ago because someone way back then had been a member of some Spanish royalty, and the land was given to reward their financial support of some early expedition.

Throughout the years, the original Spanish had mixed with the indigenous Indians that had lived here before the explorers from Spain arrived. Some of the still pure Spanish descendants felt they were superior to those who had interbred with the natives. Most of those called 'Mexican' were a result of the mixing of the races, and those closer to the original Spanish bloodlines could still have red hair and green eyes.

Of course, the Mexican population had far exceeded those with no mixing, and today, those who had married some of the whites coming into Texas made it even less likely to find a pure Spanish descendant. Pablo was very proud of his Spanish ancestors but was equally proud of his Indian and Texan heritage.

"What about Sancudo?" Kevin asked. "What is his relationship to you?"

"Oh," Pablo said, "he is the son of a cousin of mine. When our great-great-grandfathers, or even before them, died, the land was passed along one line of the family. It was the custom for the oldest son to inherit, and he was expected to make accommodations for his brothers and sisters."

"So, he would divide the land and give them some of it?" Kevin asked.

"Not necessarily so," Pablo explained. "Usually, he kept all of the land but provided for the rest of them to have an income or a job. The land was to be kept intact, but the revenue could be divided. The custom dates back to early Spain or other European countries and is used in the US as well."

"I see," Kevin replied. "I know of some ranches like that in Texas, such as the King Ranch. I can understand that after several generations of dividing the land, there would be little left of the original ranch. And, if some of the heirs wanted to sell their part, it would be impossible to control what happened or who got control of the land."

"That is correct," Pablo replied. "Now, Sancudo's side of the family has always had access to our lands, and several generations have benefited from the original land grant. One thing about Mexican families is that they tend to be very loyal to each other. We value that above all else; our family is the reason we exist."

"I wish I could say the same for our country," Kevin said. "I've seen more families divided over inheritance than anything else. I've even watched sisters fighting over who got which flowers off of the grave the minute the services were over. We could certainly use a little more family closeness."

"Is there anything else you'd like to see this morning?" Pablo asked. "Or, is there anything you and your family need?"

"I'd like to just walk around with Gene and show him how different the land is around here," Kevin said. "He's never seen mountains before, and I know he hasn't seen the different types of plants you have down here."

"And, by the way," Kevin told him, "they aren't really my family, but I like to think of them as if they were."

"Sometimes our closest family has no blood ties," Pablo said knowingly. "It is important to have a family regardless of who bred who. You are a lucky man to have people who care for you, even if they aren't related."

"Yes," Kevin admitted. "I've become very attached to those two kids and their little boy."

"Is there anything special we need to do for the baby?" Pablo asked. "I noticed that he was somewhat different."

"No," Kevin answered. "For right now, everything seems to be going all right. He's only three days old, and we don't know what problems may arise, but for now, we just watch over him."

"Well, if there is anything we can do, please just let us know," Pablo told him as they walked back toward the house.

"There is one question I have," Kevin said.

"What is that, senor?" Pablo asked.

"If we do need to get the child to a doctor, how would we do it?" Kevin asked.

"We've had several emergencies over the years," Pablo told him. "If possible, we take care of it by bringing a doctor, who is also related to our family, to see the patient. If it is necessary to take them to a hospital, we always have an airplane."

"What about if the airplane is busy, like when we were brought in?" Kevin asked.

"A true emergency always takes priority," Pablo said. "The airplane is normally used to take our guests out, either from here or one of our other locations. But, sometimes, it is better not to be seen crossing the border so often and going to the same location. Your government has ways of watching the skies that make it more susceptible to following us than a single car among hundreds crossing the border."

Kevin had been wondering if Butch knew where they were and had some plan to get them out quickly if necessary, and an airplane would be the best way to get them out. However, knowing Butch, Kevin figured that he didn't have the exact location and had left that to Sancudo. That way, if Butch was caught, he couldn't reveal exactly where they were.

"I guess you folks have got it worked out pretty well," Kevin said as they neared the house. "One other thing, is it possible to contact a friend of mine back in the States?"

"No, Senor," Pablo told him as he opened the door leading into the kitchen. "No one may contact anyone outside the ranch. If absolutely necessary, I can contact Sancudo, and he may pass a message. But it is seldom that he will do so. If he has news for you, he will call someone, who will call me, and I will tell you."

Stepping into the kitchen, Kevin saw Leslie and Gene watching Rosy as she held BK and rocked him back and forth. Rosy was smiling down at BK as she held him, and you could tell she had a special affection for children and obviously cared for them regardless of whose child they were.

"Don't you be getting any ideas, old woman," Pablo said as he walked in and saw them. "I'll be having no more children."

Rosy looked up, smiling, and told him, "You are not the only stud on the ranch, old man. I may just take after another since soon you'll need to be put out to pasture anyway."

"An old woman like you can't compete with all the pretty young fillies out there," Pablo chided. "You're lucky I let you stay around anyway; I may just take after one of the young ones myself!"

"If you want to be a gelding," Rosy joked, "just let me catch you rolling your lip up around any other female!"

Gene had been standing beside Leslie, listening to them, and looked questioningly at Kevin. Kevin just shook his head and said, "Gene, see what you have to look forward to? Constant arguing and threats, are you sure you want to hang around Leslie and face that in the coming years?"

"Leslie and I will never argue," Gene replied.

"Oh yes, you will," Rosy told him. "Pablo and I have had more fights than a stray tomcat in Juarez, but I've always forgiven him and made him understand that I'm always right."

"You've been right about as many times as there are lips on a chicken, old woman," Pablo said, turning to leave. "Now, I'll let you just stand there and cackle while I go take care of the work that keeps this place going."

"Don't you kids be fooled by her," he said, walking out of the door. "I'm the man around here, and she'll do as I say."

Pablo ducked as Rosy threw a wet towel at his head and left laughing. "The old fool," Rosy said. "But, I don't know what I'd do if he were to ever not be here."

Kevin smiled and said, "Gene, since you've never been around married couples, especially those that have spent so many years together, you need to understand that what looks like wrestling to some is dancing to another."

Leslie walked over and took BK from Rosy and told them she was going back to their bedroom to feed him. As Rosy handed him to her, Kevin noticed that the baby looked a little paler than before.

"Let me have a look at him," Kevin said, walking over to Leslie's side.

Pulling the blanket from around BK, Kevin looked at his skin and asked, "Have you noticed anything different about him?"

"No," Leslie replied. "He seems to be nursing just fine, and everything else seems to be working all right."

"I just don't like the color of his skin," Kevin said. "He looks a little lighter, and I'm not sure if it's normal. I know babies are redder when they're born, and sometimes it takes a day or so for them to adjust to life outside of the womb."

Kevin covered BK and said, "Just pay close attention to him, and if he seems to have any fever or if his body starts feeling too cool, let me know."

"Do you think there's a problem?" Gene asked anxiously.

"I don't know," Kevin admitted. "But we need to be prepared to get him to a doctor if necessary. I'll see if I can talk to Pablo about it."

Gene followed Leslie out of the kitchen as Kevin walked out to where he had seen Pablo headed. Now might be the time to let Sancudo start making arrangements to get them back to the States. If the health of the baby hung in the balance, they may just have to give themselves up.

At the very least, Kevin had to get word to Butch that things could necessitate some changes in whatever plans he had made. If he couldn't reach Butch, he'd have to make the decision himself. Either way, he needed to contact Sancudo.

CHAPTER 47

Jerry had sent the text to Butch's phone, and now he had to just wait. He didn't know if Butch would try to contact him, but by sending *'UR Frnd nds cnct,'* he hoped Butch *would use the phone he had given him, the one he had used to warn him* and call back. Maybe he should let Colonel Erickson know that he was trying this, but first, he wanted to hear from Butch what he wanted.

Jerry knew that Butch's cell phone was still being monitored and that the message would be seen almost immediately by the people at the facility. The phone he had just purchased couldn't be traced to him, and if they determined the location the call came from, it wouldn't be unusual to see that it came from Boyd. They'd wonder who had sent it but dismiss it as some friend of Butch's and probably think it was some lady that didn't want to be known about.

Jerry drove from the Dollar General Store back into Boyd and parked on the side of the cantina where Butch normally had an afternoon beer. He tossed the phone he had used for the text message into the open dumpster and waited for any contact. Although it was just barely past noon, there

351

were a few people going in and out of the side door of the cantina. Not knowing if his cell phone would get a signal inside, Jerry resigned himself to sitting in his car instead of going in and asking the people if they'd seen Butch.

Less than five minutes later, his phone rang, and he answered, "It's me. Can you talk?"

"Yes," Butch told him.

"Where are you?" Jerry asked.

"Somewhere," Butch replied. "What do you want?"

"The question is, what do you want?" Jerry told him.

"I want this over," Butch said.

"So do we," Jerry replied. "We want our product back."

"Agreed," Butch said, "but only on my conditions."

"And the baby?" Jerry asked.

"Yes," Butch answered. "Again, only on my conditions."

"What are your conditions?" Jerry asked.

"I'll lay them out tomorrow," Butch told him.

"When?" Jerry wanted to know.

"You'll receive a call from the Base Commander when I'm ready," Butch answered.

"What about the packages you sent?" Jerry wanted to know.

"The rest of them are safe," Butch responded. "But they *will* be opened if you guys screw with me on this."

"Who did you send them to?" Jerry asked.

"People that can make your lives miserable," Butch replied. "That's all I'll tell you for now. You can tell your friends back at the base that this either ends tomorrow, or your secret will be revealed in the most effective way I know."

"Can I call your personal cell phone from the base?" Jerry asked.

"Yes," Butch hesitated and then answered. "But, wait a couple of hours and make it short. I'll give you that one call as proof of my willingness to cooperate, but as I've said twice already, only on my conditions."

Jerry's phone went dead as Butch hung up, and he sat staring at it for a moment, wondering again if he should call Rick. He knew he had stuck his neck out, and he also knew that there was mounting suspicion of some of his remarks. Maybe reporting this would serve two purposes; remove any doubt as to his loyalty and give his bosses some hope that things would be favorably resolved.

Although Jerry was as dedicated to the project as the rest of the team, he just couldn't continue sitting by and watching people trying to do what they thought was right be pursued the way Butch had been. He had no qualms about so-called *violations of people's rights* when it came to dealing with people who were breaking the law.

If a person was guilty of a crime, Jerry didn't care how you got your information or how vigorously you pursued them. This was an entirely different matter. Butch and Kevin weren't really breaking any law since Jerry knew that the charges against Gene were bogus. He also knew that Butch knew it too, and so must Kevin. Those two just weren't the types to break any law, such as aiding a terrorist.

And as for Leslie, she probably didn't know why this was happening. And it certainly wasn't the baby's fault that Butch had tried to protect someone he thought was innocent of the government's charges.

He finally decided that there was no way to explain how Butch had gotten his private phone number without revealing the whole story of his contacting Butch in David's

Western Wear months ago. Even more damning was how he had warned Butch about their discovery of the baby. Jerry knew the only way to make this work would be to go back to the base and pretend that the call to Butch was the first contact he had ever made with the man.

That decided, Jerry started his pickup, pulled back onto 114, and headed east toward Rhome. It would take about an hour to drive back to the base, and he needed at least that much time to devise a story that would convince both Colonel Erickson and General Nelson that contacting Butch directly would be to their benefit. And more importantly, that he should be the person to do it.

Jerry knew that the conversation would be recorded and on the speakers. He had to trust that Butch would know that also and not give any hint that they had ever talked before. This was not the first time since this had started that Jerry was placing his career in Butch's hands. One slip and everyone would know what Jerry had done, and that might end more than just his career.

When Jerry arrived back at the facility, he went directly to the operations room and looked for Colonel Erickson. Rick wasn't there, but Colonel Lynch was reviewing the photos from the bank and making sure the computer had enhanced Butch's face as much as possible.

"Where'd those come from?" Jerry asked, looking at an excellent picture of Butch wearing a ball cap.

"They came in this morning," Karyn told him. "They're from the drive-through area of the bank in Rome. We sent them to be enhanced, and the computer removed the sunglasses Butch had on when the picture was taken."

"Can I see the originals?" Jerry asked.

"Sure," Karyn said, handing him several un-retouched photos. "It would be difficult to identify him in these pictures if we didn't have a face recognition program."

"I'd never have recognized him from these photos," Jerry admitted. "It's amazing how much such small changes made in his appearance."

"Yes, but with the enhanced pictures beside the originals, it's easy to tell that it is Butch," Karyn remarked. "Now, with us knowing his new look, Mr. North might not hide so easily."

Colonel Erickson walked in as they were discussing how they were planning on distributing the pictures and whether or not to provide them to the news media.

"How'd it go up there?" Rick asked, seeing Jerry.

"Not much help," Jerry told him. "But I have an idea that I'd like for you and General Nelson to consider."

"What's that?" Rick questioned.

"I'd like to try making direct contact with Mr. North," Jerry answered. "We know he isn't at home, but I'd bet he still has his original cell phone, and we have that number."

"What makes you think he'd answer?" Rick wondered.

"Well, he's already said that he plans on contacting us," Jerry explained. "For now, we're waiting on him to make the first move. I think we'd be better off if we made it."

Rick stood looking at Jerry and finally said, "Let me get General Nelson and see what he thinks. I think we'd be running the risk of Mr. North taking our calling as an admission of our inability to control the situation."

"Yes, sir," Jerry said. "But, our only other option is to wait. And I think General Modelle and his bosses are about out of patience with waiting."

Rick picked up the phone on the desk and dialed Mike's number, saying, "I'll let General Nelson make the decision," as he waited for the call to be answered.

"Yes, Kathy," Rick said into the phone, "I need to talk to General Nelson, please."

Hearing that Mike was in his office talking to General Modelle, Rick said, "Would you please interrupt them? I think General Modelle also needs to be here with General Nelson when they get a chance."

"Thanks, Kathy. Just tell them Major Fleenor is back and wants to discuss something with them at their convenience," Rick said as he hung up.

A few minutes later, as he came into the operations room with Paul, Mike asked, "What'd you find out up in Boyd, Jerry?"

"Not much," Jerry answered. "But I have an idea that might expedite the situation."

"What's that?" Mike asked.

"I want to try contacting Mr. North," Jerry cautiously answered. "I think he might be receptive to our call. As you already know, he plans on contacting us at some point. I think we'd be better off making the first move."

"What do you think, Rick?" Mike asked.

"I just wonder if it wouldn't show weakness on our part, sir," Rick answered. "It just might make him think he has us cornered and start making demands we can't meet."

"General Modelle," Mike asked, turning, "what's your opinion?"

"I think Jerry's right," Paul said, nodding. "Rick, I understand your opinion, but in reality, Mr. North does have us cornered. The only question is, as you've noted, will he use his information to place unreasonable demands on us."

"Sir, if I may," Karyn interrupted. "We've just gotten these photos back from Washington, and they might provide us a better chance of finding Mr. North without waiting for him to call us."

"They might help us catch him. I agree they're more likely to have him spotted than the others we've published," Paul told her. "We'll get them out to the media and law enforcement as quickly as possible. But I don't want to dismiss an option that seems to be consistent with what we already know of Mr. North's intentions."

"I agree," Mike said. "If Mr. North intends on contacting us, we'll accommodate him and make the call. At the same time, we show him that we know how he looks by having these photos on the news as soon as we can."

"Sir," Jerry interrupted. "I'd like for you to reconsider putting these photos on the news."

"Why not?" Rick asked.

"Judging from his response the other night to the news broadcasts about his involvement," Jerry explained, "I'd say it would have a negative effect on his willingness to cooperate."

"I think Jerry's right," Paul said, nodding. "At this point, we don't want him to change his mind about cooperating and possibly retaliate against what he must see as defamation."

"We'll provide the pictures to all the law enforcement people," Paul continued. "But there'll be no further broadcasts about Mr. North's involvement until after we talk to him."

"When do you want to attempt contact?" Mike asked.

"Now's as good a time as ever," Jerry said. "And, with your permission, I'd like to be the one to do it."

"I think we all agree that you'd probably be the best one of us to talk to him," Mike said. "Just be careful of what you say and try to keep him on the phone as long as you can. We might be able to get a fix on his location and get there before he can leave."

"I wouldn't count on him giving us that opportunity," Paul said, turning to Jerry. "What's your plan, Major?"

"Well, sir," Jerry answered as he picked up the phone, "I plan on asking him what he wants from us. I think he knows we can keep pressure on him forever, and he probably thinks he can keep our product from us forever."

Jerry glanced at the list of known numbers for Butch and started dialing as he continued saying, "A stalemate does neither of us any good. I think the best approach is to try to negotiate from a neutral position. He has something we want, and we control something he wants."

Mike nodded at Karyn, signaling for her to activate the speakers and the recorders as they waited anxiously for the phone to be answered. As the ringing sounded lightly throughout the room, they all held their collective breaths as they waited for what might be their only hope.

"Butch North," came the answer as the ringing stopped.

"Mr. North, this is Major Jerry Fleenor from the NAS/JRB," Jerry said, looking at the expectant faces around him.

"What do you want, Major Fleenor?" Butch asked.

"Sir, I want to know what you want," Jerry said.

"If you're from where I think you are, I want for you folks to quit lying to me or about me," Butch announced. "I want you to leave me and my friends alone."

"When can we discuss this?" Jerry asked. "Would you like to come meet with us here?"

"I'll let you know," Butch said. "You can expect a call from the Base Commander tomorrow regarding a meeting."

"Now, before you can get a trace on my location," Butch said, "I'll tell you one other thing. I don't want to expose your little problem. But I won't sit by and watch you do what you've been doing to the young man I know as Gene or the rest of us. I think you know that by now."

Following a slight pause, Butch continued, "Now, here're the rules; I want the two officers I met last year to attend. I want you there also, Major. And I want whoever has the authority to make the final decision to be there. This will be resolved before I leave, or I will release the information that you've had time to verify. There will be no future negotiations; this is the only time I will try to help you. And my demands will be reasonable but final. Do we have an agreement?"

Jerry looked at Mike and Paul for their approval. Once they both nodded yes, he said, "Mr. North, we'll wait for your call."

The line went dead before Jerry got to finish his sentence, and he stood looking at the phone in his hand. Finally replacing it, he turned to the rest, saying, "Well, I guess we know he's not going to go public for now."

"I think we can view this as a step forward," Paul said, greatly relieved after hearing that Butch didn't plan on releasing their secret unless things changed.

"I agree," Mike said. "I'd just like to know beforehand what his demands will be."

"I think you've heard them, sir," Jerry said. "I think he just wants to be left alone and provide some protection for Gene."

"Mike, call General Brown and ask if he has an appointment with anyone scheduled for tomorrow," Paul said. "If he doesn't, tell him to expect a call from Mr. North."

"Yes, sir," Mike said as he dialed his office. "Kathy, get the Base Commander on the phone for me, please. I'll hold on to this line."

Moments later, Mike heard General Brown say, "Good afternoon, Mike. How can I help you?"

"General, do you have any appointments with anyone for tomorrow?" Mike asked.

"Yes, I do," General Brown answered. "I just finished looking at my schedule, and I have one with retired U.S. Senator Larry Burklow scheduled for tomorrow morning."

"If you don't mind my asking, what's the purpose of the Senator's visit?" Mike asked.

"His secretary arranged it," Gary answered. "She said it had something to do with some special project he wanted the base to help sponsor. I just assumed it had something to do with his involvement in that charity for special needs children. Would you like for me to find out more?"

"No," Mike told him. "We were just wondering if Mr. North had contacted you. As you probably saw on the news last night, he said he'd do so. Since he can't possibly know how to contact us, you're the logical one to call."

"Haven't heard a thing," Gary said. "I'll let you know if I do. Anything else?"

"No, that'll do it, I guess. Thanks." Mike said, hanging up.

"Do you think that visit from the Senator has anything to do with our issue?" Paul asked.

"I don't see how," Mike answered. "Besides, that appointment was probably made weeks ago."

Mike looked around and said, "Well, folks, I think we've made some progress. How it ends is still to be determined. Karyn, get those photos out as soon as you can, but not to the media yet. Now, unless anyone has something to add, I think we might as well take off for the night. Or, at least until we hear from Mr. North."

"That sounds about the size of it," Paul said. "I'll give the folks at Washington a call and try to breathe some hope into their opinion of how this operation is going."

Jerry watched as everyone was leaving and breathed a silent sigh of relief. Butch had kept his remarks succinct and didn't offer a clue as to any previous contacts with him. He just hoped that Butch could just keep that information secret for a few more days.

CHAPTER 48

Butch had driven from Cristina's east on Highway 114 into Grapevine while he waited for the call from the base. In Grapevine, he had gone north on Main Street and parked in a large lot across the street from Willhoite's Restaurant. Checking the clock on the dash, he still had almost an hour before he expected the call.

Locking the car, Butch glanced at all of the motorcycles parked in front of Willhoite's and decided to wait at another restaurant about a block away. Cutting through an opening in a chain link fence, he went into the back door of Esparza's Restaurante Mexicano and stepped up to the bar. Esparza's was a local hangout for many of the airline crews that lived in the surrounding area, and Butch had been here with both of his kids several times.

After paying for his Budweiser, Butch walked through the restaurant and went out onto the patio, where several tables were filled with people eating chips and salsa with their drinks. Looking around, he saw a table with a group of folks he knew from American Airlines. As he stepped over to their table, he pulled his sunglasses off and nodded at one of the men he had flown with months earlier.

"Hey, Kerry," he said. "You folks have room for one more?"

Kerry looked up and finally recognized him, saying, "Butch, what're you doing out without your hat? Except on the airplane, I don't think I've ever seen you without it."

"Just trying to fit in with you city slickers," Butch replied as he took an empty chair.

"It's not working," said Patty, one of the flight attendants sitting there. "How are you, Butch? Haven't seen you around here very much lately."

"Well," Butch said, "since my darling daughter Jeannie finally finished spending all of my money getting educated up at The University of North Texas, she's moved back to Washington and deprived me of our weekly beer and dinner evenings here."

"It's too far for me to drive very often unless there's a good reason to come in," Butch then told her.

"Isn't seeing your friends a good enough reason?" Patty asked. "Don't you enjoy seeing me?"

"I love it," Butch said. "But, if I start hanging out with a bunch of pretty ladies like you, someone I know will get jealous and start accusing me of going 'walkabout.'"

Kerry looked surprised and asked, "Since when did you let some lady tell you when you could go have a beer? Don't tell me you've found that special lady you promised your mother you'd hold out for!"

"Well," Butch admitted. "This one doesn't exactly have all the required qualifications, but I do have waiver authority. For now, let's just say I've issued her a temporary waiver."

Butch sat there talking with them while he drank his beer and heard all the latest rumors and tales of rude passengers, horrible layover hotels, upcoming contract negotiations, and everything airline people discuss. Finally finishing the beer, he stood up and told them all goodbye and headed back toward the front door.

Shortly after he had gone, a man from an adjoining table leaned over and asked, "Who was that guy that just left?"

Kerry looked at him and answered, "Butch North. Why do you think you know him?"

"I just thought I recognized him," the man said. "I think I saw his picture and that name on the news last night. I'm pretty sure it was the same man."

"What was he on the news about?" Patty asked.

"Something about being wanted by the FBI for helping someone they were looking for," the man told her.

"I doubt that," Kerry said. "You must be mistaken, or there's someone else that looks a lot like him or something."

"You could be right," the man said. "You're sure that isn't the guy that was on the news?"

"I haven't seen the news in a couple of days," Kerry answered. "I've been on a trip down to Brazil. But you've got to be mistaken. I've known Butch for a long time, and he wouldn't be helping any fugitives."

"Thanks, maybe I'm mistaken," the man said as he turned back to his table.

Butch had continued through the restaurant, out the back door, and was almost to his car when his phone rang. Glancing at the number, he could tell that it wasn't someone he knew and it had a Ft Worth prefix. Guessing that it was from the base, he unlocked the car and got in before answering it.

He had just finished the short conversation and was pulling out of the parking lot when two Grapevine police cars with their blue lights flashing passed and made a right turn toward Esparza's. *"Crap,"* he thought as he headed south on Main Street, *"That friggin' news thing. Someone must have recognized me and called the police."*

Driving as fast as he thought he could get away with, he hurried back toward 114 and turned west on the access road. Hitting the traffic light just as it turned red, he sat there nervously and watched another police car with lights and sirens blaring heading toward the exit that led to Main Street.

When the light finally turned green, he merged with the traffic on 114 and slid over into the left lanes to exit on Highway 121 south into Ft Worth. Thinking that he had been an idiot for taking a chance being out in public unnecessarily, he drove back to Loop 820 and then took I-30 to the west side of Ft Worth. As he pulled into the motel parking lot, he killed the engine and sat there while he waited for the adrenaline to leave his system.

Finally calmed down from the near disaster of being caught, Butch locked the car and snuck back into the hotel, and ran up the stairs to his room. Locked inside, he stripped down and took a hot shower to try and relax. Finally, having washed the smelly nervous perspiration from his body, he made a large Jack and Coke and turned on the TV.

Not really caring what he watched, Butch flipped to a local news station and watched a reporter broadcasting from the patio at Esparza's. He was surprised to see how fast the media had responded to the call that must have alerted the police.

Tired and drained from the excitement, Butch sat his alarm for six o'clock in the morning and crawled into bed. Mentally reviewing what he wanted to accomplish when he confronted the people from the base, he finally fell asleep, wondering if tomorrow would end this nightmare.

Butch woke before the alarm went off and headed straight for the bathroom. After starting his small coffeepot to make a couple of cups, he showered, shaved, and pulled on a crisply starched shirt. Taking the last pair of clean jeans from the closet, he ran his belt through the loops and stepped into the stiff legs. If he was going to be meeting the people from the base, he had already decided that he would meet them dressed the way he felt the most comfortable.

It was only 6:30 when Butch pulled on his cowboy boots, left his room, and headed for the stairs. Passing through the lobby, he nodded at Ann as she stood behind the counter. Once in his car, he took his familiar black hat from the rear seat and put it on. Getting into the front seat and looking in the mirror, he quietly said, "Well, cowboy, it's ride or get thrown. Either way, it's time to mount up and give it a go."

Not knowing if he was driving into captivity or freedom, Butch started his car and headed toward the What-a-Burger and what he hoped would be the beginning of the end of this long-running battle with an unknown foe. He had a lot of suspicions but very little actual knowledge.

As he pulled into the parking lot, he saw only a single pickup sitting there. Knowing that Senator Burklow wouldn't be driving a truck and not seeing any of the familiar Suburbans, he parked and went in. With almost an hour to wait, Butch ordered a cup of coffee and grabbed a paper that someone had left on the counter. As he waited for the waiter to get his coffee, he watched an older man toss an empty cup into the trash as he was leaving and get into the pickup parked beside Butch's car.

Sitting at a booth facing the door, Butch read the front page and sipped the gradually cooling coffee. As the pickup left, another car pulled into the parking lot, and he watched anxiously as the driver stepped out. Still wondering who would arrive to meet him, Butch watched the man enter and place his order. Carrying two large coffees from the counter, the man passed Butch and nodded before taking a seat close to the windows that faced the road.

Although the man was wearing a pair of slacks, and a sport coat and had a tie loosely knotted around his neck, he appeared to be paying no attention to Butch. A few minutes later, another car arrived, and the driver walked in. He was also wearing slacks and a sports coat. After walking directly to the other man, he took a seat, picked up the extra cup of coffee, and they began talking quietly.

Still, almost 30 minutes before the Senator was due to arrive, Butch was beginning to get nervous and started wondering if he had made a mistake in trusting the man. There was nothing that really appeared too unusual, just those two men, and they hadn't even glanced his way since sitting together.

Butch rose, went to the counter, and got a refill of his coffee. Wishing there was a mirror for him to see if the men were watching him, Butch took his cup back to his seat and continued to wait. Now almost through with the paper, he glanced at the clock on his cell phone and saw that it was now five minutes until the Senator was due to arrive.

Just then, a black sedan pulled into the parking lot, and Butch watched as one of the men sitting at the other table got up, walked outside, and opened the door of the sedan. Senator Burklow stepped from the car and nodded at the man holding the car door for him. The other man at the table had turned and was watching the employees behind the counter.

Larry walked in and came directly toward Butch, saying, "Good morning, Butch. I hope I haven't kept you waiting."

Butch stood up and said, "No, sir. I just got here myself."

Shaking Butch's extended hand, Larry smiled and said, "Don't start lying to me this early, son. My people have been watching you since you arrived."

"Okay," Butch said, grinning nervously, "I'll admit that I've been here a few minutes, but just for some coffee."

"Sure, sure," Larry said. "Now, are you about ready? I've got other things to do today besides trying to get your name out of the papers and off the news."

"Yes, sir," Butch said. "I'm ready whenever you are."

"Fine," Larry said as he nodded at the two other men, who promptly nodded in return and left. "We'll take my car. Do you need to get anything before we leave?"

"Yes, sir," Butch answered. "I need to grab a package from my car right quick, and I'll be ready."

Unlocking the trunk, Butch pulled out the envelope containing duplicates of all the material he had sent to the base and mailed to the other addresses. Slamming the trunk closed, he carried it to where Larry was standing and said, "I guess I'm ready, sir."

As they got to the Senator's car, one of the men opened Larry's door, and they spoke quietly as Butch walked to the other side. When Larry got in, Butch watched as both men sat in their cars, watching them until Larry started the engine and pulled out onto the access road.

"Have you called the base this morning?" Larry asked as he merged onto Loop 820.

"No, sir," Butch answered. "I thought I'd wait until I was at the Base Commander's office before I told them I was there. I didn't want to give them a chance to have me stopped at the gate."

"I understand," Larry said as they approached White Settlement Road. "I made previous arrangements to meet with the Base Commander this morning, so I'll be expected, and we should have no problems getting on base."

"You didn't mention me to him, did you?" Butch asked.

"Oh, no," Larry said as he exited the loop and headed east toward the base. "I want to see the expression on his face when you walk in with me. That should be exciting, don't you think?"

"Yeah, that should be a shocker," Butch replied, glad that the Senator had made some preparations to expedite the process of getting onto the base.

"I do have one favor to ask of you," Butch said as they turned right off White Settlement Road and headed for the main gate to the base.

"You don't think you've asked enough of me?" Larry asked, glancing at Butch.

"I know I've imposed on you for a lot," Butch told him. "But I really need to have a little talk with the folks that will be coming to see us without you being present."

"Who do you expect to be coming to see you?" Larry asked as they pulled up to the guard shack and waited for the uniformed guard to approach.

"A couple of Air Force officers that I met when they brought me down here last year," Butch said as Larry rolled his window down and gave the guard his name.

Waiting for the guard to check the Senator's name against a list of approved visitors, Butch continued. "I've also requested a couple of other people to attend our little conference."

The guard finally gave Larry directions to the Base Commander's headquarters, stepped back, and waved them through the gate as he saluted. They could see the guard on the phone as they drove away, probably calling to report their arrival.

Larry pulled into one of the visitor's spots at the base headquarters building and somberly said, "I'd take off the hat once we get inside, Butch. I believe that if you truly want these folk's help, you need to show a little humility."

"Yes, sir," Butch said as he opened his car door and picked up the envelope. "I intend on giving them all the respect they deserve. Regardless of my current feelings about the problems, I still have the utmost respect for the officers of our military."

"I thought so," Larry said, getting out of the car. "Now, as to letting you have your private conference, I guess you have your reasons. So, I'll stay with the Base Commander unless you need me."

Butch held the front door open for the Senator as he continued saying, "Now, once this is over, I want a complete briefing from those folks. If you want to listen in, that'll be all right."

They walked down the brightly shining hall and entered the Commander's secretary's office, and Larry announced, "Good morning, ma'am. Would you please tell General Brown that Senator Larry Burklow and another gentleman are here for our appointment?"

The secretary picked her phone up, punched a button, and told the Commander that Larry was waiting. Almost immediately, she hung up and said, "General Brown will be right out, sir."

A few seconds later, the oak door to the Commander's office opened, and Gary came out saying, "Good morning, Senator Burklow. Please come into my office."

As he pointed to two comfortable-looking leather chairs in front of his desk, Gary asked, "Would either of you care for some coffee or anything else?"

Butch removed his hat as they entered the office and stood quietly as Larry answered the General, saying, "No, thanks. But I'd like for you to meet my friend here."

Watching to see General Brown's expression, Larry said, "General, this is Mr. Butch North, whom I believe you've heard of. Butch, please say hello to General Brown."

The shock registered plainly on General Brown's face as he froze the hand he had been extending. Finally regaining his composure, General Brown said, "Mr. North, I've definitely heard about you," and shook Butch's hand.

"Now, gentlemen," Gary said as he stood behind his desk. "Please be seated and tell me why you're here."

Gary waited until Larry had sat down and then continued, "I'll just assume that the original stated purpose of your visit isn't the real reason you're here."

Once Gary had sat down, Larry looked at Butch and said, "It's your show, son. Tell the General what you are requesting."

Butch held his hat in his hands and said, "Sir, I'd like for you to contact the Commander of one of your facilities here on the base and request him to meet me here."

Gary looked disbelieving at Butch and asked, "Just which facility are you referring to, Mr. North? There are several of them on the base."

"Sir, with all due respect," Butch said, looking directly into Gary's eyes, "I believe you know full well which facility I'm referring to."

"And that would be?" Gary asked.

"Let's just say it's probably the only one that has any interest in locating me," Butch said. "And I'm sure that you, or the previous Commander, arranged the conference I had with a couple of officers from that facility last year."

"General Brown," Larry interrupted. "Let's not start playing games here. If you aren't aware of the facility Mr. North is referring to, then you must not be doing a very good job of running this base. And, since I'm sure you're a very good Commander, I suggest that you call the people Mr. North wants, and let's not waste anymore of my time."

Gary looked at Larry for a moment and then finally asked Butch, "Who do you want to speak to?"

"I've already spoken to someone from there," Butch said. "All you need to do is call their Commander and tell him that I'm waiting here with Senator Burklow. I believe they'll also want the use of your conference room for a few minutes if you don't mind."

Gary reluctantly picked up his phone and told his secretary, "Please call General Nelson for me. I'll wait for him to answer."

Less than a minute later, Gary spoke into the phone and said, "General Nelson, Mr. Butch North is sitting here in my office with Senator Larry Burklow. Mr. North says he's expecting some people from your office to meet him here. Is that true?"

Gary listened for a minute and then said, "Yes, sir. I'll have the conference room ready for you when you get here."

Gary hung up the phone and said, "They'll be here in about five minutes. Now, is there anything else I can do for you while we're waiting?"

Butch placed the envelope he had been holding on Gary's desk and said, "I don't believe so, sir. But, if you keep this envelope while I'm talking to General Nelson and the other people that are on their way, I'd appreciate it."

Gary looked at the package on his desk as Butch turned to Larry and continued, "If I can't come to an understanding with General Nelson and his people, I'd like for you to use the information in that envelope as you feel necessary, sir."

CHAPTER 49

Kevin found Pablo down by the barns, feeding a small herd of goats that were milling around the corral, eating the grain that was thrown over the fence. "Can I have a word with you?" Kevin asked as Pablo slung the last of the grain onto the ground in front of the goats.

"Sure, Senor," Pablo said, carrying the empty bucket back toward the barn. "What is it you need?"

"I'm beginning to worry about the baby," Kevin told him. "He seems to be losing some color, you know, looks sort of pale."

"What do you want me to do?" Pablo asked as he hung the bucket on a nail over an open sack of oats.

Pablo turned and looked carefully at Kevin and suggested, "If you think we need a doctor, I'll see if we can get one here tomorrow morning."

"I'm not sure if that's the best answer," Kevin said, shaking his head. "I think we're going to need a specialist."

"We don't normally have small children here," Pablo explained. "For problems such as those, we would have to go to one of the larger cities. Maybe back to Piedras Negras, and I'm not sure that would be the wisest thing to do."

"Could you contact Sancudo and ask him what he thinks?" Kevin asked. "And, if the doctors in Piedras Negras can't handle this, then make arrangements for us to get back into the U.S. to see someone there?"

"How serious do you think this is?" Pablo asked. "If you believe that the child is in great danger, then we will do it."

"However," Pablo continued, "if it is just a minor thing, we would be risking too much."

"I really don't know right now," Kevin admitted. "I'd just like to have some preparations made if we need to leave sooner than expected. And, if it seems to be getting worse, to have an airplane ready to take us."

"I understand, Senor," Pablo said. "Maybe you can have Rosita look at the child; she has a lot of experience with babies. I'll ask her if you want me to."

"Yes, please," Kevin replied. "It's been years since I've had to deal with them and my wife was the one that really knew the most about it."

"Ah, yes," Pablo said, nodding his head. "The mothers know much more about their babies than us fathers."

"I know," Kevin agreed. "I'm surprised that Leslie doesn't see anything wrong."

"Maybe there isn't anything wrong, Senor," Pablo replied. "Maybe you're just seeing things. Have you thought about that?"

"Yes," Kevin said. "But, since this is her first child, I wonder if maybe she hasn't developed the ability to detect something wrong."

"I think women have that ability from the very beginning," Pablo told him. "I've seen how many of the animals around here know instinctively what to do to protect and nurture their young. Mother nature seems to know how to provide what's best."

"Well," Kevin said, "let's at least have Rosita take a look. If she doesn't see anything wrong, then we'll wait another day. But I'd still like to let Sancudo know that the potential exists for us to need a quick trip either to Piedras Negras or maybe San Antonio."

"I'll send him a message," Pablo said as they walked back toward the house.

"And, if you would also see if he can get word to Butch North that we may have a problem developing," Kevin told him.

"I will let Mel know of your concerns, Senor," Pablo said, opening the door to the kitchen.

"Rosita," Pablo called as they entered the house. "Where are you?"

The men walked through the kitchen and into the dining room, seeing no one. As they continued back toward the bedrooms, he called out again and heard voices coming from Gene and Leslie's room. When they arrived at the door, they saw Rosita sitting on the bed holding BK and looking at him as Leslie was getting a new diaper from the package.

"He is such a cute little thing," Rosy was saying. "I just love looking at his eyes, so big and dark."

"Rosita," Pablo said, "Kevin has a question for you."

Rosy looked up and asked, "What is it that you want to ask me, Señor Kevin?"

"I was just wondering if you think that BK is getting sick or something," Kevin asked.

Rosy looked at BK again and said, "I don't think so; he seems to be just fine."

Leslie took BK from Rosy and added, "I don't think so either. He doesn't seem to have a fever, and he's not crying as if something was hurting him."

"I'm just worried about his color," Kevin said. "Maybe I'm being overly cautious, but I'd like to have a doctor look at him."

"I think Senora Leslie is correct," Rosy announced firmly. "The mother will always be the first one to know if her child is ill."

"All right," Kevin finally gave in, "I just wanted to be extra cautious and be ready to get the little fellow to a doctor if we see anything wrong."

Pablo turned to leave and said, "I'll let Mel know of your concerns, Senor. But now I must return to work."

Rosy watched Pablo leave and then said, "Now, if you will excuse me, I also have things to do."

As Rosy headed for the door, she turned to Leslie and said, "Pay the men no mind, Senorita. But if you think the little one is getting sick, come get me."

"I'm sorry," Kevin said as Rosy left. "I just want to make sure BK gets whatever care he needs. Most newborn children have a doctor check them thoroughly when they're born, and we haven't been in the most ideal circumstances since he arrived."

"I understand," Leslie said. "I wish we could have had him examined by a pediatrician also. But, unless I see something wrong, I don't want to take any chances of losing either him or Gene if we were to get caught."

"Okay," Kevin said, looking at Gene, who had remained silent throughout the entire discussion. "But I've asked Pablo to try to get word to Butch that we may have a problem and try to get an airplane available if we need to get BK to a doctor quickly."

Turning to Gene, Kevin said, "Well, little buddy, what say you to some exploring?"

Gene was wondering if he was missing something he should be seeing or doing about his son and said, "I don't know. Don't you think I need to stay here with Leslie if there's something wrong with BK?"

"I just told you," Leslie said as she wrapped the blanket around BK, "there's nothing wrong. You two get out of here and let me take care of my baby."

"Let's go," Kevin said. "If Leslie says BK's okay, then he is. I want to take one of Pablo's Jeeps up into the mountains and look around."

Gene looked questioningly at Leslie, and she smiled, saying, "Go, go. If I need you, I'll let you know."

Kevin reached out and took Gene's arm and pulled him toward the door, telling him, "You need to get some fresh air, my boy. Let the women folk do what they do best, and we'll go exploring."

Kevin and Gene spent the rest of the day wandering about the ranch and looking at the different plants and terrain they encountered. Finally, after spending several hours exploring the countryside, they headed back for the house.

When they drove in and parked the Jeep beside the barn, Pablo met them and said, "Señor Kevin, I have talked to Mel and told him of your concerns."

"What did he have to say?" Kevin asked as he and Gene followed Pablo toward the house.

"Mel says that he will try to contact Mr. North tomorrow morning," Pablo told him as he opened the door to the house. "He has someone in Ft Worth that will pass the message to him and ask him to call."

"What about having an airplane ready?" Kevin asked as they walked into the kitchen.

"That will not be a problem," Pablo told him. "Unless something else comes up, he told me that Gil will be bringing some supplies later today that I have asked for."

When they entered the dining room, Rosy was busy setting their dinner on the table, and Leslie was helping by putting plates and glasses in front of each of the chairs. "Get washed," Rosy ordered as she wiped her hands on her apron. "Dinner is almost ready."

After dinner, they sat around in the front room talking and drinking some Caffé Lolita that Pablo had taken from a large liquor cabinet. Kevin and Pablo discussed the differences in what types of livestock did better in the sparse country down here as opposed to the wetter climate up north.

Gene sat with the men, but not having much knowledge of the ranching business, he just listened. When the discussion finally came around to fishing, he finally got a chance to add to the conversation. Although all of his experience was limited to catching catfish on the Red River and some of the smaller streams that joined it north of Ringgold, he enthusiastically described in great detail how much fun he had and how large the fish was.

Rosy finally stood and said, "You men have told enough lies for one night. Leslie and I are the only ones that did any work today, and we're getting tired."

As everyone got up, she continued, "Breakfast will be ready when you get up tomorrow, as it always is."

Smiling and looking at BK sleeping in Leslie's arms, she told her, "If you need anything, call me."

The next morning, Kevin was up early as usual and headed for the kitchen after he washed and brushed his teeth. Pablo was standing beside the stove, drinking coffee and watching Rosy cooking.

"Good morning," Pablo said as he walked in. "Coffee?"

"Please," Kevin said. "And good morning to both of you."
Pablo poured him a cup and passed it over, saying, "I called Mel again last night, and he said that Sanacudo will try to contact Butch later today."

"Good," Kevin said as he took a sip. "When do you think you will hear back from him?"

"Probably before noon," Pablo answered. "It just depends on when he can talk to his man in Ft Worth and how soon that man can call Mr. North. But usually, it takes no more than a couple of hours."

"Good," Kevin replied. "I just hope I'm wrong about the baby, but I'd like for Butch to know. And, maybe he's gotten things taken care of, so we can go home soon anyway."

CHAPTER 50

Colonel Lynch was on duty the morning after they had gotten the enhanced pictures of Butch at the bank in Rhome back from Washington. Although they weren't sharing the photos with the news media, she had forwarded them to every law enforcement agency and had instructed her own teams to canvas all the areas where Butch had been spotted, or they had determined that he had visited.

It was just a few minutes before eight o'clock when she got a call from a member of one of the teams that were staying at the same motel where Butch had been hiding. Ann, the clerk at the motel, had been contacted by an officer from the local police just moments earlier that morning and had been shown the newest photos of Butch. She immediately recognized him and told the officer that she was sure the man in the picture was staying there.

That officer had already called for police backup and was waiting for them when the member of the team came down in the elevator. Seeing the officer standing by the desk, he walked over to see what was going on. When he asked Ann what was happening, she told him about seeing the pictures of Butch and recognized him as the man who had registered as Mr. Wrexion.

The agent immediately identified himself as being with the FBI and asked for the registration form. As soon as Ann gave it to him, he asked the police officer if he had called for assistance. Hearing that he had and that he had also called the local FBI office, the agent told him to keep everyone away from Mr. Wrexion's room as he called Colonel Lynch and reported the sighting.

Karyn, wanting to ensure that her agents made the arrest and to keep Butch out of either police or regular FBI custody, told the agent to gather the rest of his team and wait for further instructions.

Karyn immediately called Colonel Erickson and gave him the news. Rick told her to make sure every exit at the motel was covered and to keep everyone else away from Butch. When she told him that she was working on it but didn't want to take a chance of not having enough people, Rick instructed her to use the local police to surround the area and any additional FBI agents to guard the halls and stairs.

Karyn called her agent back and gave him the orders Rick had given and then told him to get a key to the room where Butch was suspected to be. To make sure only her people made the arrest, she told him to use their people on the floor the room was on and let the other FBI agents cover the rest of the motel.

Rick called back a few minutes later and told her that he had called General Nelson, and they were both on their way to the facility. Rick then instructed her to call General Modelle's room and let him know that they had found where Butch was hiding and had him trapped.

Karyn dialed the number for General Modelle and told him what was happening and that Rick and Mike were on their way. Paul told her he would be there in just a few minutes and to make sure there were no mistakes this time in capturing Mr. North.

Karyn sat waiting for some word from the agents at the motel when Colonel Erickson walked in and asked, "Are we sure it's Mr. North?"

"Almost positive," Karyn answered. "The desk clerk recognized him and told our man that a Mr. Wrexion had registered a couple of days ago and hadn't checked out."

"Get that registration form sent to us," Rick told her. "What's happening with the police and FBI?"

Karyn told him what she had ordered them to do while she was attempting to make contact with the agent at the motel. When the agent answered, she told him to have the clerk fax the form to them at the facility. Hearing that it would be there shortly, Karyn nodded at Rick as he listened and waited to see if he wanted anything else.

She had just set the microphone on the desk when General Modelle walked in, asking, "Do we have him?" "Not yet, sir," Rick said as he and Karyn came to attention.

"What's our status?" Paul asked as he watched the registration form slide from the fax machine.

"We have the motel surrounded," Karyn said as Rick retrieved the form and looked it over. "The local police are controlling the exterior, and the FBI is covering the inside."

Rick handed the form to General Modelle and waited for him to read it before saying, "That's our man, sir."

"What makes you so sure?" Paul asked as Mike entered.

"I don't know if you remember, sir," Rick said as Paul handed the form to General Nelson, "but that name is just the sort of thing we saw back when we got the sign-in sheets from the VFW last year."

Mike nodded as he read and said, "Yep, that time it was probably Kevin that used 'Won Dum Phuc.'"

"Karyn," Mike said, handing the form to Rick, "give me a quick update on when the teams will try to take Mr. North."

"Yes, sir," Karyn said as she picked the microphone up and called. The agent that answered said they would be in place in about 15 minutes, and there would be no chance of escape.

Rick smiled as he heard the report and said, "Looks like Mr. North will be contacting us sooner than he expected."

"We don't have him yet," Mike told him. "And, even if we get the man the clerk identified, it may not be Mr. North."

"I'd bet my life on it being him," Rick said. "And, as for having him, it's just a matter of a few minutes now."

"Mike's right," Paul said. "We've been this close before, and we're still empty-handed. Let's not start celebrating until Mr. North's sitting here."

Major Fleenor came in, looked around at the expectant faces, and asked, "Something new?"

"Jerry," Rick told him, "I think you're about to get the chance you've been wanting."

"What's that?" Jerry asked.

"We've got Mr. Butch North trapped in a motel," Rick answered. "And, to make it even more ironic, it's the same motel where our agents have been staying."

"You've got to be kidding me," Jerry said, amazed.

"That's just like him, too," Rick said. "That man likes to taunt us every chance he gets. I'll bet he found out where our people were and snuck in just so he could watch us chase our tails."

They were still waiting for the trap to be sprung when the phone on Karyn's desk rang. Expecting it to be from the motel, she answered it, saying, "Colonel Lynch."

Surprised at finding out who it was, she said, "General Nelson, it's General Brown for you, sir."

Mike took the call and got the news that Butch North was sitting in General Brown's office with Senator Larry Burklow. Stunned, he thanked Gary and hung up.

"You'll never believe this," Mike said, looking at Paul. "Mr. North is right here on base."

"What?" Paul asked, sounding as shocked as he looked.

"Yes," Mike told them. "He's in General Brown's office with Senator Burklow and has asked for us to meet him in Gary's conference room this morning."

"How the hell did he get there?" Rick demanded. "He's supposed to be at the motel."

No sooner than Rick had spoken, Karyn's radio announced that the room had been entered, found empty and that the articles left behind were being brought in for identification.

"I guess he's still a step ahead of us," Paul said to the now-silent group.

Looking at Mike, Paul asked, "What's he asking for?"

"Same as he asked for yesterday; he wants me, Colonel Erickson, and Major Fleenor to meet with him," Mike answered.

Mike paused and then said, "And he still wants someone with the authority to agree to the requests that he will make when we get there."

"Is Senator Burklow going to be there?" Paul asked.

"I don't think so," Mike told him. "Mr. North didn't mention him. But we better get a quick biography of the Senator anyway. I'm not sure what part he may play in this, but I want to be prepared."

Paul looked around the room and said, "I guess I'd better make a call. In the meantime, I suggest you folks get your dress blues on and figure out how you're going to handle this meeting."

Paul was turning to leave when Mike reminded him, "Sir, he also asked for someone in authority to be there."

Paul stopped and looked at Mike, saying, "I think that's going to be me for now, Mike. But I have to clear this up with my boss. Depending on Mr. North's demands, even my boss may not have the authority to approve them."

CHAPTER 51

Hearing that the people he wanted to see would be here in about five minutes, Butch asked, "Senator, could I have a word with you privately, please?"

"Certainly," Larry said as he rose from his chair. "General, you'll excuse me for a moment."

Butch looked at the package on Gary's desk and then looked at the General, saying, "Sir, we'll just be a minute. I'll leave the envelope with you for safekeeping if you don't mind."

Gary nodded and replied, "It'll be here when you return. Will you need anything in the conference room?"

"No, sir," Butch said as he held the door open for the Senator. "Unless the other people have any requests, I can't think of anything I'll need."

Just as they walked through the secretary's office, Butch's phone rang. Glancing at it, Butch said, "Excuse me, Senator; this won't take but a minute or so."

Butch walked a few feet down the hall toward the front door and answered the phone, "Hello, this is Butch."

He listened for just a moment and said, "I'll call you back in about 30 minutes with an answer."

Hanging up, Butch went back to where the Senator was walking along the wall and looking at pictures of the various aircraft that had been stationed at the base dating back to World War II.

"Sir," Butch said as he approached him, "I'll ask them to remain in the conference room after we've had our discussion so you can be briefed on their operations. I shouldn't need more than half an hour or so. Will that be all right with you?"

"That'll be fine," Larry said. "I don't suppose you're ready to tell me all of your side of the story, are you?"

"No, sir," Butch answered. "I'll talk to you after I'm satisfied with the arrangements I make with them. I think it would be better for them to meet with you after I tell you what we've decided."

"It may take a few hours after we talk for them to prepare the necessary paperwork," Butch said. "But I'm hoping that I have their verbal guarantees that any agreements will be followed. I'll give you a quick synopsis when I get out."

As they were talking, Butch and Larry saw a group of Air Force officers enter the hall from one of the side doors. The group headed for the conference room and entered without showing any recognition of having noticed Butch or Larry watching them.

"I guess that's your people," Larry said as they watched the door close on the conference room."

"I suppose so, sir," Butch said, hoping that his problems would soon be over.

"I wouldn't keep them waiting, Butch," Larry advised. "I'm surprised that they have given you their time on such short notice anyway. You must have something they really want."

"I hope so," Butch said. "I surely do."

"Well, good luck," Larry said as he started walking back to Gary's office. "I'll be in with the General until you finish. Come get me when you're ready."

"Thanks, sir," Butch said as he nervously headed down the hall.

Butch opened the door to the conference room and saw the four officers standing at the end of a long polished oak table that had at least 20 stuffed leather armchairs sitting around it.

"Good morning, gentlemen," Butch said as he walked toward them. "As I'm sure you know, I'm Butch North."

General Modelle nodded and said, "Good morning, Mr. North. I'm General Modelle."

"And this is General Nelson," he continued, pointing to Mike.

"General," Butch said, nodding to him.

"This is Colonel Erickson," Paul said, "and this is Major Fleenor."

"Colonel, Major," Butch said, nodding at them. "Thank you for agreeing to meet with me this morning."

Butch walked to the chair at the head of the table and asked, "Shall we get started? I'm sure you have more important business this morning than dealing with my small problems."

Butch remained standing behind the chair as Mike and Paul went to his right, and Rick and Jerry went to the left side. Butch stood respectfully until the two Generals were seated and then pulled his chair out and sat down.

"First, General Modelle," Butch said, looking at the impressive array of ribbons below the silver command pilot wings on Paul's chest, "I'm assuming that you're the one that has the authority to approve any agreements we reach."

Paul nodded and said, "That's correct, Mr. North. However, even my authority has its limits."

"I understand that, sir," Butch said. "I'm just hoping that what I'm proposing will be so minor compared with any alternative that you will either have the authority or can quickly obtain it."

"What are your demands?" Rick asked.

Butch turned and looked at him and said, "Colonel Erickson, it's good to see you again. Before I get into my '*requests,*' I have a few questions."

"Now, I'm not absolutely positive of the entire scope of your operation," Butch started, "but I have a pretty good idea."

"Your knowledge of our operations isn't important, sir," Rick countered. "Your possession of our property is!"

Butch looked at Rick and said, "Colonel, I don't want this to be an adversarial discussion. I was hoping that we could agree that the situation can't continue as it currently is without any further bitterness."

Mike leaned forward and said, "Mr. North, Colonel Erickson is just concerned about protecting our operation, as we all are. With your background, I'm sure you understand the need for protecting sensitive programs."

Butch continued to stare at Rick for a second and then turned to Mike and said, "General Nelson, I completely understand. What I'm trying to do is sort of set a basic understanding of the situation and show how what I'm going to propose will be of benefit to both of us, as well as other interested parties."

"I suppose you're referring to the Senator," Paul said.

"Yes, sir," Butch acknowledged, "as well as your '*product*' and a few others."

Butch paused a second and then said, "Now, back to the beginning, I don't know everything about your operation, but I'm sure it isn't something that would meet with the public's approval. And, I'm equally positive that the public doesn't need to know about it."

"At least we agree on that," Mike said.

"Now, let me ask you something," Butch said. "How successful has your program been? And, how important is it to you to have Gene, and that's his name, back along with his son?"

"Very," Paul answered. "As to the success of our program, that's not to be negotiated."

"I'm not trying to negotiate that, sir," Butch told him. "I'm just suggesting that if Gene is the single success after all the years you must have put into this, maybe you would appreciate having him and his son."

"Very well," Paul said. "Regardless of other issues regarding this program, we will acknowledge that Gene is our primary successful product."

"A small point," Butch said, "I'd prefer that we quit referring to Gene as a product. He *is* a human, regardless of how he came to be. And his son is also a human."

"Agreed," Mike said. "Now, what do we need to do to get Gene back?"

"Before we get to that," Butch said, "I'd like to thank Major Fleenor for having the insight to call me directly. If you folks had been direct with me when we first met, I think we could have avoided a lot of misery and needless effort on both of our parts."

Jerry nodded and said, "Thank you, Mr. North. But I can't take the credit; it was a joint decision."

"I'm sure it was," Butch conceded, "But I'm just as sure it was your idea."

"Now, to the crux of the problem," Butch said. "I'm willing to bring Gene, his wife Leslie, and his son BK, back here. I do request, no, in this case, I demand, that certain things be guaranteed."

"What are those?" Paul asked.

"I want your guarantee that no further experiments on any of them will be conducted without their express consent," Butch said. "By that, I mean that they can be used as advisors or consultants on any issue you want, within certain constraints."

"And, those would be?" Mike asked.

"I know you've taken Gene to one of the government's classified locations and used him to help determine the function of various pieces of *'confiscated'* equipment," Butch answered. "That's fine, and later, if you wish to use his son, BK, in the same manner, that will be acceptable."

Butch paused while they considered his demand and then continued, "Gene has told me that he has been unable to provide you with any worthwhile information. Maybe his son will have more of the capabilities than he does."

"Now, in order for you to have access to whatever abilities those two may possess," Butch told them, "I want them to have as much of a normal life as possible."

"I want you to put Gene, and his son, on a retainer," Butch said. "I want them to have a chance to raise their son as any other American family does."

"What did you have in mind?" Paul asked.

"I want Gene to be given a Civil Service rating that would provide him with an annual income of $100,000 per year for as long as he lives. Of course, he has the option to retire the same as any other employee should he elect to do so," Butch told him. "That will guarantee his service for at least 20 more years. If he's not able to help you during that time, he's of no use further to you."

"I can guarantee you that," Paul said. "What about his son?"

"The same applies to him," Butch answered. "His services will be made available at a rate of $1000 per day until he reaches the age of 21. He will then be hired at the same pay scale as Gene, with the same conditions."

"We can do that," Paul said, nodding.

"Now, I'm sure you noticed some, let's say, abnormal features when you saw the photographs of BK," Butch said. "Along with Gene's status as a civil service member, he and his family will have access to your medical facilities."

"Included in the normal routine doctor services any average family requires, BK will need very special reconstructive surgery," Butch continued. "These, as well as other medical requirements, will be provided by your facility. I think you'd prefer to restrict the family's access to medical care to your own doctors anyway, so this shouldn't be anything that you wouldn't already want to do."

"Again, not a problem," Paul said. "Anything else?"

"Of course," Butch said, smiling. "Along with their salaries, consultation fees, medical services, and basic humane treatment, the government will provide a five million dollar life insurance policy on each member of the family. They're obviously worth that much since you've probably spent more than that trying to get them back."

"Of course," Paul agreed, smiling as well. "And, I hate to ask, what about your own requirements."

"Those are simple," Butch told him. "But first, let's take care of Mr. Kevin Knox. I want him to be given a full military retirement based on 20 years of service at the highest rank he held during his previous service. Along with that, he is to be the final authority as to what is being done for, or to, Gene and his family."

"Basically, he is the guardian of the family, the beneficiary of their insurance, and will have the right to deny any unreasonable request by the government," Butch said.

"What's to prevent him from denying us any access?" Rick wanted to know.

"Colonel, maybe you should learn to have a little more faith in those of us who served before you did," Butch replied. "I think you'll find Kevin to be as patriotic as I am and just as willing to help you. But, at the same time, I wouldn't cross him. He can be just as resourceful as I can if need be."

"That's acceptable," Paul said. "Now, what about you?"

"I want the government to put as much effort into clearing my name, as well as those of the rest of us, as it did in portraying us as terrorists or traitors," Butch said. "I would suggest that you get all of your media friends together in a press conference and explain how we, including Gene, were part of a massive government program to infiltrate other suspected terrorist organizations here in the U.S. that may be plotting actions such as those done in the 9-11 attacks."

"We were working undercover, and we're the reason you finally caught whatever dumb smuck or group you want to parade around as terrorists," Butch told them. "And it would be just wonderful if you gave each of us some minor public award in a nationally televised ceremony."

"You've got to be kidding me," Rick said. "After all the trouble you've put us through?"

"Never mind, Rick," Paul said. "I suppose you want the President to present the award?"

"That'd be nice," Butch said, smiling and nodding. "I like ol' George Dubya. I think we could live with that."

"But, regardless of who presents the award or just tells the press without presenting any award," Butch said seriously, "the main point is to exert the same effort in clearing our names as you did in defaming us."

"I get your drift, son," Paul said. "I'll see if I can get President Bush to either be present at the news conference or at least make sure his Press Secretary is involved, and you'll get the full attention of the media."

"Is that it?" Mike asked.

"Pretty much," Butch answered. "I just want Gene, his family, and Kevin taken care of as you would any valuable asset of the government and be given the same opportunities as any other citizen of this country."

"Me?" Butch continued, "I want just to be left alone."

It grew silent in the room, and Butch finally asked, "By the way, is Gene's nurse, Ms. Vicki Grubbs, still alive?"

"I believe so," Mike replied. "What does she have to do with this?"

"As far as Gene's concerned," Butch said, "she's his mother. And I know he'd like for her to know that he's going to be taken care of. And, I think he'd like to see her and tell her that you wonderful people have given him a birth certificate showing that he was born to her and her husband, who I don't know the name of, on whatever date you *'conceived'* him or produced him. Or, maybe, allow her to adopt him. As long as Gene gets her last name, it doesn't really matter."

"Now, sir," Butch asked Paul, "can you authorize the things I've asked for? Or shall we continue the game?"

"I can do so," Paul answered. "But it is contingent upon the safe return of Gene and his son. Can you guarantee that?"

"Unless I get any interference from anyone, and I mean *anyone*, I can probably have him here tomorrow," Butch told him. "But, if I think there's any effort to hinder me or interfere with our agreement, they will disappear forever."

"Oh, yes," Butch menacingly said, "all of those other packages will be opened, and your little secret will no longer be so."

"Speaking of those," Mike asked, "how do we know you won't use that information against us in the future?"

"Sir, I have tried to show you my intentions about this up to now," Butch replied, "If I'd wanted to expose you, I'd have done so months ago. If you uphold your end of our agreement, I'll contact all of the addressees and have the material returned in accordance with the instructions I placed in each envelope."

"If I find anyone has tampered with the material," Butch told him, "I'll give you their name and address. But I can almost guarantee their strict compliance with my instructions."

"Are there any others, such as with the Senator?" Paul asked.

"There is one other," Butch acknowledged. "It is on General Brown's desk, and I will remain in possession of it. Speaking of the Senator, I'd suggest that you be ready to brief him on whatever story you normally use to describe your mission."

"How much does he already know?" Mike asked.

"Only that I have suspicions that your facility is performing genetic experiments that I think are contrary to the public interest," Butch answered. "And no, I didn't mention where I really think your genetic material actually originated.”

“And just where do you think we got it?” Rick asked.

“Let’s just leave that to the science fiction writers, okay?” Butch replied. “Now, I know you can’t provide the documents that will enact our agreements right away. So, until you do, Gene and the rest of them will remain where they are.”

“Where is that?” Mike asked.

“To be perfectly honest,” Butch said smiling, “I don’t know. But, just before I came in here, I received a call from an individual who can provide that answer and will be the first person I call when I walk out.”

Butch stood and said, “One other thing, if I ever get so much as a suspicion that you are monitoring me or my calls, you’ll wish you hadn’t. And that goes for the one I told you that I just received and the one I’m about to make. So, in the interest of good faith, please notify your people to shut down any and all intrusive measures on me and my friends.”

General Modelle stood first, followed by the rest of them, and Paul said, holding out his hand, “Mr. North, I appreciate your sincerity and reasonableness. I will have the required documents no later than noon today.”

Butch shook Paul’s hand and said, “Sir, I can’t say it’s been a pleasure for the last few months, but I appreciate you taking the time to finally listen to me and take care of some people I’m quite fond of.”

“Now, while you folks get the paperwork I need and brief Senator Burklow, I’ll be having lunch at the Officer’s Club,” Butch told them. “If you need more time to prepare a full briefing for the Senator, maybe you can delay it some by having him join me at the club. Of course, you’re all welcome, too.”

"General Nelson," Paul said, looking directly at Mike, "I'm giving you a direct order to cease all activity involved with the program enacted originally to find Gene."

"Yes, sir," Mike said, coming to attention.

Shaking Butch's hand, Paul continued, "I'll take care of clearing your names myself, son. I'm also going to appoint Lieutenant Colonel Jerry Fleenor to be your personal liaison with our unit here. By the way, Jerry, the promotion list came out this morning. Congratulations."

Butch looked at Jerry's surprised face and said, "Congratulations on the promotion, sir."

"Thanks, Mr. North," Jerry said as he shook Butch's hand.

Jerry handed Butch a card and said, "Here is my personal number and the number at the facility where I can be reached. Call me if you have any questions."

"Thanks, Major Fleenor; I mean *Lieutenant Colonel Fleenor*. Now, if you gentlemen will remain for just a little while longer," Butch said as he turned to leave. "I promised Senator Burklow that you'd brief him on your efforts to find a cure for genetic defects in children. Personally, I think you'd be wise to tailor your efforts in that direction in the future."

Butch walked across the floor and opened the door. The officers remained standing quietly as the door closed behind Butch until General Modelle finally said, "Son of a Bitch, why didn't we do that sooner?"

Everyone turned to look at Jerry, and he said, "I wish I'd spoken up a little quicker, sir. But I'm just glad we finally found a workable solution for all of us."

Rick looked at Jerry and stuck his hand out, saying, "You were right, Jerry. I'm sorry if I doubted you. And congratulations on the promotion."

Paul cleared his throat and said, "Now, Mike, take care of getting the program shut down. Then, call Colonel Moore and have her prepare some slides and a briefing for the Senator."

"Also," he continued, "have Kathy prepare the conference room. This thing isn't over until we get Gene and his son back. If there was ever a time not to screw things up, it's now. Let's try not to piss off Mr. North again."

Butch went directly to General Brown's office and asked as he entered, "Senator, if you're ready, I've reached an agreement with them and they're ready to talk to you."

Larry stood and told Gary, "General Brown, I appreciate your hospitality, but I need to discuss a few things with those other officers."

Gary rose from behind his desk and shook Larry's hand, saying, "I'm glad I could be of some assistance, Senator. Please feel free to call again if I can help you in the future."

Butch took the envelope from the desk, thanked Gary, and said, "Senator, it'll only take me a couple of minutes to tell you the basics of the agreement we've reached."

Moments later, having briefed Larry, Butch walked out of the building and pulled his cell phone from the case on his belt. Redialing the number in the phone's memory of received calls, Butch waited until it was answered and said, "Please tell Sancudo and my friends that the end is in sight. I will begin preparations for their return tomorrow morning."

Butch listened for a moment and then said, "Please ask Sancudo to call me this afternoon to coordinate the return."

After hanging up, Butch walked down the street in the direction of the Officer's Club and dialed Tammy's number. Smiling, he waited until she answered and then asked, "How'd you like to have a dinner guest over this evening?

Maybe if you're really, really, really nice and prepare a feast for him, you can persuade him to spend at least one night."

Hearing her reply, he smiled and continued walking as he told her that things seemed to be going well. Finally hanging up, he really hoped he was correct.

Butch was almost to the front door of the club when his phone rang again. Looking at the number, he answered, "Norte."

"Listo?" Sancudo answered, asking him if he was ready.

"Almost," Butch said. "Donde y cuando?" he asked, wondering where and when.

"The infant is not far," Sancudo told him. "And there is a tailwind."

Butch knew from what Mel said that he was referring to Rancho El Infante, where he and Mel had gone hunting while he was stationed at Laughlin AFB in Del Rio. He also figured that Sancudo was planning on flying them to Piedras Negras and then driving them across. Now, all Butch needed to do was either drive them from Eagle Pass or get an airplane to pick them up.

"Maverick manana," Butch said.

He waited for Mel to acknowledge that the location for Butch to meet them tomorrow was the Maverick County Municipal Airport at Eagle Pass. Then Butch said, "The early bird gets the worm, you know. That is if you like worms," and hung up.

Trusting that the tap on his phone had been lifted, Butch called a former American Airlines pilot he had flown with when he had first been hired and asked, "Ronald, Butch North here. Is the Bonanza available tomorrow morning?"

Hearing that it was, Butch asked, "How about renting it to me for a few hours?"

Once they had agreed on the price and the time, Butch thanked him and hung up. Now, even if all of the different agencies hadn't gotten the word that Kevin, Gene, and Leslie were no longer wanted, Sancudo would get them across the Rio Grande, avoiding any Border Patrol or Customs Agents. Then, Butch would fly them back to Hicks Field, where the Bonanza was hanged, and then drive them to the base if all the required documents were furnished by noon today as promised.

If the documents weren't ready, Butch would have to call Sancudo and cancel their plans. Knowing that Kevin and the rest of them were being told that tomorrow was their day of freedom, Butch really hoped he didn't have to disappoint them.

CHAPTER 52

Butch was sitting in the dining room at the Officer's Club and drinking iced tea when Senator Burklow walked in. As Larry approached the table, Butch rose and searched his face for any clue as to how things had gone.

"Please, have a seat," Butch said.

After Larry had sat down, Butch asked, "How'd it go?"

"Pretty good," Larry said as Butch sat back down.

"You were right about a genetic program," Larry continued. "After you left, we went over to their facility, and they gave me the briefing that they used for updating Congress. They're doing some pretty amazing stuff."

The waitress walked up, asking, "Anything to drink, sir?"

"Iced tea, please," Larry told her. "Unsweet."

"Yes, sir," she replied. "Will you be having lunch with us?"

"Yes, ma'am," Larry said. "But we'll need a larger table; there are six others joining us."

"Would you be dining with General Modelle?" she asked. "He just called to reserve a private room for eight."

"Yes, ma'am," Larry answered.

"If you'll just follow me," the waitress said as she turned to walk away.

Butch picked up his glass and the envelope he had been carrying all day and followed them to a large room that would seat 50 or more. A table for eight was being set up, and two young ladies wearing white aprons were busy placing silverware and plates along the sides.

"I'll bring your tea in here, sir," the waitress said. "Please, have a seat, and I'll be right back."

"Now, back to the briefing," Larry said, looking around the room. "I don't know if they really give that same brief to Congress as they said, but I think there's more to it than they showed me."

"Really?" Butch asked. "What do you think they're hiding?"

"I don't know," Larry answered. "But you can bet that I'll be keeping my eyes open. I may be retired, but I still have friends on the hill who wield a lot of power."

The door to their dining area swung open, and General Modelle and the rest of the staff came in, still wearing their dress uniforms. Jerry was carrying a briefcase and came directly to Butch, saying, "I think that you'll find everything in here that you've asked for."

"Great," Butch said. "Do we have time to review them before we eat?"

Jerry turned to Paul and said, "General, Mr. North would like to review the documents before we eat, if that's okay with you."

"Fine," Paul said, "you two sit down and get the paperwork out of the way so we can enjoy our meal later."

Butch and Jerry walked to another table a few feet away, and Jerry began pulling stacks of paper from the briefcase. As he handed them to Butch, he explained what each of them were and what they meant. Butch scanned each page and then set it on the table, keeping them in the same order that Jerry had handed them to him.

Every sheet of paper had the appropriate letterhead and signatures of either General Modelle or another person whose official title was on the form. After making sure everything had been covered, Butch asked, "Do you have copies for the Senator, Kevin, and the rest of them?"

"Yes," Jerry said, pulling five stuffed envelopes from his briefcase. "Here are duplicates, all bearing original signatures, for all of you, including Senator Burklow."

"You folks have been busy," Butch said, looking at one sheet bearing the signature of President George W. Bush.

"Especially this one," he said, holding it up.

Jerry smiled and told him, "The President was more than happy to get this resolved."

Butch put the paper back into the stack and jokingly said, "Damn, I should have asked for more. I might have gotten to be the Ambassador somewhere!"

Jerry laughed and admitted, "We were really surprised at how little you really wanted. We were half expecting to have to pay millions."

"Simple men have simple needs, my friend," Butch said, looking Jerry in the eyes. "My only concern right now is how to carry all this crap you've brought me."

Jerry pushed the briefcase over to him and said, "Take this one; I think the Air Force can afford to get me a new one anyway."

After putting all of the documents and his own envelope in the case, they got up and shook hands before walking back to where the rest of the people were still milling around. Knowing that the staff of the club was waiting for them to be seated before interrupting, Butch walked up to General Modelle and said, "Sir, everything seems to be as you promised."

Paul looked at Butch for a second and said, "Now, I expect you to do everything you promised."

"Sir," Butch told him, "my father taught me that a man's word should be the only thing that matters. I firmly believe that. I gave you my word, and to me, that's better than any contract a lawyer can provide."

Paul took Butch's extended hand and said with sincerity, "It's good to know some of the old values are still alive. It's rare to meet a man these days who thinks more about others than he does himself."

"Now," Paul said, looking around, "I believe it's time to eat. I've taken the liberty of ordering sirloin steaks, medium rare baked potatoes, green beans, and a salad with ranch dressing for all of us. I hope that's satisfactory with you."

Everyone nodded, and they headed for their chairs. Butch, Jerry, Larry, and Karyn stood on one side of the table as Paul, Mike, Rick, and Amy walked to the other. Standing, Paul asked for a moment of silence for the troops and then motioned for the Senator to sit first.

Throughout lunch, they discussed several issues but stayed away from the subject that had brought them together today. Butch and Jerry talked about growing up on farms or ranches and how similar their fathers had been, and how that had shaped their character.

After finishing their meals, General Nelson stood and announced that President Bush couldn't make the presentation himself but had asked Vice President Cheney to do it. The ceremony would be scheduled to take place here at the base as soon as Butch could get Kevin and the rest of them back.

After a final round of hand-shaking and goodbyes, Larry was just telling Butch that he would take him back to his car at What-A-Burger when Jerry interrupted him.

"I'm sorry to tell you this, Mr. North," Jerry said. "It seems that we found out about your room at the motel this morning, and some of our agents managed to collect all of the items you left behind."

"And where are they now?" Butch asked, not surprised that he had finally been seen there.

"After we reached our agreement," Jerry answered, "I had them taken to one of the suites at the Visiting Officer's Quarters (VOQ) and placed in the rooms we reserved for you. At our expense, of course."

"Well, I still need to go get my car," Butch said. "If you'll tell me which room, I'll come get my things. I believe I've had a better offer for tonight if you don't mind."

"Of course," Jerry said. "If it's alright with the Senator, I'll come with you to get your car and make sure you have no problems getting back on base."

"That would be appreciated," Butch said. "Senator, is that okay with you?"

"Sure," Larry answered. "But we need to get going. I do have other appointments this afternoon."

Larry turned to leave and then asked, "Where're the documents you promised, Lieutenant Colonel Fleenor?"

"I have them, sir," Butch said, holding up the briefcase. "I'll give you yours in the car."

"Well then," Larry said as he headed for the door, passing Paul and Mike, "thanks for the lunch, Generals; I'll be in touch."

"I don't suppose your better offer has something to do with a certain Ms. Tammy Terbush, does it?" Jerry asked as they walked down the hall.

"Are you telling me that you're still monitoring my calls," Butch asked, almost stopping.

"Oh, no," Jerry quickly replied. "It's just that we've known about y'all's relationship since it started, I guess. I just naturally assumed that was what you meant. Trust me, that program is over."

"It'd better be," Butch told him, continuing down the hall. "I trust you, Jerry. But, if I were you, I'd be careful around Colonel Erickson. I've seen too many like him in the past, more concerned with their next promotion than taking care of their people."

"I think Rick and I have come to an understanding," Jerry said. "We had some difficulties a while back, but I think that's over."

"I hope so, for your sake," Butch said as they got to Larry's car. "Just remember that most snakes give no warning. A diamondback is the only honest snake I know of; he'll let you know when he's around and ready to strike."

Larry drove them back to where Butch had left his car and told him to call again if he needed any help. Butch thanked him and left one of the envelopes with him as he and Jerry got out of the car. As Larry drove away, Butch pointed to the little white sedan and told Jerry to get in.

After they got back on base, Jerry directed him to the VOQ office and went in with him to get the keys to the room. After Butch collected all of the things they had brought over, he drove Jerry back to the hangar, where he asked to be dropped off.

Butch watched as Jerry headed for a small guard shack just inside the hangar and then drove away. Winding back towards the exit to the base, he decided to go to the Class Six store and get a couple of bottles of wine for dinner tonight. Not knowing what Tammy was going to make, he purchased a bottle of Fat Bastard Chardonnay, a bottle of Three Dudes, and a dog, Texas Merlot.

Walking back to his car he thought, "The prices are good, but those folks just aren't as friendly as at Wise Liquor. I think I'd rather spend my money where folks like me." He drove away thinking, *'Maybe they like me* because *I spend my money there. Nah, they like me! I know it!'"*

CHAPTER 53

Rosy had just called everyone in for lunch when Pablo came into the dining room and said, "Señor Kevin, I have some news for you."

"What's that?" Kevin asked.

"All of you will be leaving this afternoon with Gil," Pablo told him.

"Where are we going?" Kevin asked, wondering if they were moving or going home.

"I don't know everything," Pablo answered. "But you will fly out with Gil later this afternoon. I think Mr. North has made arrangements for you to go home tomorrow."

"Are we going back to the place where we were living?" Gene asked.

"I don't know," Kevin told him. "But I'd bet that Butch has made some other arrangements. If he accomplished what he told me he was planning, I think it will mean that it will have something to do with the base."

"I'm not going back to the base!" Gene said. "I won't let them have BK!"

"Hold on," Kevin quickly said. "I'm sure that Butch would never agree to anything that put you or BK in danger."

"What about me?" Leslie asked. "I'm going wherever they take Gene and BK."

"All right," Kevin told them. "Let's slow down a little. Like I said, Butch wouldn't do anything that separated you guys. Now, I'm not sure exactly what he's arranged, but it'll be in everybody's best interest."

Kevin paused and let their emotions settle and then said, "We'll just have to wait until we see Butch, and then we'll find out what's going to happen. But the important thing to remember is that he's taken care of us so far. We've got to keep trusting him now."

"What could he do that would keep the people at the base from taking us wherever they wanted?" Leslie asked. "Maybe they've lied to Butch, and we're walking into a trap."

"Look," Kevin said. "I've known Butch for a long time, and I've never seen him do something without analyzing every angle. Sometimes, he's a little too cautious, but I'm sure that he's figured out some way of preventing the government from double-crossing him."

"You remember all of those samples of hair and stuff he took?" Kevin continued. "Well, I know he planned on sending those to a lot of different people who would be able to use them against the people at the base if they don't keep their agreement."

"What if they find all of those other samples and take them?" Gene wanted to know.

"I don't know," Kevin admitted. "But I still think Butch has something he can use if the government doesn't keep their word. I don't know what that is, but you can bet that he isn't leaving it to chance."

Rosy brought in a plate of steaming tamales and placed it on the table, saying, "You folks are spending a lot of time worrying about something that you have no control over."

She wiped her hands on her apron and told them, "I don't know Mr. North, but I do know Sancudo and his people. Mel has always managed to take care of his customers, and I'd assume that Mr. North does the same. Now, until Gil gets here with something more to tell you, I suggest you eat lunch and wait."

"My little Rosita is right," Pablo said, sitting down. "Worrying will do you no good. If you trusted Mr. North in the past, I think you should continue to do so. He seems to have done well so far, so what makes you think he would do any less now?"

"Pablo's right," Kevin said, taking his seat and putting two tamales on his plate. "Let's just wait until Gil gets here, and maybe he'll know where we're going."

After lunch, Leslie and Gene took BK back to their room while Kevin followed Pablo around the ranch, helping with the chores. It was getting late when they finally heard the sound of an airplane coming in from the south.

Pablo told Kevin to get into the Jeep, and they headed for the runway where the Cessna had just landed and was taxiing to the end. They pulled up just as the propeller had stopped spinning, and Gil was stepping out.

"Hola, Gil," Pablo said, stepping out of the Jeep. "What's the plan for our guests?"

Gil walked over and said, "First, we need to get the supplies out of the plane and loaded into your Jeep. Then, I will take all of them to Piedras Negras."

"What are we going to do in Piedras Negras?" Kevin asked.

Gil walked back to the plane and started taking out sacks and handing them to Pablo, saying, "You will be spending the night at the house of a cousin of mine. Then, early tomorrow morning, you will be taken across the river where Mel crossed over with Gene the other day."

"Is Butch going to meet us there?" Kevin asked, carrying a couple of sacks to Pablo's Jeep.

"He will meet you at the airport in Eagle Pass, Senor," Gil told him. "After that, I don't know where you will be going."

"What about the car we came in," Kevin asked. "How am I supposed to get that back to the man that owns it?"

"I don't know," Gil said. "But I think that you should worry more about yourselves than an old car. Maybe Sancudo has bought it from Mr. North; we can always use another car."

Putting the last of the sacks in the Jeep, Gil said, "Now, we must hurry and get all of you on the plane. I can't fly after it gets dark."

"Why don't you just fly us to Eagle Pass tomorrow morning?" Kevin asked as they got into the Jeep.

"I would have to clear customs," Gil said. "And that would include having to show passports, visas, and other things that we can't provide."

"What about just flying us somewhere that doesn't have customs?" Kevin asked as they drove toward the house.

"Not worth the risk of being discovered," Gil said. "Your government has too many ways of watching the sky to take such a chance when there are other less dangerous ways."

After carrying in the supplies at the house, Pablo told them, "You folks need to grab whatever you need and get ready to go to the airplane. I'll help Rosy put this stuff away, and then we'll take you down there."

Kevin walked down the hall and told Gene and Leslie to start packing their things and not to take anything that was unnecessary. He stepped into his room and looked around to see what he needed to take. Seeing only a pair of pants, a shirt, and his toiletries, he stuffed them into a plastic sack that lined a trashcan and headed back to where Gene and Leslie were packing.

Rosy was there helping them put everything in plastic sacks as Leslie changed BK's diaper. When they had finished, Pablo came in and helped them carry the sacks out to his Jeep. Everyone and everything onboard, they headed down to the airplane while Rosy held BK for the last time and told them how much she would miss them.

After parking beside the airplane, Gil helped Gene and Leslie into the back seat with BK while Kevin loaded their meager possessions behind it. Pablo and Rosy stood beside the Jeep watching until Kevin walked back to tell them goodbye and thank them.

"You've been wonderful to us," he said. "I hope we can come back sometime and visit a little longer."

"It's been our pleasure, Senor," Pablo said, shaking his hand. "You are always welcome."

Kevin hugged Rosy and told her, "Keep an eye on Pablo, Tia Rosita. You'll never find another one like him."

Rosy smiled and replied, "I wouldn't want another one, and you take care of those children."

"I will," Kevin answered as he headed back to the plane.

After Kevin was in his seat, Gil waved and started the engine, blowing dust out behind the airplane. As he turned it around and headed for the opposite end of the runway, Pablo and Rosy stood waving goodbye.

A few minutes later, they took off and headed south down the valley as the sun was just touching the mountains to the west. Out of the valley, they turned east and flew low across the barren countryside they had driven through just a couple of days ago. From the air, they could see numerous small dry creek beds, small herds of goats, and dirt roads crisscrossing the land.

About 30 minutes later, they flew over a small asphalt runway and circled it before Gil swung around and landed. As they taxied to a parking spot beside a few other single-engine airplanes, a familiar Bronco came over to meet them.

When the propeller finally stopped, Mel stepped out of the Bronco and walked over to open Kevin's door. "Look what we have here," Mel said as he helped Kevin out of the plane. "You certainly smell better than you did the last time I saw you."

Kevin shook Sancudo's hand and said, "And you look much friendlier. What're we supposed to do now?"

They went to help Gene and Leslie out of the plane, and Mel said, "You will spend the night here in town, and then very early tomorrow morning, I will take you across the river up by Quemado."

"Then, we will drive back down to the little airport at Eagle Pass, and Butch will fly you to somewhere around Ft Worth," Sancudo told them as they were getting into the Bronco with their things.

"Did Butch tell you what was going to happen once we get back to Ft Worth?"

Gene asked, climbing into the back seat with Leslie.

"No, he just told me that he would land at the airport in Eagle Pass and take you back," Sancudo answered as he waved goodbye to Gil and drove off.

Mel took them to a small residential development on the north side of Piedras Negras and pulled up in front of a modest house with a stucco wall across the front. Killing the engine, he opened his door and told Kevin to help get everything out and follow him into the house.

Inside, Mel showed them their rooms and the bathroom and told them that the refrigerator had sandwich meat and other things to make for supper if they got hungry. After telling them to be ready to leave as soon as he arrived early in the morning, Sancudo headed for the door and left.

"Well," Kevin said, "I guess we might as well get some sleep. Try not to worry about what's going to happen tomorrow. At least we'll get to see Butch, and he'll finally get to tell us everything. Until then, try to have a good night."

CHAPTER 54

Butch woke early the next morning, having set the alarm for four o'clock just to make sure he wasn't late. Tammy had been home when he arrived early the previous evening, and he spent the first hour or so telling her about Gene, Leslie, their son BK, and Kevin. Once she knew what had been happening for the past several months, she began to understand why the government had gone to such extreme measures to find Butch.

He didn't tell her what he really suspected; that was part of his agreement as he understood it. He would help protect the government's secret, and they would leave him alone. Now that it was almost over, he didn't want to invoke their ire if the secret was leaked and have them take revenge on any of them.

At the first sound of the alarm, Butch silenced it and quietly slipped out of the bed, hoping not to wake Tammy. She made some unrecognizable noise as she rolled over but didn't open her eyes as Butch walked to the bathroom. Shutting the door, he showered, shaved, brushed his teeth, and then snuck back into the bedroom for his clothes.

Tammy was awake watching as he came out of the bathroom and asked, "Can't I go with you?"

Butch pulled on his shirt and snapped it as he explained, "It's a four-seat airplane, and there's already five of us, counting BK. Where do you intend to sit?"

"On your lap," she answered, smiling.

Butch smiled back and pulled on his Wrangler jeans, saying, "This isn't the time to be joining the mile-high club; maybe another day."

Turning serious, she asked, "When will you be back?"

"I hope we'll get back here by 10 or 11 o'clock," Butch answered as he put on his Tony Lama boots and pulled the legs of his jeans over the tops.

"But," he continued, "when we get back to the airport, I have to drive them to the base and take care of some final business. Getting back here is just the start of the agreement. We still have to finalize all of the paperwork, set up accounts for their money, find them a place to live, and all the other things that need to be done to start their new lives."

Butch walked over to the bed and bent over to kiss her goodbye, and said, "I'll call you when I can. You can go back to sleep and then go to work like you normally do; I'll be back this evening for sure."

Butch grabbed his hat and briefcase from the table in the living room as he headed for the door to leave. Tammy had gotten out of bed and was following him when he opened the door, and she told him, "Be careful, Butch. I'm not done with you yet."

Butch turned and smiled, saying, "Maybe I'd better be careful about what you have in mind. Sometimes, the greatest dangers are in the prettiest packages!"

After a final kiss goodbye, Butch climbed into the little white rental sedan and headed for Hicks Airport. There was little traffic this early, and it only took about 20 minutes to make the drive. As he drove in, he saw Ronald's car sitting beside the open doors of his hanger, and the Bonanza was already on the taxiway in front.

Butch parked behind Ronald's car and said, "Good morning, Ronald. How's the bird?"

"Morning, Butch," Ronald said. "She's ready to go; I topped off the tanks last night and checked everything else this morning."

"Thanks," Butch said as he climbed onto the right wing and put the briefcase on the rear seat. "I'll just do a quick walk around, not that I don't trust you, but I like to do my own preflight."

"I figured you would," Ronald told him. "By the way, where are you going?"

Butch was opening the gas cap to check the fuel level and answered, "Eagle Pass."

Ronald followed Butch as he finished checking the rest of the airplane and told him, "I put my bag of aeronautical charts and approaches in the left side panel for you. I've checked them, and they're all current. The GPS was updated last week, so it's good to go. There's also a thermos of coffee on the floor behind your seat."

"Thanks again," Butch said, shaking Ronald's hand. "I should be back around 10 o'clock or so. Do you want me to put the plane back in the hangar?"

"No, just call me when you land, and I'll meet you over at the restaurant," Ronald answered. "Maybe we'll have lunch when you get back."

"Sounds good," Butch said as he stepped onto the wing. "I'll give you a shout as soon as we land. Thanks again."

Butch crawled over into the left seat and pulled the door closed as Ronald stepped away from the airplane. After a look around the instrument panel, Butch made sure the area around the propeller was clear and started the engine. As soon as it was running, he waved at Ronald and headed toward the runway.

Butch made a quick radio call to advise any other aircraft around that he was taking off from Hicks and pulled onto the runway as he shoved the throttle forward. Accelerating rapidly, he eased the yoke back to lift the airplane smoothly into the air. After retracting the landing gear, he turned south as he climbed and watched the sky for other aircraft.

Once he was 3,000 feet in the air, he called the Ft Worth approach control and advised them of his direction of flight and requested flight following to Eagle Pass. Reaching 8,500 feet, he engaged the autopilot and reached behind his seat for the coffee Ronald had thoughtfully provided. Nothing to do now for the next couple of hours; he opened the briefcase and reread all of the material regarding Kevin's and Gene's new lives.

Kevin had gotten little sleep during the night and was awake when the lights of Sancudo's Bronco came through the front windows of the house. He had made a pot of coffee and was sitting in a chair in the living room while he was wondering just what was going to happen today. Setting his cup on the small table beside the chair, he got up and walked to the bedroom where Gene and Leslie were sleeping.

Kevin knocked on their door and told them to get up as he heard the front door opening and Sancudo walking in. After hearing Gene answering his knock, Kevin walked back to the living room and said, "Good morning, Sancudo. Do you want some coffee?"

"No, thanks," Mel said. "We don't have a lot of time. Are the others ready?"

"Almost," Kevin answered. "I just woke them, and it won't take long for them to grab their stuff."

"Good," Mel replied. "I want to get across up by Quemado before the sun comes up. I think Butch plans on being at the airport around seven or so, and I don't want to make him wait too long."

Gene came into the room, tucking his shirttail into his pants, and said, "Are we leaving?"

"Yes, little man," Sancudo said. "As soon as you get your wife and kid, we need to go."

Gene walked back to his bedroom and began helping Leslie pack their things and bundle BK in a couple of blankets. Moments later, they walked into the living room, and Gene said, "We're ready. How long until we see Butch?"

Sancudo turned toward the door and said, "Maybe an hour, maybe a little more. But it will be even longer if we don't get started."

Kevin helped them carry their things to the Bronco and climbed in after tossing the plastic bags with their worldly possessions into the back. As soon as everyone was in, Sancudo backed out of the short driveway and headed north. There was almost no traffic as they drove up toward where they would cross just north of Quemado on the other side of the border. The sun was just beginning to lighten the sky in the east when Sancudo pulled off the road onto a trail leading into the brush.

Sancudo turned off the lights and drove slowly along the almost invisible dirt trail until they reached the gravel bank of the Rio Grande. Still almost hidden in the brush, he stopped and waited for a signal that it was safe to cross. Pulling his CB radio from under the seat, he checked the frequency and keyed the microphone three short times.

Immediately, he heard an answering three bursts of static and saw a flash of light from across the river. He replaced the radio and pulled into the shallow water, heading for the opposite shore. Once across, he continued along the trail until he exited the undergrowth about half of a mile from US Highway 277.

Clear of the brush and on a well-established dirt road, Sancudo turned the lights back on and quickly made it to 277. There, he turned south, passed through Quemado, heading toward Eagle Pass, and said, "Welcome to the United States of America."

Twenty minutes later, they drove through Eagle Pass and pulled into the airport just as the sun finally broke loose from the horizon. Looking around the parking ramp, they couldn't see any airplanes that weren't tied down. Sancudo pulled over to the small building that served as the operations room and killed the engine.

"Well," he said, turning to look at Kevin, "it appears that we're early, but I need for you to take your things from the car so I can get going if Butch doesn't get here soon. I have other work that requires my attention this morning."

Kevin nodded and opened the door, saying, "All right, kids, let's get our stuff. It shouldn't be long until Butch gets here."

They pulled their things from the back of the Bronco and set them on the ground beside the car. Sancudo was standing by the open door as Kevin walked around and said, "Thanks. I hope we get to meet again someday."

Sancudo shook his hand and replied, "Maybe so, Senor. Maybe you and Butch will come down, and we will go back over to Rancho El Infante for some hunting."

"I would like that," Kevin told him. "I really do appreciate what you've done for us."

"Just business, Senor," Mel said. "Just business."

"I understand," Kevin said as they heard the sound of an airplane coming from the north. "But I think what you've done for us is more than just business."

"A man helps his friends," Sancudo said as they watched the airplane land and head toward them. "Without good friends, a man lives a lonely life."

The Bonanza came to a stop beside the gas pumps, and the engine died as they stood watching. Seconds later, the door over the right wing opened, and they saw Butch step out. Seeing him, Kevin smiled and headed over with Gene and the rest of them following.

Butch walked toward them and asked, "You folks looking for a lift?"

When they met, everyone hugged Butch as Sancudo walked up and said, "I would like to stay for the reunion party, but there just isn't time."

Butch broke away from the rest and shook Mel's hand, saying, "Thanks, old friend, I owe you one."

"And you know I will collect it someday," Mel answered before turning away and waving as he walked back to the Bronco.

"All right, folks," Butch said, picking up one of the plastic bags they had set down. "Let's get loaded and head home."

Tossing the bags into the small storage compartment in the rear of the airplane, Butch helped get Gene, Leslie, and BK buckled into the rear seats before refilling the gas tanks.

After replacing the hose on the pump, he did a quick walk around the airplane and climbed back onto the wing to get in.

Kevin had followed him around the airplane and watched as Butch checked the oil and made sure all of the latches were fastened. Once Butch was inside the airplane, Kevin climbed onto the wing and into the right front seat.

Butch waited until the door was securely fastened and then ensured that the area around the propeller was clear before starting the engine. Releasing the parking brake, he swung the plane around and headed back toward the runway as he made a radio call stating his intentions.

Once airborne, he repeated the process of contacting the FAA and telling them that he was climbing to 9,500 feet for the flight to Hicks Field. After leveling off, he engaged the autopilot and turned to Kevin, saying, "Well, I think it's finally almost over."

For the rest of the flight, Butch told them what he and the government had agreed to, how it was to be done, and gave them each one of the packages that contained all of the documents for them to read.

It was almost 10:30 when Butch finally began his descent toward Hicks and notified Ft Worth Approach Control that he had the field in sight. Switching frequencies, he stated his intentions to land and lined up with the runway. Once on the ground, he pulled his cell phone from its case and called Ronald to let him know they had made it back safely.

Butch taxied to the gas pumps that were a short distance from the restaurant and parked. As soon as the propeller quit spinning, he told Kevin to open the door and help everyone out. As they were pulling their things from the storage compartment, Butch used his credit card and refilled the gas tanks.

He was just replacing the hose when Ronald drove up and parked beside the restaurant. "Well, I see you made it back all right," Ronald said as he walked over to his airplane. "I don't see any major damage, so I guess you haven't forgotten how to fly one of these little planes."

"Just like riding a bike," Butch said. "Do you want to take it back to the hangar now?"

"No," Ronald said as he walked around the plane, "I'm taking the wife down to Stephenville in a couple of hours for some Bar-B-Q at the Hard Eight. You want to come with us?"

"No thanks," Butch answered. "I was just down there a few days ago. I've got to get these folks home pretty soon. Do you want some breakfast with us?"

"I'll come in and have a cup of coffee after I move the plane from the pumps in case someone else wants to get gas," Ronald said as he climbed onto the wing. "Then I'll take you over to get your car."

Butch helped Kevin and Gene carry their things to the side of the restaurant and told them to go inside and get a table while he went to get the car. As soon as he and Ronald had parked the airplane and put chocks around the wheels, he came over and told Butch to climb into his pickup. Back at the hangar, Ronald told Butch he would meet him back at the restaurant and went inside.

Butch started his car, drove back, and loaded everything into the trunk before walking in to join Kevin and the others. Looking at all of them sitting together at the table, watching him anxiously, he smiled and said, "You guys should really learn to relax. Not to mention, I'd suggest a

shower and a change of clothes. Where've you folks been,
trying to hide out in the desert somewhere?"

425

CHAPTER 55

After they had eaten, Butch stepped outside to thank Ronald as he was leaving and to call Jerry and let him know that Gene and his family were back. "Good morning, Lieutenant Colonel Fleenor," Butch said as the phone was answered. "I have some people I think you'd like to talk to."

"I assume you're referring to Gene and the others," Jerry said.

"You are correct," Butch told him. "But I have a couple of requests before any actual meeting."

"What's that?" Jerry asked.

"I need to get some clothes for all of them, and they need to get a shower and clean up a little," Butch told him.

"That's not a problem," Jerry replied. "The suite we had for you is still available; they can use it."

"How about one for Kevin?" Butch asked.

"I'll take care of it," Jerry said. "Anything else?"

"That's about it for now," Butch told him.

"When do you expect to get here?" Jerry asked.

"I'd guess about an hour and a half or so," Butch told him. "Depending on how long it takes Leslie to pick out her clothes. Kevin and Gene will be through shopping as soon as they find the right size jeans and a shirt."

"I know what you mean," Jerry answered. "I'll schedule General Brown's conference room for a couple of hours starting at one o'clock. And, if you'll give me a call when you get close to the base, I'll come escort you to the rooms."

"Okay, I'll talk to you in an hour or so," Butch replied.

"By the way, Butch," Jerry said. "Please call me Jerry when it's just us, okay?"

"All right, Jerry. I'll call you when we're ready to come on base," Butch replied and hung up.

Kevin had walked out just as Butch was finishing his conversation and asked, "Who was that?"

"My friend from the base," Butch said.

"The one that warned you?" Kevin asked.

"Yes," Butch told him. "But, never mention anything about being warned or us having someone helping us. If the subject ever comes up, just say you got spooked when the State Trooper spotted Leslie."

"Sure," Kevin answered. "But, do you really trust this guy?"

"Yes, I trust him," Butch said. "He put his career on the line for us, and I think you'll like him too. He's sort of like us, comes from a ranching background, really down to earth, and pretty much just a good ol' boy."

"We'll see," Kevin said as Gene came out with Leslie and BK.

"All right, folks," Butch said as they walked up. "We're off to the mall, gotta get some new duds for you folks. Can't have you meeting the Generals looking like you do now."

"Are we going back to the base?" Gene asked.

"Yep, sure are," Butch told him as he opened the car door.

"Are you sure it'll be all right?" Leslie asked as she got in the car.

"I'm positive," Butch told her as Gene got in beside her and Kevin got in the front seat.

Butch drove south on Business 287 and joined Loop 820 headed west. When they got to White Settlement Road, he exited and drove east for a couple of miles until they arrived at Ridgmar Mall. After finding a parking spot not too far from the entrance, Butch led them in and begged Leslie not to take too long.

"By the way, Butch," Kevin said as they were walking down the wide aisle, "I've got something for you."

"What's that?" Butch asked as Kevin stepped to the side.

Kevin reached into his shirt and pulled out what remained of the cash Butch had given him. "I thought you might need this to cover Leslie's shopping."

Butch looked at it and smiled, saying, "I hope we don't need this much. Thanks, though; I'm sure I can find a way to spend it."

"Just don't let Tammy know you've got that much cash," Kevin laughed. "I'm sure she'd know how to spend it."

Butch handed one stack of $100 bills back to Kevin, saying, "I'll keep that in mind. You keep this; I think you'll need it until things are settled."

He slid the rest of the money into his shirt and replied, "Now, let's just get you folks some clothes and get out of here."

Leslie finally selected a dress, shoes, a purse, various undergarments, and a few other things. Kevin and Gene had found jeans, new shirts, and socks and were standing waiting patiently for Leslie to get some new things for BK. After everyone was satisfied with their selections, Butch led them to the front and paid with his credit card. In another store, they found deodorant, toothbrushes, and other toiletries they would need after they got to their rooms.

As they walked back to the car, Butch called Jerry and told him they were leaving the mall and should be at the gate in about five minutes. Butch unlocked the car, and after they got in with their packages, he started and drove out of the parking lot toward the base.

Jerry was waiting in his car beside the guard as they approached and waved for them to follow him. Once parked in front of their rooms, Jerry walked over to meet them, saying, "Good afternoon, I'm Lieutenant Colonel Jerry Fleenor."

Butch introduced all of them, and once they had shaken hands, Jerry handed them the keys to their rooms. Butch and Jerry stood outside talking as Gene took Leslie and BK into their suite. Kevin told them he'd be back out in a few minutes and went into his room.

Jerry and Butch talked about some of Butch's concerns as they waited for everyone to finish cleaning up and get dressed. Finally, everyone was outside, and Jerry told them to follow him over to the Base Headquarters. Once there, he led them into the conference room where General Modelle was waiting with the rest of the people who had been present at their last meeting.

Gene nervously greeted everyone and introduced them to Leslie and BK. Kevin cautiously shook everyone's hand, and they all finally sat down to take care of the business that brought them here.

After almost an hour of arranging temporary housing on base for Kevin and Gene, signing papers to implement all the agreements, providing bank accounts for each of them, and setting up medical examinations for Leslie and BK, they finally looked at each other and relaxed.

"Is all of this satisfactory, Mr. North?" Paul asked as the last document was signed.

"I think so," Butch said. "How about you, Kevin?"

"Fine by me," he said, nodding his head, amazed at what had been accomplished in such a short amount of time.

"Gene, is this acceptable for you and your family?" Butch asked.

"Yes, sir," Gene replied gratefully. "I'm just glad we can finally settle down, and Leslie can get back in touch with her family."

"Leslie, do you have any questions?" Butch asked.

"Probably," she answered, shocked at knowing the running was finally over. "But I don't know what they are right now."

Mike smiled and said, "Well, I'm sure we can take care of anything you think of later. Is there anything else anyone can think of before we get to work?"

"One thing," Butch answered. "When's the press conference?"

"Tomorrow morning," Paul told him. "The President decided that he would hold it in Washington thinking that it would get more attention up there than down here."

"I suppose that means no awards for us," Butch replied.

"If you want, we'll fly all of you up there, or we'll have a ceremony here to present them," Paul said. "But it would take another day or two to set that up. I just wanted to get the statement out clearing your reputations as we had agreed as quickly as possible."

Butch nodded and said, "I think the press conference will be enough; award ceremonies aren't really necessary."

Paul stood and said, "Fine, it's settled. Jerry will spend the next few days helping you get settled and take care of any problems that arise. It's been a pleasure to meet all of you, but now I need to get back to Washington and brief a few people who have been very concerned about this for several months."

Everyone stood, shook hands, and said goodbye as Paul led his officers out of the room. Jerry remained with Butch and the others as they watched them leave, saying, "What're your plans, Mr. North?"

"I plan on returning this car, finding my truck, and staying home with no interruptions for the rest of my life," Butch answered, shaking Jerry's hand. "And hopefully, I'll never have to see any of you folks again unless it's purely social."

Butch looked at Kevin and said, "Well, buddy, I'm done. It's all in your hands now. If you and Jerry can't handle it, I might help a little. But, until then, I just want to go home."

Kevin shook Butch's hand and said, "We'll talk about all this later over a beer or twelve. I'll let you know if we have any problems."

Butch turned to Gene and Leslie and said, "Kids, you take care of little BK. Let Uncle Kevin know if you need anything. I'll come visit when you've found a house and get settled."

They both hugged Butch with tears running down their faces and thanked him for getting everything taken care of.

Butch took one final look at all of them and said, "That's enough sentimental farewells for now. I'm going home."

Butch walked back to his car as they watched, climbed in, waved goodbye and drove off.

EPILOGUE

Over the next few months, Kevin and Jerry helped Gene and Leslie find a house, arranged for them to get financing, provided furnishings and made sure they were on their way to a normal life. Leslie's mother came down and spent a lot of time with BK and, of course, gave her opinion of everything that was going on.

Kevin spent most of his time with them unless Leslie's mom was there, but he headed back to Vashti when she arrived. Occasionally he would call Butch, and they would meet to discuss how things were going.

Jerry became close friends with Butch and Kevin, deciding he would retire when his 20 years were up and move somewhere around Decatur. On most weekends, he could be found looking at land and frequently met Butch and Kevin at one of the local bars.

The government kept their promise, but ultimately was disappointed in the amount of information they could get from either Gene or BK. They brought in one of the military's finest plastic surgeons after evaluating BK's needs, and he spent the next few years reconstructing all of the abnormalities.

Butch and Tammy continued to see each other, mainly on weekends, but plans for marriage were never really discussed. Although they enjoyed seeing each other, neither of them was willing to give up their private lives and live together.

After many years of limited success and enormous expense in the GENE program, the government finally abandoned that aspect of research and concentrated on other areas. Or so they say.